BITS OF PARADISE

D0937300

Bits of Paradise

21 UNCOLLECTED STORIES BY

F. SCOTT AND ZELDA

FITZGERALD

Selected by

Matthew J. Bruccoli
with the assistance of

Scottie Fitzgerald Smith

Charles Scribner's Sons
New York

To Wanda Randall

CONTENTS

FOREWORD

Though it was Professor Bruccoli who conceived, delivered, and nursed this volume—he loves 'his' authors so much I do believe if he found all their grocery bills he'd put them out in an annotated edition—it is I who claim the credit for the title. It's a bit corny, but then so are some of the things in these stories, which have some mighty unbelievable heroes and heroines. The only way you'll get through them all, I think, is to imagine my father and mother as two bright meteors streaking across a starry sky back in the days when wars and moons seemed equally far away, and then these stories as a sort of fall-out. For they all have one thing in common: a sense of breathlessness, as if even their authors still were gasping at the wonders glimpsed as they flew past Heaven.

The title has two even more personal meanings for me, however. First, it brings to mind my mother's description of my father in her novel, *Save Me The Waltz*, which tells the story of their romance better than anything else which has been written: 'There seemed to be some heavenly support beneath his shoulder blades that lifted his feet from the ground in ecstatic suspension, as if he secretly enjoyed the ability to fly but was walking as a compromise to convention.'

Secondly, this is the last book which will ever be published devoted to previously uncollected writings of my parents. It's the end of an era, really, marked by the monumental scholarship of Professor Bruccoli and many others, which began about twenty-five years ago and has brought my father from relative obscurity as an artifact of the Jazz Age to his present secure nook in literature. Now everything that's fit to print—and even some that's borderline!—is out on the table for all to see, for the thesis writers to deduce from, and the moralists to point to, and the women's libbers to be shocked by. This is the last addition to the Scott and Zelda story as told by those who lived it, and for this reason I find it a little sad, like an attic which has been emptied of all its secret treasures.

It was in this mood of sentimental leave-taking that I went up to my real-life attic to see what I could find in the way of tangible mementoes still lurking about among the camp trunks and the children's bird cages. Despite a friend's remark that I am the luckiest person she knows because whenever my fortunes take a turn for the worse, I can always try to write myself another batch of undiscovered letters from my father, the fact is that everything of literary interest —the scrapbooks, the photograph albums, the ledgers and notebooks which my father so meticulously kept—has gradually been turned over to the Princeton University Library. The attic is now mostly populated with such unfamiliar titles as *Kultahattu* (Helsinki, 1959): '. . . ja Gatsby riensi sisään pukeutuneena valkoiseen flanellipukuun ja hopeanhohtoiseen paitaan . . .' and *Lepi I Prokleti* (Belgrade, 1969): '. . . jer je Glorija zamahnula rukom brzo ispusti i ona pade na pod . . ..'

But there are a few things which are special, bits and pieces of the child's paradise which my parents created for me, and which is far more vivid to me than any of our later worlds in Alabama, Maryland, or Hollywood.

Item: The paper dolls on which my mother lavished so much time. Some of them represented the three of us. Once upon a time these dolls had wardrobes of which Rumpelstiltskin could be proud. My mother and I had dresses of pleated wallpaper, and one party frock of mine had ruffles of real lace cut from a Belgian handkerchief. More durable were the ball dresses of Mesdames de Maintenon and Pompadour and the coats-of-mail of Galahad and Launcelot, for these were lavishly painted in the most minute detail in water color so thick that it has scarcely faded. Perfectly preserved are the proud members of the courts of both Louis XIV and King Arthur (figures of haughty mien and aristocratic bearing), a jaunty Goldilocks, an *insouciante* Red Riding Hood, an Errol Flynn-like D'Artagnan, and other personages familiar to all little well-instructed boys and girls of that time. It is characteristic of my mother that these exquisite dolls, each one requiring hours of artistry, should have been created for the delectation of a six-year-old; at the time she died, she was working on a series of Bible illustrations for her oldest grandchild, then eighteen months.

Item: A stamp collection with about a third of its spaces filled in, and in the same box two disconsolate toy soldiers in uniforms of the Wars of the Roses . . . all that's left of the armies from Hannibal's to Napoleon's which used to be put through their battle paces on the dining-room table. These Daddy bought at the *Nain Bleu* in Paris in the vain hope, I suppose, that I would become as fascinated by military history as he was. Very little of my extra-curricular education took—some of it backfired, in fact, for I was made to recite so much Keats and Shelley that I came to look upon them as personal enemies—but I do have some occasionally useful bits of information learned at the parental knee, such as what King Solomon said. 'Solomon said,' Daddy loved to declaim very seriously, 'that all men are liars. Therefore, Solomon was a liar. Therefore what Solomon said was not true. Therefore all men are not liars. Therefore Solomon was not a liar. Therefore what Solomon said was true. Therefore all men are liars. Therefore . . .' You can imagine how frequently I have been reminded of King Solomon during the political events of the past two years.

I'm happy to report, by the way, that insofar as my father was a political creature in any way (as he wrote in 1931, 'It

(3)

was characteristic of the Jazz Age that it had no interest in politics at all.'), he was a Franklin D. Roosevelt Democrat. His dismissal of the idea that Roosevelt was 'a traitor to his class' as pure nonsense was his single most influential legacy to me, and I expect to go to my grave, as he did to his, with the rare distinction of never having voted for a Republican candidate for President.

Item: A handful of Christmas ornaments, peeling here and there but still in use, along with the tiny skaters who were brought out every year to glide across my mother's pocket-mirrors under the tree. They were carried everywhere with us like talismans, for Christmas was a major production with the Fitzgeralds: railroad tracks would be laid down, mountains would be built out of papier mâché, towns would be constructed to look like mediaeval villages. My mother described her feeling best in one of the letters which I copied before they, too, were sent to Princeton:

'The tree [in Rome] was cooled with silver bells which rang hauntedly through the night by themselves . . . and we had a tree in Paris covered with mushrooms and with snowy houses which was fun. There were myriad birds of paradise on the tree with spun glass tails, and Nanny kept busily admonishing us about the French customs: how they did not give gifts at Christmas but at New Year's . . . then we had a tree on the Avenue McMahon which Nanny and I decorated between sips of champagne until neither we nor the tree could hold any more of fantaisie or decor. We kept our decorations for years in painted toy boxes and when the last of the tails wilted and the last house grew lopsided, it was almost a bereavement.'

That was a slight exaggeration; three of the birds, tails as sleek as ever, still perch on my own family's tree every Christmas. But Nanny—If only Nanny, our symbol of order and respectability, would come back into my life, I could recapture the past as well as Proust! I don't know her married name, or where she lives now; perhaps she will read

(4)

these musings and phone. 'You and Nanny,' my mother wrote, 'had so much paraphernalia and were such an official entourage that going some place was always an auspicious pilgrimage. By the time we had been on a boat half an hour she had the staff up to the chief officers running errands and finding all those so comfortable items which give life a completely mastered and domestic flavor in the British Isles.'

There is a blue ostrich feather fan with most of the feathers missing, and there are some postcards addressed to me from all over, usually just signed 'The man with the three noses' in my father's handwriting. This was one of his favorite jokes and I don't remember thinking it particularly funny, though it was better than the ones in which I had to play an active role. For company, I would inevitably be placed on his knee, where the following dialogue would ensue:

> FSF: Do you know the story of three holes in the ground?
> ME   (gravely): No, I don't. What is it?
> FSF   (triumphantly): Well, well, well!

or——and this one usually went over a little better:

> FSF: Do you know the story of the three eggs?
> ME   (gravely): No, I don't. What is it?
> FSF   (in mock sorrow): Too bad!

and finally, as the grand climax to his performance:

> FSF: Do you know the story of the dirty shirt?
> ME   (gravely): No, I don't. What is it?
> FSF   (tossing me off his knee): That's one on you-oo!

He told me why the chicken crossed the road and what's black and white and red all over, and showed me how to make a handkerchief disappear up your sleeve and how to make rabbit ears with your fingers against the light; he loved games and false faces and make-believe and his favorite children's story was *The Rose and The Ring*. That's what *I* remember about the paradise years, but here's a version from

(5)

my mother, written after I got back from a trip to Europe just before World War II:

'I suppose that few people have seen more varied aspects of life at first hand than we did; known more different kinds of people or participated in more compelling destinies. The truncate wails of the nightingale echoing melancholily through those first years on a deserted Riviera; Paris in the roseate glow of early street lights with violets being sold over the Cafe Weber and dyed roses about the foot of the Madeleine; the blatant prerogative of taxi horns and hotels full of new people all freed from weary sequences of life somewhere else. Do you, by any chance, remember the sparrows at the Cafe Dauphine and how you fed them bread crumbs on those gala mornings?

'Then, too, we saw Rome before the new gilt of Fascism had begun to fade and sipped aperitifs in the eternal glooms of the Piazza Cologna and swept like wraiths through the dim passageways to obscure hotels. We went to London to see a fog and saw Tallulah Bankhead which was, perhaps, about the same effect. Then the fog blew up and we reconstituted Arnold Bennett's *Pretty Lady* and the works of Compton McKenzie which Daddy loved so, and we had a curious nocturnal bottle of champagne with members of the British polo team. We dined with Galsworthy and lunched with Lady Randolph Churchill and had tea in the mellow remembrances of Shane Leslie's house, who later took us to see the pickpockets pick in Wopping. They did.

'I don't know how many other things we saw; we saw Venice and visited the Murphys at Salzburg in the dwarf-haunted fastnesses of inky black lakes and fir-fragrant lanes and we stayed in the royal suite at Munich . . . courtesy of the proprietors. Your generation is the last to bear witness of the grace and gala of those days of the doctrine of free will. I am so glad that you saw where the premium lay and savoured its properties before the end.'

Some of these stories may come as a disappointment to

lovers of *Tender Is The Night*, 'The Rich Boy,' or even some of the devastatingly self-revealing articles in *Esquire*. But if one thinks of them less as literature than as reports from another, more romantic world, one will find bits in them that evoke the best of both Fitzgeralds . . . they will at least lay to rest what is in my opinion a popular misconception about their relationship: the notion that they plagiarized from one another in a tense, sometimes hostile, spirit of competition. As can be seen in this collection, their styles, attitudes, and modes of story-telling were so completely different that the only thing they have in common is the material from which they were molded: in 'Southern Girl,' for instance, you find the same theme—Alabama girl feels intimidated and ill-at ease in Yankee territory—the well-known FSF story, *The Ice Palace*. To be sure, when it came to drawing upon their experiences in Europe, a serious conflict of interest arose between the characters in *Tender Is The Night* and those in my mother's novel, *Save Me The Waltz*. But that is another story, and the one told in this book is of the brighter side of their personal paradise, a mutually complementary sense of humor and zest for living.

Scottie Fitzgerald Smith
21 August 1973

PREFACE

Bits of Paradise began as two collections: a volume of F. Scott Fitzgerald's uncollected stories, and a volume of Zelda Fitzgerald's work. The decision to combine them arose naturally in view of the intimate and complex relationship between the Fitzgeralds' fiction. They drew on a common store of material; and although they rarely collaborated in the act of writing, their work reflects an emotional collaboration. The feelings that went into their fiction were the feelings generated by their life together.

This volume includes all of Zelda Fitzgerald's published stories—none of which has been collected—and a sampling of F. Scott Fitzgerald's buried magazine stories that merit a new audience. Of F. Scott Fitzgerald's 160-odd published stories (there are borderline sketches and parodies), only 46 were collected by him in the four volumes he prepared; and 50 more have been posthumously collected. From the remaining stories, eleven are reprinted here. Fitzgerald did not reprint some of his best stories from the post-*Gatsby* period, for he had a strong feeling about the impropriety of 'serving warmed-over fare'—i.e., of using the same passages in a collected story and in a novel. Beginning in 1925 there is a cluster of stories related to *Tender Is The Night* (1934) which he designated as 'stripped' or 'scrapped' because he had drawn upon them in that novel. Readers who know *Tender* will recognise material in 'Love in the Night,' 'The Swimmers,' and 'Jacob's Ladder'—indeed, the latter adumbrates much of the Dick Diver-Rosemary Hoyt plot line.

It is not accidental that eight of the nine stories here that were published during Fitzgerald's lifetime appeared in *The Saturday Evening Post*. Sixty-six of his stories appeared in the *Post* between 1920–1936, for this magazine was his favorite market and provided the basis for his career as a popular writer. Even a thrifty man would have found it difficult to support a family on Fitzgerald's book royalties. *The Great Gatsby* (1925) earned him $9,861 in the year of its publication.* Fitzgerald's strategy was to write popular stories for the money that would allow him time to write his novels. The *Post* paid $400 for the first Fitzgerald story it published in 1920 and regularly increased his price until a peak of $4,000 was reached in 1929. His strategy did not work, as he usually borrowed against the price of his next unwritten story.

F. Scott Fitzgerald's work for the prosperous slick magazines is a much misunderstood aspect of his career. His work for the *Post* and its competitors was not simply hack work. It was highly professional commercial writing for magazines that could afford the best that money could buy. The *Post* had a roster of important writers, and Fitzgerald's very successful *Post* fiction required hard work and good writing. He was competing in an intensely competitive field. As Fitzgerald noted at a later time when he found it difficult to write *Post* stories: 'I have asked a lot of my emotions—one hundred and twenty stories. The price was high, right up there with Kipling, because there was one little drop of something—not blood, not a tear, not my seed, but me more intimately than these, in every story, it was the extra I had.' Within the requirements of his market, Fitzgerald wrote brilliant stories. Moreover, he managed to evade some editorial proscriptions—notably the obligatory happy ending,

* Fitzgerald received 30¢ per copy on 23,870 sold in America in 1925.

(9)

which he frequently modified into only an ominously happy ending. It is doubtful that he was troubled by restrictions on material, because strong language and frank sexuality never had much appeal to him as a writer.

Most of the *Post* stories in *Bits of Paradise* deserve reprinting for their own literary merit, apart from any sentimental considerations; and three—'The Swimmers,' 'A New Leaf,' and 'What a Handsome Pair!'—are major Fitzgerald stories. 'The Swimmers,' despite its over-plotting and unlikely climax, may well be the most significant of the heretofore buried stories. Fitzgerald described it as 'the hardest story I ever wrote, too big for its space + not even now satisfactory.' Into it he put his deepest feelings about America after five years of interrupted expatriation. The eloquent coda ('. . . America, having about it still that quality of the idea, was harder to utter. . . . It was a willingness of the heart.') has been widely quoted—often by people who have never read the story. Of particular interest in 'The Swimmers' is Fitzgerald's redefinition of the Stein-Hemingway 'lost generation' label, which he identifies with the generation *before* the war. It is typical of the ironies that permeate Fitzgerald's career that this patriotic story with its confidence in the war generation and its declaration, 'The best of America was the best of the world', appeared just before the October 1929 Wall Street crash.

'A New Leaf' with its suicide ending is another example of how Fitzgerald managed to evade *Post* restrictions. Written in 1931 after Zelda Fitzgerald's collapse, it derives its 'extra' from the author's contemplation of his alcoholism and his own resolutions. 'What A Handsome Pair!' could serve as the theme story for *Bits of Paradise*. It was written in 1932, after the tragedy of Zelda Fitzgerald's attempts to make her own career as a dancer, painter, and writer (her only novel, *Save Me The Waltz*, was published in October 1932); and it is an obvious response to the rivalry within the Fitzgerald marriage: 'He hated the conflict that had grown out of their wanting the same excellences, the same prizes from life.'

The inclusion of the two posthumously published stories may require explanation. 'Last Kiss' and 'Dearly Beloved' were written in 1940—at which time they were unsalable —during the final burst of creativity that accompanied Fitzgerald's work on *The Last Tycoon*. Both have connections with that unfinished novel, 'Last Kiss' more obviously. They have been collected here because they are superb, and because they provide examples of Fitzgerald's short fiction during his Hollywood period when he was thought to be finished as a short-story writer. 'Last Kiss' is one of those delayed-reaction Fitzgerald stories that gets better as the reader remembers it. When it was first published in 1969, 'Dearly Beloved' attracted considerable attention as Fitzgerald's only story with a black protagonist, but it is significant as a perfect specimen of the so-called 'short-short' form that Fitzgerald was experimenting with near the end of his life.

It is absurdly sentimental to equate F. Scott and Zelda Fitzgerald as writers. In literature, as in everything else, there is a crucial distinction between the gifted amateur and the professional. The blunt fact is that Zelda Sayre Fitzgerald's work is interesting today mainly because she was F. Scott Fitzgerald's wife. But within her limits, she wrote remarkable prose. She did not imitate her husband. Her style was her own. She had wit, an astonishing vocabulary, and the ability to see life from her own angle.

Bits of Paradise collects for the first time all ten of Zelda Fitzgerald's published stories. The extent of her work has been obscured because magazine editors made it a condition of publication that F. Scott Fitzgerald's name appear on her stories as co-author. The five 'girl' stories in *College Humor* were credited to both Fitzgeralds, although they were almost entirely Zelda Fitzgerald's. Harold Ober, Fitzgerald's agent, judged one of the stories in this series, 'A Millionaire's

Girl,' as too good for the $500 *College Humor* was paying, so he sold it to the *Post* for $4,000; but it appeared as by F. Scott Fitzgerald alone.*

Most of Zelda Fitzgerald's pieces are best described as sketches, for they do not have the usual short-story structure. Her treatment of a plot is essayistic and impressionistic. She depends little on dialogue to advance action or create character, preferring to describe action and analyze character. They are mood pieces in which atmosphere and place are evoked in surprising—occasionally puzzling—language. The style is remarkable, but undisciplined. With the exception of 'Our Own Movie Queen,' written in 1923, Zelda Fitzgerald's sketches or stories are never trivial, never mere entertainment. 'Our Own Movie Queen,' the only story here that seems to have been a collaborative effort, shows that the Fitzgeralds did not work successfully as collaborators. It is a routine piece of popular fiction that displays none of the best abilities of either of its authors. In contrast, the 'girl' sketches, which were written around the time of Zelda Fitzgerald's April 1930 breakdown, are immediately recognizable as her own work. The subjects are women who have gotten less from life—and from men and love—than they anticipated. Although 'Miss Ella' has its advocates, 'A Couple of Nuts' is Zelda Fitzgerald's best effort—and it is closer to a real story than any of the others. Written in 1932 after the Fitzgeralds had lost hope, it is a moving assessment of *les années folles* and the people who wasted 'love and success and beauty' during 'the greatest, gaudiest spree in history.' It is an indictment of the destructiveness of expatriate life, a recurring theme in this collection.

* Ober explained: 'I really felt a little guilty about dropping Zelda's name from that story, THE MILLIONAIRE'S GIRL, but I think she understands that using the two names would have tied the story up with the College Humor stories and might have got us into trouble.' The record of the Fitzgeralds' dealings with magazines through Harold Ober is contained in *As Ever, Scott Fitz-*, ed. Matthew J. Bruccoli and Jennifer McCabe Atkinson (London: Woburn Press, 1973).

The favorite subjects of the Fitzgeralds' fiction are love and money, material which some commentators have felt precludes 'all dealing with mature persons in a mature world.' If the Fitzgeralds insist that love requires money, well then so did Jane Austen. It hardly seems necessary to claim that these stories are not predictable romances for mindless readers. The best stories of both Fitzgeralds are marked by an element of disaster. The disaster may be overcome—sometimes by an obvious concession to the canons of popular fiction—but nonetheless it lurks in the story, like a destitute classmate at a college reunion whose presence reminds the revelers of the vanity of human wishes, the mutability of fortune, and the impermanence of youth, success, love, money—and happiness.

Matthew J. Bruccoli
University of South Carolina

TEXTUAL NOTE: These stories are reprinted from their first published appearances. Spelling and punctuation errors in the magazine texts have been silently corrected, and a list of these emendations will be published in the *Fitzgerald/ Hemingway Annual*.

SCOTT

The Popular Girl

(The Saturday Evening Post,
11 & 18 February 1922)

Along about half past ten every Saturday night Yanci Bowman eluded her partner by some graceful subterfuge and
from the dancing floor went to a point of vantage overlooking
the country-club bar. When she saw her father she would
either beckon to him, if he chanced to be looking in her
direction, or else she would dispatch a waiter to call attention to her impendent presence. If it were no later than half
past ten—that is, if he had had no more than an hour of
synthetic gin rickeys—he would get up from his chair and
suffer himself to be persuaded into the ballroom.

'Ballroom,' for want of a better word. It was that room,
filled by day with wicker furniture, which was always con-
notated in the phrase 'Let's go in and dance.' It was referred
to as 'inside' or 'downstairs.' It was that nameless chamber
wherein occur the principal transactions of all the country
clubs in America.

Yanci knew that if she could keep her father there for an
hour, talking, watching her dance, or even on rare occasions
dancing himself, she could safely release him at the end of that
time. In the period that would elapse before midnight ended
the dance he could scarcely become sufficiently stimulated to
annoy anyone.

All this entailed considerable exertion on Yanci's part,
and it was less for her father's sake than for her own that she
went through with it. Several rather unpleasant experiences
were scattered through this past summer. One night when

she had been detained by the impassioned and impossible-to-interrupt speech of a young man from Chicago her father had appeared swaying gently in the ballroom doorway; in his ruddy handsome face two faded blue eyes were squinted half shut as he tried to focus them on the dancers, and he was obviously preparing to offer himself to the first dowager who caught his eye. He was ludicrously injured when Yanci insisted upon an immediate withdrawal.

After that night Yanci went through her Fabian maneuver to the minute.

Yanci and her father were the handsomest two people in the Middle Western city where they lived. Tom Bowman's complexion was hearty from twenty years spent in the service of good whisky and bad golf. He kept an office downtown, where he was thought to transact some vague real-estate business; but in point of fact his chief concern in life was the exhibition of a handsome profile and an easy well-bred manner at the country club, where he had spent the greater part of the ten years that had elapsed since his wife's death.

Yanci was twenty, with a vague die-away manner which was partly the setting for her languid disposition and partly the effect of a visit she had paid to some Eastern relatives at an impressionable age. She was intelligent, in a flitting way, romantic under the moon and unable to decide whether to marry for sentiment or for comfort, the latter of these two abstractions being well enough personified by one of the most ardent among her admirers. Meanwhile she kept house, not without efficiency, for her father, and tried in a placid unruffled tempo to regulate his constant tippling to the sober side of inebriety.

She admired her father. She admired him for his fine appearance and for his charming manner. He had never quite lost the air of having been a popular Bones man at Yale. This charm of his was a standard by which her susceptible temperament unconsciously judged the men she knew. Nevertheless, father and daughter were far from that sentimental family relationship which is a stock plant in fiction, but in life usually exists in the mind of only the older party to it. Yanci Bowman had decided to leave her home by marriage within the year. She was heartily bored.

Scott Kimberly, who saw her for the first time this November evening at the country club, agreed with the lady whose house guest he was that Yanci was an exquisite little beauty. With a sort of conscious sensuality surprising in such a young man—Scott was only twenty-five—he avoided an introduction that he might watch her undisturbed for a fanciful hour, and sip the pleasure or the disillusion of her conversation at the drowsy end of the evening.

'She never got over the disappointment of not meeting the Prince of Wales when he was in this country,' remarked Mrs Orrin Rogers, following his gaze. 'She said so, anyhow; whether she was serious or not I don't know. I hear that she has her walls simply plastered with pictures of him.'

'Who?' asked Scott suddenly.

'Why, the Prince of Wales.'

'Who has plaster pictures of him?'

'Why, Yanci Bowman, the girl you said you thought was so pretty.'

'After a certain degree of prettiness, one pretty girl is as pretty as another,' said Scott argumentatively.

'Yes, I suppose so.'

Mrs Rogers' voice drifted off on an indefinite note. She had never in her life compassed a generality until it had fallen familiarly on her ear from constant repetition.

'Let's talk her over,' Scott suggested.

With a mock reproachful smile Mrs Rogers lent herself agreeably to slander. An encore was just beginning. The orchestra trickled a light overflow of music into the pleasant green-latticed room and the two score couples who for the evening comprised the local younger set moved placidly into time with its beat. Only a few apathetic stags gathered one by one in the doorways, and to a close observer it was apparent that the scene did not attain the gayety which was its aspiration. These girls and men had known each other from childhood; and though there were marriages incipient upon the floor to-night, they were marriages of environment, of resignation, or even of boredom.

Their trappings lacked the sparkle of the seventeen-year-old affairs that took place through the short and radiant holidays. On such occasions as this, thought Scott as his eyes still sought casually for Yanci, occurred the matings of the left-overs, the plainer, the duller, the poorer of the social world; matings actuated by the same urge toward perhaps a more glamorous destiny, yet, for all that, less beautiful and less young. Scott himself was feeling very old.

But there was one face in the crowd to which his generalization did not apply. When his eyes found Yanci Bowman among the dancers he felt much younger. She was the incarnation of all in which the dance failed—graceful youth, arrogant, languid freshness and beauty that was sad and perishable as a memory in a dream. Her partner, a young man with one of those fresh red complexions ribbed with white streaks, as though he had been slapped on a cold day, did not appear to be holding her interest, and her glance fell here and there upon a group, a face, a garment, with a far-away and oblivious melancholy.

'Dark-blue eyes,' said Scott to Mrs Rogers. 'I don't know that they mean anything except that they're beautiful, but that nose and upper lip and chin are certainly aristocratic —if there is any such thing,' he added apologetically.

'Oh, she's very aristocratic,' agreed Mrs Rogers. 'Her grandfather was a senator or governor or something in one of the Southern States. Her father's very aristocratic looking too. Oh, yes, they're very aristocratic; they're aristocratic people.'

'She looks lazy.'

Scott was watching the yellow gown drift and submerge among the dancers.

'She doesn't like to move. It's a wonder she dances so well. Is she engaged? Who is the man who keeps cutting in on her, the one who tucks his tie under his collar so rakishly and affects the remarkable slanting pockets?'

He was annoyed at the young man's persistence, and his sarcasm lacked the ring of detachment.

'Oh, that's'—Mrs Rogers bent forward, the tip of her tongue just visible between her lips—'that's the O'Rourke boy. He's quite devoted, I believe.'

'I believe,' Scott said suddenly, 'that I'll get you to introduce me if she's near when the music stops.'

They arose and stood looking for Yanci—Mrs Rogers, small, stoutening, nervous, and Scott Kimberly her husband's cousin, dark and just below medium height. Scott was an orphan with half a million of his own, and he was in this city for no more reason than that he had missed a train. They looked for several minutes, and in vain. Yanci, in her yellow dress, no longer moved with slow loveliness among the dancers.

The clock stood at half past ten.

II

'Good evening,' her father was saying to her at that moment in syllables faintly slurred. 'This seems to be getting to be a habit.'

They were standing near a side stairs, and over his shoulder through a glass door Yanci could see a party of half a dozen men sitting in familiar joviality about a round table.

'Don't you want to come out and watch for a while?' she suggested, smiling and affecting a casualness she did not feel.

'Not to-night, thanks.'

Her father's dignity was a bit too emphasized to be convincing.

'Just come out and take a look,' she urged him. 'Everybody's here, and I want to ask you what you think of somebody.'

This was not so good, but it was the best that occurred to her.

'I doubt very strongly if I'd find anything to interest me out there,' said Tom Bowman emphatically. 'I observe that f'some insane reason I'm always taken out and aged on the wood for half an hour as though I was irresponsible.'

'I only ask you to stay a little while.'

'Very considerate, I'm sure. But to-night I happ'n be interested in a discussion that's taking place in here.'

'Come on, father.'

Yanci put her arm through his ingratiatingly; but he released it by the simple expedient of raising his own arm and letting hers drop.

'I'm afraid not.'

'I'll tell you,' she suggested lightly, concealing her annoyance at this unusually protracted argument, 'you come in and look, just once, and then if it bores you you can go right back.'

He shook his head.

'No thanks.'

Then without another word he turned suddenly and re-entered the bar. Yanci went back to the ballroom. She glanced easily at the stag line as she passed, and making a quick selection murmured to a man near her, 'Dance with me, will you, Carty? I've lost my partner.'

'Glad to,' answered Carty truthfully.

'Awfully sweet of you.'

'Sweet of me? Of you, you mean.'

She looked up at him absently. She was furiously annoyed at her father. Next morning at breakfast she would radiate a consuming chill, but for to-night she could only wait, hoping that if the worst happened he would at least remain in the bar until the dance was over.

Mrs Rogers, who lived next door to the Bowmans, appeared suddenly at her elbow with a strange young man. 'Yanci,' Mrs Rogers was saying with a social smile. 'I want to introduce Mr Kimberly. Mr Kimberly's spending the weekend with us, and I particularly wanted him to meet you.'

'How perfectly slick!' drawled Yanci with lazy formality.

Mr Kimberly suggested to Miss Bowman that they dance, to which proposal Miss Bowman dispassionately acquiesced. They mingled their arms in the gesture prevalent and stepped into time with the beat of the drum. Simultaneously it seemed to Scott that the room and the couples who danced up and down upon it converted themselves into a background behind her. The commonplace lamps, the rhythm of the music playing some paraphrase of a paraphrase, the faces of many girls, pretty, undistinguished or absurd, assumed a certain solidity as though they had grouped themselves in a retinue for Yanci's languid eyes and dancing feet.

'I've been watching you,' said Scott simply. 'You look rather bored this evening.'

'Do I?' Her dark-blue eyes exposed a borderland of fragile iris as they opened in a delicate burlesque of interest. 'How perfectly kill-ing!' she added.

Scott laughed. She had used the exaggerated phrase without smiling, indeed without any attempt to give it verisimilitude. He had heard the adjectives of the year—'hectic,' 'marvelous' and 'slick'—delivered casually, but never before without the faintest meaning. In this lackadaisical young beauty it was inexpressibly charming.

The dance ended. Yanci and Scott strolled toward a lounge set against the wall, but before they could take possession there was a shriek of laughter and a brawny damsel dragging an embarrassed boy in her wake skidded by them and plumped down upon it.

'How rude!' observed Yanci.

(20)

'I suppose it's her privilege.'

'A girl with ankles like that has no privileges.'

They seated themselves uncomfortably on two stiff chairs.

'Where do you come from?' she asked of Scott with polite disinterest.

'New York.'

This having transpired, Yanci deigned to fix her eyes on him for the best part of ten seconds.

'Who was the gentleman with the invisible tie,' Scott asked rudely, in order to make her look at him again, 'who was giving you such a rush? I found it impossible to keep my eyes off him. Is his personality as diverting as his haberdashery?'

'I don't know,' she drawled; 'I've only been engaged to him for a week.'

'My Lord!' exclaimed Scott, perspiring suddenly under his eyes.

'I beg your pardon. I didn't——'

'I was only joking,' she interrupted with a sighing laugh. 'I thought I'd see what you'd say to that.'

Then they both laughed, and Yanci continued, 'I'm not engaged to anyone. I'm too horribly unpopular.' Still the same key, her languorous voice humorously contradicting the content of her remark. 'No one'll ever marry me.'

'How pathetic!'

'Really,' she murmured; 'because I have to have compliments all the time, in order to live, and no one thinks I'm attractive any more, so no one ever gives them to me.'

Seldom had Scott been so amused.

'Why, you beautiful child,' he cried, 'I'll bet you never hear anything else from morning till night!'

'Oh, yes I do,' she responded, obviously pleased. 'I never get compliments unless I fish for them.'

'Everything's the same,' she was thinking as she gazed around her in a peculiar mood of pessimism. Same boys sober and same boys tight; same old women sitting by the walls—and one or two girls sitting with them who were dancing this time last year.

Yanci had reached the stage where these country-club dances seemed little more than a display of sheer idiocy. From being an enchanted carnival where jeweled and immaculate maidens rouged to the pinkest propriety displayed themselves to strange and fascinating men, the picture had faded to a medium-sized hall where was an almost indecent display of unclothed motives and obvious failures. So much for several years! And the dance had changed scarcely by a ruffle in the fashions or a new flip in a figure of speech.

Yanci was ready to be married.

Meanwhile the dozen remarks rushing to Scott Kimberly's lips were interrupted by the apologetic appearance of Mrs Rogers.

'Yanci,' the older woman was saying, 'the chauffeur's just telephoned to say that the car's broken down. I wonder if you and your father have room for us going home. If it's the slightest inconvenience don't hesitate to tell——'

'I know he'll be terribly glad to. He's got loads of room, because I came out with someone else.'

She was wondering if her father would be presentable at twelve.

He could always drive at any rate—and, besides, people who asked for a lift could take what they got.

'That'll be lovely. Thank you so much,' said Mrs Rogers.

Then, as she had just passed the kittenish late thirties when women still think they are *persona grata* with the young and entered upon the early forties when their children convey to them tactfully that they no longer are, Mrs Rogers obliterated herself from the scene. At that moment the music started and the unfortunate young man with white streaks in his red complexion appeared in front of Yanci.

Just before the end of the end of the next dance Scott Kimberly cut in on her again.

'I've come back,' he began, 'to tell you how beautiful you are.'

'I'm not, really,' she answered. 'And besides, you tell everyone that.'

The music gathered gusto for its finale, and they sat down upon the comfortable lounge.

'I've told no one that for three years,' said Scott.

There was no reason why he should have made it three years, yet somehow it sounded convincing to both of them. Her curiosity was stirred. She began finding out about him. She put him to a lazy questionnaire which began with his relationship to the Rogerses and ended, he knew not by what steps, with a detailed description of his apartment in New York.

'I want to live in New York,' she told him; 'on Park Avenue, in one of those beautiful white buildings that have twelve big rooms in each apartment and cost a fortune to rent.'

'That's what I'd want, too, if I were married. Park Avenue —it's one of the most beautiful streets in the world, I think, perhaps chiefly because it hasn't any leprous park trying to give it an artificial suburbanity.'

'Whatever that is,' agreed Yanci. 'Anyway, father and I go to New York about three times a year. We always go to the Ritz.'

This was not precisely true. Once a year she generally pried her father from his placid and not unbeneficent existence that she might spend a week lolling by the Fifth Avenue shop windows, lunching or having tea with some former school friend from Farmover, and occasionally going to dinner and the theater with boys who came up from Yale or Princeton for the occasion. These had been pleasant adventures—not one but was filled to the brim with colorful hours—dancing at Mont Martre, dining at the Ritz, with some movie star or supereminent society woman at the next table, or else dreaming of what she might buy at Hempel's or

Waxe's or Thrumble's if her father's income had but one additional naught on the happy side of the decimal. She adored New York with a great impersonal affection—adored it as only a Middle Western or Southern girl can. In its gaudy bazaars she felt her soul transported with turbulent delight, for to her eyes it held nothing ugly, nothing sordid, nothing plain.

She had stayed once at the Ritz—once only. The Manhattan, where they usually registered, had been torn down. She knew that she could never induce her father to afford the Ritz again.

After a moment she borrowed a pencil and paper and scribbled a notification 'To Mr Bowman in the grill' that he was expected to drive Mrs Rogers and her guest home, 'by request'—this last underlined. She hoped that he would be able to do so with dignity. This note she sent by a waiter to her father. Before the next dance began it was returned to her with a scrawled O.K. and her father's initials.

The remainder of the evening passed quickly. Scott Kimberly cut in on her as often as time permitted, giving her those comforting assurances of her enduring beauty which, not without a whimsical pathos, she craved. He laughed at her also, and she was not sure that she liked that. In common with all vague people, she was unaware that she was vague. She did not entirely comprehend when Scott Kimberly told her that her personality would endure long after she was too old to care whether it endured or not.

She liked best to talk about New York, and each of their interrupted conversations gave her a picture or a memory of the metropolis on which she speculated as she looked over the shoulder of Jerry O'Rourke or Carty Braden or some other beau, to whom, as to all of them, she was comfortably anæsthetic. At midnight she sent another note to her father, saying that Mrs Rogers and Mrs Rogers' guest would meet him immediately on the porch by the main driveway. Then, hoping for the best, she walked out into the

(24)

starry night and was assisted by Jerry O'Rourke into his roadster.

III

'Good night, Yanci.' With her late escort she was standing on the curbstone in front of the rented stucco house where she lived. Mr O'Rourke was attempting to put significance into his lingering rendition of her name. For weeks he had been straining to boost their relations almost forcibly onto a sentimental plane; but Yanci, with her vague impassivity, which was a defense against almost anything, had brought to naught his efforts. Jerry O'Rourke was an old story. His family had money; but he—he worked in a brokerage house along with most of the rest of his young generation. He sold bonds—bonds were the new thing; real estate was once the thing—in the days of the boom; then automobiles were the thing. Bonds were the thing now. Young men sold them who had nothing else to go into.

'Don't bother to come up, please.' Then as he put his car into gear, 'Call me up soon!'

A minute later he turned the corner of the moonlit street and disappeared, his cut-out resounding voluminously through the night as it declared that the rest of two dozen weary inhabitants was of no concern to his gay meanderings.

Yanci sat down thoughtfully upon the porch steps. She had no key and must wait for her father's arrival. Five minutes later a roadster turned into the street, and approaching with an exaggerated caution stopped in front of the Rogers' large house next door. Relieved, Yanci arose and strolled slowly down the walk. The door of the car had swung open and Mrs Rogers, assisted by Scott Kimberly, had alighted safely upon the sidewalk; but to Yanci's surprise Scott Kimberly, after escorting Mrs Rogers to her steps, returned to the car. Yanci was close enough to notice that he took the driver's seat. As he drew up at the Bowmans' curbstone

Yanci saw that her father was occupying the far corner, fighting with ludicrous dignity against a sleep that had come upon him. She groaned. The fatal last hour had done its work—Tom Bowman was once more *hors de combat*.

'Hello,' cried Yanci as she reached the curb.

'Yanci,' muttered her parent, simulating, unsuccessfully, a brisk welcome. His lips were curved in an ingratiating grin.

'Your father wasn't feeling quite fit, so he let me drive home,' explained Scott cheerfully as he got himself out and came up to her.

'Nice little car. Had it long?'

Yanci laughed, but without humor.

'Is he paralyzed?'

'Is who paralyze'?' demanded the figure in the car with an offended sigh.

Scott was standing by the car.

'Can I help you out, sir?'

'I c'n get out. I c'n get out,' insisted Mr Bowman. 'Just step a li'l' out my way. Someone must have given me some stremely bad wisk'.'

'You mean a lot of people must have given you some,' retorted Yanci in cold unsympathy.

Mr Bowman reached the curb with astonishing ease; but this was a deceitful success, for almost immediately he clutched at a handle of air perceptible only to himself, and was saved by Scott's quickly proffered arm. Followed by the two men, Yanci walked toward the house in a furor of embarrassment. Would the young man think that such scenes went on every night? It was chiefly her own presence that made it humiliating for Yanci. Had her father been carried to bed by two butlers each evening she might even have been proud of the fact that he could afford such dissipation; but to have it thought that she assisted, that she was burdened with the worry and the care! And finally she was annoyed with Scott Kimberly for being there, and for his officiousness in helping to bring her father into the house.

Reaching the low porch of tapestry brick, Yanci searched in Tom Bowman's vest for the key and unlocked the front door. A minute later the master of the house was deposited in an easy-chair.

'Thanks very much,' he said, recovering for a moment. 'Sit down. Like a drink? Yanci, get some crackers and cheese, if there's any, won't you, dear?'

At the unconscious coolness of this Scott and Yanci laughed.

'It's your bedtime, father,' she said, her anger struggling with diplomacy.

'Give me my guitar,' he suggested, 'and I'll play you tune.'

Except on such occasions as this, he had not touched his guitar for twenty years. Yanci turned to Scott.

'He'll be fine now. Thanks a lot. He'll fall asleep in a minute and when I wake him he'll go to bed like a lamb.'

'Well——'

They strolled together out the door.

'Sleepy?' he asked.

'No, not a bit.'

'Then perhaps you'd better let me stay here with you a few minutes until you see if he's all right. Mrs Rogers gave me a key so I can get in without disturbing her.'

'It's quite all right,' protested Yanci. 'I don't mind a bit, and he won't be any trouble. He must have taken a glass too much, and this whisky we have out here—you know! This has happened once before—last year,' she added.

Her words satisfied her; as an explanation it seemed to have a convincing ring.

'Can I sit down for a moment, anyway?' They sat side by side upon a wicker porch settee.

'I'm thinking of staying over a few days,' Scott said.

'How lovely!' Her voice had resumed its die-away note.

'Cousin Pete Rogers wasn't well today, but to-morrow he's going duck shooting, and he wants me to go with him.'

'Oh, how thrill-ing! I've always been mad to go, and father's always promised to take me, but he never has.'

'We're going to be gone about three days, and then I thought I'd come back here and stay over the next week-end——' He broke off suddenly and bent forward in a listening attitude.

'Now what on earth is that?'

The sounds of music were proceeding brokenly from the room they had lately left—a ragged chord on a guitar and half a dozen feeble starts.

'It's father!' cried Yanci.

And now a voice drifted out to them, drunken and murmurous, taking the long notes with attempted melancholy:

> *Sing a song of cities,*
> *Ridin' on a rail,*
> *A niggah's ne'er so happy*
> *As when he's out-a jail.*

'How terrible!' exclaimed Yanci. 'He'll wake up everybody in the block.'

The chorus ended, the guitar jangled again, then gave out a last harsh spang! and was still. A moment later these disturbances were followed by a low but quite definite snore. Mr Bowman, having indulged his musical proclivity, had dropped off to sleep.

'Let's go to ride,' suggested Yanci impatiently. 'This is too hectic for me.'

Scott arose with alacrity and they walked down to the car.

'Where'll we go?' she wondered.

'I don't care.'

'We might go up half a block to Crest Avenue—that's our show street—and then ride out to the river boulevard.'

IV

As they turned into Crest Avenue the new cathedral, immense and unfinished, in imitation of a cathedral left unfinished by accident in some little Flemish town, squatted just across the way like a plump white bulldog on its haunches. The ghosts of four moonlit apostles looked down at them wanly from wall niches still littered with the white dusty trash of the builders. The cathedral inaugurated Crest Avenue. After it came the great brownstone mass built by R. R. Comerford, the flour king, followed by a half mile of pretentious stone houses put up in the gloomy 90's. These were adorned with monstrous driveways and porte-cochères which had once echoed to the hoofs of good horses and with huge circular windows that corseted the second stories.

The continuity of these mausoleums was broken by a small park, a triangle of grass where Nathan Hale stood ten feet tall with his hands bound behind his back by stone cord and stared over a great bluff at the slow Mississippi. Crest Avenue ran along the bluff, but neither faced it nor seemed aware of it, for all the houses fronted inward toward the street. Beyond the first half mile it became newer, essayed ventures in terraced lawns, in concoctions of stucco or in granite mansions which imitated through a variety of gradual refinements the marble contours of the Petit Trianon. The houses of this phase rushed by the roadster for a succession of minutes; then the way turned and the car was headed directly into the moonlight which swept toward it like the lamp of some gigantic motorcycle far up the avenue.

Past the low Corinthian lines of the Christian Science Temple, past a block of dark frame horrors, a deserted row of grim red brick—an unfortunate experiment of the late 90's—then new houses again, bright-red brick now, with trimmings of white, black iron fences and hedges binding flowery lawns. These swept by, faded, passed, enjoying their moment of grandeur; then waiting there in the moonlight to be outmoded as had the frame, cupolaed mansions of lower town and the brownstone piles of older Crest Avenue in their turn.

The roofs lowered suddenly, the lots narrowed, the houses

shrank up in size and shaded off into bungalows. These held the street for the last mile, to the bend in the river which terminated the prideful avenue at the statue of Chelsea Arbuthnot. Arbuthnot was the first governor—and almost the last of Anglo-Saxon blood.

All the way thus far Yanci had not spoken, absorbed still in the annoyance of the evening, yet soothed somehow by the fresh air of Northern November that rushed by them. She must take her fur coat out of storage next day, she thought.

'Where are we now?'

As they slowed down Scott looked up curiously at the pompous stone figure, clear in the crisp moonlight, with one hand on a book and the forefinger of the other pointing, as though with reproachful symbolism directly at some construction work going on in the street.

'This is the end of Crest Avenue,' said Yanci, turning to him. 'This is our show street.'

'A museum of American architectural failures.'

'What?'

'Nothing,' he murmured.

'I should have explained it to you. I forgot. We can go along the river boulevard if you'd like—or are you tired?'

Scott assured her that he was not tired—not in the least.

Entering the boulevard, the cement road twisted under darkling trees.

'The Mississippi—how little it means to you now!' said Scott suddenly.

'What?' Yanci looked around. 'Oh, the river.'

'I guess it was once pretty important to your ancestors up here.'

'My ancestors weren't up here then,' said Yanci with some dignity. 'My ancestors were from Maryland. My father came out here when he left Yale.'

'Oh!' Scott was politely impressed.

'My mother was from here. My father came out here from Baltimore because of his health.'

'Oh!'

'Of course we belong here now, I suppose'—this with faint condescension— 'as much as anywhere else.'

'Of course.'

'Except that I want to live in the East and I can't persuade father to,' she finished.

It was after one o'clock and the boulevard was almost deserted. Occasionally two yellow disks would top a rise ahead of them and take shape as a late-returning automobile. Except for that they were alone in a continual rushing dark. The moon had gone down.

'Next time the road goes near the river let's stop and watch it,' he suggested.

Yanci smiled inwardly. This remark was obviously what one boy of her acquaintance had named an international petting cue, by which was meant a suggestion that aimed to create naturally a situation for a kiss. She considered the matter. As yet the man had made no particular impression on her. He was good-looking, apparently well-to-do and from New York. She had begun to like him during the dance, increasingly as the evening had drawn to a close; then the incident of her father's appalling arrival had thrown cold water upon this tentative warmth; and now—it was November, and the night was cold. Still——

'All right,' she agreed suddenly.

The road divided; she swerved around and brought the car to a stop in an open place high above the river.

'Well?' she demanded in the deep quiet that followed the shutting off of the engine.

'Thanks.'

'Are you satisfied here?'

'Almost. Not quite.'

'Why not?'

'I'll tell you in a minute,' he answered. 'Why is your name Yanci?'

'It's a family name.'

'It's very pretty.' He repeated it several times caressingly. 'Yanci—it has all the grace of Nancy, and yet it isn't prim.'

'What's your name?' she inquired.

'Scott.'

'Scott what?'

'Kimberly. Didn't you know?'

'I wasn't sure. Mrs Rogers introduced you in such a mumble.'

There was a slight pause.

'Yanci,' he repeated; 'beautiful Yanci, with her dark-blue eyes and her lazy soul. Do you know why I'm not quite satisfied, Yanci?'

'Why?'

Imperceptibly she had moved her face nearer until as she waited for an answer with her lips faintly apart he knew that in asking she had granted.

Without haste he bent his head forward and touched her lips.

He sighed, and both of them felt a sort of relief—relief from the embarrassment of playing up to what conventions of this sort of thing remained.

'Thanks,' he said as he had when she first stopped the car.

'Now are you satisfied?'

Her blue eyes regarded him unsmilingly in the darkness.

'After a fashion; of course, you can never say—definitely.'

Again he bent toward her, but she stooped and started the motor. It was late and Yanci was beginning to be tired. What purpose there was in the experiment was accomplished. He had had what he asked. If he liked it he would want more, and that put her one move ahead in the game which she felt she was beginning.

'I'm hungry,' she complained. 'Let's go down and eat.'

'Very well,' he acquiesced sadly. 'Just when I was so enjoying—the Mississippi.'

'Do you think I'm beautiful?' she inquired almost plaintively as they backed out.

'What an absurd question!'

'But I like to hear people say so.'

'I was just about to—when you started the engine.'

Downtown in a deserted all-night lunch room they ate bacon and eggs. She was pale as ivory now. The night had drawn the lazy vitality and languid color out of her face. She encouraged him to talk to her of New York until he was beginning every sentence with, 'Well, now, let's see——'

The repast over, they drove home. Scott helped her put the car in the little garage, and just outside the front door she lent him her lips again for the faint brush of a kiss. Then she went in.

The long living room which ran the width of the small stucco house was reddened by a dying fire which had been high when Yanci left and now was faded to a steady undancing glow. She took a log from the fire box and threw it on the embers, then started as a voice came out of the half darkness at the other end of the room.

'Back so soon?'

It was her father's voice, not yet quite sober, but alert and intelligent.

'Yes. Went riding,' she answered shortly, sitting down in a wicker chair before the fire. 'Then went down and had something to eat.'

'Oh!'

Her father left his place and moved to a chair nearer the fire, where he stretched himself out with a sigh. Glancing at him from the corner of her eye, for she was going to show an appropriate coldness, Yanci was fascinated by his complete recovery of dignity in the space of two hours. His graying hair was scarcely rumpled; his handsome face was ruddy as ever. Only his eyes, crisscrossed with tiny red lines, were evidence of his late dissipation.

'Have a good time?'

'Why should you care?' she answered rudely.

'Why shouldn't I?'

'You didn't seem to care earlier in the evening. I asked

you to take two people home for me, and you weren't able to drive your own car.'

'The deuce I wasn't!' he protested. 'I could have driven in—in a race in an arana, areaena. That Mrs Rogers insisted that her young admirer should drive, so what could I do?'

'That isn't her young admirer,' retorted Yanci crisply. There was no drawl in her voice now. 'She's as old as you are. That's her niece—I mean her nephew.'

'Excuse me!'

'I think you owe me an apology.' She found suddenly that she bore him no resentment. She was rather sorry for him and it occurred to her that in asking him to take Mrs Rogers home she had somehow imposed on his liberty. Nevertheless, discipline was necessary—there would be other Saturday nights. 'Don't you?' she concluded.

'I apologize, Yanci.'

'Very well, I accept your apology,' she answered stiffly.

'What's more, I'll make it up to you.'

Her blue eyes contracted. She hoped—she hardly dared to hope that he might take her to New York.

'Let's see,' he said. 'November, isn't it? What date?'

'The twenty-third.'

'Well, I'll tell you what I'll do.' He knocked the tips of his fingers together tentatively. 'I'll give you a present. I've been meaning to let you have a trip all fall, but business has been bad.' She almost smiled—as though business was of any consequence in his life. 'But then you need a trip. I'll make you a present of it.'

He rose again, and crossing over to his desk sat down.

'I've got a little money in a New York bank that's been lying there quite a while,' he said as he fumbled in a drawer for a check book. 'I've been intending to close out the the account. Let—me—see. There's just——' His pen scratched. 'Where the devil's the blotter? Uh!'

He came back to the fire and a pink oblong paper fluttered into her lap.

(34)

'Why, father!'

It was a check for three hundred dollars.

'But can you afford this?' she demanded.

'It's all right,' he reassured her, nodding. 'That can be a Christmas present, too, and you'll probably need a dress or a hat or something before you go.'

'Why,' she began uncertainly, 'I hardly know whether I ought to take this much or not! I've got two hundred of my own downtown, you know. Are you sure——'

'Oh, yes!' He waved his hand with magnificent carelessness. 'You need a holiday. You've been talking about New York, and I want you to go down there. Tell some of your friends at Yale and the other colleges and they'll ask you to the prom or something. That'll be nice. You'll have a good time.'

He sat down abruptly in his chair and gave vent to a long sigh. Yanci folded up the check and tucked it into the low bosom of her dress.

'Well,' she drawled softly with a return to her usual manner, 'you're a perfect lamb to be so sweet about it, but I don't want to be horribly extravagant.'

Her father did not answer. He gave another little sigh and relaxed sleepily into his chair.

'Of course I do want to go,' went on Yanci.

Still her father was silent. She wondered if he were asleep.

'Are you asleep?' she demanded, cheerfully now. She bent toward him; then she stood up and looked at him.

'Father,' she said uncertainly.

Her father remained motionless; the ruddy color had melted suddenly out of his face.

'Father!'

It occurred to her—and at the thought she grew cold, and a brassière of iron clutched at her breast—that she was alone in the room. After a frantic instant she said to herself that her father was dead.

V

Yanci judged herself with inevitable gentleness—judged herself very much as a mother might judge a wild, spoiled child. She was not hard-minded, nor did she live by any ordered and considered philosophy of her own. To such a catastrophe as the death of her father her immediate reaction was a hysterical self-pity. The first three days were something of a nightmare; but sentimental civilization, being as infallible as Nature in healing the wounds of its more fortunate children, had inspired a certain Mrs Oral, whom Yanci had always loathed, with a passionate interest in all such crises. To all intents and purposes Mrs Oral buried Tom Bowman. The morning after his death Yanci had wired her maternal aunt in Chicago, but as yet that undemonstrative and well-to-do lady had sent no answer.

All day long, for four days, Yanci sat in her room upstairs hearing steps come and go on the porch, and it merely increased her nervousness that the doorbell had been disconnected. This by order of Mrs Oral! Doorbells were always disconnected! After the burial of the dead the strain relaxed. Yanci, dressed in her new black, regarded herself in the pier glass, and then wept because she seemed to herself very sad and beautiful. She went downstairs and tried to read a moving-picture magazine, hoping that she would not be alone in the house when the winter dark came down just after four.

This afternoon Mrs Oral had said *carpe diem* to the maid and Yanci was just starting for the kitchen to see whether she had yet gone when the reconnected bell rang suddenly through the house. Yanci started. She waited a minute, then went to the door. It was Scott Kimberly.

'I was just going to inquire for you,' he said.

'Oh! I'm much better, thank you,' she responded with the quiet dignity that seemed suited to her rôle.

They stood there in the hall awkwardly, each reconstructing the half-facetious, half-sentimental occasion on which they had last met. It seemed such an irreverent prelude to such a somber disaster. There was no common ground for them now, no gap that could be bridged by a slight reference to their mutual past, and there was no foundation on which he could adequately pretend to share her sorrow.

'Won't you come in?' she said, biting her lip nervously. He followed her to the sitting room and sat beside her on the lounge. In another minute, simply because he was there and alive and friendly, she was crying on his shoulder.

"There, there!' he said, putting his arm behind her and patting her shoulder idiotically. 'There, there, there!'

He was wise enough to attribute no ulterior significance to her action. She was overstrained with grief and loneliness and sentiment; almost any shoulder would have done as well. For all the biological thrill to either of them he might have been a hundred years old. In a minute she sat up.

'I beg your pardon,' she murmured brokenly. 'But it's—it's so dismal in this house to-day.'

'I know just how you feel, Yanci.'

'Did I—did I—get—tears on your coat?'

In tribute to the tenseness of the incident they both laughed hysterically, and with the laughter she momentarily recovered her propriety.

'I don't know why I should have chosen you to collapse on,' she wailed. 'I really don't just go round doing it indiscriminately on anyone who comes in.'

'I consider it a—a compliment,' he responded soberly, 'and I can understand the state you're in.' Then, after a pause, 'Have you any plans?'

She shook her head.

'Va-vague ones,' she muttered between little gasps. 'I tho-ought I'd go down and stay with my aunt in Chicago a while.'

'I should think that'd be best—much the best thing.' Then, because he could think of nothing else to say, he added, 'Yes, very much the best thing.'

'What are you doing—here in town?' she inquired,

taking in her breath in minute gasps and dabbing at her eyes with a handkerchief.

'Oh, I'm here with—with the Rogerses. I've been here.'

'Hunting?'

'No, I've just been here.'

He did not tell her that he had stayed over on her account. She might think it fresh.

'I see,' she said. She didn't see.

'I want to know if there's any possible thing I can do for you, Yanci. Perhaps go downtown for you, or do some errands—anything. Maybe you'd like to bundle up and get a bit of air. I could take you out to drive in your car some night, and no one would see you.'

He clipped his last word short as the inadvertency of this suggestion dawned on him. They stared at each other with horror in their eyes.

'Oh, no, thank you!' she cried. 'I really don't want to drive.'

To his relief the outer door opened and an elderly lady came in. It was Mrs Oral. Scott rose immediately and moved backward toward the door.

'If you're sure there isn't anything I can do——'

Yanci introduced him to Mrs Oral; then leaving the elder woman by the fire walked with him to the door. An idea had suddenly occurred to her.

'Wait a minute.'

She ran up the front stairs and returned immediately with a slip of pink paper in her hand.

'Here's something I wish you'd do,' she said. 'Take this to the First National Bank and have it cashed for me. You can leave the money here for me any time.'

Scott took out his wallet and opened it.

'Suppose I cash it for you now,' he suggested.

'Oh, there's no hurry.'

'But I may as well.' He drew out three new one-hundred-dollar bills and gave them to her.

(38)

'That's awfully sweet of you,' said Yanci.

'Not at all. May I come in and see you next time I come West?'

'I wish you would.'

'Then I will. I'm going East to-night.'

The door shut him out into the snowy dusk and Yanci returned to Mrs Oral. Mrs Oral had come to discuss plans.

'And now, my dear, just what do you plan to do? We ought to have some plan to go by, and I thought I'd find out if you had any definite plan in your mind.'

Yanci tried to think. She seemed to herself to be horribly alone in the world.

'I haven't heard from my aunt. I wired her again this morning. She may be in Florida.'

'In that case you'd go there?'

'I suppose so.'

'Would you close this house?'

'I suppose so.'

Mrs Oral glanced around with placid practicality. It occurred to her that if Yanci gave the house up she might like it for herself.

'And now,' she continued, 'do you know where you stand financially?'

'All right, I guess,' answered Yanci indifferently; and then with a rush of sentiment, 'There was enough for t-two; there ought to be enough for o-one.'

'I didn't mean that,' said Mrs Oral. 'I mean, do you know the details?'

'No.'

'Well, I thought you didn't know the details. And I thought you ought to know all the details—have a detailed account of what and where your money is. So I called up Mr Haedge, who knew your father very well personally, to come up this afternoon and glance through his papers. He was going to stop in your father's bank, too, by the way, and get all the details there. I don't believe your father left any will.'

Details! Details! Details!

'Thank you,' said Yanci. 'That'll be—nice.'

Mrs Oral gave three or four vigorous nods that were like heavy periods. Then she got up.

'And now if Hilma's gone out I'll make you some tea. Would you like some tea?'

'Sort of.'

'All right, I'll make you some ni-ice tea.'

Tea! Tea! Tea!

Mr Haedge, who came from one of the best Swedish families in town, arrived to see Yanci at five o'clock. He greeted her funereally; said that he had been several times to inquire for her; had organized the pallbearers and would now find out how she stood in no time. Did she have any idea whether or not there was a will? No? Well, there probably wasn't one.

There was one. He found it almost at once in Mr Bowman's desk—but he worked there until eleven o'clock that night before he found much else. Next morning he arrived at eight, went down to the bank at ten, then to a certain brokerage firm, and came back to Yanci's house at noon. He had known Tom Bowman for some years, but he was utterly astounded when he discovered the condition in which that handsome gallant had left his affairs.

He consulted Mrs Oral, and that afternoon he informed a frightened Yanci in measured language that she was practically penniless. In the midst of the conversation a telegram from Chicago told her that her aunt had sailed the week previous for a trip through the Orient and was not expected back until late spring.

The beautiful Yanci, so profuse, so debonair, so careless with her gorgeous adjectives, had no adjectives for this calamity. She crept upstairs like a hurt child and sat before a mirror, brushing her luxurious hair to comfort herself. One hundred and fifty strokes she gave it, as it said in the treatment, and then a hundred and fifty more—she was too distraught to stop the nervous motion. She brushed it until her arm ached, then she changed arms and went on brushing.

The maid found her next morning, asleep, sprawled across the toilet things on the dresser in a room that was heavy and sweet with the scent of spilled perfume.

VI

To be precise, as Mr Haedge was to a depressing degree, Tom Bowman left a bank balance that was more than ample—that is to say, more than ample to supply the post-mortem requirements of his own person. There was also twenty years' worth of furniture, a temperamental roadster with asthmatic cylinders and two one-thousand-dollar bonds of a chain of jewelry stores which yielded 7.5 per cent interest. Unfortunately these were not known in the bond market.

When the car and the furniture had been sold and the stucco bungalow sublet, Yanci· contemplated her resources with dismay. She had a bank balance of almost a thousand dollars. If she invested this she would increase her total income to about fifteen dollars a month. This, as Mrs Oral cheerfully observed, would pay for the boarding-house room she had taken for Yanci as long as Yanci lived. Yanci was so encouraged by this news that she burst into tears.

So she acted as any beautiful girl would have acted in this emergency. With rare decision she told Mr Haedge that she would leave her thousand dollars in a checking account, and then she walked out of his office and across the street to a beauty parlor to have her hair waved. This raised her morale astonishingly. Indeed, she moved that very day out of the boarding house and into a small room at the best hotel in town. If she must sink into poverty she would at least do so in the grand manner.

Sewed into the lining of her best mourning hat were the three new one-hundred-dollar bills, her father's last present. What she expected of them, why she kept them in such a way, she did not know, unless perhaps because they had come to her under cheerful auspices and might through some gayety inherent in their crisp and virgin paper buy happier things than solitary meals and narrow hotel beds. They were hope and youth and luck and beauty; they began, somehow, to stand for all the things she had lost in that November night when Tom Bowman, having led her recklessly into space, had plunged off himself, leaving her to find the way back alone.

Yanci remained at the Hiawatha Hotel for three months, and she found that after the first visits of condolence her friends had happier things to do with their time than to spend it in her company. Jerry O'Rourke came to see her one day with a wild Celtic look in his eyes, and demanded that she marry him immediately. When she asked for time to consider he walked out in a rage. She heard later that he had been offered a position in Chicago and had left the same night.

She considered, frightened and uncertain. She had heard of people sinking out of place, out of life. Her father had once told her of a man in his class at college who had become a worker around saloons, polishing brass rails for the price of a can of beer; and she knew also that there were girls in this city with whose mothers her own mother had played as a little girl, but who were poor now and had grown common; who worked in stores and had married into the proletariat. But that such a fate should threaten her—how absurd! Why, she knew everyone! She had been invited everywhere; her great-grandfather had been governor of one of the Southern States!

She had written to her aunt in India and again in China, receiving no answer. She concluded that her aunt's itinerary had changed, and this was confirmed when a post card arrived from Honolulu which showed no knowledge of Tom Bowman's death, but announced that she was going with a party to the east coast of Africa. This was a last straw. The languorous and lackadaisical Yanci was on her own at last.

(42)

'Why not go to work for a while?' suggested Mr Haedge with some irritation. 'Lots of nice girls do nowadays, just for something to occupy themselves with. There's Elsie Prendergast, who does society news on the Bulletin, and that Semple girl——'

'I can't,' said Yanci shortly with a glitter of tears in her eyes. 'I'm going East in February.'

'East? Oh, you're going to visit someone?'

She nodded.

'Yes, I'm going to visit,' she lied, 'so it'd hardly be worth while to go to work.' She could have wept, but she managed a haughty look. 'I'd like to try reporting sometime, though, just for the fun of it.'

'Yes, it's quite a lot of fun,' agreed Mr Haedge with some irony. 'Still, I suppose there's no hurry about it. You must have plenty of that thousand dollars left.'

'Oh, plenty!'

There were a few hundred, she knew.

'Well, then I suppose a good rest, a change of scene would be the best thing for you.'

'Yes,' answered Yanci. Her lips were trembling and she rose, scarcely able to control herself. Mr Haedge seemed so impersonally cold. 'That's why I'm going. A good rest is what I need.'

'I think you're wise.'

What Mr Haedge would have thought had he seen the dozen drafts she wrote that night of a certain letter is problematical. Here are two of the earlier ones. The bracketed words are proposed substitutions:

Dear Scott: Not having seen you since that day I was such a silly ass and wept on your coat, I thought I'd write and tell you that I'm coming East pretty soon and would like you to have lunch [dinner] with me or something. I have been living in a room [suite] at the Hiawatha Hotel, intending to meet my aunt, with whom I am going to

(43)

live [stay], and who is coming back from China this month [spring]. Meanwhile I have a lot of invitations to visit, etc., in the East, and I thought I would do it now. So I'd like to see you——

This draft ended here and went into the wastebasket. After an hour's work she produced the following:

My dear Mr Kimberly: I have often [sometimes] wondered how you've been since I saw you. I am coming East next month before going to visit my aunt in Chicago, and you must come and see me. I have been going out very little, but my physician advises me that I need a change, so I expect to shock the proprieties by some very gay visits in the East——

Finally in despondent abandon she wrote a simple note without explanation or subterfuge, tore it up and went to bed. Next morning she identified it in the wastebasket, decided it was the best one after all and sent him a fair copy. It ran:

Dear Scott: Just a line to tell you I will be at the Ritz-Carlton Hotel from February seventh, probably for ten days. If you'll phone me some rainy afternoon I'll invite you to tea.
Sincerely,
Yanci Bowman.

VII

Yanci was going to the Ritz for no more reason than that she had once told Scott Kimberly that she always went there. When she reached New York—a cold New York, a strangely menacing New York, quite different from the gay city of theaters and hotel-corridor rendezvous that she had known—there was exactly two hundred dollars in her purse.

It had taken a large part of her bank account to live, and she had at last broken into her sacred three hundred dollars to substitute pretty and delicate quarter-mourning clothes for the heavy black she had laid away.

Walking into the hotel at the moment when its exquisitely dressed patrons were assembling for luncheon, it drained at her confidence to appear bored and at ease. Surely the clerks at the desk knew the contents of her pocketbook. She fancied even that the bell boys were snickering at the foreign labels she had steamed from an old trunk of her father's and pasted on her suitcase. This last thought horrified her. Perhaps the very hotels and steamers so grandly named had long since been out of commission!

As she stood drumming her fingers on the desk she was wondering whether if she were refused admittance she could muster a casual smile and stroll out coolly enough to deceive two richly dressed women standing near. It had not taken long for the confidence of twenty years to evaporate. Three months without security had made an ineffaceable mark on Yanci's soul.

'Twenty-four sixty-two,' said the clerk callously.

Her heart settled back into place as she followed the bell boy to the elevator, meanwhile casting a nonchalant glance at the two fashionable women as she passed them. Were their skirts long or short?—longer, she noticed.

She wondered how much the skirt of her new walking suit could be let out.

At luncheon her spirits soared. The head waiter bowed to her. The light rattle of conversation, the subdued hum of the music soothed her. She ordered supreme of melon, eggs Susette and an artichoke, and signed her room number to the check with scarcely a glance at it as it lay beside her plate. Up in her room, with the telephone directory open on the bed before her, she tried to locate her scattered metropolitan acquaintances. Yet even as the phone numbers, with their supercilious tags, Plaza, Circle and Rhinelander, stared out

(45)

at her, she could feel a cold wind blow at her unstable confidence. These girls, acquaintances of school, of a summer, of a house party, even of a week-end at a college prom—what claim or attraction could she, poor and friendless, exercise over them? They had their loves, their dates, their week's gayety planned in advance. They would almost resent her inconvenient memory.

Nevertheless, she called four girls. One of them was out, one at Palm Beach, one in California. The only one to whom she talked said in a hearty voice that she was in bed with grippe, but would phone Yanci as soon as she felt well enough to go out. Then Yanci gave up the girls. She would have to create the illusion of a good time in some other manner. The illusion must be created—that was part of her plan.

She looked at her watch and found that it was three o'clock. Scott Kimberly should have phoned before this, or at least left some word. Still, he was probably busy—at a club, she thought vaguely, or else buying some neckties. He would probably call at four.

Yanci was well aware that she must work quickly. She had figured to a nicety that one hundred and fifty dollars carefully expended would carry her through two weeks, no more. The idea of failure, the fear that at the end of that time she would be friendless and penniless had not begun to bother her.

It was not the first time that for amusement, for a coveted invitation or for curiosity she had deliberately set out to capture a man; but it was the first time she had laid her plans with necessity and desperation pressing in on her.

One of her strongest cards had always been her background, the impression she gave that she was popular and desired and happy. This she must create now, and apparently out of nothing. Scott must somehow be brought to think that a fair portion of New York was at her feet.

At four she went over to Park Avenue, where the sun was out walking and the February day was fresh and odorous of

spring and the high apartments of her desire lined the street
with radiant whiteness. Here she would live on a gay schedule
of pleasure. In these smart not-to-be-entered-without-a-card
women's shops she would spend the morning hours acquiring and acquiring, ceaselessly and without thought of expense; in these restaurants she would lunch at noon in
company with other fashionable women, orchid-adorned
always, and perhaps bearing an absurdly dwarfed Pomeranian
in her sleek arms.

In the summer—well, she would go to Tuxedo, perhaps to
an immaculate house perched high on a fashionable eminence, where she would emerge to visit a world of teas and
balls, of horse shows and polo. Between the halves of the
polo game the players would cluster around her in their
white suits and helmets, admiringly, and when she swept
away, bound for some new delight, she would be followed
by the eyes of many envious but intimidated women.

Every other summer they would, of course, go abroad.
She began to plan a typical year, distributing a few months
here and a few months there until she—and Scott Kimberly,
by implication—would become the very auguries of the
season, shifting with the slightest stirring of the social
barometer from rusticity to urbanity, from palm to pine.

She had two weeks, no more, in which to attain to this
position. In an ecstasy of determined emotion she lifted
up her head toward the tallest of the tall white apartments.

'It will be too marvelous!' she said to herself.

For almost the first time in her life her words were not too
exaggerated to express the wonder shining in her eyes.

VIII

About five o'clock she hurried back to the hotel, demanding
feverishly at the desk if there had been a telephone message
for her. To her profound disappointment there was nothing.
A minute after she had entered her room the phone rang.

(47)

'This is Scott Kimberly.'

At the words a call to battle echoed in her heart.

'Oh, how do you do?'

Her tone implied that she had almost forgotten him. It was not frigid—it was merely casual.

As she answered the inevitable question as to the hour when she had arrived a warm glow spread over her. Now that, from a personification of all the riches and pleasure she craved, he had materialized as merely a male voice over the telephone, her confidence became strengthened. Male voices were male voices. They could be managed; they could be made to intone syllables of which the minds behind them had no approval. Male voices could be made sad or tender or despairing at her will. She rejoiced. The soft clay was ready to her hand.

'Won't you take dinner with me to-night?' Scott was suggesting.

'Why'—perhaps not, she thought; let him think of her to-night—'I don't believe I'll be able to,' she said. 'I've got an engagement for dinner and the theater. I'm terribly sorry.'

Her voice did not sound sorry—it sounded polite. Then as though a happy thought had occurred to her as to a time and place where she could work him into her list of dates, 'I'll tell you: Why don't you come around here this afternoon and have tea with me?'

He would be there immediately. He had been playing squash and as soon as he took a plunge he would arrive. Yanci hung up the phone and turned with a quiet efficiency to the mirror, too tense to smile.

She regarded her lustrous eyes and dusky hair in critical approval. Then she took a lavender tea gown from her trunk and began to dress.

She let him wait seven minutes in the lobby before she appeared; then she approached him with a friendly, lazy smile.

'How do you do?' she murmured. 'It's marvelous to

(48)

see you again. How are you?' And, with a long sigh, 'I'm frightfully tired. I've been on the go ever since I got here this morning; shopping and then tearing off to luncheon and a matinée. I've bought everything I saw. I don't know how I'm going to pay for it all.'

She remembered vividly that when they had first met she had told him, without expecting to be believed, how unpopular she was. She could not risk such a remark now, even in jest. He must think that she had been on the go every minute of the day.

They took a table and were served with olive sandwiches and tea. He was so good-looking, she thought, and marvelously dressed. His gray eyes regarded her with interest from under immaculate ash-blond hair. She wondered how he passed his days, how he liked her costume, what he was thinking of at that moment.

'How long will you be here?' he asked.

'Well, two weeks, off and on. I'm going down to Princeton for the February prom and then up to a house party in Westchester County for a few days. Are you shocked at me for going out so soon? Father would have wanted me to, you know. He was very modern in all his ideas.'

She had debated this remark on the train. She was not going to a house party. She was not invited to the Princeton prom. Such things, nevertheless, were necessary to create the illusion. That was everything—the illusion.

'And then,' she continued, smiling, 'two of my old beaus are in town, which makes it nice for me.'

She saw Scott blink and she knew that he appreciated the significance of this.

'What are your plans for this winter?' he demanded. 'Are you going back West?'

'No. You see, my aunt returns from India this week. She's going to open her Florida house, and we'll stay there until the middle of March. Then we'll come up to Hot Springs and we may go to Europe for the summer.'

(49)

This was all the sheerest fiction. Her first letter to her aunt, which had given the bare details of Tom Bowman's death, had at last reached its destination. Her aunt had replied with a note of conventional sympathy and the announcement that she would be back in America within two years if she didn't decide to live in Italy.

'But you'll let me see something of you while you're here,' urged Scott, after attending to this impressive program. 'If you can't take dinner with me to-night, how about Wednesday—that's the day after to-morrow?'

'Wednesday? Let's see.' Yanci's brow was knit with imitation thought. 'I think I have a date for Wednesday, but I don't know for certain. How about phoning me to-morrow, and I'll let you know? Because I want to go with you, only I think I've made an engagement.'

'Very well, I'll phone you.'

'Do—about ten.'

'Try to be able to—then or any time.'

'I'll tell you—if I can't go to dinner with you Wednesday I can go to lunch surely.'

'All right,' he agreed. 'And we'll go to a matinée.'

They danced several times. Never by word or sign did Yanci betray more than the most cursory interest in him until just at the end, when she offered him her hand to say good-by.

'Good-by, Scott.'

For just the fraction of a second—not long enough for him to be sure it had happened at all, but just enough so that he would be reminded, however faintly, of that night on the Mississippi boulevard—she looked into his eyes. Then she turned quickly and hurried away.

She took her dinner in a little tea room around the corner. It was an economical dinner which cost a dollar and a half. There was no date concerned in it at all, and no man—except an elderly person in spats who tried to speak to her as she came out the door.

IX

Sitting alone in one of the magnificent moving-picture
theaters—a luxury which she thought she could afford—
Yanci watched Mae Murray swirl through splendidly
imagined vistas, and meanwhile considered the progress of
the first day. In retrospect it was a distinct success. She had
given the correct impression both as to her material prosperity
and as to her attitude toward Scott himself. It seemed best to
avoid evening dates. Let him have the evenings to himself, to
think of her, to imagine her with other men, even to spend a
few lonely hours in his apartment, considering how much more
cheerful it might be if—— Let time and absence work for her.

Engrossed for a while in the moving picture, she calculated the cost of the apartment in which its heroine endured
her movie wrongs. She admired its slender Italian table,
occupying only one side of the large dining room and flanked
by a long bench which gave it an air of medieval luxury. She
rejoiced in the beauty of Mae Murray's clothes and furs, her
gorgeous hats, her short-seeming French shoes. Then after
a moment her mind returned to her own drama; she wondered if Scott were already engaged, and her heart dipped at
the thought. Yet it was unlikely. He had been too quick to
phone her on her arrival, too lavish with his time, too responsive that afternoon.

After the picture she returned to the Ritz, where she slept
deeply and happily for almost the first time in three months.
The atmosphere around her no longer seemed cold. Even
the floor clerk had smiled kindly and admiringly when Yanci
asked for her key.

Next morning at ten Scott phoned. Yanci, who had been up
for hours, pretended to be drowsy from her dissipation of the
night before.

No, she could not take dinner with him on Wednesday.
She was terribly sorry; she had an engagement, as she had
feared. But she could have luncheon and go to a matinée if
he would get her back in time for tea.

She spent the day roving the streets. On top of a bus, though not on the front seat, where Scott might possibly spy her, she sailed out Riverside Drive and back along Fifth Avenue just at the winter twilight, and her feeling for New York and its gorgeous splendors deepened and redoubled. Here she must live and be rich, be nodded to by the traffic policemen at the corners as she sat in her limousine—with a small dog—and here she must stroll on Sunday to and from a stylish church, with Scott, handsome in his cutaway and tall hat, walking devotedly at her side.

At luncheon on Wednesday she described for Scott's benefit a fanciful two days. She told of a motoring trip up the Hudson and gave him her opinion of two plays she had seen with—it was implied—adoring gentlemen beside her. She had read up very carefully on the plays in the morning paper and chosen two concerning which she could garner the most information.

'Oh,' he said in dismay, 'you've seen Dulcy? I have two seats for it—but you won't want to go again.'

'Oh, no, I don't mind,' she protested truthfully. 'You see, we went late, and anyway I adored it.'

But he wouldn't hear of her sitting through it again—besides, he had seen it himself. It was a play Yanci was mad to see, but she was compelled to watch him while he exchanged the tickets for others, and for the poor seats available at the last moment. The game seemed difficult at times.

'By the way,' he said afterwards as they drove back to the hotel in a taxi, 'you'll be going down to the Princeton prom to-morrow, won't you?'

She started. She had not realized that it would be so soon or that he would know of it.

'Yes,' she answered coolly. 'I'm going down to-morrow afternoon.'

'On the 2:20, I suppose,' Scott commented; and then, 'Are you going to meet the boy who's taking you down—at Princeton?'

For an instant she was off her guard.

'Yes, he'll meet the train.'

'Then I'll take you to the station,' proposed Scott. 'There'll be a crowd, and you may have trouble getting a porter.'

She could think of nothing to say, no valid objection to make. She wished she had said that she was going by automobile, but she could conceive of no graceful and plausible way of amending her first admission.

'That's mighty sweet of you.'

'You'll be at the Ritz when you come back?'

'Oh, yes,' she answered. 'I'm going to keep my rooms.'

Her bedroom was the smallest and least expensive in the hotel.

She concluded to let him put her on the train for Princeton; in fact, she saw no alternative. Next day as she packed her suitcase after luncheon the situation had taken such hold of her imagination that she filled it with the very things she would have chosen had she really been going to the prom. Her intention was to get out at the first stop and take the train back to New York.

Scott called for her at half past one and they took a taxi to the Pennsylvania Station. The train was crowded as he had expected, but he found her a seat and stowed her grip in the rack overhead.

'I'll call you Friday to see how you've behaved,' he said.

'All right. I'll be good.'

Their eyes met and in an instant, with an inexplicable, only half-conscious rush of emotion, they were in perfect communion. When Yanci came back, the glance seemed to say, ah, then——

A voice startled her ear:

'Why, Yanci!'

Yanci looked around. To her horror she recognized a girl named Ellen Harley, one of those to whom she had phoned upon her arrival.

'Well, Yanci Bowman! You're the last person I ever expected to see. How are you?'

Yanci introduced Scott. Her heart was beating violently.

'Are you coming to the prom? How perfectly slick!' cried Ellen. 'Can I sit here with you? I've been wanting to see you. Who are you going with?'

'No one you know.'

'Maybe I do.'

Her words, falling like sharp claws on Yanci's sensitive soul, were interrupted by an unintelligible outburst from the conductor. Scott bowed to Ellen, cast at Yanci one level glance and then hurried off.

The train started. As Ellen arranged her grip and threw off her fur coat Yanci looked around her. The car was gay with girls whose excited chatter filled the damp, rubbery air like smoke. Here and there sat a chaperon, a mass of decaying rock in a field of flowers, predicting with a mute and somber fatality the end of all gayety and all youth. How many times had Yanci herself been one of such a crowd, careless and happy, dreaming of the men she would meet, of the battered hacks waiting at the station, the snow-covered campus, the big open fires in the clubhouses, and the imported orchestra beating out defiant melody against the approach of morning.

And now—she was an intruder, uninvited, undesired. As at the Ritz on the day of her arrival, she felt that at any instant her mask would be torn from her and she would be exposed as a pretender to the gaze of all the car.

'Tell me everything!' Ellen was saying. 'Tell me what you've been doing. I didn't see you at any of the football games last fall.'

This was by way of letting Yanci know that she had attended them herself.

The conductor was bellowing from the rear of the car, 'Manhattan Transfer next stop!'

Yanci's cheeks burned with shame. She wondered what she had best do—meditating a confession, deciding against it, answering Ellen's chatter in frightened monosyllables—

then, as with an ominous thunder of brakes the speed of the train began to slacken, she sprang on a despairing impulse to her feet.

'My heavens!' she cried. 'I've forgotten my shoes! I've got to go back and get them.'

Ellen reacted to this with annoying efficiency.

'I'll take your suitcase,' she said quickly, 'and you can call for it. I'll be at the Charter Club.'

'No!' Yanci almost shrieked. 'It's got my dress in it!'

Ignoring the lack of logic in her own remark, she swung the suitcase off the rack with what seemed to her a super-human effort and went reeling down the aisle, stared at curiously by the arrogant eyes of many girls. When she reached the platform just as the train came to a stop she felt weak and shaken. She stood on the hard cement which marks the quaint old village of Manhattan Transfer and tears were streaming down her cheeks as she watched the unfeeling cars speed off to Princeton with their burden of happy youth.

After half an hour's wait Yanci got on a train and returned to New York. In thirty minutes she had lost the confidence that a week had gained for her. She came back to her little room and lay down quietly upon the bed.

X

By Friday Yanci's spirits had partly recovered from their chill depression. Scott's voice over the telephone in mid-morning was like a tonic, and she told him of the delights of Princeton with convincing enthusiasm, drawing vicariously upon a prom she had attended there two years before. He was anxious to see her, he said. Would she come to dinner and the theater that night? Yanci considered, greatly tempted. Dinner—she had been economizing on meals, and a gor-geous dinner in some extravagant show place followed by a musical comedy appealed to her starved fancy, indeed; but instinct told her that the time was not yet right. Let him wait. Let him dream a little more, a little longer.

'I'm too tired, Scott,' she said with an air of extreme frankness; 'that's the whole truth of the matter. I've been out every night since I've been here, and I'm really half dead. I'll rest up on this house party over the week-end and then I'll go to dinner with you any day you want me.'

There was a minute's silence while she held the phone expectantly.

'Lot of resting up you'll do on a house party,' he replied; 'and, anyway, next week is so far off. I'm awfully anxious to see you, Yanci.'

'So am I, Scott.'

She allowed the faintest caress to linger on his name. When she had hung up she felt happy again. Despite her humiliation on the train her plan had been a success. The illusion was still intact; it was nearly complete. And in three meetings and half a dozen telephone calls she had managed to create a tenser atmosphere between them than if he had seen her constantly in the moods and avowals and beguilements of an out-and-out flirtation.

When Monday came she paid her first week's hotel bill. The size of it did not alarm her—she was prepared for that—but the shock of seeing so much money go, of realizing that there remained only one hundred and twenty dollars of her father's present, gave her a peculiar sinking sensation in the pit of her stomach. She decided to bring guile to bear immediately, to tantalize Scott by a carefully planned incident, and then at the end of the week to show him simply and definitely that she loved him.

As a decoy for Scott's tantalization she located by telephone a certain Jimmy Long, a handsome boy with whom she had played as a little girl and who had recently come to New York to work. Jimmy Long was deftly maneuvered into asking her to go to a matinée with him on Wednesday afternoon. He was to meet her in the lobby at two.

On Wednesday she lunched with Scott. His eyes followed her every motion, and knowing this she felt a great rush of tenderness toward him. Desiring at first only what he represented, she had begun half unconsciously to desire him also. Nevertheless, she did not permit herself the slightest relaxation on that account. The time was too short and the odds too great. That she was beginning to love him only fortified her resolve.

'Where are you going this afternoon?' he demanded.

'To a matinée—with an annoying man.'

'Why is he annoying?'

'Because he wants me to marry him and I don't believe I want to.'

There was just the faintest emphasis on the word 'believe.' The implication was that she was not sure—that is, not quite.

'Don't marry him.'

'I won't—probably.'

'Yanci,' he said in a low voice, 'do you remember a night on that boulevard——'

She changed the subject. It was noon and the room was full of sunlight. It was not quite the place, the time. When he spoke she must have every aspect of the situation in control. He must say only what she wanted said; nothing else would do.

'It's five minutes to two,' she told him, looking at her wrist watch. 'We'd better go. I've got to keep my date.'

'Do you want to go?'

'No,' she answered simply.

This seemed to satisfy him, and they walked out to the lobby. Then Yanci caught sight of a man waiting there, obviously ill at ease and dressed as no habitué of the Ritz ever was. The man was Jimmy Long, not long since a favored beau of his Western city. And now—his hat was green, actually! His coat, seasons old, was quite evidently the product of a well-known ready-made concern. His shoes, long and narrow, turned up at the toes. From head to foot everything that could possibly be wrong about him was wrong. He was embarrassed by instinct only, unconscious of his *gaucherie*, an obscene specter, a Nemesis, a horror.

'Hello, Yanci!' he cried, starting toward her with evident relief.

With a heroic effort Yanci turned to Scott, trying to hold his glance to herself. In the very act of turning she noticed the impeccability of Scott's coat, his tie.

'Thanks for luncheon,' she said with a radiant smile. 'See you to-morrow.'

Then she dived rather than ran for Jimmy Long, disposed of his outstretched hand and bundled him bumping through the revolving door with only a quick 'Let's hurry!' to appease his somewhat sulky astonishment.

The incident worried her. She consoled herself by remembering that Scott had had only a momentary glance at the man, and that he had probably been looking at her anyhow. Nevertheless, she was horrified, and it is to be doubted whether Jimmy Long enjoyed her company enough to compensate him for the cut-price, twentieth-row tickets he had obtained at Black's Drug Store.

But if Jimmy as a decoy had proved a lamentable failure, an occurrence of Thursday offered her considerable satisfaction and paid tribute to her quickness of mind. She had invented an engagement for luncheon, and Scott was going to meet her at two o'clock to take her to the Hippodrome. She lunched alone somewhat imprudently in the Ritz dining room and sauntered out almost side by side with a good-looking young man who had been at the table next to her. She expected to meet Scott in the outer lobby, but as she reached the entrance to the restaurant she saw him standing not far away.

On a lightning impulse she turned to the good-looking man abreast of her, bowed sweetly and said in an audible, friendly voice, 'Well, I'll see you later.'

Then before he could even register astonishment she faced about quickly and joined Scott.

'Who was that?' he asked, frowning.

'Isn't he darling-looking?'

'If you like that sort of looks.'

Scott's tone implied that the gentleman referred to was effete and overdressed. Yanci laughed, impersonally admiring the skillfulness of her ruse.

It was in preparation for that all-important Saturday night that on Thursday she went into a shop on Forty-second Street to buy some long gloves. She made her purchase and handed the clerk a fifty-dollar bill so that her lightened pocketbook would feel heavier with the change she could put in. To her surprise the clerk tendered her the package and a twenty-five-cent piece.

'Is there anything else?'

'The rest of my change.'

'You've got it. You gave me five dollars. Four-seventy-five for the gloves leaves twenty-five cents.'

'I gave you fifty dollars.'

'You must be mistaken.'

Yanci searched her purse.

'I gave you fifty!' she repeated frantically.

'No, ma'am, I saw it myself.'

They glared at each other in hot irritation. A cash girl was called to testify, then the floor manager; a small crowd gathered.

'Why, I'm perfectly sure!' cried Yanci, two angry tears trembling in her eyes. 'I'm positive!'

The floor manager was sorry, but the lady really must have left it at home. There was no fifty-dollar bill in the cash drawer. The bottom was creaking out of Yanci's rickety world.

'If you'll leave your address,' said the floor manager, 'I'll let you know if anything turns up.'

'Oh, you damn fools!' cried Yanci, losing control. 'I'll get the police!'

And weeping like a child she left the shop. Outside, helplessness overpowered her. How could she prove anything?

(59)

It was after six and the store was closing even as she left it. Whichever employee had the fifty-dollar bill would be on her way home now before the police could arrive, and why should the New York police believe her, or even give her fair play?

In despair she returned to the Ritz, where she searched through her trunk for the bill with hopeless and mechanical gestures. It was not there. She had known it would not be there. She gathered every penny together and found that she had fifty-one dollars and thirty cents. Telephoning the office, she asked that her bill be made out up to the following noon—she was too dispirited to think of leaving before then.

She waited in her room, not daring even to send for ice water. Then the phone rang and she heard the room clerk's voice, cheerful and metallic.

'Miss Bowman?'

'Yes.'

'Your bill, including to-night, is ex-act-ly fifty-one twenty.'

'Fifty-one twenty?' Her voice was trembling.

'Yes, ma'am.'

'Thank you very much.'

Breathless, she sat there beside the telephone, too frightened now to cry. She had ten cents left in the world!

XI

Friday. She had scarcely slept. There were dark rings under her eyes, and even a hot bath followed by a cold one failed to arouse her from a despairing lethargy. She had never fully realized what it would mean to be without money in New York; her determination and vitality seemed to have vanished at last with her fifty-dollar bill. There was no help for it now —she must attain her desire to-day or never.

(60)

She was to meet Scott at the Plaza for tea. She wondered—was it her imagination, or had his manner been consciously cool the afternoon before? For the first time in several days she had needed to make no effort to keep the conversation from growing sentimental. Suppose he had decided that it must come to nothing—that she was too extravagant, too frivolous. A hundred eventualities presented themselves to her during the morning—a dreary morning, broken only by her purchase of a ten-cent bun at a grocery store.

It was her first food in twenty hours, but she self-consciously pretended to the grocer to be having an amusing and facetious time in buying one bun. She even asked to see his grapes, but told him, after looking at them appraisingly—and hungrily—that she didn't think she'd buy any. They didn't look ripe to her, she said. The store was full of prosperous women who, with thumb and first finger joined and held high in front of them, were inspecting food. Yanci would have liked to ask one of them for a bunch of grapes. Instead she went up to her room in the hotel and ate her bun.

When four o'clock came she found that she was thinking more about the sandwiches she would have for tea than of what must occur there, and as she walked slowly up Fifth Avenue toward the Plaza she felt a sudden faintness which she took several deep breaths of air to overcome. She wondered vaguely where the bread line was. That was where people in her condition should go—but where was it? How did one find out? She imagined fantastically that it was in the phone book under *B*, or perhaps under *N*, for New York Bread Line.

She reached the Plaza. Scott's figure, as he stood waiting for her in the crowded lobby, was a personification of solidity and hope.

'Let's hurry!' she cried with a tortured smile. 'I feel rather punk and I want some tea.'

She ate a club sandwich, some chocolate ice cream and six tea biscuits. She could have eaten much more, but she dared not. The eventuality of her hunger having been disposed of, she must turn at bay now and face this business of life, represented by the handsome young man who sat opposite watching her with some emotion whose import she could not determine just behind his level eyes.

But the words, the glance, subtle, pervasive and sweet, that she had planned, failed somehow to come.

'Oh, Scott,' she said in a low voice, 'I'm so tired.'

'Tired of what?' he asked coolly.

'Of—everything.'

There was a silence.

'I'm afraid,' she said uncertainly—'I'm afraid I won't be able to keep that date with you to-morrow.'

There was no pretense in her voice now. The emotion was apparent in the waver of each word, without intention or control.

'I'm going away.'

'Are you? Where?'

His tone showed a strong interest, but she winced as she saw that that was all.

'My aunt's come back. She wants me to join her in Florida right away.'

'Isn't this rather unexpected?'

'Yes.'

'You'll be coming back soon?' he said after a moment.

'I don't think so. I think we'll go to Europe from—from New Orleans.'

'Oh!'

Again there was a pause. It lengthened. In the shadow of a moment it would become awkward, she knew. She had lost—well? Yet, she would go on to the end.

'Will you miss me?'

'Yes.'

One word. She caught his eyes, wondered for a moment if she saw more there than that kindly interest; then she dropped her own again.

'I like it—here at the Plaza,' she heard herself saying.

They spoke of things like that. Afterwards she could never remember what they said. They spoke—even of the tea, of the thaw that was ended and the cold coming down outside. She was sick at heart and she seemed to herself very old. She rose at last.

'I've got to tear,' she said. 'I'm going out to dinner.'

To the last she would keep on—the illusion, that was the important thing. To hold her proud lies inviolate—there was only a moment now. They walked toward the door.

'Put me in a taxi,' she said quietly. 'I don't feel equal to walking.'

He helped her in. They shook hands.

'Good-by, Scott,' she said.

'Good-by, Yanci,' he answered slowly.

'You've been awfully nice to me. I'll always remember what a good time you helped to give me this two weeks.'

'The pleasure was mine. Shall I tell the driver the Ritz?'

'No. Just tell him to drive out Fifth. I'll tap on the glass when I want him to stop.'

Out Fifth! He would think, perhaps, that she was dining on Fifth. What an appropriate finish that would be! She wondered if he were impressed. She could not see his face clearly, because the air was dark with the snow and her own eyes were blurred by tears.

'Good-by,' he said simply.

He seemed to realize that any pretense of sorrow on his part would be transparent. She knew that he did not want her.

The door slammed, the car started, skidding in the snowy street.

Yanci leaned back dismally in the corner. Try as she might, she could not see where she had failed or what it was that had changed his attitude toward her. For the first time in her life she had ostensibly offered herself to a man—and he had not wanted her. The precariousness of her position paled beside the tragedy of her defeat.

(63)

She let the car go on—the cold air was what she needed, of course. Ten minutes had slipped away drearily before she realized that she had not a penny with which to pay the driver.

'It doesn't matter,' she thought. 'They'll just send me to jail, and that's a place to sleep.'

She began thinking of the taxi driver.

'He'll be mad when he finds out, poor man. Maybe he's very poor, and he'll have to pay the fare himself.' With a vague sentimentality she began to cry.

'Poor taxi man,' she was saying half aloud. 'Oh, people have such a hard time—such a hard time!'

She rapped on the window and when the car drew up at a curb she got out. She was at the end of Fifth Avenue and it was dark and cold.

'Send for the police!' she cried in a quick low voice. 'I haven't any money!'

The taxi man scowled down at her.

'Then what'd you get in for?'

She had not noticed that another car had stopped about twenty-five feet behind them. She heard running footsteps in the snow and then a voice at her elbow.

'It's all right,' someone was saying to the taxi man. 'I've got it right here.'

A bill was passed up. Yanci slumped sideways against Scott's overcoat.

Scott knew—he knew because he had gone to Princeton to surprise her, because the stranger she had spoken to in the Ritz had been his best friend, because the check of her father's for three hundred dollars had been returned to him marked 'No funds.' Scott knew—he had known for days.

But he said nothing; only stood there holding her with one arm as her taxi drove away.

'Oh, it's you,' said Yanci faintly. 'Lucky you came along. I left my purse back at the Ritz, like an awful fool. I do such ridiculous things——'

(64)

Scott laughed with some enjoyment. There was a light snow falling, and lest she should slip in the damp he picked her up and carried her back toward his waiting taxi.

'Such ridiculous things,' she repeated.

'Go to the Ritz first,' he said to the driver. 'I want to get a trunk.'

SCOTT

Love in the Night

(The Saturday Evening Post,
14 March 1925)

The words thrilled Val. They had come into his mind sometime during the fresh gold April afternoon and he kept repeating them to himself over and over: 'Love in the night; love in
the night.' He tried them in three languages—Russian, French
and English—and decided that they were best in English. In
each language they meant a different sort of love and a different
sort of night—the English night seemed the warmest and softest
with a thinnest and most crystalline sprinkling of stars. The
English love seemed the most fragile and romantic—a white
dress and a dim face above it and eyes that were pools of light.
And when I add that it was a French night he was thinking
about, after all, I see I must go back and begin over.

Val was half Russian and half American. His mother was
the daughter of that Morris Hasylton who helped finance the
Chicago World's Fair in 1892, and his father was—see the
Almanach de Gotha, issue of 1910—Prince Paul Serge Boris
Rostoff, son of Prince Vladimir Rostoff, grandson of a grand
duke—'Jimber-jawed Serge'—and third-cousin-once-re-
moved to the czar. It was all very impressive, you see, on
that side—house in St Petersburg, shooting lodge near
Riga, and swollen villa, more like a palace, overlooking the
Mediterranean. It was at this villa in Cannes that the Rostoffs
passed the winter—and it wasn't at all the thing to remind
Princess Rostoff that this Riviera villa, from the marble
fountain—after Bernini—to the gold cordial glasses—after
dinner—was paid for with American gold.

The Russians, of course, were gay people on the Continent in the gala days before the war. Of the three races that used Southern France for a pleasure ground they were easily the most adept at the grand manner. The English were too practical, and the Americans, though they spent freely, had no tradition of romantic conduct. But the Russians—there was a people as gallant as the Latins, and rich besides! When the Rostoffs arrived at Cannes late in January the restaurateurs telegraphed north for the Prince's favorite labels to paste on their champagne, and the jewelers put incredibly gorgeous articles aside to show to him—but not to the princess—and the Russian Church was swept and garnished for the season that the Prince might beg orthodox forgiveness for his sins. Even the Mediterranean turned obligingly to a deep wine color in the spring evenings, and fishing boats with robin-breasted sails loitered exquisitely offshore.

In a vague way young Val realized that this was all for the benefit of him and his family. It was a privileged paradise, this white little city on the water, in which he was free to do what he liked because he was rich and young and the blood of Peter the Great ran indigo in his veins. He was only seventeen in 1914, when this history begins, but he had already fought a duel with a young man four years his senior, and he had a small hairless scar to show for it on top of his handsome head.

But the question of love in the night was the thing nearest his heart. It was a vague pleasant dream he had, something that was going to happen to him some day that would be unique and incomparable. He could have told no more about it than that there was a lovely unknown girl concerned in it, and that it ought to take place beneath the Riviera moon.

The odd thing about all this was not that he had this excited and yet almost spiritual hope of romance, for all boys of any imagination have just such hopes, but that it actually came true. And when it happened, it happened so unexpectedly; it was such a jumble of impressions and emotions, of curious phrases that sprang to his lips, of sights and sounds and moments that were here, were lost, were past, that he scarcely understood it at all. Perhaps its very vagueness preserved it in his heart and made him forever unable to forget.

There was an atmosphere of love all about him that spring—his father's loves, for instance, which were many and indiscreet, and which Val became aware of gradually from overhearing the gossip of servants, and definitely from coming on his American mother unexpectedly one afternoon, to find her storming hysterically at his father's picture on the salon wall. In the picture his father wore a white uniform with a furred dolman and looked back impassively at his wife as if to say 'Were you under the impression, my dear, that you were marrying into a family of clergymen?'

Val tiptoed away, surprised, confused—and excited. It didn't shock him as it would have shocked an American boy of his age. He had known for years what life was among the Continental rich, and he condemned his father only for making his mother cry.

Love went on around him—reproachless love and illicit love alike. As he strolled along the seaside promenade at nine o'clock, when the stars were bright enough to compete with the bright lamps, he was aware of love on every side. From the open-air cafés, vivid with dresses just down from Paris, came a sweet pungent odor of flowers and chartreuse and fresh black coffee and cigarettes—and mingled with them all he caught another scent, the mysterious thrilling scent of love. Hands touched jewel-sparkling hands upon the white tables. Gay dresses and white shirt fronts swayed together, and matches were held, trembling a little, for slow-lighting cigarettes. On the other side of the boulevard lovers less fashionable, young Frenchmen who worked in the stores of Cannes, sauntered with their fiancées under the dim trees, but Val's young eyes seldom turned that way.

(68)

The luxury of music and bright colors and low voices—they were all part of his dream. They were the essential trappings of Love in the night.

But assume as he might the rather fierce expression that was expected from a young Russian gentleman who walked the streets alone, Val was beginning to be unhappy. April twilight had succeeded March twilight, the season was almost over, and he had found no use to make of the warm spring evenings. The girls of sixteen and seventeen whom he knew, were chaperoned with care between dusk and bedtime—this, remember, was before the war—and the others who might gladly have walked beside him were an affront to his romantic desire. So April passed by—one week, two weeks, three weeks——

He had played tennis until seven and loitered at the courts for another hour, so it was half-past eight when a tired cab horse accomplished the hill on which gleamed the façade of the Rostoff villa. The lights of his mother's limousine were yellow in the drive, and the princess, buttoning her gloves, was just coming out the glowing door. Val tossed two francs to the cabman and went to kiss her on the cheek.

'Don't touch me,' she said quickly. 'You've been handling money.'

'But not in my mouth, mother,' he protested humorously.

The princess looked at him impatiently.

'I'm angry,' she said. 'Why must you be so late tonight? We're dining on a yacht and you were to have come along too.'

'What yacht?'

'Americans.' There was always a faint irony in her voice when she mentioned the land of her nativity. Her America was the Chicago of the nineties which she still thought of as the vast upstairs to a butcher shop. Even the irregularities of Prince Paul were not too high a price to have paid for her escape.

'Two yachts,' she continued; 'in fact we don't know which one. The note was very indefinite. Very careless indeed.'

Americans. Val's mother had taught him to look down on Americans, but she hadn't succeeded in making him dislike them. American men noticed you, even if you were seventeen. He liked Americans. Although he was thoroughly Russian he wasn't immaculately so—the exact proportion, like that of a celebrated soap, was about ninety-nine and three-quarters per cent.

'I want to come,' he said, 'I'll hurry up, mother. I'll——'

'We're late now.' The princess turned as her husband appeared in the door. 'Now Val says he wants to come.'

'He can't,' said Prince Paul shortly. 'He's too outrageously late.'

Val nodded. Russian aristocrats, however indulgent about themselves, were always admirably Spartan with their children. There were no arguments.

'I'm sorry,' he said.

Prince Paul grunted. The footman, in red and silver livery, opened the limousine door. But the grunt decided the matter for Val, because Princess Rostoff at that day and hour had certain grievances against her husband which gave her command of the domestic situation.

'On second thought you'd better come, Val,' she announced coolly. 'It's too late now, but come after dinner. The yacht is either the Minnehaha or the Privateer.' She got into the limousine. 'The one to come to will be the gayer one, I suppose—the Jacksons' yacht——'

'Find got sense,' muttered the Prince cryptically, conveying that Val would find it if he had any sense. 'Have my man take a look at you 'fore you start. Wear tie of mine 'stead of that outrageous string you affected in Vienna. Grow up. High time.'

As the limousine crawled crackling down the pebbled drive Val's face was burning.

II

It was dark in Cannes harbor, rather it seemed dark after the brightness of the promenade that Val had just left behind. Three frail dock lights glittered dimly upon innumerable fishing boats heaped like shells along the beach. Farther out in the water there were other lights where a fleet of slender yachts rode the tide with slow dignity, and farther still a full ripe moon made the water bosom into a polished dancing floor. Occasionally there was a swish! creak! drip! as a rowboat moved about in the shallows, and its blurred shape threaded the labyrinth of hobbled fishing skiffs and launches. Val, descending the velvet slope of sand, stumbled over a sleeping boatman and caught the rank savor of garlic and plain wine. Taking the man by the shoulders he shook open his startled eyes.

'Do you know where the Minnehaha is anchored, and the Privateer?'

As they slid out into the bay he lay back in the stern and stared with vague discontent at the Riviera moon. That was the right moon, all right. Frequently, five nights out of seven, there was the right moon. And here was the soft air, aching with enchantment, and here was the music, many strains of music from many orchestras, drifting out from the shore. Eastward lay the dark Cape of Antibes, and then Nice, and beyond that Monte Carlo, where the night rang chinking full of gold. Some day he would enjoy all that, too, know its every pleasure and success—when he was too old and wise to care.

But tonight—tonight, that stream of silver that waved like a wide strand of curly hair toward the moon; those soft romantic lights of Cannes behind him, the irresistible ineffable love in this air—that was to be wasted forever.

'Which one?' asked the boatman suddenly.

'Which what?' demanded Val, sitting up.

'Which boat?'

He pointed. Val turned; above hovered the gray, sword-like

prow of a yacht. During the sustained longing of his wish they had covered half a mile.

He read the brass letters over his head. It was the Privateer, but there were only dim lights on board, and no music and no voices, only a murmurous k-plash at intervals as the small waves leaped at the sides.

'The other one,' said Val; 'the Minnehaha.'

'Don't go yet.'

Val started. The voice, low and soft, had dropped down from the darkness overhead.

'What's the hurry?' said the soft voice. 'Thought maybe somebody was coming to see me, and have suffered terrible disappointment.'

The boatman lifted his oars and looked hesitatingly at Val. But Val was silent, so the man let the blades fall into the water and swept the boat out into the moonlight.

'Wait a minute!' cried Val sharply.

'Good-by,' said the voice. 'Come again when you can stay longer.'

'But I am going to stay now,' he answered breathlessly.

He gave the necessary order and the rowboat swung back to the foot of the small companionway. Someone young, someone in a misty white dress, someone with a lovely low voice, had actually called to him out of the velvet dark. 'If she has eyes!' Val murmured to himself. He liked the romantic sound of it and repeated it under his breath—'If she has eyes.'

'What are you?' She was directly above him now; she was looking down and he was looking up as he climbed the ladder, and as their eyes met they both began to laugh.

She was very young, slim, almost frail, with a dress that accentuated her youth by its blanched simplicity. Two wan dark spots on her cheeks marked where the color was by day.

'What are you?' she repeated, moving back and laughing again as his head appeared on the level of the deck. 'I'm frightened now and I want to know.'

'I am a gentleman,' said Val, bowing.

'What sort of a gentleman? There are all sorts of gentlemen. There was a—there was a colored gentleman at the table next to ours in Paris, and so——' She broke off. 'You're not American, are you?'

'I'm Russian,' he said, as he might have announced himself to be an archangel. He thought quickly and then added, 'And I am the most fortunate of Russians. All this day, all this spring I have dreamed of falling in love on such a night, and now I see that heaven has sent me to you.'

'Just one moment!' she said, with a little gasp. 'I'm sure now that this visit is a mistake. I don't go in for anything like that. Please!'

'I beg your pardon.' He looked at her in bewilderment, unaware that he had taken too much for granted. Then he drew himself up formally.

'I have made an error. If you will excuse me I will say good night.'

He turned away. His hand was on the rail.

'Don't go,' she said, pushing a strand of indefinite hair out of her eyes. 'On second thoughts you can talk any nonsense you like if you'll only not go. I'm miserable and I don't want to be left alone.'

Val hestitated; there was some element in this that he failed to understand. He had taken it for granted that a girl who called to a strange man at night, even from the deck of a yacht, was certainly in a mood for romance. And he wanted intensely to stay. Then he remembered that this was one of the two yachts he had been seeking.

'I imagine that the dinner's on the other boat,' he said.

'The dinner? Oh, yes, it's on the Minnehaha. Were you going there?'

'I was going there—a long time ago.'

'What's your name?'

He was on the point of telling her when something made him ask a question instead.

'And you? Why are you not at the party?'

'Because I preferred to stay here. Mrs Jackson said there would be some Russians there—I suppose that's you.' She looked at him with interest. 'You're a very young man, aren't you?'

'I am much older than I look,' said Val stiffly. 'People always comment on it. It's considered rather a remarkable thing.'

'How old are you?'

'Twenty-one,' he lied.

She laughed.

'What nonsense! You're not more than nineteen.'

His annoyance was so perceptible that she hastened to reassure him. 'Cheer up! I'm only seventeen myself. I might have gone to the party if I'd thought there'd be anyone under fifty there.'

He welcomed the change of subject.

'You preferred to sit and dream here beneath the moon.'

'I've been thinking of mistakes.' They sat down side by side in two canvas deck chairs. 'It's a most engrossing subject —the subject of mistakes. Women very seldom brood about mistakes—they're much more willing to forget than men are. But when they do brood——'

'You have made a mistake?' inquired Val.

She nodded.

'Is it something that cannot be repaired?'

'I think so,' she answered. 'I can't be sure. That's what I was considering when you came along.'

'Perhaps I can help in some way,' said Val. 'Perhaps your mistake is not irreparable, after all.'

'You can't,' she said unhappily. 'So let's not think about it. I'm very tired of my mistake and I'd much rather you'd tell me about all the gay, cheerful things that are going on in Cannes tonight.'

They glanced shoreward at the line of mysterious and alluring lights, the big toy banks with candles inside that

(74)

were really the great fashionable hotels, the lighted clock in the old town, the blurred glow of the Café de Paris, the pricked-out points of villa windows rising on slow hills toward the dark sky.

'What is everyone doing there?' she whispered. 'It looks as though something gorgeous was going on, but what it is I can't quite tell.'

'Everyone there is making love,' said Val quietly.

'Is that it?' She looked for a long time, with a strange expression in her eyes. 'Then I want to go home to America,' she said. 'There is too much love here. I want to go home tomorrow.'

'You are afraid of being in love then?'

She shook her head.

'It isn't that. It's just because—there is no love here for me.'

'Or for me either,' added Val quietly. 'It is sad that we two should be at such a lovely place on such a lovely night and have—nothing.'

He was leaning toward her intently, with a sort of inspired and chaste romance in his eyes—and she drew back.

'Tell me more about yourself,' she inquired quickly. 'If you are Russian where did you learn to speak such excellent English?'

'My mother was American,' he admitted. 'My grandfather was American also, so she had no choice in the matter.'

'Then you're American too!'

'I am Russian,' said Val with dignity.

She looked at him closely, smiled and decided not to argue. 'Well then,' she said diplomatically, 'I suppose you must have a Russian name.'

But he had no intention now of telling her his name. A name, even the Rostoff name, would be a desecration of the night. They were their own low voices, their two white faces —and that was enough. He was sure, without any reason for being sure but with a sort of instinct that sang triumphantly through his mind, that in a little while, a minute or an hour, he was going to undergo an initiation into the life of romance. His name had no reality beside what was stirring in his heart.

'You are beautiful,' he said suddenly.

'How do you know?'

'Because for women moonlight is the hardest light of all.'

'Am I nice in the moonlight?'

'You are the loveliest thing that I have ever known.'

'Oh.' She thought this over. 'Of course I had no business to let you come on board. I might have known what we'd talk about—in this moon. But I can't sit here and look at the shore—forever. I'm too young for that. Don't you think I'm too young for that?'

'Much too young,' he agreed solemnly.

Suddenly they both became aware of new music that was close at hand, music that seemed to come out of the water not a hundred yards away.

'Listen!' she cried. 'It's from the Minnehaha. They've finished dinner.'

For a moment they listened in silence.

'Thank you,' said Val suddenly.

'For what?'

He hardly knew he had spoken. He was thanking the deep low horns for singing in the breeze, the sea for its warm murmurous complaint against the bow, the milk of the stars for washing over them until he felt buoyed up in a substance more taut than air.

'So lovely,' she whispered.

'What are we going to do about it?'

'Do we have to do something about it? I thought we could just sit and enjoy——'

'You didn't think that,' he interrupted quietly. 'You know that we must do something about it. I am going to make love to you—and you are going to be glad.'

'I can't,' she said very low. She wanted to laugh now, to make some light cool remark that would bring the situation

(76)

back into the safe waters of a casual flirtation. But it was too late now. Val knew that the music had completed what the moon had begun.

'I will tell you the truth,' he said. 'You are my first love. I am seventeen—the same age as you, no more.'

There was something utterly disarming about the fact that they were the same age. It made her helpless before the fate that had thrown them together. The deck chairs creaked and he was conscious of a faint illusive perfume as they swayed suddenly and childishly together.

III

Whether he kissed her once or several times he could not afterward remember, though it must have been an hour that they sat there close together and he held her hand. What surprised him most about making love was that it seemed to have no element of wild passion—regret, desire, despair—but a delirious promise of such happiness in the world, in living, as he had never known. First love—this was only first love! What must love itself in its fullness, its perfection be. He did not know that what he was experiencing then, that unreal, undesirous medley of ecstasy and peace, would be unrecapturable forever.

The music had ceased for some time when presently the murmurous silence was broken by the sound of a rowboat disturbing the quiet waves. She sprang suddenly to her feet and her eyes strained out over the bay.

'Listen!' she said quickly. 'I want you to tell me your name.'

'No.'

'Please,' she begged him. 'I'm going away tomorrow.' He didn't answer.

'I don't want you to forget me,' she said. 'My name is——'

'I won't forget you. I will promise to remember you always. Whoever I may love I will always compare her to

(77)

you, my first love. So long as I live you will always have that much freshness in my heart.'

'I want you to remember,' she murmured brokenly. 'Oh, this has meant more to me than it has to you—much more.'

She was standing so close to him that he felt her warm young breath on his face. Once again they swayed together. He pressed her hands and wrists between his as it seemed right to do, and kissed her lips. It was the right kiss, he thought, the romantic kiss—not too little or too much. Yet there was a sort of promise in it of other kisses he might have had, and it was with a slight sinking of his heart that he heard the rowboat close to the yacht and realized that her family had returned. The evening was over.

'And this is only the beginning,' he told himself. 'All my life will be like this night.'

She was saying something in a low quick voice and he was listening tensely.

'You must know one thing—I am married. Three months ago. That was the mistake that I was thinking about when the moon brought you out here. In a moment you will understand.'

She broke off as the boat swung against the companionway and a man's voice floated up out of the darkness.

'Is that you, my dear?'

'Yes.'

'What is this other rowboat waiting?'

'One of Mrs Jackson's guests came here by mistake and I made him stay and amuse me for an hour.'

A moment later the thin white hair and weary face of a man of sixty appeared above the level of the deck. And then Val saw and realized too late how much he cared.

IV

When the Riviera season ended in May the Rostoffs and all the other Russians closed their villas and went north for the summer. The Russian Orthodox Church was locked up and so were the bins of rarer wine, and the fashionable spring moonlight was put away, so to speak, to wait for their return.

'We'll be back next season,' they said as a matter of course.

But this was premature, for they were never coming back any more. Those few who straggled south again after five tragic years were glad to get work as chambermaids or *valets de chambre* in the great hotels where they had once dined. Many of them, of course, were killed in the war or in the revolution; many of them faded out as spongers and small cheats in the big capitals, and not a few ended their lives in a sort of stupefied despair.

When the Kerensky government collapsed in 1917, Val was a lieutenant on the eastern front, trying desperately to enforce authority in his company long after any vestige of it remained. He was still trying when Prince Paul Rostoff and his wife gave up their lives one rainy morning to atone for the blunders of the Romanoffs—and the enviable career of Morris Hasylton's daughter ended in a city that bore even more resemblance to a butcher shop than had Chicago in 1892.

After that Val fought with Denikin's army for a while until he realized that he was participating in a hollow farce and the glory of Imperial Russia was over. Then he went to France and was suddenly confronted with the astounding problem of keeping his body and soul together.

It was, of course, natural that he should think of going to America. Two vague aunts with whom his mother had quarreled many years ago still lived there in comparative affluence. But the idea was repugnant to the prejudices his mother had implanted in him, and besides he hadn't sufficient money left to pay for his passage over. Until a possible counter-revolution should restore to him the Rostoff properties in Russia he must somehow keep alive in France.

So he went to the little city he knew best of all. He went to Cannes. His last two hundred francs bought him a third-class ticket and when he arrived he gave his dress suit to an obliging party who dealt in such things and received in return money for food and bed. He was sorry afterward that he had sold the dress suit, because it might have helped him to a position as a waiter. But he obtained work as a taxi driver instead and was quite as happy, or rather quite as miserable, at that.

Sometimes he carried Americans to look at villas for rent, and when the front glass of the automobile was up, curious fragments of conversation drifted out to him from within.

'——heard this fellow was a Russian prince.' . . . 'Sh!' . . . 'No, this one right here.' . . . 'Be quiet, Esther!'— followed by subdued laughter.

When the car stopped, his passengers would edge around to have a look at him. At first he was desperately unhappy when girls did this; after a while he didn't mind any more. Once a cheerfully intoxicated American asked him if it were true and invited him to lunch, and another time an elderly woman seized his hand as she got out of the taxi, shook it violently and then pressed a hundred-franc note into his hand.

'Well, Florence, now I can tell 'em back home I shook hands with a Russian prince.'

The inebriated American who had invited him to lunch thought at first that Val was a son of the czar, and it had to be explained to him that a prince in Russia was simply the equivalent of a British courtesy lord. But he was puzzled that a man of Val's personality didn't go out and make some real money.

'This is Europe,' said Val gravely. 'Here money is not made. It is inherited or else it is slowly saved over a period of many years and maybe in three generations a family moves up into a higher class.'

'Think of something people want—like we do.'

'That is because there is more money to want with in America. Everything that people want here has been thought of long ago.'

(80)

But after a year and with the help of a young Englishman he had played tennis with before the war, Val managed to get into the Cannes branch of an English bank. He forwarded mail and bought railroad tickets and arranged tours for impatient sight-seers. Sometimes a familiar face came to his window; if Val was recognized he shook hands; if not he kept silence. After two years he was no longer pointed out as a former prince, for the Russians were an old story now—the splendor of the Rostoffs and their friends was forgotten.

He mixed with people very little. In the evenings he walked for a while on the promenade, took a slow glass of beer in a café, and went early to bed. He was seldom invited anywhere because people thought that his sad, intent face was depressing—and he never accepted anyhow. He wore cheap French clothes now instead of the rich tweeds and flannels that had been ordered with his father's from England. As for women, he knew none at all. Of the many things he had been certain about at seventeen, he had been most certain about this—that his life would be full of romance. Now after eight years he knew that it was not to be. Somehow he had never had time for love—the war, the revolution and now his poverty had conspired against his expectant heart. The springs of his emotion which had first poured forth one April night had dried up immediately and only a faint trickle remained.

His happy youth had ended almost before it began. He saw himself growing older and more shabby, and living always more and more in the memories of his gorgeous boyhood. Eventually he would become absurd, pulling out an old heirloom of a watch and showing it to amused young fellow clerks who would listen with winks to his tales of the Rostoff name.

He was thinking these gloomy thoughts one April evening in 1922 as he walked beside the sea and watched the never-changing magic of the awakening lights. It was no longer for his benefit, that magic, but it went on, and he was somehow glad. Tomorrow he was going away on his vacation, to a cheap hotel farther down the shore where he could bathe and rest and read; then he would come back and work some more. Every year for three years he had taken his vacation during the last two weeks in April, perhaps because it was then that he felt the most need for remembering. It was in April that what was destined to be the best part of his life had come to a culmination under a romantic moonlight. It was sacred to him—for what he had thought of as an initiation and a beginning had turned out to be the end.

He paused now in front of the Café des Étrangers and after a moment crossed the street on impulse and sauntered down to the shore. A dozen yachts, already turned to a beautiful silver color, rode at anchor in the bay. He had seen them that afternoon, and read the names painted on their bows— but only from habit. He had done it for three years now, and it was almost a natural function of his eye.

'*Un beau soir*,' remarked a French voice at his elbow. It was a boatman who had often seen Val here before. 'Monsieur finds the sea beautiful?'

'Very beautiful.'

'I too. But a bad living except in the season. Next week, though, I earn something special. I am paid well for simply waiting here and doing nothing more from eight o'clock until midnight.'

'That's very nice,' said Val politely.

'A widowed lady, very beautiful, from America, whose yacht always anchors in the harbor for the last two weeks in April. If the Privateer comes tomorrow it will make three years.'

V

All night Val didn't sleep—not because there was any question in his mind as to what he should do, but because his long stupefied emotions were suddenly awake and alive. Of course he must not see her—not he, a poor failure with a name that was now only a shadow—but it would make him a little happier always to know that she remembered. It gave his own memory another dimension, raised it like those stereopticon glasses that bring out a picture from the flat paper. It made him sure that he had not deceived himself—he had been charming once upon a time to a lovely woman, and she did not forget.

An hour before train time next day he was at the railway station with his grip, so as to avoid any chance encounter in the street. He found himself a place in a third-class carriage of the waiting train.

Somehow as he sat there he felt differently about life—a sort of hope, faint and illusory, that he hadn't felt twenty-four hours before. Perhaps there was some way in these next few years in which he could make it possible to meet her once again—if he worked hard, threw himself passionately into whatever was at hand. He knew of at least two Russians in Cannes who had started over again with nothing except good manners and ingenuity and were now doing surprisingly well. The blood of Morris Hasylton began to throb a little in Val's temples and made him remember something he had never before cared to remember—that Morris Hasylton, who had built his daughter a palace in St Petersburg, had also started from nothing at all.

Simultaneously another emotion possessed him, less strange, less dynamic but equally American—the emotion of curiosity. In case he did—well, in case life should ever make it possible for him to seek her out, he should at least know her name.

He jumped to his feet, fumbled excitedly at the carriage handle and jumped from the train. Tossing his valise into the check room he started at a run for the American consulate.

'A yacht came in this morning,' he said hurriedly to a clerk, 'an American yacht—the Privateer. I want to know who owns it.'

'Just a minute,' said the clerk, looking at him oddly. 'I'll try to find out.'

After what seemed to Val an interminable time he returned.

'Why, just a minute,' he repeated hesitantly. 'We're—it seems we're finding out.'

'Did the yacht come?'

'Oh, yes—it's here all right. At least I think so. If you'll just wait in that chair.'

After another ten minutes Val looked impatiently at his watch. If they didn't hurry he'd probably miss his train. He made a nervous movement as if to get up from his chair.

'Please sit still,' said the clerk, glancing at him quickly from his desk. 'I ask you. Just sit down in that chair.'

Val stared at him. How could it possibly matter to the clerk whether or not he waited?

'I'll miss my train,' he said impatiently. 'I'm sorry to have given you all this bother——'

'Please sit still! We're glad to get it off our hands. You see, we've been waiting for your inquiry for—ah—three years.'

Val jumped to his feet and jammed his hat on his head.

'Why didn't you tell me that?' he demanded angrily.

'Because we had to get word to our—our client. Please don't go! It's—ah, it's too late.'

Val turned. Someone slim and radiant with dark frightened eyes was standing behind him, framed against the sunshine of the doorway.

'Why——'

Val's lips parted, but no words came through. She took a step toward him.

'I——' She looked at him helplessly, her eyes filling with tears. 'I just wanted to say hello,' she murmured. 'I've come back for three years just because I wanted to say hello.'

Still Val was silent.

'You might answer,' she said impatiently. 'You might answer when I'd—when I'd just about begun to think you'd been killed in the war.' She turned to the clerk. 'Please

(84)

introduce us!' she cried. 'You see, I can't say hello to him when we don't even know each other's names.'

It's the thing to distrust these international marriages, of course. It's an American tradition that they always turn out badly, and we are accustomed to such headlines as: 'Would Trade Coronet for True American Love, Says Duchess,' and 'Claims Count Mendicant Tortured Toledo Wife.' The other sort of headlines are never printed, for who would want to read: 'Castle is Love Nest, Asserts Former Georgia Belle,' or 'Duke and Packer's Daughter Celebrate Golden Honeymoon.'

So far there have been no headlines at all about the young Rostoffs. Prince Val is much too absorbed in that string of moonlight-blue taxicabs which he manipulates with such unusual efficiency, to give out interviews. He and his wife only leave New York once a year—but there is still a boatman who rejoices when the Privateer steams into Cannes harbor on a mid-April night.

SCOTT & ZELDA

Our Own Movie Queen

(*Chicago Sunday Tribune*,
7 June 1925*)

The Mississippi river came carelessly down through the pine forests and phlegmatic villages of Minnesota to the city of New Heidelberg, for the express purpose of dividing the ladies and gentlemen of the town from their laundresses and their butchers and their charioteers of the ash can—who dwelt in sodden bad taste upon thither bank. On the high and fashionable side an avenue lined with well bred trees pushed itself out to where the river, by a series of dexterous swoops, brought the city to a tidy end.

On the low side there were huge chalk cliffs where the people grew mushrooms and made incompetent whisky, and there were cobblestone streets where casual water lay incessantly in dull little pools. Here, too, was the morgue, with its pale barred windows, and here were rows of sinister, dull red houses that no one was ever seen entering or leaving. Back further from the water were railroad yards and stockyards and the spot (mark it now with an X) where Gracie Axelrod lived—Gracie who backed into local publicity a short year since as 'our movie queen.' This is the story of her screen career, and of a picture the memory of which still causes bursts of crazy laughter, but which, alas, will never be shown again in this world.

Gracie's neighbors were fat Italians and cheerless Poles and Swedes who conducted themselves as though they were

---

* Published as by F. Scott Fitzgerald, but Fitzgerald's *Ledger* notes: 'Two thirds by Zelda. Only my climax and revision'. Written November 1923.

conversant with the Nordic theory. Her father may or may not have been a Swede. He did not speak the language certainly, and his deplorable personal appearance cannot with justice be ascribed to any nationality. He was the sole owner of a tumbledown shanty where fried chicken of dubious antecedents might be washed down by cold beer, any time between ten o'clock at night and eight o'clock in the morning. Gracie fried the chicken with such brown art that complaints were unknown.

For seven months a year New Heidelberg was covered with sooty snow, and mere zero weather was considered a relief from the true cold: citizens were glad to get home at night and there was little inducement to linger late around the streets. But dances were given in the best hotel and even Gracie had heard tales about the gaiety of the dwellers on the upper river bank. She had seen them, too, arrive in closed automobiles and come shouting into the shanty at small hours, behaving as if it were a daring thing to do.

Gracie was pretty, but too full blown for a girl of twenty. Her flaxen hair was a glorious smooth color, and would have been beautiful if she had not snarled it and brushed it out over her ears until the shape of her head was entirely distorted. Her skin was radiantly pale, her large blue eyes were faintly inclined to bulge. Her teeth were small and very white. There was a warm moist look about her, as if she had materialized out of hot milk vapor—and perhaps she had, for no one had ever seen or heard of her mother. Her whole appearance was as voluptuous as that of a burlesque show prima donna—that was the way Gracie felt about it anyhow, and if Mr Zeigfeld (of whom she had never heard) had wired her to join his show, she would have been only faintly surprised. She quietly expected great things to happen to her, and no doubt that's one of the reasons why they did.

Now on Gracie's side of the river Christmas eve was celebrated with no more display than the Dante centennial.

But on the high bank where the snow lay along the fashionable avenue as if it had just been unwound from a monster bolt of cotton batting, every model home set out a tree adorned with electric bulbs. It was a gorgeous sight, and Gracie and her father always came every year and walked a few blocks in the icy cold. They compared each tree to the last one, and were scornful and superior toward the trees that had no stars on top.

Tonight was the fifth time that Gracie could remember having taken this walk, and as she bustled about after the excursion and filled the shack with greasy, pleasant smelling smoke, she discussed it thoroughly with her vague parent.

'Honest,' she complained, 'if people ain't going to have better trees than them, I don't see why they want to get you out on a cold night like this for. There was only one place that didn't look like somebody was dead in it.'

The place to which she referred was a great white house adorned with stone animal heads and Greek friezes which tonight had had suspended proudly from its arched porte-cochere, a huge electric sign which wished the passers-by a Merry Christmas.

'Who lives there, daddy?' she asked abruptly.

'B'longs to the feller that owns the Blue Ribbon,' elucidated Mr Axelrod. 'I guess he must be worth a good lot of money.'

'Who says so?' demanded Gracie.

'O, some people told me,' her father answered vaguely. He was propped up back of the stove, his hat shading his eyes as he read the evening pink sheet. Just at the moment the paper was open over his knees at a full page advertisement: the Blue Ribbon Department store wished every one a happy New Year, and hoped they would attend the sale of white goods immediately after the holidays.

Mr Axelrod read the composition to his daughter. He always read her everything in the big type. They liked to hear each other's voices, and as Gracie was too busy with the

(88)

chicken and her father with the reading to pay much attention to the content, it was a successful arrangement. To Mr Axelrod reading in itself was enough and he would have enjoyed a Chinese newspaper just as much had the hieroglyphics aroused as familiar and soothing a sensation.

'He's a swell looking fella, too,' Gracie remarked after a moment. 'Every time I go in there I see him walking up and down the store. B'lieve me, I'd just as soon marry a man like that. Then you could just walk in the store and say gimme this or gimme that and you wouldn't have to pay nothing for 'em.'

This was worth thinking about apparently, for Mr Axelrod discontinued his reading, and looked Gracie over appraisingly.

In the long interval between the completion of the evening's preparation and the appearance of the first customer they speculated upon the advantages of being married to a man who owned a store like the Blue Ribbon. No wonder Gracie was as surprised and as disconcerted as if she had been caught breaking his huge plate glass window when Mr Blue Ribbon himself walked into the shack, demanding, in a loud and supercilious voice, chicken that was all white meat.

I say that this respectable gentleman walked in, but perhaps this is an understatement, for what he literally did was to reel in. And Gracie recognized the man she had seen walking up and down the Blue Ribbon's gorgeous aisles.

He was an officious little man, fat in spots and not unlike one of those bottom-heavy dolls which refuse to lie down. Tonight the illusion was increased, for he swayed faintly with no partiality as to direction, as though if some one removed the weights from his great round abdomen he would keel permanently over and never again stand on his own initiative. There was a small cranium, a large jaw, and two superhuman ears—a comic valentine of a man with a pig's head. But he was affable, and tonight he was obsessed with the idea of himself, not as a comic valentine, but as a person of importance.

He announced that he was celebrating, and asked at large if it were possible that Gracie and her father did not know him.

'I should say,' answered Gracie, reassuringly, 'why, you own the Blue Ribbon. I always notice you around every time I go in there.'

If Gracie had made this speech in full possession of the facts in the case, it would have indicated an extraordinary subtlety and tact. For Mr Albert Pomeroy did not own the city's biggest and best department store. But from eight in the morning until six at night he owned the departments of which he was in charge—notions, perfumes, hosiery, gloves, umbrellas, dress goods, and men's wear. Gracie had flattered not only him but his position in life. He beamed. For a moment he stopped bobbing around and focused unblinking eyes on Gracie.

'Not exactly,' he managed, resuming his teetering. 'I don't exactly own it. I run it. Blue Ribbon's got the money and I got the brains.' Mr Pomeroy's voice rose to a sort of confidential shout and Gracie was impressed in spite of her disappointment.

'You any relation to him?' she asked curiously.

'Not exactly relation,' explained Mr Pomeroy, 'but close— very, very close.' He implied that they were in all but complete physical juxtaposition.

'Can you just go and say, "This looks pretty good to me. I guess I'll take it," and walk right out of the store with anything you want?'

She was now engrossed by the man himself. Her father was also listening intently.

'Not exactly,' admitted Mr Pomeroy, 'I can't exactly take things, but I can get 'em for about twenty or twenty-five dollars less than the people who don't have the influence and don't work there.'

'O, I see.' Gracie enthusiastically handed a platter of chicken to her important customer. 'I suppose that's why them girls work in there. I'd like to try it for a while myself. I'd get what I wanted cheap and then quit.'

Mr Pomeroy's head waggled and his cheeks blew out, and he busied himself with his feed.

'O, no, you wouldn't,' he managed to say. 'You wouldn't quit. You just say you'd quit.' He waved a greasy drumstick in Gracie's face.

'How do you know I wouldn't quit, I'd like to know?' cried Gracie indignantly. 'If I say I'm gonna quit, I'm gonna quit. I guess I can quit if I want to quit.'

She became animated by the thought of quitting. She wanted passionately to quit, and doubtless would have done so immediately had there been anything to quit. Mr Pomeroy, on his part, was incredulous toward the idea. It was inconceivable and beyond all reason to him that Gracie should quit.

'You just come down and see,' he insisted. 'Come down tomorrow and I'll give you a job. Just between you and me— our candidate's gonna win the Grand Popularity contest. Mr Blue Ribbon says to me, "Albert, old man, you pick out the girl and I'll make her the Grand Popularity queen."'

Now one of the news items which Gracie's father had habitually read aloud of late bore always the headline, 'Our City's Queen.' The reading matter which followed explained how the Blue Ribbon, our largest department store, together with the New Heidelberg Tribune, our city's foremost newspaper, and the Tick-tock Jewelry emporium, and a dozen other business establishments were going to give some lucky young woman the opportunity for which every girl has always longed. She would be selected from the whole city of New Heidelberg, would 'lead' all the affairs which centered around the winter carnival and, last and best of all, would win a chance to distinguish herself in the movies.

'Who's your girl and how do you know she's gonna win?'
Gracie demanded.

'Well, the folks from all the stores that's in on the thing
each choose their own girl. Mr Blue Ribbon, he says to me,
"Albert, the jane that represents this store wins the whole
contest." Everybody can't win, can they?'

Mr Pomeroy was growing eloquent. He would probably
have talked about himself through the waning night, but
Gracie's interest was aroused in another direction.

'Aw, can it!' she interrupted. 'I bet I'd quit anyhow,
whether you or Mr Blue Ribbon wanted me to or not. I'd
just quit and show you I'd quit.'

Mr Pomeroy had finished his chicken, and an automobile
horn was blowing furiously outside the shanty demanding
Gracie's attention, so he spoke one parting line.

'You come in tomorrow and see, Miss—Miss Quit,' he
remarked oracularly, and reeled out into the cold just as he
had reeled in—with all the motion above the knees.

And that was how it happened that on Christmas night
Gracie retired early and left Mr Axelrod to shift for himself.
She slept as determinedly as she usually fried chicken and for
about the same length of time. She was drinking coffee when
she heard the first trolley pass a block below her house
and, putting on a coat of some indeterminate fur that in damp
weather smelled like a live animal, she minced over the ice
and crusted snow to the trolley stop. The street she came
along was steeply down hill, and if she had been an exu-
berant person she might have taken a little skip and slid all
the way. But she didn't—she walked sideways to keep from
falling.

The car was filled with steamy heat and melted snow, and
workingmen puffing their ways to far parts of the city. Gracie
reached the Blue Ribbon at the opening hour, and after some
wandering among aisles and elevators located Mr Albert
Pomeroy.

He was more pompous and less verbose than when she had seen him before—but he remembered her perfectly and for the best part of an hour he initiated her, with severe finger shakings into the art of being a saleslady.

Before Gracie had time to consider the question of quitting, a momentous occasion arose that drove the thought out of her head. She had been a participant in the activities of the store for less than a week when a general massmeeting of all the employees was held in the restroom after hours. Mr Pomeroy standing on a bench, acted as general chairman.

'We are gathered here,' he announced from his rostrum, 'for the purpose of discussing the subject of selecting the Blue Ribbon's representative in the popularity contest now being held under the auspices of Mr Blue Ribbon, one of the town's leading business men, and several other of the town's leading business men.' He paused here and took a long breath as one slightly dizzy.

'We must choose our queen—with honesty,' he went on, and then added surprisingly, 'which is always the best policy. Everybody knows that we have here in this store the most beautiful ladies that can be found in this town, and we must choose the best one among them all to represent us. You have until this time tomorrow to decide who you will vote for. I want to thank you on behalf of myself and Mr Blue Ribbon for your attention and——' he had prepared a strong finish for his speech, but it was considerably marred by the fact that just at this moment a stray thought of the haberdashery department flashed into his mind.

'In clothing, I wish to say——' He paused. 'In clothing, I wish——' Then he gave up and ended somewhat tamely with, 'And that's the way it is.'

As Gracie went out through the employees' entrance behind the tittering file of females she saw Mr Pomeroy on the corner under the white arc light. She walked quickly over and spoke to him.

'Honest,' she said, 'that was a great speech you made. I

don't see how some people can all of a sudden just make up a speech.'

She smiled and disappeared into the winter lights and the furry crowds and hurried toward her street car. Unwittingly, she had made up a good speech herself. Mr Pomeroy, though impervious both to ridicule and insult, was a sensitive man to compliments.

The next afternoon in the Blue Ribbon restroom, Gracie was somehow being heralded as a leading candidate for the honor of representing the store. She was surprised—and in the same breath she was not surprised. She never doubted that she would win, although she was a newcomer and there were five girls competing against her. Two of the five were prettier than Gracie and the other three were not pretty at all. But the ballot found a spirit of irritable perversity in possession. The pretty women were jealous of each other and voted for the ugly ones. The ugly ones were jealous of the pretty ones and voted for the newcomer, Gracie—and ugly ones were in the majority. No one was envious of Gracie, for no one knew her. And no one believed she could possibly win the contest—but she did.

And Mr Blue Ribbon was as good as Mr Pomeroy's indiscreet and intoxicated word. He 'fixed it,' and at the end of a month came the day of the coronation. It was to proceed up the main business street and then along the fashionable avenue to the river. In effect Queen Gracie Axelrod, in her royal coach, was to be borne through shouting mobs of faithful citizenry.

On a cold noon the cohorts gathered in front of the New Heidelberg hotel, where there was much scraping of fenders and blowing of horns. Gracie sat in her car beside Mr Pomeroy, whose title was 'Blue Ribbon Courtier Dedicated to the Queen of Popularity.' Behind Gracie a blue pole arose, balancing over her head a bright, insecure star. She carried a sceptre and wore a crown made by the local costumer, but

(94)

due to the cold air the crown had undergone a peculiar chemical change and faded to an inconspicuous roan. Of this Gracie was unaware.

From time to time she glanced tenderly at Mr Pomeroy, and it occurred to her how nice it would be if his gloved hand should hold hers under the heavy robe. The thought was delicious, and she reached out experimentally until her finger barely touched his, just faintly suggesting an amour of digits to take place later in the ride.

The less important cars—loaded with representatives of fraternal orders and assistant queens from other stores—had begun to move slowly off, following the brass band, and now the chauffeurs of the principal floats were coaxing roars of white steam from their engines. The mayor's car set up a cloud of noise and vapor.

'What's the matter?' demanded Mr Pomeroy anxiously of Gracie's chauffeur. 'We don't want to be left behind.'

'I'm afraid it's a little bit froze up.' The chauffeur was unscrewing the radiator cap. 'I guess maybe I'd better get some hot water from the hotel.'

'Well, hurry up, then,' complained Gracie. The car ahead of them was pulling out. 'Let's start anyhow,' she went on excitedly. 'You can fix it when we get back.'

'Start!' exclaimed the chauffeur, indignantly. 'Start! How can I start when it's froze up?'

The tail of the procession was a hundred yards up the street, and several automobiles that had no connection with the celebration had turned in and followed behind it.

Another car, containing a stout young man in the back seat, drove up alongside Gracie.

'Are you stuck?' asked the young man politely.

'Of course we are, you crazy fool!' shouted Gracie, whereupon the crowd laughed.

'You better get in this here car,' suggested the young man, unabashed.

'Maybe we better jump in,' said Mr Pomeroy uncertainly.

'When these things freeze up——'

'But how about all them decorations?' interrupted Gracie.

Willing onlookers began to tug at the ornamental star with the idea of transferring it to the other automobile, whereupon the support creaked, groaned and collapsed neatly into four pieces.

The tail of the parade had by this time rounded a bend and was passing out of sight far up the street; the music of the band was already faint and faraway.

'Here!' commanded Mr Pomeroy, breathing hard, 'get in!'

Gracie got in, and some one threw the star in after her for good luck. The young man drew the robe over them and they set off at full speed—but in less than a block the long delayed cross traffic brought them to another halt. When they overcame this obstacle a quarter of a mile of tight packed cars still interposed between Gracie and the procession ahead.

'Tell your chauffeur to honk!' said Gracie indignantly to the fat young man.

'He isn't mine. They gave me this car. I just got into town, you see. I'm Joe Murphy, the assistant director.'

'We got to get up to our place, ain't we?' shouted the queen. 'What do you suppose everybody's going to say when they don't see me?'

The chauffeur obediently honked, but as everybody else was honking, too, it produced little effect. The other cars, having attained a place in line, were not disposed to relinquish it to an undecorated machine containing an obviously intoxicated young woman who kept threatening them with a long blue stick.

When the procession turned into the fashionable avenue Gracie began to bow right and left to the crowds that should have lined the way. She bowed to groups or individuals impartially, to babies, to responsive dogs, and even to several of the more pretentious houses, which answered her with cold plate glass stares. Here and there some one nodded back at her politely, and one group gave her a short cheer—but they obviously failed to connect her with the colorful display ahead.

Gracie bowed for over a mile. Then two young men on a corner yelled something that was perfectly audible to her. They yelled it over and over again, and several small boys on the sidewalk took up the cry:

'Where'd you get the gin, sister? Where'd you get the gin?'

Then Gracie gave up and burst into tears and told Mr Murphy to take her home.

The movie, 'New Heidelberg, the Flower City of the Middle West,' was being filmed in the outskirts of the city. On a morning of February thaw Gracie stepped gingerly from the street car at the end of the line and, with the other city queens, navigated the melted snow and mud puddles that almost obliterated the ground. The lot was already crowded and Gracie, as leading lady, tried to locate those in charge. Some one pointed out a platform in the center, and told her that the active little man who was pacing nervously back and forth upon it was the director, Mr Decourcey O'Ney. Gracie elbowed her way in that direction.

Mr Decourcey O'Ney had come early into the pictures and back in 1916 had been known as a 'big' director. Then, due to one of those spasms of hysteria which periodically seize upon the industry, he had found himself suddenly out of work. His acquisition by the 'Our Own Movie' committee was especially played up by the New Heidelberg Tribune.

He was commenting to his assistant director on the undeniably swampy condition of the ground when a plump young lady with a big suit box under her arm appeared beside him on the platform.

'What can I do for you?' he asked absently.

'I'm the movie queen,' announced Gracie.

Mr Joe Murphy, 'assistant director' and man of all work, confirmed this fact.

'Why, sure,' he said warmly, 'this girl was elected the most popular girl in the city. Don't you remember me, Miss Axelrod?'

'Yeah,' said Gracie, grudgingly. She had no wish to be reminded of the late fiasco.

'Have you had any experience in pictures?' inquired Mr O'Ney.

'O, I seen a lot of 'em and I know just about how the leading lady ought to act.'

'Well,' murmured Mr O'Ney, alarmingly, 'I think I'll have you gilded to start with.'

'Mr O'Ney means that he'll show you how to do,' said Joe Murphy, hastily.

'By the bye,' said Mr O'Ney politely. 'Can you scream?'

'What?'

'Have you ever done any screaming?' And then he added in explanatory fashion, 'The only reason I ask you is because I want to know.'

'Why—sure,' answered Gracie hesitantly, 'I guess I can scream good enough, if you want somebody to scream.'

'All right.' Mr O'Ney seemed greatly pleased. 'Then scream!'

Before Gracie could believe her ears, much less open her mouth, Joe Murphy again interjected: 'Mr O'Ney means later. You go over to that house and put on your costume.'

Somewhat bewildered, Gracie set out for the ladies' dressing rooms, and Joe Murphy looked after her admiringly. He liked blondes as full blown as himself—and especially those who seemed to have materialized out of the vapor from warm milk.

The picture, written by a local poetess, commemorated the settling of New Heidelberg by the brave pioneers. Three days were spent in the rehearsal of the mob scenes. Gracie, relieved from work at the store, came every morning and sat shivering in the back of a prairie schooner. It was all very confusing, and she had little idea of what her part was to be. When the day came for the actual shooting she acted as she had never acted before. Entering the covered wagon, she violently elevated her eyebrows and crooked her little fingers into grotesque hooks. During the Indian attack she rushed about in the center of a blank cartridge bedlam, waving her arms and pointing here and there at the circling redskins as if to indicate startling tactical dispositions. At the end of the second day Mr O'Ney announced that the shooting was done. He thanked them all for their willingness, and told them their services were no longer required. Not once during the whole course of the picture had Gracie been required to scream.

Since Gracie had been 'working days,' Mr Axelrod's business had fallen off. He went to bed at midnight just when he should have been most alert. It was lonely when Gracie wasn't there to fill the shack with warm chicken smoke, and he had no one to read the newspaper at. But he was vaguely proud of his daughter, and his drowsy mind grasped the fact that something apart from him was going on in her life.

He was flattered when Gracie asked him to accompany her one Thursday night to the private showing of the picture. Only the people closely concerned were to be there. The real showing would take place in grand style at the city auditorium.

The preliminary showing was at the Bijou, and when the small, select audience was seated and the red velvet curtains parted to show the screen, Gracie and her father became rigid with excitement. The first title flashed suddenly on.

NEW HEIDELBERG

THE FLOWERY CITY OF THE MIDDLE WEST

AN EPIC OF PAST AND PRESENT

GROWTH AND PROSPERITY

BY

HARRIET DINWIDDIE HILLS CRAIG

DIRECTED BY

DECOURCEY O'NEY

There followed a cast of characters. Gracie thrilled when she found her name:

MISS GRACE AXELROD

WINNER OF THE POPULARITY CONTEST

And, after a line of dots:

AS AN EARLY QUEEN OF NEW HEIDELBERG

The word 'Prologue' danced before her eyes, and Gracie felt in her stomach the sinking sensation that preceded dental work. She looked steadfastly at the clumsy covered wagons creeping across the plain and she gasped as there was a sudden close-up of herself, acting, in the canvas oval at a wagon's back.

LET US NEVER FORGET THE NOBLE MEN AND

WOMEN WHOSE SUPREME SACRIFICE MADE

POSSIBLE OUR GLORIOUS CITY.

There were the Indians in the distance now—it was much more exciting than it had been on the suburban lot. The battle, looking desperately real, was in full swing. She sought herself anxiously amid the heat of conflict, but she might have been any one of a score of girls who it seemed had been acting just as violently as herself.

And here was the climax already. A savage rode up threateningly. Bang! And Gracie, or some one who looked like Gracie, sank wounded to the ground.

'See that? See that?' she whispered excitedly to her father. 'That was hard to do let me tell you!'

Someone said 'Sh!' and Gracie's eyes again sought the screen. The Indians were driven off, a hearty prayer was said by all, and the fields were expeditiously plowed for corn. Then to Gracie's astonishment the whole scene began to change. The suburban plain disappeared, and one of the covered wagons faded before her eyes into a handsome limousine. From the limousine stepped out a modern young girl in a fur coat with hat to match. It was none other than Miss Virginia Blue Ribbon, the pretty daughter of the owner of the Blue Ribbon store.

Gracie stared. Was the pioneer part over, she wondered—in less than fifteen minutes? And what did this limousine have to do with the picture?

'They must of left out some,' she whispered to her father. 'I guess they'll have me doing some more in a minute. But they shouldn't have showed so soon how I got wounded.'

Even now she did not realize the truth—that she was in the prologue and the prologue was over. She saw Miss Blue Ribbon standing in front of her father's store and then she saw her shopping in the Blue Ribbon aisles. Now she was in a limousine again bound for the fashionable avenue, and later in a beautiful evening dress she was dancing with many young men in the ballroom of the big hotel.

In the dim light Gracie looked at her program. 'Miss Virginia Blue Ribbon,' it stated, 'representing the Queen of Today.'

'They must be saving some of that western stuff for the end,' Gracie said in an uncertain voice.

Two reels flickered by. Miss Blue Ribbon manifested an unnatural interest in factories, jewelry stores, and even statistics. Gracie's bewilderment was fading now and a heavy burning lump had arisen in her throat. When the parade itself was thrown on the screen she watched through a blurry glaze that had gathered over her eyes. There went the automobiles through cheering crowds—the minor queens, the mayor, Mr Blue Ribbon, and his daughter in their limousine—then the scene ended—and she thought of her car, lost somewhere back two miles in the crowd.

Gracie wanted to leave, but she still felt that all the audience were watching her. She waited, stunned and unseeing, until in a few minutes more the screen flashed white and the movie was over.

Then she slipped into the aisle and ran quickly toward the exit, trying to bury her head in her coat collar. She had hoped to evade the crowd, but the closed door detained her and she came out into the lobby simultaneously with a score of people.

'Let me by,' she said gruffly to a portly person who had wedged her against a brass rail. The portly person turned, and she recognized Mr Blue Ribbon himself.

'Isn't this the carnival queen?' he asked jovially.

Gracie straightened up and seemed to draw the half ejected tears back into her eyes. She saw Mr Pomeroy just behind his employer, and she realised that the floorwalker's leer was but a copy, on a small scale, of Mr Blue Ribbon's business grin.

Then rage gave her dignity, gave her abandon, and Mr Blue Ribbon and his employee started back as they saw the expression that transformed her face.

'Say!' she cried, incredulously, 'just let me tell you one thing right to your face. I think the picture was rotten and I wouldn't pay a cent to see anything so rotten as that.'

A lobby full of people were listening now; even the fountain in the center seemed puffing with excitement. Mr Pomeroy made a move forward as if he would have seized her, but Gracie raised her hand threateningly.

'Don't you touch me!' she shouted. 'I told you if I didn't like your old store I'd quit, and now I quit! When they go out and elect somebody queen they ought to make her queen of something except an old broken down wagon.' Her voice was soaring now to the highest pitch it had ever reached.

'I resign from the moving pictures!' she cried passionately, and with the gesture of one tearing up a million dollar contract, she pulled a program ferociously from her pocket, tore it once, twice—and hurled the white segments into Mr Blue Ribbon's astonished face.

Two o'clock that night. There were no customers in the chicken shanty and Mr Axelrod, worn out with the excitement of the evening, was long gone to bed when the door opened suddenly and a stout young man with a baby's face stepped inside. It was Joe Murphy.

'Get out of here!' cried Gracie quickly. 'You go on out of this chicken joint!'

'I want to speak to you about the movie.'

'I wouldn't be in another movie if you gave me a million dollars! I hate movies, see? I wouldn't dirty my hands being in one. And, besides, you get out!'

She looked wildly about her, and as Joe Murphy saw her eyes fall on a dish of sizzling chicken gravy he took an instinctive step toward the door.

'I didn't have nothing to do with it. They fixed up the whole thing. Say, I wouldn't keep you out of a picture,' and then he blurted out suddenly, 'Why—why, I'm in love with you.'

Gracie's plate rattled to the floor, where it vibrated for a moment like a top.

'Well,' she snapped, 'this is a fine time of night to come telling me about it!'

But she indicated that he should come in.

'Look here, Gracie,' he began, 'that was a dirty trick they did you and I was wondering wouldn't you like a chance to get back at 'em.'

'I'd like to smash 'em in the face.'

'That's the way Decourcey O'Ney feels about it,' confided Joe. He ain't a good business man, you see, and they beat him out of some of the cash they said they'd pay him.'

'Why didn't he let me be the leading lady when I should of been?' demanded Gracie.

'He says they told him not to,' said Joe eagerly. 'They said you was just an accident and wasn't important at all and not to waste any footage on you.'

'O, they did, did they?' cried Gracie, red with rage. 'Wait till the people who elected me queen see what they done to that picture!'

'That's what I think,' agreed Joe, 'and my idea is that we ought to fix that picture up. Because, like you say, I been thinking how sore those people are going to be.'

'Gosh, they're going to be sore,' said Gracie, drawing a pleasant warmth from the idea. 'I bet they'll get after old Blue Ribbon. They'll all get together and never buy nothing more in his store,' she added, hopefully.

'That's right,' agreed Joe with tact, 'and that's why I think the thing for us to do is to try and fix that picture up. Mr O'Ney, he's so mad he don't care what happens. He says for me to go ahead and do anything I want to. He don't care.'

Gracie hesitated.

'I'd rather have it so nobody would ever go to the Blue Ribbon no more.'

She visualized Mr Pomeroy, out of a job, bobbing into the shack after a scrap of charity chicken. But Joe shook his head.

'I got a better scheme,' he insisted. 'I'll come around

tomorrow morning at nine o'clock. Have your costume in a box—the one you wore in the movie.'

When he went out, she stood in the doorway and followed his retreating figure with her eyes. The roofs were dripping, and the stars were out, and there was a soft, moist breeze. An earlier remark he had made was reverberating persistently in her head.

'Say,' Gracie called after him, 'what did you mean when you said all that stuff about being in love with me?'

Joe stopped and turned.

'Me? Why—I just meant it, that's all!'

'That's funny,' and then she added, 'Say, come back here a minute, will you—Joe?'

Joe came back.

As the public performance drew near, the pavements grew sloppier and the snow in the gutters melted into dirty sherbet. On the great Saturday night the auditorium was jammed to capacity. There was a big orchestra this time, which played a stupendous overture, after which Mr Blue Ribbon himself appeared on the lighted stage and advanced to the footlights.

'Fellow New Heidelbergians!' he began in an inspiring voice, 'to make a long story as short as possible this movie is a real—a real epoch in the life of our city. It shows first in a great sweeping epic a picture of what I may call an epic of our pioneer days when our grandfathers and grandmothers yoked up their oxen and came over here from—from Europe—looking for gold!'

He seemed to realize that there was some slight inaccuracy in his last observation, but as there was a burst of applause from a line of old, deaf, white haired people in the middle of the house, he let it pass, and now turned to those without whose efforts this picture could never have been made. He wanted to thank first of all the splendid spirit of every one who participated. This spirit had convinced Mr Blue Ribbon that New Heidelberg could act as a unit. Next he turned to that distinguished director, Mr Decourcey O'Ney. After constant triumphs in Hollywood Mr O'Ney had come here because he had heard of the splendid spirit of the inhabitants.

Applause! Every one turned to look at Mr O'Ney. Mr O'Ney on being located stood up and bowed. It was afterwards remarked by those nearest him that he glanced somewhat nervously around and that his eyes fell with most approval upon the red exit lamps over the doors.

'Then,' continued Mr Blue Ribbon, and this was true magnanimity, 'let us not forget the young lady who was chosen by public acclaim as the fairest in our city and who adorns this work of art with her graces—Miss Grace Axelrod —Our Own Movie Queen!'

There was a storm of applause. Gracie stood up, bowed, and then sat down quickly, uttering a subdued ironic sound.

Mr Blue Ribbon rambled on for some moments. Finally he ceased with a benign smile, and bobbing off the stage took his seat down in front. The house grew dark, the orchestra struck up the national anthem, and the silver rectangle appeared upon the blue screen:

NEW HEIDELBERG, THE FLOWERY CITY

OF THE MIDDLE WEST

The preliminary titles were all as before. The wagons set off on the journey to outbursts of applause as the passengers were recognized by proud relatives and friends.

Then, to the surprise of those who had witnessed the private showing, a brand new title flashed on:

MISS GRACE AXELROD

CHOSEN BY EVERYBODY IN THE CITY

TO BE QUEEN AND STAR OF THE PICTURE.

A PIONEER GIRL . . . MISS AXELROD.

Mr Blue Ribbon gasped faintly. The audience, unconscious of a change, applauded.

Here were the Indians now, shading their eyes with their hands and beginning their immemorial tactics of riding around their prey in concentric circles. The battle began, the wagon train was brought to a stop, the bedlam of blank cartridges was so real as to be almost audible. Clapping broke out. A title:

WHEN THE WHITE PEOPLE WERE GETTING
BEATEN, MISS GRACE AXELROD, THE CITY'S
QUEEN, SHOOTS THE INDIAN CHIEF WITH A
GUN SHE GOT.

The applause which greeted this was punctuated with an occasional gasp and somebody snickered. But the action which followed was even more curious. It showed Miss Axelrod snatching a rifle from some one who leapt quickly out of the picture, but who gave the undeniable impression of having been a young man in a derby hat. Miss Axelrod knelt and fired the gun in the direction of a telegraph pole, which had sprung up suddenly on the prairie. There followed a scene, so short as to be scarcely distinguishable, of a man falling down. This was obviously the Indian chief shot by Miss Axelrod, but again the realists in the audience perceived that the aborigine, though he wore feathers in his hair, was dressed in modern trousers rolled up above modern garters.

This time a long restrained titter broke out, but the audience were still far from the suspicion that this was not the film as originally planned.

AS THE INDIANS WERE NOT YET BEATEN OFF
BY MISS GRACE AXELROD'S ATTACK, SHE
SHOOTS THE SECOND IN COMMAND AND THUS
COMPLETES THEIR DISMAY.

The shooting of the second in command was remarkably like the shooting of the chief. There was the lean telegraph pole in the distance, and there was the be-gartered Sioux who in the next flash fell to the ground. The resemblance indicated that the second in command might be the chief's twin brother.

The whispering had now thickened to a buzz, and a suspicion was abroad that somewhere, somehow, something had gone awry.

On the screen, however, the action had returned to normality. The Indians, dismayed by the fall of the second in command—apparently he was the real power behind the throne—began to retreat in earnest, and the settlers, after embracing each other with shouts of joy, sang a hymn of thanksgiving and went about building New Heidelberg.

Mr Blue Ribbon had for some time been stirring wildly in his seat, casting distraught glances rearward and then glaring back at the screen with unbelieving eyes. The prologue was over, and Miss Virginia Blue Ribbon's triumphant progress among the marts and emporiums should now have been recorded.

MISS GRACE AXELROD, WINNER OF THE CITY'S

POPULARITY CONTEST, GOES ON A TOUR TO

THE CITY'S BIG STORES.

And as the flickering letters flashed out, Mr Blue Ribbon found himself gazing on an episode that was so cut as to expose only a back view of his daughter. She entered shops as before, she fingered materials, she admired jewelry—but whenever she seemed about to turn her face to the audience the scene ended.

Then the astounding information blazed across the silver sheet that:

MISS GRACE AXELROD LOOKS THINNER HERE
BECAUSE SHE'S GOT ON A BETTER CORSET
THAN YOU COULD EVER BUY AT THE BLUE
RIBBON STORE.

For a moment there was no sound except a long sigh from Miss Virginia Blue Ribbon as she fainted away. Then with a low flabbergasted roar that increased to a din, pandemonium burst forth in the auditorium. Mr Blue Ribbon rose choking from his seat and dashed for the back of the house, leaving a little path of awe that marked his passage through.

To the rest of the audience, history was being made before their eyes. A full close-up of Miss Blue Ribbon appeared, following the comment:

ONE WHO STUCK HER NOSE IN

After that the picture went on, but no one cared. It was a crazed howl from the gallery for 'More Gracie!' which really terminated the entertainment. No one saw the end of the picture, in which the school children's black and white handkerchiefs spelled out the name of the city. The crowd was on its feet looking up at the balcony, where Mr Blue Ribbon and other inarticulate, half-crazy citizens were trying to climb over the operator's back and stop the projector. A mob had gathered around Mr Decourcey O'Ney, who stood calmly trembling. The only remark he was heard to make was that it would have been a bigger picture if he could have had everyone gilded.

Joe Murphy turned and whispered to Gracie.

'We better beat it before they turn up the lights.'

'Do you think it went off good?' she asked anxiously, as they came out by a side exit into the almost warm night. 'I thought it was a swell picture, and I guess anybody would of but a lot of soreheads.'

'Poor O'Ney,' said Joe thoughtfully as they walked toward the street car.

'Do you suppose them people will put Mr O'Ney in prison?'

'Well, not in prison.' He pronounced the last word so that Gracie demanded:

'Where will they put him?'

Joe took Gracie's hand and squeezed it comfortably.

'They'll put him in a nice, quiet asylum,' he said. 'He's a good director, you know, when he's right. The only trouble with him is that he's raving crazy.'

Gracie Axelrod and Joe Murphy were married late in March, and all the department stores, except the Blue Ribbon, sent her elaborate wedding presents. For their honeymoon they went to Sioux City, where every night they went to the picture show. Since they've been back in New Heidelberg and started the restaurant, which has made them rather more than prosperous, Gracie has become the neighbourhood authority on the subject of pictures. She buys all the movie magazines, 'Screen Sobs,' 'Photo Passion,' and 'Motion Picture Scandal,' and she winks a cynical eye when a new opportunity contest is announced in Wichita, Kansas.

Mr Decourcey O'Ney has been released from the asylum and engaged by 'Films Par Excellence,' at two thousand a week. His first picture is to be called 'Hearts A-Craze.' Gracie can hardly wait to see it.

SCOTT

A Penny Spent

(*The Saturday Evening Post*,
10 October 1925)

The Brix Grill in Paris is one of those places where things happen—like the first bench as you enter Central Park South, or Herrin, Illinois. I have seen marriages broken up there at an ill-considered word and blows struck between a professional dancer and a British baron, and I know personally of at least two murders that would have been committed on the spot but for the fact that it was July and there was no room. Even murders require a certain amount of space, and in July the Brix Grill has no room at all.

Go in at six o'clock of a summer evening, planting your feet lightly lest you tear some college boy bag from bag, and see if you don't find the actor who owes you a hundred dollars or the stranger who gave you a match once in Red Wing, Minnesota, or the man who won your girl away from you with silver phrases just ten years ago. One thing is certain—that before you melt out into the green-and-cream Paris twilight you will have the feel of standing for a moment at one of the predestined centers of the world.

At 7:30, walk to the center of the room and stand with your eyes shut for half an hour—this is a merely hypothetical suggestion—and then open them. The gray and blue and brown and slate have faded out of the scene and the prevailing note, as the haberdashers say, has become black and white. Another half hour and there is no note at all—the room is nearly empty. Those with dinner engagements have gone to keep them and those without any have gone to pretend they have. Even the two Americans who opened up the bar that morning have been led off by kind friends. The clock makes one of those quick little electric jumps to nine. We will too.

It is nine o'clock by Brix time, which is just the same as any other time. Mr Julius Bushmill; manufacturer; b. Canton, Ohio, June 1, 1876; m., 1899, Jessie Pepper; Mason; Republican; Congregationalist; Delegate M. A. of A. 1908; pres. 1909–1912; director Grimes, Hansen Co. since 1911; director Midland R. R. of Indiana—all that and more—walks in, moving a silk handkerchief over a hot scarlet brow. It is his own brow. He wears a handsome dinner coat, but has no vest on because the hotel valet has sent both his vests to the dry-cleaners by mistake, a fact which has been volubly explained to Mr Bushmill for half an hour. Needless to say, the prominent manufacturer is prey to a natural embarrassment at this discrepancy in his attire. He has left his devoted wife and attractive daughter in the lounge while he seeks something to fortify his entrance into the exclusive and palatial dining room.

The only other man in the bar was a tall, dark, grimly handsome young American, who slouched in a leather corner and stared at Mr Bushmill's patent-leather shoes. Self-consciously Mr Bushmill looked down at his shoes, wondering if the valet had deprived him of them too. Such was his relief to find them in place that he grinned at the young man and his hand went automatically to the business card in his coat pocket.

'Couldn't locate my vests,' he said cordially. 'That blamed valet took both my vests. See?'

He exposed the shameful overexpanse of his starched shirt.

'I beg your pardon?' said the young man, looking up with a start.

'My vests,' repeated Mr Bushmill with less gusto—'lost my vests.'

The young man considered.

'I haven't seen them,' he said.

'Oh, not here!' exclaimed Bushmill. 'Upstairs.'

'Ask Jack,' suggested the young man, and waved his hand toward the bar.

Among our deficiencies as a race is the fact that we have no respect for the contemplative mood. Bushmill sat down, asked the young man to have a drink, obtained finally the grudging admission that he would have a milk shake; and after explaining the vest matter in detail, tossed his business card across the table. He was not the frock-coated and impressive type of millionaire which has become so frequent since the war. He was rather the 1910 model—a sort of cross between Henry VIII and 'our Mr Jones will be in Minneapolis on Friday.' He was much louder and more provincial and warm-hearted than the new type.

He liked young men, and his own young man would have been about the age of this one, had it not been for the defiant stubbornness of the German machine gunners in the last days of the war.

'Here with my wife and daughter,' he volunteered. 'What's your name?'

'Corcoran,' answered the young man pleasantly, but without enthusiasm.

'You American—or English?'

'American.'

'What business you in?'

'None.'

'Been here long?' continued Bushmill stubbornly.

The young man hesitated.

'I was born here,' he said.

Bushmill blinked and his eyes roved involuntarily around the bar.

'Born here!' he repeated.

Corcoran smiled.

'Up on the fifth floor.'

The waiter set the two drinks and a dish of Saratoga

(113)

chips on the table. Immediately Bushmill became aware of an interesting phenomenon—Corcoran's hand commenced to flash up and down between the dish and his mouth, each journey transporting a thick layer of potatoes to the eager aperture, until the dish was empty.

'Sorry,' said Corcoran, looking rather regretfully at the dish. He took out a handkerchief and wiped his fingers. 'I didn't think what I was doing. I'm sure you can get some more.'

A series of details now began to impress themselves on Bushmill—that there were hollows in this young man's cheeks that were not intended by the bone structure, hollows of undernourishment or ill health; that the fine flannel of his unmistakably Bond Street suit was shiny from many pressings—the elbows were fairly gleaming—and that his whole frame had suddenly collapsed a little as if the digestion of the potatoes and milk shake had begun immediately instead of waiting for the correct half hour.

'Born here, eh?' he said thoughtfully. 'Lived a lot abroad, I guess.'

'Yes.'

'How long since you've had a square meal?'

The young man started.

'Why, I had lunch,' he said. 'About one o'clock I had lunch.'

'One o'clock last Friday,' commented Bushmill skeptically. There was a long pause.

'Yes,' admitted Corcoran, 'about one o'clock last Friday.'

'Are you broke? Or are you waiting for money from home?'

'This is home.' Corcoran looked around abstractedly. 'I've spent most of my life in the Brix hotels of one city or another. I don't think they'd believe me upstairs if I told them I was broke. But I've got just enough left to pay my bill when I move out tomorrow.'

Bushmill frowned.

'You could have lived a week at a small hotel for what it costs you here by the day,' he remarked.

'I don't know the names of any other hotels.'

Corcoran smiled apologetically. It was a singularly charming and somehow entirely confident smile, and Julius Bushmill was filled with a mixture of pity and awe. There was something of the snob in him, as there is in all self-made men, and he realized that this young man was telling the defiant truth.

'Any plans?'

'No.'

'Any abilities—or talents?'

Corcoran considered.

'I can speak most languages,' he said. 'But talents—I'm afraid the only one I have is for spending money.'

'How do you know you've got that?'

'I can't very well help knowing it.' Again he hesitated. 'I've just finished running through a matter of half a million dollars.'

Bushmill's exclamation died on its first syllable as a new voice, impatient, reproachful and cheerfully anxious, shattered the seclusion of the grill.

'Have you seen a man without a vest named Bushmill? A very old man about fifty? We've been waiting for him about two or three hours.'

'Hallie,' called Bushmill, with a groan of remorse, 'here I am. I'd forgotten you were alive.'

'Don't flatter yourself it's you we missed,' said Hallie, coming up. 'It's only your money. Mamma and I want food—and we must look it; two nice French gentlemen wanted to take us to dinner while we were waiting in the hall.'

'This is Mr Corcoran,' said Bushmill. 'My daughter.'

Hallie Bushmill was young and vivid and light, with boy's hair and a brow that bulged just slightly, like a baby's brow, and under it small perfect features that danced up and down when she smiled. She was constantly repressing their tendency toward irresponsible gayety, as if she feared that, once encouraged, they would never come back to kindergarten under that childish brow any more.

'Mr Corcoran was born here in the Brix,' announced her father. 'I'm sorry I kept you and your mother waiting, but to tell the truth we've been fixing up a little surprise.' He looked at Corcoran and winked perceptibly. 'As you know, I've got to go to England day after tomorrow and do some business in those ugly industrial towns. My plan was that you and your mother should make a month's tour of Belgium and Holland and end up at Amsterdam, where Hallie's— where Mr Nosby will meet you.'

'Yes, I know all that,' said Hallie. 'Go on. Let's have the surprise.'

'I had planned to engage a courier,' continued Mr Bushmill, 'but fortunately I ran into my friend Corcoran this evening and he's agreed to go instead.'

'I haven't said a word——' interrupted Corcoran in amazement, but Bushmill continued with a decisive wave of his hand:

'Brought up in Europe, he knows it like a book; born in the Brix, he understands hotels; taught by experience'— here he looked significantly at Corcoran—'taught by experience, he can prevent you and your mother from being extravagant and show you how to observe the happy mean.'

'Great!' Hallie looked at Corcoran with interest. 'We'll have a regular loop, Mr ——'

She broke off. During the last few minutes a strange expression had come into Corcoran's face. It spread suddenly now into a sort of frightened pallor.

'Mr Bushmill,' he said with an effort, 'I've got to speak to you alone—at once. It's very important. I——'

Hallie jumped to her feet.

'I'll wait with mother,' she said with a curious glance. 'Hurry—both of you.'

As she left the bar, Bushmill turned to Corcoran anxiously.

'What is it?' he demanded. 'What do you want to say?'

'I just wanted to tell you that I'm going to faint,' said Corcoran.

And with remarkable promptitude he did.

II

In spite of the immediate liking that Bushmill had taken to young Corcoran, a certain corroboratory investigation was, of course, necessary. The Paris branch of the New York bank that had handled the last of the half million told him what he needed to know. Corcoran was not given to drink, heavy gambling or vice; he simply spent money—that was all. Various people, including certain officers of the bank who had known his family, had tried to argue with him at one time or another, but he was apparently an incurable spendthrift. A childhood and youth in Europe with a wildly indulgent mother had somehow robbed him of all sense of value or proportion.

Satisfied, Bushmill asked no more—no one knew what had become of the money and, even if they had, a certain delicacy would have prevented him from inquiring more deeply into Corcoran's short past. But he did take occasion to utter a few parting admonitions before the expedition boarded the train.

'I'm letting you hold the purse strings because I think you've learned your lesson,' he said; 'but just remember that this time the money isn't your own. All that belongs to you is the seventy-five dollars a week that I pay you in salary. Every other expenditure is to be entered in that little book and shown to me.'

'I understand.'

'The first thing is to watch what you spend, and prove to me that you've got the common sense to profit by your mistake. The second and most important thing is that my wife and daughter are to have a good time.'

With the first of his salary Corcoran supplied himself with histories and guidebooks of Holland and Belgium, and on the night before their departure, as well as on the night of their arrival in Brussels, he sat up late absorbing a mass of information that he had never in his travels with his mother been aware of before. They had not gone in for sight-seeing. His mother had considered it something which only school-teachers and vulgar tourists did, but Mr Bushmill had impressed upon him that Hallie was to have all the advantages of travel; he must make it interesting for her by keeping ahead of her every day.

In Brussels they were to remain five days. The first morning Corcoran took three seats in a touring bus, and they inspected the guild halls and the palaces and the monuments and the parks, while he corrected the guide's historical slips in stage whispers and congratulated himself on doing so well.

But during the afternoon it drizzled as they drove through the streets and he grew tired of his own voice, of Hallie's conventional 'Oh, isn't that interesting,' echoed by her mother, and he wondered if five days wasn't too long to stay here after all. Still, he had impressed them, without doubt; he had made a good start as the serious and well-informed young man. Moreover, he had done well with the money. Resisting his first impulse to take a private limousine for the day, which would certainly have cost twelve dollars, he had only three bus tickets at one dollar each to enter in the little book. Before he began his nightly reading he put it down for Mr Bushmill to see. But first of all he took a steaming hot bath—he had never ridden in a rubber-neck wagon with ordinary sightseers before and he found the idea rather painful.

The next day the tour continued, but so did the drizzling rain, and that evening, to his dismay, Mrs Bushmill came down with a cold. It was nothing serious, but it entailed two doctor's visits at American prices, together with the cost of the dozen remedies which European physicians order under any circumstances, and it was a discouraging note which he made in the back of his little book that night:

> *One ruined hat—she claimed it was an old hat,*
> *   but it didn't look old to me* $10.00
> *3 bus tickets for Monday.* 3.00
> *3 bus tickets for Tuesday.* 2.00
> *Tips to incompetent guide* 1.50
> *2 doctor's visits* 8.00
> *Medicines* 2.25
>
> *Total for two days' sight-seeing* . . . $26.75

And, to balance that, Corcoran thought of the entry he might have made had he followed his first instinct: ·

> *One comfortable limousine for two days, in-*
> *cluding tip to chauffeur* $26.00

Next morning Mrs Bushmill remained in bed while he and Hallie took the excursion train to Waterloo. He had diligently mastered the strategy of the battle, and as he began his explanation of Napoleon's maneuvers, prefacing it with a short account of the political situation, he was rather disappointed at Hallie's indifference. Luncheon increased his uneasiness. He wished he had brought along the cold-lobster luncheon, put up by the hotel, that he had extravagantly considered. The food at the local restaurant was execrable and Hallie stared desolately at the hard potatoes and vintage steak, and then out the window at the melancholy rain. Corcoran wasn't hungry, either, but he forced himself to eat with an affectation of relish. Two more days in Brussels! And then Antwerp! And Rotterdam! And The Hague! Twenty-five more days of history to get up in the still hours of the night, and all for an unresponsive young person who did not seem to appreciate the advantages of travel.

They were coming out of the restaurant, and Hallie's voice, with a new note in it, broke in on his meditations.

'Get a taxi; I want to go home.'

He turned to her in consternation.

'What? You want to go back without seeing the famous indoor panorama, with paintings of all the actions and the life-size figures of the casualties in the foreground?'

'There's a taxi,' she interrupted. 'Quick!'

'A taxi!' he groaned, running after it through the mud. 'And these taxis are robbers—we might have had a limousine out and back for the same price.'

In silence they returned to the hotel. As Hallie entered the elevator she looked at him with suddenly determined eyes.

'Please wear your dinner coat tonight. I want to go out somewhere and dance—and please send flowers.'

Cocoran wondered if this form of diversion had been included in Mr Bushmill's intentions—especially since he had gathered that Hallie was practically engaged to the Mr Nosby who was to meet them in Amsterdam.

Distraught with doubt, he went to a florist and priced orchids. But a corsage of three would come to twenty-four dollars, and this was not an item he cared to enter in the little book. Regretfully, he compromised on sweet peas and was relieved to find her wearing them when she stepped out of the elevator at seven, in a pink-petaled dress.

Corcoran was astounded and not a little disturbed by her loveliness—he had never seen her in full evening dress before. Her perfect features were dancing up and down in delighted anticipation, and he felt that Mr Bushmill might have afforded the orchids after all.

'Thanks for the pretty flowers,' she cried eagerly. 'Where are we going?'

'There's a nice orchestra here in the hotel.'

Her face fell a little.

'Well, we can start here——'

They went down to the almost-deserted grill, where a few scattered groups of diners swooned in midsummer languor, and only a half dozen Americans arose with the music and stalked defiantly around the floor. Hallie and Corcoran danced. She was surprised to find how well he danced, as all tall, slender men should, with such a delicacy of suggestion that she felt as though she were being turned here and there as a bright bouquet or a piece of precious cloth before five hundred eyes.

But when they had finished dancing she realized that there were only a score of eyes; after dinner even these began to melt apathetically away.

'We'd better be moving on to some gayer place,' she suggested.

He frowned.

'Isn't this gay enough?' he asked anxiously. 'I rather like the happy mean.'

'That sounds good. Let's go there!'

'It isn't a café—it's a principle I'm trying to learn. I don't know whether your father would want——'

She flushed angrily.

'Can't you be a little human?' she demanded. 'I thought when father said you were born in the Brix you'd know something about having a good time.'

He had no answer ready. After all, why should a girl of her conspicuous loveliness be condemned to desolate hotel dances and public-bus excursions in the rain?

'Is this your idea of a riot?' she continued. 'Do you ever think about anything except history and monuments? Don't you know anything about having fun?'

'Once I knew quite a lot.'

'What?'

'In fact—once I used to be rather an expert at spending money.'

'Spending money!' she broke out. 'For these?'

She unpinned the corsage from her waist and flung it on the table. 'Pay the check, please. I'm going upstairs to bed.'

'All right,' said Corcoran suddenly, 'I've decided to give you a good time.'

'How?' she demanded with frozen scorn. 'Take me to the movies?'

'Miss Bushmill,' said Corcoran grimly, 'I've had good times beyond the wildest flights of your very provincial, Middle-Western imagination. I've entertained from New York to Constantinople—given affairs that have made Indian rajahs weep with envy.

'I've had prima donnas break ten-thousand-dollar engagements to come to my smallest dinners. When you were still playing who's got the button back in Ohio I entertained on a cruising trip that was so much fun that I had to sink my yacht to make the guests go home.'

'I don't believe it. I——' Hallie gasped.

'You're bored,' he interrupted. 'Very well, I'll do my stuff. I'll do what I know how to do. Between here and Amsterdam you're going to have the time of your life.'

III

Corcoran worked quickly. That night, after taking Hallie to her room, he paid several calls—in fact, he was extraordinarily busy up to eleven o'clock next morning. At that hour he tapped briskly at the Bushmills' door.

'You are lunching at the Brussels Country Club,' he said to Hallie directly, 'with Prince Abrisini, Countess Perimont and Major Sir Reynolds Fitz-Hugh, the British attaché. The Bolls-Ferrari landaulet will be ready at the door in half an hour.'

'But I thought we were going to the culinary exhibit,' objected Mrs Bushmill in surprise. 'We had planned——'

'You are going,' said Corcoran politely, 'with two nice

ladies from Wisconsin. And afterward you are going to an American tea room and have an American luncheon with American food. At twelve o'clock, a dark conservative town car will be waiting downstairs for your use.'

He turned to Hallie.

'Your new maid will arrive immediately to help you dress. She will oversee the removal of your things in your absence so that nothing will be mislaid. This afternoon you entertain at tea.'

'Why, how can I entertain at tea?' cried Hallie. 'I don't know a soul in the place.'

'The invitations are already issued,' said Corcoran.

Without waiting for further protests, he bowed slightly and retired through the door.

The next three hours passed in a whirl. There was the gorgeous landaulet with a silk-hatted, satin-breeched, plum-colored footman beside the chauffeur, and a wilderness of orchids flowering from the little jars inside. There were the impressive titles that she heard in a daze at the country club as she sat down at a rose-littered table; and out of no-where a dozen other men appeared during luncheon and stopped to be introduced to her as they went by. Never in her two years as the belle of a small Ohio town had Hallie had such attention, so many compliments; her features danced up and down with delight. Returning to the hotel, she found that they had been moved dexterously to the royal suite, a huge high salon and two sunny bedrooms overlooking a garden. Her capped maid—exactly like the French maid she had once impersonated in a play—was in attendance, and there was a new deference in the manner of all the servants in the hotel. She was bowed up the steps—other guests were gently brushed aside for her—and bowed into the elevator, which clanged shut in the faces of two irate Englishwomen and whisked her straight to her floor.

Tea was a great success. Her mother, considerably encouraged by the pleasant two hours she had spent in congenial company, conversed with the clergyman of the American church, while Hallie moved enraptured through a swarm of charming and attentive men. She was surprised to learn that she was giving a dinner dance that night at the fashionable Café Royal, and even the afternoon faded before the glories of the night. She was not aware that two specially hired entertainers had left Paris for Brussels on the noon train until they bounced hilariously in upon the shining floor. But she knew that there were a dozen partners for every dance, and chatter that had nothing to do with monuments or battlefields. Had she not been so thoroughly and cheerfully tired, she would have protested frantically at midnight when Corcoran approached her and told her he was taking her home.

Only then, half asleep in the luxurious depths of the town car, did she have time to wonder.

'How on earth—how did you do it?'

'It was nothing—I had no time,' said Corcoran disparagingly. 'I knew a few young men around the embassies. Brussels isn't very gay, you know, and they're always glad to help stir things up. All the rest was—even simpler. Did you have a good time?'

No answer.

'Did you have a good time?' he repeated a little anxiously. 'There's no use going on, you know, if you didn't have a——'

'The Battle of Wellington was won by Major Sir Corcoran Fitz-Hugh Abrisini,' she muttered, decisively but indistinctly.

Hallie was asleep.

IV

After three more days, Hallie finally consented to being torn away from Brussels, and the tour continued through Antwerp, Rotterdam and The Hague. But it was not the same sort of tour that had left Paris a short week before. It traveled in two limousines, for there were always at least one pair of attentive cavaliers in attendance—not to mention a quartet of hirelings who made the jumps by train. Corcoran's guidebooks and histories appeared no more. In Antwerp they did not stay at a mere hotel, but at a famous old shooting box on the outskirts of the city which Corcoran hired for six days, servants and all.

Before they left, Hallie's photograph appeared in the Antwerp papers over a paragraph which spoke of her as the beautiful American heiress who had taken Brabant Lodge and entertained so delightfully that a certain royal personage had been several times in evidence there.

In Rotterdam, Hallie saw neither the Boompjes nor the Groote Kerk—they were both obscured by a stream of pleasant young Dutchmen who looked at her with soft blue eyes. But when they reached The Hague and the tour neared its end, she was aware of a growing sadness—it had been such a good time and now it would be over and put away. Already Amsterdam and a certain Ohio gentleman, who didn't understand entertaining on the grand scale, were sweeping toward her, and though she tried to be glad she wasn't glad at all. It depressed her, too, that Corcoran seemed to be avoiding her—he had scarcely spoken to her or danced with her since they left Antwerp. She was thinking chiefly of that on the last afternoon, as they rode through the twilight toward Amsterdam and her mother drowsed sleepily in a corner of the car.

'You've been so good to me,' she said. 'If you're still angry about that evening in Brussels, please try to forgive me now.'

'I've forgiven you long ago.'

The rode into the city in silence, and Hallie looked out the window in a sort of panic. What would she do now with no one to take care of her, to take care of that part of her that wanted to be young and gay forever? Just before they drew up at the hotel, she turned again to Corcoran and their eyes met in a strange, disquieting glance. Her hand reached out for his and pressed it gently, as if this was their real good-by.

Mr Claude Nosby was a stiff, dark, glossy man, leaning hard toward forty, whose eyes rested for a hostile moment upon Corcoran almost as he helped Hallie from the car.

'Your father arrives tomorrow,' he said portentously. 'His attention has been called to your picture in the Antwerp papers and he is hurrying over from London.'

'Why shouldn't my picture be in the Antwerp papers, Claude?' inquired Hallie innocently.

'It seems a bit unusual.'

Mr Nosby had had a letter from Mr Bushmill which told him of the arrangement. He looked upon it with profound disapproval. All through dinner he listened without enthusiasm to the account which Hallie, rather spiritedly assisted by her mother, gave of the adventure; and afterward when Hallie and her mother went to bed he informed Corcoran that he would like to speak to him alone.

'Ah—Mr Corcoran,' he began, 'would you be kind enough to let me see the little account book you are keeping for Mr Bushmill?'

'I'd rather not,' answered Corcoran pleasantly. 'I think that's a matter between Mr Bushmill and me.'

'It's the same thing,' said Nosby impatiently. 'Perhaps you are not aware that Miss Bushmill and I are engaged.'

'I had gathered as much.'

'Perhaps you can gather, too, that I am not particularly pleased at the sort of good time you chose to give her.'

'It was just an ordinary good time.'

'That is a matter of opinion. Will you give me the note-book?'

'Tomorrow,' said Corcoran, still pleasantly, 'and only to Mr Bushmill. Good night.'

Corcoran slept late. He was awakened at eleven by the telephone, through which Nosby's voice informed him coldly that Mr Bushmill had arrived and would see him at once.

(126)

When he rapped at his employer's door ten minutes later, he found Hallie and her mother also were there, sitting rather sulkily on a sofa. Mr Bushmill nodded at him coolly, but made no motion to shake hands.

'Let's see that account book,' he said immediately.

Corcoran handed it to him, together with a bulky packet of vouchers and receipts.

'I hear you've all been out raising hell,' said Bushmill.

'No,' said Hallie, 'only mamma and me.'

'You wait outside, Corcoran. I'll let you know when I want you.'

Corcoran descended to the lobby and found out from the porter that a train left for Paris at noon. Then he bought a New York Herald and stared at the headlines for half an hour. At the end of that time he was summoned upstairs.

Evidently a heated discussion had gone on in his absence. Mr Nosby was staring out the window with a look of patient resignation. Mrs Bushmill had been crying, and Hallie, with a triumphant frown on her childish brow, was making a camp stool out of her father's knee.

'Sit down,' she said sternly.

Corcoran sat down.

'What do you mean by giving us such a good time?'

'Oh, drop it, Hallie!' said her father impatiently. He turned to Corcoran: 'Did I give you any authority to lay out twelve thousand dollars in six weeks? Did I?'

'You're going to Italy with us,' interrupted Hallie reassuringly. 'We——'

'Will you be quiet?' exploded Bushmill. 'It may be funny to you, but I don't like to make bad bets, and I'm pretty sore.'

'What nonsense!' remarked Hallie cheerfully. 'Why, you were laughing a minute ago!'

'Laughing! You mean at that idiotic account book? Who wouldn't laugh? Four titles at five hundred francs a head! One baptismal font to American church for presence of clergyman at tea. It's like the log book of a lunatic asylum!'

'Never mind,' said Hallie. 'You can charge the baptismal font off your income tax.'

'That's consoling,' said her father grimly. 'Nevertheless, this young man will spend no more of my money for me.'

'But still he's a wonderful guide. He knows everything—don't you? All about the monuments and catacombs and the Battle of Waterloo.'

'Will you please let me talk to Mr Corcoran?' Hallie was silent. 'Mrs Bushmill and my daughter and Mr Nosby are going to take a trip through Italy as far as Sicily, where Mr Nosby has some business, and they want you—that is, Hallie and her mother think they would get more out of it if you went along. Understand—it isn't going to be any royal fandango this time. You'll get your salary and your expenses and that's all you'll get. Do you want to go?'

'No, thanks, Mr Bushmill,' said Corcoran quietly. 'I'm going back to Paris at noon.'

'You're not!' cried Hallie indignantly. 'Why—why how am I going to know which is the Forum and the—the Acropolis and all that?' She rose from her father's knee. 'Look here, daddy, I can persuade him.' Before they guessed her intentions she had seized Corcoran's arm, dragged him into the hall and closed the door behind her.

'You've got to come,' she said intensely. 'Don't you understand? I've seen Claude in a new light and I can't marry him and I don't dare tell father, and I'll go mad if we have to go away with him alone.'

The door opened and Mr Nosby peered suspiciously out into the hall.

'It's all right,' cried Hallie. 'He'll come. It was just a question of more salary and he was too shy to say anything about it.'

As they went back in Bushmill looked from one to the other.

'Why do you think you ought to get more salary?'

'So he can spend it, of course,' explained Hallie triumphantly. 'He's got to keep his hand in, hasn't he?'

This unanswerable argument closed the discussion. Corcoran was to go to Italy with them as courier and guide at three hundred and fifty dollars a month, an advance of some fifty dollars over what he had received before. From Sicily they were to proceed by boat to Marseilles, where Mr Bushmill would meet them. After that Mr Corcoran's services would be no longer required—the Bushmills and Mr Nosby would sail immediately for home.

They left next morning. It was evident even before they reached Italy that Mr Nosby had determined to run the expedition in his own way. He was aware that Hallie was less docile and less responsive than she had been before she came abroad, and when he spoke of the wedding a curious vagueness seemed to come over her, but he knew that she adored her father and that in the end she would do whatever her father liked. It was only a question of getting her back to America before any silly young men, such as this unbalanced spendthrift, had the opportunity of infecting her with any nonsense. Once in the factory town and in the little circle where she had grown up, she would slip gently back into the attitude she had held before.

So for the first four weeks of the tour he was never a foot from her side, and at the same time he managed to send Corcoran on a series of useless errands which occupied much of his time. He would get up early in the morning, arrange that Corcoran should take Mrs Bushmill on a day's excursion and say nothing to Hallie until they were safely away. For the opera in Milan, the concerts in Rome, he bought tickets for three, and on all automobile trips he made it plain to Corcoran that he was to sit with the chauffeur outside.

In Naples they were to stop for a day and take the boat trip to the Island of Capri in order to visit the celebrated Blue Grotto. Then, returning to Naples, they would motor south and cross to Sicily. In Naples Mr Nosby received a telegram from Mr Bushmill, in Paris, which he did not read to the others, but folded up and put into his pocket. He told them, however, that on their way to the Capri steamer he must stop for a moment at an Italian bank.

Mrs Bushmill had not come along that morning, and Hallie and Corcoran waited outside in the cab. It was the first time in four weeks that they had been together without Mr Nosby's stiff, glossy presence hovering near.

'I've got to talk to you,' said Hallie in low voice. 'I've tried so many times, but it's almost impossible. He got father to say that if you molested me, or even were attentive to me, he could send you immediately home.'

'I shouldn't have come,' answered Corcoran despairingly. 'It was a terrible mistake. But I want to see you alone just once—if only to say good-by.'

As Nosby hurried out of the bank, he broke off and bent his glance casually down the street, pretending to be absorbed in some interesting phenomenon that was taking place there. And suddenly, as if life were playing up to his subterfuge, an interesting phenomenon did immediately take place on the corner in front of the bank. A man in his shirt sleeves rushed suddenly out of the side street, seized the shoulder of a small, swarthy hunchback standing there and, swinging him quickly around, pointed at their taxicab. The man in his shirt sleeves had not even looked at them—it was as if he had known that they would be there.

The hunchback nodded and instantly both of them disappeared, the first man into the side street which had yielded him up, the hunchback into nowhere at all. The incident took place so quickly that it made only an odd visual impression upon Corcoran—he did not have occasion to think of it again until they returned from Capri eight hours later.

The Bay of Naples was rough as they set out that morning, and the little steamer staggered like a drunken man through the persistent waves. Before long Mr Nosby's complexion was running through a gamut of yellows, pale creams and ghostly whites, but he insisted that he scarcely noticed the motion and forced Hallie to accompany him in an incessant promenade up and down the deck.

When the steamer reached the coast of the rocky, cheerful little island, dozens of boats put out from shore and swarmed about dizzily in the waves as they waited for passengers to the Blue Grotto. The constant Saint Vitus' dance which they performed in the surf turned Mr Nosby from a respectable white to a bizarre and indecent blue and compelled him to a sudden decision.

'It's too rough,' he announced. 'We won't go.'

Hallie, watching fascinated from the rail, paid no attention. Seductive cries were floating up from below:

'Theesa a good boat, lady an' ge'man!'

'I spik American—been America two year!'

'Fine sunny day for go to see Blue Grotte!'

The first passengers had already floated off, two to a boat, and now Hallie was drifting with the next batch down the gangway.

'Where are you going, Hallie?' shouted Mr Nosby. 'It's too dangerous today. We're going to stay on board.'

Hallie, half down the gangway, looked back over her shoulder.

'Of course I'm going!' she cried. 'Do you think I'd come all the way to Capri and miss the Blue Grotto?'

Nosby took one more look at the sea, then he turned hurriedly away. Already Hallie, followed by Corcoran, had stepped into one of the small boats and was waving him a cheerful good-by.

They approached the shore, heading for a small dark opening in the rocks. When they arrived, the boatman ordered them to sit on the floor of the boat to keep from being bumped against the low entrance. A momentary passage through darkness, then a vast space opened up around them and they were in a bright paradise of ultramarine, a cathedral cave where the water and air and the high-vaulted roof were of the most radiant and opalescent blue.

(131)

'Ver' pret',' singsonged the boatman. He ran his oar through the water and they watched it turn to an incredible silver.

'I'm going to put my hand in!' said Hallie, enraptured. They were both kneeling now, and as she leaned forward to plunge her hand under the surface the strange light enveloped them like a spell and their lips touched—then all the world turned to blue and silver, or else this was not the world, but a delightful enchantment in which they would dwell forever.

'Ver' beaut'ful,' sang the boatman. 'Come back see Blue Grotte tomorrow, next day. Ask for Frederico, fine man for Blue Grotte. Oh, chawming!'

Again their lips sought each other, and blue and silver seemed to soar like rockets above them, burst and shower down about their shoulders in protective atoms of color, screening them from time, from sight. They kissed again. The voices of tourists were seeking echoes here and there about the cave. A brown naked boy dived from a high rock, cleaving the water like a silver fish, and starting a thousand platinum bubbles to churn up through the blue light.

'I love you with all my heart,' she whispered. 'What shall we do? Oh, my dear, if you only had a little common sense about money!'

The cavern was emptying, the small boats were feeling their way out, one by one, to the glittering restless sea.

'Good-by, Blue Grotte!' sang the boatman. 'Come again soo-oon!'

Blinded by the sunshine, they sat back apart and looked at each other. But though the blue and silver was left behind, the radiance about her face remained.

'I love you,' rang as true here under the blue sky.

Mr Nosby was waiting on the deck, but he said not a word—only looked at them sharply and sat between them all the way back to Naples. But for all his tangible body, they were no longer apart. He had best be quick and interpose his four thousand miles.

(132)

It was not until they had docked and were walking from the pier that Corcoran was jerked sharply from his mood of rapture and despair by something that sharply recalled to him the incident of the morning. Directly in their path, as if waiting for them, stood the swarthy hunchback to whom the man in the shirt sleeves had pointed out their taxi. No sooner did he see them, however, than he stepped quickly aside and melted into a crowd. When they had passed, Corcoran turned back, as if for a last look at the boat, and saw in the sweep of his eye that the hunchback was pointing them out in his turn to still another man.

As they got into a taxi Mr Nosby broke the silence.

'You'd better pack immediately,' he said. 'We're leaving by motor for Palermo right after dinner.'

'We can't make it tonight,' objected Hallie.

'We'll stop halfway.'

It was plain that he wanted to bring the trip to an end at the first possible moment. After dinner he asked Corcoran to come to the hotel garage with him while he engaged an automobile for the trip, and Corcoran understood that this was because Hallie and he were not to be left together. Nosby, in an ill-humor, insisted that the garage price was too high; finally he walked out and up to a dilapidated taxi in the street.

The taxi agreed to make the trip for twenty-five dollars.

'I don't believe this old thing will make the grade,' ventured Corcoran. 'Don't you think it would be wiser to pay the difference and take the other car?'

Nosby stared at him, his anger just under the surface.

'We're not all like you,' he said dryly. 'We can't all afford to throw it away.'

Corcoran took the snub with a cool nod.

'Another thing,' he said. 'Did you get money from the bank this morning—or anything that would make you likely to be followed?'

'What do you mean?' demanded Nosby quickly.

'Somebody's been keeping pretty close track of our movements all day.'

Nosby eyed him shrewdly.

'You'd like us to stay here in Naples a day or so more, wouldn't you?' he said. 'Unfortunately, you're not running this party. If you stay, you can stay alone.'

'And you won't take the other car?'

'I'm getting a little weary of your suggestions.'

At the hotel, as the porters piled the bags into the high old-fashioned car, Corcoran was again possessed by a feeling of being watched. With an effort, he resisted the impulse to turn his head and look behind. If this was a product of his imagination, it was better to put it immediately from his mind.

It was already eight o'clock when they drove off into a windy twilight. The sun had gone behind Naples, leaving a sky of pigeon's-blood and gold, and as they rounded the bay and climbed slowly toward Torre dell' Annunziata, the Mediterranean momentarily toasted the fading splendor in pink wine. Above them loomed Vesuvius and from its crater a small persistent fountain of smoke contributed darkness to the gathering night.

'We ought to reach our destination about twelve,' said Nosby.

No one answered. The city had disappeared behind a rise of ground, and now they were alone, tracing down the hot mysterious shin of the Italian boot where the Mafia sprang out of rank human weeds and the Black Hand rose to throw its ominous shadow across two continents. There was something eerie in the sough of the wind over these gray mountains, crowned with the decayed castles. Hallie suddenly shivered.

'I'm glad I'm American,' she said. 'Here in Italy I feel that everybody's dead. So many people dead and all watching from up on those hills—Carthaginians and old Romans and Moorish pirates and medieval princes with poisoned rings——'

The solemn gloom of the countryside communicated itself to all of them. The wind had come up stronger and was groaning through the dark-massed trees along the way. The engine labored painfully up the incessant slopes and then coasted down winding spiral roads until the brakes gave out a burning smell. In the dark little village of Eboli they stopped for gasoline, and while they waited for their change another car came quickly out of the darkness and drew up behind.

Corcoran looked at it closely, but the lights were in his face and he could distinguish only the pale blots of four faces which returned his insistent stare. When the taxi had driven off and toiled a mile uphill in the face of the sweeping wind, he saw the lamps of the other car emerge from the village and follow. In a low voice he called Nosby's attention to the fact whereupon Nosby leaned forward nervously and tapped on the front glass.

'*Piu presto!*' he commanded. '*Il sera sono tropo tarde!*'

Corcoran translated the mutilated Italian and then fell into conversation with the chauffeur. Hallie had dozed off to sleep with her head on her mother's shoulder. It might have been twenty minutes later when she awoke with a start to find that the car had stopped. The chauffeur was peering into the engine with a lighted match, while Corcoran and Mr Nosby were talking quickly in the road.

'What is it?' she cried.

'He's broken down,' said Corcoran, 'and he hasn't got the proper tools to make the repair. The best thing is for all of you to start out on foot for Agropoli. That's the next village —it's about two miles away.'

'Look!' said Nosby uneasily. The lights of another car had breasted a rise less than a mile behind.

'Perhaps they'll pick us up?' asked Hallie.

'We're taking no such chances,' answered Corcoran. 'This is the special beat of one of the roughest gangs of holdup men in Southern Italy. What's more, we're being followed. When I asked the chauffeur if he knew that car that drove up behind us in Eboli, he shut right up. He's afraid to say.'

As he spoke, he was helping Hallie and her mother from the car. Now he turned authoritatively to Nosby.

'You better tell me what you got in that Naples bank.'

'It was ten thousand dollars in English bank notes,' admitted Nosby in a frightened voice.

'I thought so. Some clerk tipped them off. Hand over those notes to me!'

'Why should I?' demanded Nosby. 'What are you going to do with them?'

'I'm going to throw them away,' said Corcoran. His head went up alertly. The complaint of a motor car taking a hill in second speed was borne toward them clearly on the night. 'Hallie, you and your mother start on with the chauffeur. Run as fast as you can for a hundred yards or so, and then keep going. If I don't show up, notify the carabinieri in Agropoli.' His voice sank lower. 'Don't worry, I'm going to fix this thing. Good-by.'

As they started off he turned again to Nosby.

'Hand over that money,' he said.

'You're going to——'

'I'm going to keep them here while you get Hallie away. Don't you see that if they got her up in these hills they could ask any amount of money they wanted?'

Nosby paused irresolute. Then he pulled out a thick packet of fifty-pound notes and began to peel half a dozen from the top.

'I want all of it,' snapped Corcoran. With a quick movement he wrested the packet violently from Nosby's hand. 'Now go on!'

Less than half a mile away, the lights of the car dipped into sight. With a broken cry Nosby turned and stumbled off down the road.

Corcoran took a pencil and an envelope from his pocket and worked quickly for a few minutes by the glow of the headlights. Then he wet one finger and held it up tentatively in the air as if he were making an experiment. The result seemed to satisfy him. He waited, ruffling the large thin notes—there were forty of them—in his hands.

The lights of the other car came nearer, slowed up, came to a stop twenty feet away.

Leaving the engine running idle, four men got out and walked toward him.

'*Buona sera!*' he called, and then continued in Italian, 'We have broken down.'

'Where are the rest of your people?' demanded one of the men quickly.

'They were picked up by another car. It turned around and took them back to Agropoli,' Corcoran said politely. He was aware that he was covered by two revolvers, but he waited an instant longer, straining to hear the flurry in the trees which would announce a gust of wind. The men drew nearer.

'But I have something here that may interest you.' Slowly, his heart thumping, he raised his hand, bringing the packet of notes into the glare of the headlight. Suddenly out of the valley swept the wind, louder and nearer; he waited a moment longer until he felt the first cold freshness on his face. 'Here are two hundred thousand lire in English bank notes!' He raised the sheaf of paper higher as if to hand it to the nearest man. Then he released it with a light upward flick and immediately the wind seized upon it and whirled the notes in forty directions through the air.

The nearest man cursed and made a lunge for the closest piece. Then they were all scurrying here and there about the road while the frail bills sailed and flickered in the gale, pirouetting like elves along the grass, bouncing and skipping from side to side in mad perversity.

From one side to the other they ran, Corcoran with them, crumpling the captured money into their pockets, then scattering always farther and farther apart in wild pursuit of the elusive beckoning symbols of gold.

Suddenly Corcoran saw his opportunity. Bending low, as if he had spotted a stray bill beneath the car, he ran toward it, vaulted over the side and hitched into the driver's seat. As he plunged the lever into first, he heard a cursing cry and then a sharp report, but the warmed car had jumped forward safely and the shot went wide.

In a moment, his teeth locked and muscles tense against the fusillade, he had passed the stalled taxi and was racing along into the darkness. There was another report close at hand and he ducked wildly, afraid for an instant that one of them had clung to the running board; then he realized that one of their shots had blown out a tire.

After three-quarters of a mile he stopped, cut off his motor and listened. There wasn't a sound, only the drip from his radiator onto the road.

'Hallie!' he called. 'Hallie!'

A figure emerged from the shadows not ten feet away, then another figure and another.

'Hallie!' he said.

She clambered into the front seat with him; her arms went about him.

'You're safe!' she sobbed. 'We heard the shots and I wanted to go back.'

Mr Nosby, very cool now, stood in the road.

'I don't suppose you brought back any of that money,' he said.

Corcoran took three crumpled bank notes from his pocket.

'That's all,' he said. 'But they're liable to be along here any minute and you can argue with them about the rest.'

Mr Nosby, followed by Mrs Bushmill and the chauffeur, stepped quickly into the car.

'Nevertheless,' he insisted shrilly, as they moved off, 'this has been a pretty expensive business. You've flung away ten thousand dollars that was to have bought goods in Sicily.'

'Those are English bank notes,' said Corcoran. 'Big notes too. Every bank in England and Italy will be watching for those numbers.'

'But we don't know the numbers!'

'I took all the numbers,' said Corcoran.

The rumor that Mr Julius Bushmill's purchasing department keeps him awake nights is absolutely unfounded. There are those who say that a once conservative business is expanding in a way that is more sensational than sound, but they are probably small, malevolent rivals with a congenital disgust for the grand scale. To all gratuitous advice, Mr Bushmill replies that even when his son-in-law seems to be throwing it away, it all comes back. His theory is that the young idiot really has a talent for spending money.

SCOTT

The Dance

(The Red Book Magazine,
June 1926)

All my life I have had a rather curious horror of small towns: not suburbs; they are quite a different matter—but the little lost cities of New Hampshire and Georgia and Kansas, and upper New York. I was born in New York City, and even as a little girl I never had any fear of the streets or the strange foreign faces—but on the occasions when I've been in the sort of place I'm referring to, I've been oppressed with the consciousness that there was a whole hidden life, a whole series of secret implications, significances and terrors, just below the surface, of which I knew nothing. In the cities everything good or bad eventually comes out, comes out of people's hearts, I mean. Life moves about, moves on, vanishes. In the small towns—those of between five and twenty-five thousand people—old hatreds, old and unforgotten affairs, ghostly scandals and tragedies, seem unable to die, but live on all tangled up with the natural ebb and flow of outward life.

Nowhere has this sensation come over me more insistently than in the South. Once out of Atlanta and Birmingham and New Orleans, I often have the feeling that I can no longer communicate with the people around me. The men and the girls speak a language wherein courtesy is combined with violence, fanatic morality with corn-drinking recklessness, in a fashion which I can't understand. In 'Huckleberry Finn' Mark Twain described some of those towns perched along the Mississippi River, with their fierce feuds and their equally fierce revivals—and some of them haven't fundamentally changed beneath their new surface of flivvers and radios. They are deeply uncivilized to this day.

I speak of the South because it was in a small Southern city of this type that I once saw the surface crack for a minute and something savage, uncanny and frightening rear its head. Then the surface closed again—and when I have gone back there since, I've been surprised to find myself as charmed as ever by the magnolia trees and the singing darkies in the street and the sensuous warm nights. I have been charmed, too, by the bountiful hospitality and the languorous easy-going outdoor life and the almost universal good manners. But all too frequently I am the prey of a vivid nightmare that recalls what I experienced in that town five years ago.

Davis—that is not its real name—has a population of about twenty thousand people, one-third of them colored. It is a cotton-mill town, and the workers of that trade, several thousand gaunt and ignorant 'poor whites,' live together in an ill-reputed section known as 'Cotton Hollow.' The population of Davis has varied in its seventy-five years. Once it was under consideration for the capital of the State, and so the older families and their kin form a proud little aristocracy, even when individually they have sunk to destitution.

That winter I'd made the usual round in New York until about April, when I decided I never wanted to see another invitation again. I was tired and I wanted to go to Europe for a rest; but the baby panic of 1921 hit Father's business, and so it was suggested that I go South and visit Aunt Musidora Hale instead.

Vaguely I imagined that I was going to the country, but on the day I arrived, the Davis *Courier* published a hilarious old picture of me on its society page, and I found I was in for another season. On a small scale, of course: there were Saturday-night dances at the little country-club with its nine-hole golf-course, and some informal dinner parties and several attractive and attentive boys. I didn't have a dull time at all, and when after three weeks I wanted to go home, it wasn't because I was bored. On the contrary I wanted to go home because I'd allowed myself to get rather interested in a good-looking young man named Charley Kincaid, without realizing that he was engaged to another girl.

We'd been drawn together from the first because he was almost the only boy in town who'd gone North to college, and I was still young enough to think that America revolved around Harvard and Princeton and Yale. He liked me too—I could see that; but when I heard that his engagement to a girl named Marie Bannerman had been announced six months before, there was nothing for me except to go away. The town was too small to avoid people, and though so far there hadn't been any talk, I was sure that—well, that if we kept meeting, the emotion we were beginning to feel would somehow get into words. I'm not mean enough to take a man away from another girl.

Marie Bannerman was almost a beauty. Perhaps she would have been a beauty if she'd had any clothes, and if she hadn't used bright pink rouge in two high spots on her cheeks and powdered her nose and chin to a funereal white. Her hair was shining black; her features were lovely; and an affection of one eye kept it always half-closed and gave an air of humorous mischief to her face.

I was leaving on a Monday, and on Saturday night a crowd of us dined at the country-club as usual before the dance. There was Joe Cable, the son of a former governor, a handsome, dissipated and yet somehow charming young man; Catherine Jones, a pretty, sharp-eyed girl with an exquisite figure, who under her rouge might have been any age from eighteen to twenty-five; Marie Bannerman; Charley Kincaid; myself and two or three others.

I loved to listen to the genial flow of bizarre neighborhood anecdote at this kind of party. For instance, one of the girls, together with her entire family, had that afternoon been evicted from her house for nonpayment of rent. She told the story wholly without self-consciousness, merely as something troublesome but amusing. And I loved the banter which presumed every girl to be infinitely beautiful and attractive, and every man to have been secretly and hopelessly in love with every girl present from their respective cradles.

'We liked to die laughin'' . . . . '—said he was fixin' to shoot him without he stayed away.' The girls ''clared to heaven;' the men 'took oath' on inconsequential statements. 'How come you nearly about forgot to come by for me—' and the incessant Honey, Honey, Honey, Honey, until the word seemed to roll like a genial liquid from heart to heart.

Outside, the May night was hot, a still night, velvet, soft-pawed, splattered thick with stars. It drifted heavy and sweet into the large room where we sat and where we would later dance, with no sound in it except the occasional long crunch of an arriving car on the drive. Just at that moment I hated to leave Davis as I never had hated to leave a town before—I felt that I wanted to spend my life in this town, drifting and dancing forever through these long, hot, romantic nights.

Yet horror was already hanging over that little party, was waiting tensely among us, an uninvited guest, and telling off the hours until it could show its pale and blinding face. Beneath the chatter and laughter something was going on, something secret and obscure that I didn't know.

Presently the colored orchestra arrived, followed by the first trickle of the dance crowd. An enormous red-faced man in muddy knee boots and with a revolver strapped around his waist, clumped in and paused for a moment at our table before going upstairs to the locker-room. It was Bill Abercrombie, the Sheriff, the son of Congressman Abercrombie. Some of the boys asked him half-whispered questions, and he replied in an attempt at an undertone.

'Yes. . . . . He's in the swamp all right; farmer saw him near the crossroads store. . . . . Like to have a shot at him myself.'

I asked the boy next to me what was the matter.

(143)

'Nigger case,' he said, 'over in Kisco, about two miles from here. He's hiding in the swamp, and they're going in after him tomorrow.'

'What'll they do to him?'

'Hang him, I guess.'

The notion of the forlorn darky crouching dismally in a desolate bog waiting for dawn and death depressed me for a moment. Then the feeling passed and was forgotten.

After dinner Charley Kincaid and I walked out on the veranda—he had just heard that I was going away. I kept as close to the others as I could, answering his words but not his eyes—something inside me was protesting against leaving him on such a casual note. The temptation was strong to let something flicker up between us here at the end. I wanted him to kiss me—my heart promised that if he kissed me, just once, it would accept with equanimity the idea of never seeing him any more; but my mind knew it wasn't so.

The other girls began to drift inside and upstairs to the dressing-room to improve their complexions, and with Charley still beside me, I followed. Just at that moment I wanted to cry—perhaps my eyes were already blurred, or perhaps it was my haste lest they should be, but I opened the door of a small card-room by mistake, and with my error the tragic machinery of the night began to function. In the card-room, not five feet from us, stood Marie Bannerman, Charley's fiancée, and Joe Cable. They were in each other's arms, absorbed in a passionate and oblivious kiss.

I closed the door quickly, and without glancing at Charley opened the right door and ran upstairs.

A few minutes later Marie Bannerman entered the crowded dressing-room. She saw me and came over, smiling in a sort of mock despair, but she breathed quickly, and the smile trembled a little on her mouth.

'You won't say a word, honey, will you?' she whispered.

'Of course not.' I wondered how that could matter, now that Charley Kincaid knew.

'Who else was it that saw us?'

'Only Charley Kincaid and I.'

'Oh!' She looked a little puzzled; then she added: 'He didn't wait to say anything, honey. When we came out, he was just going out the door. I thought he was going to wait and romp all over Joe.'

'How about his romping all over you?' I couldn't help asking.

'Oh, he'll do that.' She laughed wryly. 'But, honey, I know how to handle him. It's just when he's first mad that I'm scared of him—he's got an awful temper.' She whistled reminiscently. 'I know, because this happened once before.'

I wanted to slap her. Turning my back, I walked away on the pretext of borrowing a pin from Katie, the negro maid. Catherine Jones was claiming the latter's attention with a short gingham garment which needed repair.

'What's that?' I asked.

'Dancing-dress,' she answered shortly, her mouth full of pins. When she took them out, she added: 'It's all come to pieces—I've used it so much.'

'Are you going to dance here tonight?'

'Going to try.'

Somebody had told me that she wanted to be a dancer—that she had taken lessons in New York.

'Can I help you fix anything?'

'No, thanks—unless—you can sew? Katie gets so excited Saturday night that she's no good for anything except fetching pins. I'd be everlasting grateful to you, honey.'

I had reasons for not wanting to go downstairs just yet, and so I sat down and worked on her dress for half an hour. I wondered if Charley had gone home, if I would ever see him again—I scarcely dared to wonder if what he had seen would set him free, ethically. When I went down finally he was not in sight.

The room was now crowded; the tables had been removed and dancing was general. At that time, just after the war, all Southern boys had a way of agitating their heels from side to side, pivoting on the ball of the foot as they danced, and to acquiring this accomplishment I had devoted many hours. There were plenty of stags, almost all of them cheerful with corn-liquor; I refused on an average at least two drinks a dance. Even when it is mixed with a soft drink, as is the custom, rather than gulped from the neck of a warm bottle, it is a formidable proposition. Only a few girls like Catherine Jones took an occasional sip from some boy's flask down at the dark end of the veranda.

I liked Catherine Jones—she seemed to have more energy than these other girls, though Aunt Musidora sniffed rather contemptuously whenever Catherine stopped for me in her car to go to the movies, remarking that she guessed 'the bottom rail had gotten to be the top rail now.' Her family were 'new and common,' but it seemed to me that perhaps her very commonness was an asset. Almost every girl in Davis confided in me at one time or another that her ambition was to 'get away and come to New York,' but only Catherine Jones had actually taken the step of studying stage dancing with that end in view.

She was often asked to dance at these Saturday night affairs, something 'classic' or perhaps an acrobatic clog—on one memorable occasion she had annoyed the governing board by a 'shimee' (then the scapegrace of jazz), and the novel and somewhat startling excuse made for her was that she was 'so tight she didn't know what she was doing, anyhow.' She impressed me as a curious personality, and I was eager to see what she would produce tonight.

At twelve o'clock the music always ceased, as dancing was forbidden on Sunday morning. So at eleven-thirty a vast fanfaronade of drum and cornet beckoned the dancers and the couples on the verandas, and the ones in the cars outside, and the stragglers from the bar, into the ballroom. Chairs were brought in and galloped up *en masse* and with a great racket to the slightly raised platform. The orchestra had evacuated this and taken a place beside. Then, as the rearward lights were lowered, they began to play a tune accompanied by a curious drum-beat that I had never heard before and simultaneously Catherine Jones appeared upon the platform. She wore the short, country girl's dress upon which I had lately labored, and a wide sunbonnet under which her face, stained yellow with powder, looked out at us with rolling eyes and a vacant negroid leer. She began to dance.

I had never seen anything like it before, and until five years later I wasn't to see it again. It was the Charleston—it must have been the Charleston. I remember the double drum-beat like a shouted '*Hey! Hey!*' and the unfamiliar swing of the arms and the odd knock-kneed effect. She had picked it up, heaven knows where.

Her audience, familiar with negro rhythms, leaned forward eagerly—even to them it was something new, but it is stamped on my mind as clearly and indelibly as though I had seen it yesterday. The figure on the platform swinging and stamping, the excited orchestra, the waiters grinning in the doorway of the bar, and all around, through many windows, the soft languorous Southern night seeping in from swamp and cottonfield and lush foliage and brown, warm streams. At what point a feeling of tense uneasiness began to steal over me I don't know. The dance could scarcely have taken ten minutes; perhaps the first beats of the barbaric music disquieted me—long before it was over, I was sitting rigid in my seat, and my eyes were wandering here and there around the hall, passing along the rows of shadowy faces as if seeking some security that was no longer there.

I'm not a nervous type; nor am I given to panic; but for a moment I was afraid that if the music and the dance didn't stop, I'd be hysterical. Something was happening all about me. I knew it as well as if I could see into these unknown souls. Things were happening, but one thing especially was leaning over so close that it almost touched us, that it did touch us. . . . . I almost screamed as a hand brushed accidentally against my back.

The music stopped. There was applause and protracted cries of encore, but Catherine Jones shook her head definitely at the orchestra leader and made as though to leave the platform. The appeals for more continued—again she shook her head, and it seemed to me that her expression was rather angry. Then a strange incident occurred. At the protracted pleading of some one in the front row, the colored orchestra leader began the vamp of the tune, as if to lure Catherine Jones into changing her mind. Instead she turned toward him, snapped out, 'Didn't you hear me say no?' and then, surprisingly, slapped his face. The music stopped, and an amused murmur terminated abruptly as a muffled but clearly audible shot rang out.

Immediately we were on our feet, for the sound indicated that it had been fired within or near the house. One of the chaperons gave a little scream, but when some wag called out, 'Cæsar's in that henhouse again,' the momentary alarm dissolved into laughter. The club manager, followed by several curious couples, went out to have a look about, but the rest were already moving around the floor to the strains of 'Good Night, Ladies,' which traditionally ended the dance.

I was glad it was over. The man with whom I had come went to get his car, and calling a waiter, I sent him for my golf-clubs, which were in the stack upstairs. I strolled out on the porch and waited, wondering again if Charley Kincaid had gone home.

Suddenly I was aware, in that curious way in which you

become aware of something that has been going on for several minutes, that there was a tumult inside. Women were shrieking; there was a cry of 'Oh, my God!' then the sounds of a stampede on the inside stairs, and footsteps running back and forth across the ballroom. A girl appeared from somewhere and pitched forward in a dead faint—almost immediately another girl did the same, and I heard a frantic male voice shouting into a telephone. Then, hatless and pale, a young man rushed out on the porch, and with hands that were cold as ice, seized my arm.

'What is it?' I cried. 'A fire? What's happened?'

'Marie Bannerman's dead upstairs in the women's dressing-room. Shot through the throat!'

The rest of that night is a series of visions that seem to have no connection with one another, that follow each other with the sharp instantaneous transitions of scenes in the movies. There was a group who stood arguing on the porch, in voices now raised, now hushed, about what should be done and how every waiter in the club, 'even old Moses,' ought to be given the third degree tonight. That a 'nigger' had shot and killed Marie Bannerman was the instant and unquestioned assumption—in the first unreasoning instant, anyone who doubted it would have been under suspicion. The guilty one was said to be Katie Golstien, the colored maid, who had discovered the body and fainted. It was said to be 'that nigger they were looking for over near Kisco.' It was any darky at all.

Within half an hour people began to drift out, each with his little contribution of new discoveries. The crime had been committed with Sheriff Abercrombie's gun—he had hung it, belt and all, in full view on the wall before coming down to dance. It was missing—they were hunting for it now. Instantly killed, the doctor said—bullet had been fired from only a few feet away.

Then a few minutes later another young man came out and made the announcement in a loud, grave voice:

'They've arrested Charley Kincaid.'

My head reeled. Upon the group gathered on the veranda fell an awed, stricken silence.

'Arrested Charley Kincaid!'

'Charley *Kincaid*?'

Why, he was one of the best, one of themselves.

'That's the craziest thing I ever heard of!'

The young man nodded, shocked like the rest, but self-important with his information.

'He wasn't downstairs when Catherine Jones was dancing —he says he was in the men's locker-room. And Marie Bannerman told a lot of girls that they'd had a row, and she was scared of what he'd do.'

Again an awed silence.

'That's the craziest thing I ever heard!' some one said again.

'Charley *Kincaid*!'

The narrator waited a moment. Then he added:

'He caught her kissing Joe Cable—'

I couldn't keep silence a minute longer.

'What about it?' I cried out. 'I was with him at the time. He wasn't—he wasn't angry at all.'

They looked at me, their faces startled, confused, unhappy. Suddenly the footsteps of several men sounded loud through the ballroom, and a moment later Charley Kincaid, his face dead white, came out the front door between the Sheriff and another man. Crossing the porch quickly, they descended the steps and disappeared in the darkness. A moment later there was the sound of a starting car.

When an instant later far away down the road I heard the eerie scream of an ambulance, I got up desperately and called to my escort, who formed part of the whispering group.

'I've got to go,' I said. 'I can't stand this. Either take me home or I'll find a place in another car.' Reluctantly he shouldered my clubs—the sight of them made me realize that I now couldn't leave on Monday after all—and followed me down the steps just as the black body of the ambulance curved in at the gate—a ghastly shadow on the bright, starry night.

The situation, after the first wild surmises, the first burst of unreasoning loyalty to Charley Kincaid, had died away, was outlined by the Davis *Courier* and by most of the State newspapers in this fashion: Marie Bannerman died in the women's dressing-room of the Davis Country Club from the effects of a shot fired at close quarters from a revolver just after eleven forty-five o'clock on Saturday night. Many persons had heard the shot; moreover it had undoubtedly been fired from the revolver of Sheriff Abercrombie, which had been hanging in full sight on the wall of the next room. Abercrombie himself was down in the ballroom when the murder took place, as many witnesses could testify. The revolver was not found.

So far as was known, the only man who had been upstairs at the time the shot was fired was Charles Kincaid. He was engaged to Miss Bannerman, but according to several witnesses they had quarreled seriously that evening. Miss Bannerman herself had mentioned the quarrel, adding that she was afraid and wanted to keep away from him until he cooled off.

Charles Kincaid asserted that at the time the shot was fired he was in the men's locker-room—where, indeed, he was found, immediately after the discovery of Miss Bannerman's body. He denied having had any words with Miss Bannerman at all. He had heard the shot but it had had no significance for him—if he thought anything of it, he thought that 'some one was potting cats outdoors.'

Why had he chosen to remain in the locker-room during the dance?

No reason at all. He was tired. He was waiting until Miss Bannerman wanted to go home.

The body was discovered by Katie Golstien, the colored maid, who herself was found in a faint when the crowd of girls surged upstairs for their coats. Returning from the kitchen, where she had been getting a bite to eat, Katie had found Miss Bannerman, her dress wet with blood, already dead on the floor.

Both the police and the newspapers attached importance to the geography of the country-club's second story. It consisted of a row of three rooms—the women's dressing-room and the men's locker-room at either end, and in the middle a room which was used as a cloak-room and for the storage of golf-clubs. The women's and men's rooms had no outlet except into this chamber, which was connected by one stairs with the ballroom below, and by another with the kitchen. According to the testimony of three negro cooks and the white caddy-master, no one but Katie Golstien had gone up the kitchen stairs that night.

As I remember it after five years, the foregoing is a pretty accurate summary of the situation when Charley Kincaid was accused of first-degree murder and committed for trial. Other people, chiefly negroes, were suspected (at the loyal instigation of Charley Kincaid's friends), and several arrests were made, but nothing ever came of them, and upon what grounds they were based I have long forgotten. One group, in spite of the disappearance of the pistol, claimed persistently that it was a suicide and suggested some ingenious reasons to account for the absence of the weapon.

Now when it is known how Marie Bannerman happened to die so savagely and so violently, it would be easy for me, of all people, to say that I believed in Charley Kincaid all the time. But I didn't. I thought that he had killed her, and at the same time I knew that I loved him with all my heart. That it was I who first happened upon the evidence which set him free was due not to any faith in his innocence but to a strange vividness with which, in moods of excitement, certain scenes stamp themselves on my memory, so that I can remember every detail and how that detail struck me at the time.

It was one afternoon early in July, when the case against Charley Kincaid seemed to be at its strongest, that the horror of the actual murder slipped away from me for a moment and I began to think about other incidents of that same haunted night. Something Marie Bannerman had said to me in the dressing-room persistently eluded me, bothered me—not because I believed it to be important, but simply because I couldn't remember. It was gone from me, as if it had been a part of the fantastic undercurrent of small-town life which I had felt so strongly that evening, the sense that things were in the air, old secrets, old loves and feuds, and unresolved situations, that I, an outsider, could never fully understand. Just for a minute it seemed to me that Marie Bannerman had pushed aside the curtain; then it had dropped into place again—the house into which I might have looked was dark now forever.

Another incident, perhaps less important, also haunted me. The tragic events of a few minutes after had driven it from everyone's mind, but I had a strong impression that for a brief space of time I wasn't the only one to be surprised. When the audience had demanded an encore from Catherine Jones, her unwillingness to dance again had been so acute that she had been driven to the point of slapping the orchestra leader's face. The discrepancy between his offense and the venom of the rebuff recurred to me again and again. It wasn't natural—or, more important, it hadn't *seemed* natural. In view of the fact that Catherine Jones had been drinking, it was explicable, but it worried me now as it had worried me then. Rather to lay its ghost than to do any investigating, I pressed an obliging young man into service and called on the leader of the band.

His name was Thomas, a very dark, very simple-hearted virtuoso of the traps, and it took less than ten minutes to find out that Catherine Jones' gesture had surprised him as much as it had me. He had known her a long time, seen her at dances since she was a little girl—why, the very dance she did that night was one she had rehearsed with his orchestra a week before. And a few days later she had come to him and said she was sorry.

'I knew she would,' he concluded. 'She's a right good-hearted girl. My sister Katie was her nurse from when she was born up to the time she went to school.'

'Your sister?'

'Katie. She's the maid out at the country-club. Katie Golstien. You been reading 'bout her in the papers in 'at Charley Kincaid case. She's the maid. Katie Golstien. She's the maid at the country-club what found the body of Miss Bannerman.'

'So Katie was Miss Catherine Jones' nurse?'

'Yes ma'am.'

Going home, stimulated but unsatisfied, I asked my companion a quick question.

'Were Catherine and Marie good friends?'

'Oh, yes,' he answered without hesitation. 'All the girls are good friends here, except when two of them are tryin' to get hold of the same man. Then they warm each other up a little.'

'Why do you suppose Catherine hasn't married? Hasn't she got lots of beaux?'

'Off and on. She only likes people for a day or so at a time. That is—all except Joe Cable.'

Now a scene burst upon me, broke over me like a dissolving wave. And suddenly, my mind shivering from the impact, I remembered what Marie Bannerman had said to me in the dressing-room: 'Who else was it that saw?' She had caught a glimpse of some one else, a figure passing so quickly that she could not identify it, out of the corner of her eye.

And suddenly, simultaneously, I seemed to see that figure, as if I too had been vaguely conscious of it at the time, just as one is aware of a familiar gait or outline on the street long before there is any flicker of recognition. On the corner of my own eye was stamped a hurrying figure—that might have been Catherine Jones.

But when the shot was fired, Catherine Jones was in full view of over fifty people. Was it credible that Katie Golstien, a woman of fifty, who as a nurse had been known and trusted by three generations of Davis people, would shoot down a young girl in cold blood at Catherine Jones' command?

'*But when the shot was fired, Catherine Jones was in full view of over fifty people.*'

That sentence beat in my head all night, taking on fantastic variations, dividing itself into phrases, segments, individual words.

'*But when the shot was fired*—Catherine Jones was in full view—of over fifty people.'

When the shot was fired! What shot? The shot we heard. When the shot was fired. . . . . When the shot was fired. . . . .

The next morning at nine o'clock, with the pallor of sleeplessness buried under a quantity of paint such as I had never worn before or have since, I walked up a rickety flight of stairs to the Sheriff's office.

Abercrombie, engrossed in his morning's mail, looked up curiously as I came in the door.

'Catherine Jones did it,' I cried, struggling to keep the hysteria out of my voice. 'She killed Marie Bannerman with a shot we didn't hear because the orchestra was playing and everybody was pushing up the chairs. The shot we heard was when Katie fired the pistol out of the window after the music was stopped. To give Catherine an alibi!'

I was right—as everyone now knows; but for a week, until Katie Golstien broke down under a fierce and ruthless inquisition, nobody believed me. Even Charley Kincaid, as he afterward confessed, didn't dare to think it could be true.

What had been the relations between Catherine and Joe Cable no one ever knew, but evidently she had determined that his clandestine affair with Marie Bannerman had gone too far.

Then Marie chanced to come into the women's room while Catherine was dressing for her dance—and there again there is a certain obscurity, for Catherine always claimed that Marie got the revolver, threatened her with it and that in the ensuing struggle the trigger was pulled. In spite of everything I always rather liked Catherine Jones, but in justice it must be said that only a simple-minded and very exceptional jury would have let her off with five years. And in just about five years from her commitment my husband and I are going to make a round of the New York musical shows and look hard at all the members of the chorus from the very front row.

After the shooting she must have thought quickly. Katie was told to wait until the music stopped, fire the revolver out the window and then hide it—Catherine Jones neglected to specify where. Katie, on the verge of collapse, obeyed instructions, but she was never able to specify where she had hid the revolver. And no one ever knew until a year later, when Charley and I were on our honeymoon and Sheriff Abercrombie's ugly weapon dropped out of my golf-bag onto a Hot Springs golf-links. The bag must have been standing just outside the dressing-room door; Katie's trembling hand had dropped the revolver into the first aperture she could see.

We live in New York. Small towns make us both uncomfortable. Every day we read about the crime-waves in the big cities, but at least a wave is something tangible that you can provide against. What I dread above all things is the unknown depths, the incalculable ebb and flow, the secret shapes of things that drift through opaque darkness under the surface of the sea.

SCOTT

Jacob's Ladder

(The Saturday Evening Post,
20 August 1927)

It was a particularly sordid and degraded murder trial, and
Jacob Booth, writhing quietly on a spectators' bench, felt that
he had childishly gobbled something without being hungry,
simply because it was there. The newspapers had humanized
the case, made a cheap, neat problem play out of an affair of
the jungle, so passes that actually admitted one to the court
room were hard to get. Such a pass had been tendered him
the evening before.

Jacob looked around at the doors, where a hundred people,
inhaling and exhaling with difficulty, generated excitement
by their eagerness, their breathless escape from their own
private lives. The day was hot and there was sweat upon the
crowd—obvious sweat in large dewy beads that would shake
off on Jacob if he fought his way through to the doors. Someone behind him guessed that the jury wouldn't be out half an
hour.

With the inevitability of a compass needle, his head swung
toward the prisoner's table and he stared once more at the
murderess' huge blank face garnished with red button eyes.
She was Mrs Choynski, *née* Delehanty, and fate had ordained
that she should one day seize a meat ax and divide her sailor
lover. The puffy hands that had swung the weapon turned an
ink bottle about endlessly; several times she glanced at the
crowd with a nervous smile.

Jacob frowned and looked around quickly; he had found a
pretty face and lost it again. The face had edged sideways

into his consciousness when he was absorbed in a mental picture of Mrs Choynski in action; now it was faded back into the anonymity of the crowd. It was the face of a dark saint with tender, luminous eyes and a skin pale and fair. Twice he searched the room, then he forgot and sat stiffly and uncomfortably, waiting.

The jury brought in a verdict of murder in the first degree; Mrs Choynski squeaked, 'Oh, my God!' The sentence was postponed until next day. With a slow rhythmic roll, the crowd pushed out into the August afternoon.

Jacob saw the face again, realizing why he hadn't seen it before. It belonged to a young girl beside the prisoner's table and it had been hidden by the full moon of Mrs Choynski's head. Now the clear, luminous eyes were bright with tears, and an impatient young man with a squashed nose was trying to attract the attention of the shoulder.

'Oh, get out!' said the girl, shaking the hand off impatiently. 'Le' me alone, will you? Le' me alone. Geeze!'

The man sighed profoundly and stepped back. The girl embraced the dazed Mrs Choynski and another lingerer remarked to Jacob that they were sisters. Then Mrs Choynski was taken off the scene—her expression absurdly implied an important appointment—and the girl sat down at the desk and began to powder her face. Jacob waited; so did the young man with the squashed nose. The sergeant came up brusquely and Jacob gave him five dollars.

'Geeze!' cried the girl to the young man. 'Can't you le' me alone?' She stood up. Her presence, the obscure vibrations of her impatience, filled the court room. 'Every day itsa same!'

Jacob moved nearer. The other man spoke to her rapidly:

'Miss Delehanty, we've been more than liberal with you and your sister and I'm only asking you to carry out your share of the contract. Our paper goes to press at——'

Miss Delehanty turned despairingly to Jacob. 'Can you beat it?' she demanded. 'Now he wants a pitcher of my sister when she was a baby, and it's got my mother in it too.'

'We'll take your mother out.'

'I want my mother though. It's the only one I got of her.'

'I'll promise to give you the picture back tomorrow.'

'Oh, I'm sicka the whole thing.' Again she was speaking to Jacob, but without seeing him except as some element of the vague, omnipresent public. 'It gives me a pain in the eye.' She made a clicking sound in her teeth that comprised the essence of all human scorn.

'I have a car outside, Miss Delehanty,' said Jacob suddenly. 'Don't you want me to run you home?'

'All right,' she answered indifferently.

The newspaper man assumed a previous acquaintance between them; he began to argue in a low voice as the three moved toward the door.

'Every day it's like this,' said Miss Delehanty bitterly. 'These newspaper guys!' Outside, Jacob signaled for his car and as it drove up, large, open and bright, and the chauffeur jumped out and opened the door, the reporter, on the verge of tears, saw the picture slipping away and launched into a peroration of pleading.

'Go jump in the river!' said Miss Delehanty, sitting in Jacob's car. 'Go—jump—in—the—river!'

The extraordinary force of her advice was such that Jacob regretted the limitations of her vocabulary. Not only did it evoke an image of the unhappy journalist hurling himself into the Hudson but it convinced Jacob that it was the only fitting and adequate way of disposing of the man. Leaving him to face his watery destiny, the car moved off down the street.

'You dealt with him pretty well,' Jacob said.

'Sure,' she admitted. 'I get sore after a while and then I can deal with anybody no matter who. How old would you think I was?'

'How old are you?'

'Sixteen.'

She looked at him gravely, inviting him to wonder. Her

face, the face of a saint, an intense little Madonna, was lifted fragilely out of the mortal dust of the afternoon. On the pure parting of her lips no breath hovered; he had never seen a texture pale and immaculate as her skin, lustrous and garish as her eyes. His own well-ordered person seemed for the first time in his life gross and well worn to him as he knelt suddenly at the heart of freshness.

'Where do you live?' he asked. The Bronx, perhaps Yonkers, Albany—Baffin's Bay. They could curve over the top of the world, drive on forever.

Then she spoke, and as the toad words vibrated with life in her voice, the moment passed: 'Eas' Hun'erd thuyty-thuyd. Stayin' with a girl friend there.'

They were waiting for a traffic light to change and she exchanged a haughty glance with a flushed man peering from a flanking taxi. The man took off his hat hilariously. 'Somebody's stenog,' he cried. 'And oh, what a stenog!'

An arm and hand appeared in the taxi window and pulled him back into the darkness of the cab.

Miss Delehanty turned to Jacob, a frown, the shadow of a hair in breadth, appearing between her eyes. 'A lot of 'em know me,' she said. 'We got a lot of publicity and pictures in the paper.'

'I'm sorry it turned out badly.'

She remembered the event of the afternoon, apparently for the first time in half an hour. 'She had it comin' to her, mister. She never had a chance. But they'll never send no woman to the chair in New York State.'

'No; that's sure.'

'She'll get life.' Surely it was not she who had spoken. The tranquillity of her face made her words separate themselves from her as soon as they were uttered and take on a corporate existence of their own.

'Did you use to live with her?'

'Me? Say, read the papers! I didn't even know she was my sister till they come and told me. I hadn't seen her since

I was a baby.' She pointed suddenly at one of the world's largest department stores. 'There's where I work. Back to the old pick and shovel day after tomorrow.'

'It's going to be a hot night,' said Jacob. 'Why don't we ride out into the country and have dinner?'

She looked at him. His eyes were polite and kind. 'All right,' she said.

Jacob was thirty-three. Once he had possessed a tenor voice with destiny in it, but laryngitis had despoiled him of it in one feverish week ten years before. In despair that concealed not a little relief, he bought a plantation in Florida and spent five years turning it into a golf course. When the land boom came in 1924 he sold his real estate for eight hundred thousand dollars.

Like so many Americans, he valued things rather than cared about them. His apathy was neither fear of life nor was it an affectation; it was the racial violence grown tired. It was a humorous apathy. With no need for money, he had tried—tried hard—for a year and a half to marry one of the richest women in America. If he had loved her, or pretended to, he could have had her; but he had never been able to work himself up to more than the formal lie.

In person, he was short, trim and handsome. Except when he was overcome by a desperate attack of apathy, he was unusually charming; he went with a crowd of men who were sure that they were the best of New York and had by far the best time. During a desperate attack of apathy he was like a gruff white bird, ruffled and annoyed, and disliking mankind with all his heart.

He liked mankind that night under the summer moonshine of the Borghese Gardens. The moon was a radiant egg, smooth and bright as Jenny Delehanty's face across the table, a salt wind blew in over the big estates collecting flower scents from their gardens and bearing them to the road-house lawn. The waiters hopped here and there like pixies through the hot night, their black backs disappearing

(162)

into the gloom, their white shirt fronts gleaming startlingly out of an unfamiliar patch of darkness.

They drank a bottle of champagne and he told Jenny Delehanty a story. 'You are the most beautiful thing I have ever seen,' he said, 'but as it happens you are not my type and I have no designs on you at all. Nevertheless, you can't go back to that store. Tomorrow I'm going to arrange a meeting between you and Billy Farrelly, who's directing a picture on Long Island. Whether he'll see how beautiful you are I don't know, because I've never introduced anybody to him before.'

There was no shadow, no ripple of a change in her expression, but there was irony in her eyes. Things like that had been said to her before, but the movie director was never available next day. Or else she had been tactful enough not to remind men of what they had promised last night.

'Not only are you beautiful,' continued Jacob, 'but you are somehow on the grand scale. Everything you do— yes, like reaching for that glass, or pretending to be self-conscious, or pretending to despair of me—gets across. If somebody's smart enough to see it, you might be something of an actress.'

'I like Norma Shearer the best. Do you?'

Driving homeward through the soft night, she put up her face quietly to be kissed. Holding her in the hollow of his arm, Jacob rubbed his cheek against her cheek's softness and then looked down at her for a long moment.

'Such a lovely child,' he said gravely.

She smiled back at him; her hands played conventionally with the lapels of his coat. 'I had a wonderful time,' she whispered. 'Geeze! I hope I never have to go to court again.'

'I hope you don't.'

'Aren't you going to kiss me good night?'

'This is Great Neck,' he said, 'that we're passing through. A lot of moving-picture stars live here.'

'You're a card, handsome.'

(163)

'Why?'

She shook her head from side to side and smiled. 'You're a card.'

She saw then that he was a type with which she was not acquainted. He was surprised, not flattered, that she thought him droll. She saw that whatever his eventual purpose he wanted nothing of her now. Jenny Delehanty learned quickly; she let herself become grave and sweet and quiet as the night, and as they rolled over Queensboro Bridge into the city she was half asleep against his shoulder.

II

He called up Billy Farrelly next day. 'I want to see you,' he said. 'I found a girl I wish you'd take a look at.'

'My gosh!' said Farrelly. 'You're the third today.'

'Not the third of this kind.'

'All right. If she's white, she can have the lead in a picture I'm starting Friday.'

'Joking aside, will you give her a test?'

'I'm not joking. She can have the lead, I tell you. I'm sick of these lousy actresses. I'm going out to the Coast next month. I'd rather be Constance Talmadge's water boy than own most of these young——' His voice was bitter with Irish disgust. 'Sure, bring her over, Jake. I'll take a look at her.'

Four days later, when Mrs Choynski, accompanied by two deputy sheriffs, had gone to Auburn to pass the remainder of her life, Jacob drove Jenny over the bridge to Astoria, Long Island.

'You've got to have a new name,' he said; 'and remember you never had a sister.'

'I thought of that,' she answered. 'I thought of a name too—Tootsie Defoe.'

'That's rotten,' he laughed; 'just rotten.'

'Well, you think of one if you're so smart.'

'How about Jenny—Jenny—oh, anything—Jenny Prince?'

'All right, handsome.'

Jenny Prince walked up the steps of the motion-picture studio, and Billy Farrelly, in a bitter Irish humor, in contempt for himself and his profession, engaged her for one of the three leads in his picture.

'They're all the same,' he said to Jacob. 'Shucks! Pick 'em up out of the gutter today and they want gold plates tomorrow. I'd rather be Constance Talmadge's water boy than own a harem full of them.'

'Do you like this girl?'

'She's all right. She's got a good side face. But they're all the same.'

Jacob bought Jenny Prince an evening dress for a hundred and eighty dollars and took her to the Lido that night. He was pleased with himself, and excited. They both laughed a lot and were happy.

'Can you believe you're in the movies?' he demanded.

'They'll probably kick me out tomorrow. It was too easy.'

'No, it wasn't. It was very good—psychologically. Billy Farrelly was in just the one mood——'

'I liked him.'

'He's fine,' agreed Jacob. But he was reminded that already another man was helping to open doors for her success. 'He's a wild Irishman, look out for him.'

'I know. You can tell when a guy wants to make you.'

'What?'

'I don't mean he wanted to make me, handsome. But he's got that look about him, if you know what I mean.' She distorted her lovely face with a wise smile. 'He likes 'em; you could tell that this afternoon.'

They drank a bottle of charged and very alcoholic grape juice.

Presently the head waiter came over to their table.

'This is Miss Jenny Prince,' said Jacob. 'You'll see a lot of her, Lorenzo, because she's just signed a big contract with the pictures. Always treat her with the greatest possible respect.'

When Lorenzo had withdrawn, Jenny said, 'You got the nicest eyes I ever seen.' It was her effort, the best she could do. Her face was serious and sad. 'Honest,' she repeated herself, 'the nicest eyes I ever seen. Any girl would be glad to have eyes like yours.'

He laughed, but he was touched. His hand covered her arm lightly. 'Be good,' he said. 'Work hard and I'll be so proud of you—and we'll have some good times together.'

'I always have a good time with you.' Her eyes were full on his, in his, held there like hands. Her voice was clear and dry. 'Honest, I'm not kidding about your eyes. You always think I'm kidding. I want to thank you for all you've done for me.'

'I haven't done anything, you lunatic. I saw your face and I was—I was beholden to it—everybody ought to be beholden to it.'

Entertainers appeared and her eyes wandered hungrily away from him.

She was so young—Jacob had never been so conscious of youth before. He had always considered himself on the young side until tonight.

Afterward, in the dark cave of the taxicab, fragrant with the perfume he had bought for her that day, Jenny came close to him, clung to him. He kissed her, without enjoying it. There was no shadow of passion in her eyes or on her mouth; there was a faint spray of champagne on her breath. She clung nearer, desperately. He took her hands and put them in her lap.

She leaned away from him resentfully.

'What's the matter? Don't you like me?'

'I shouldn't have let you have so much champagne.'

'Why not? I've had a drink before. I was tight once.'

'Well, you ought to be ashamed of yourself. And if I hear of your taking any more drinks, you'll hear from me.'

'You sure have got your nerve, haven't you?'

'What do you do? Let all the corner soda jerkers maul you around whenever they want?'

'Oh, shut up!'

For a moment they rode in silence. Then her hand crept across to his. 'I like you better than any guy I ever met, and I can't help that, can I?'

'Dear little Jenny.' He put his arm around her again.

Hesitating tentatively, he kissed her and again he was chilled by the innocence of her kiss, the eyes that at the moment of contact looked beyond him out into the darkness of the night, the darkness of the world. She did not know yet that splendor was something in the heart; at the moment when she should realize that and melt into the passion of the universe he could take her without question or regret.

'I like you enormously,' he said; 'better than almost anyone I know. I mean that about drinking though. You mustn't drink.'

'I'll do anything you want,' she said; and she repeated, looking at him directly, 'Anything.'

The car drew up in front of her flat and he kissed her good night.

He rode away in a mood of exultation, living more deeply in her youth and future than he had lived in himself for years. Thus, leaning forward a little on his cane, rich, young and happy, he was borne along dark streets and light toward a future of his own which he could not foretell.

III

A month later, climbing into a taxicab with Farrelly one night, he gave the latter's address to the driver. 'So you're in love with this baby,' said Farrelly pleasantly. 'Very well, I'll get out of your way.'

Jacob experienced a vast displeasure. 'I'm not in love with her,' he said slowly. 'Billy, I want you to leave her alone.'

'Sure! I'll leave her alone,' agreed Farrelly readily. 'I didn't know you were interested—she told me she couldn't make you.'

'The point is you're not interested either,' said Jacob. 'If I thought that you two really cared about each other, do you think I'd be fool enough to try to stand in the way? But you don't give a darn about her, and she's impressed and a little fascinated.'

'Sure,' agreed Farrelly, bored. 'I wouldn't touch her for anything.'

Jacob laughed. 'Yes, you would. Just for something to do. That's what I object to—anything—anything casual happening to her.'

'I see what you mean. I'll let her alone.'

Jacob was forced to be content with that. He had no faith in Billy Farrelly, but he guessed that Farrelly liked him and wouldn't offend him unless stronger feelings were involved. But the holding hands under the table tonight had annoyed him. Jenny lied about it when he reproached her; she offered to let him take her home immediately, offered not to speak to Farrelly again all evening. Then he had seemed silly and pointless to himself. It would have been easier, when Farrelly said 'So you're in love with this baby,' to have been able to answer simply, 'I am.'

But he wasn't. He valued her now more than he had ever thought possible. He watched in her the awakening of a sharply individual temperament. She liked quiet and simple things. She was developing the capacity to discriminate and shut the trivial and the unessential out of her life. He tried giving her books; then wisely he gave up that and brought her into contact with a variety of men. He made situations and then explained them to her, and he was pleased, as appreciation and politeness began to blossom before his eyes. He valued, too, her utter trust in him and the fact that she used him as a standard for judgments on other men.

Before the Farrelly picture was released, she was offered a

two-year contract on the strength of her work in it—four hundred a week for six months and an increase on a sliding scale. But she would have to go to the Coast.

'Wouldn't you rather have me wait?' she said, as they drove in from the country one afternoon. 'Wouldn't you rather have me stay here in New York—near you?'

'You've got to go where your work takes you. You ought to be able to look out for yourself. You're seventeen.'

Seventeen—she was as old as he; she was ageless. Her dark eyes under a yellow straw hat were as full of destiny as though she had not just offered to toss destiny away.

'I wonder if you hadn't come along, someone else would of,' she said—'to make me do things, I mean.'

'You'd have done them yourself. Get it out of your head that you're dependent on me.'

'I am. Everything is, thanks to you.'

'It isn't, though,' he said emphatically, but he brought no reasons; he liked her to think that.

'I don't know what I'll do without you. You're my only friend'—and she added—'that I care about. You see? You understand what I mean?'

He laughed at her, enjoying the birth of her egotism implied in her right to be understood. She was lovelier that afternoon than he had ever seen her, delicate, resonant and, for him, undesirable. But sometimes he wondered if that sexlessness wasn't for him alone, wasn't a side that, perhaps purposely, she turned toward him. She was happiest of all with younger men, though she pretended to despise them. Billy Farrelly, obligingly and somewhat to her mild chagrin, had left her alone.

'When will you come out to Hollywood?'

'Soon,' he promised. 'And you'll be coming back to New York.'

She began to cry. 'Oh, I'll miss you so much! I'll miss you so much!' Large tears of distress ran down her warm ivory cheeks. 'Oh, geeze!' she cried softly. 'You been good to me!

Where's your hand? Where's your hand? You been the best friend anybody ever had. Where am I ever going to find a friend like you?'

She was acting now, but a lump arose in his throat and for a moment a wild idea ran back and forth in his mind, like a blind man, knocking over its solid furniture—to marry her. He had only to make the suggestion, he knew, and she would become close to him and know no one else, because he would understand her forever.

Next day, in the station, she was pleased with her flowers, her compartment, with the prospect of a longer trip than she had ever taken before. When she kissed him good-by her deep eyes came close to his again and she pressed against him as if in protest against the separation. Again she cried, but he knew that behind her tears lay the happiness of adventure in new fields. As he walked out of the station, New York was curiously empty. Through her eyes he had seen old colors once more; now they had faded back into the gray tapestry of the past. The next day he went to an office high in a building on Park Avenue and talked to a famous specialist he had not visited for a decade.

'I want you to examine the larynx again,' he said. 'There's not much hope, but something might have changed the situation.'

He swallowed a complicated system of mirrors. He breathed in and out, made high and low sounds, coughed at a word of command. The specialist fussed and touched. Then he sat back and took out his eyeglass. 'There's no change,' he said. 'The cords are not diseased—they're simply worn out. It isn't anything that can be treated.'

'I thought so,' said Jacob, humbly, as if he had been guilty of an impertinence. 'That's practically what you told me before. I wasn't sure how permanent it was.'

He had lost something when he came out of the building on Park Avenue—a half hope, the love child of a wish, that some day——

'New York desolate,' he wired her. 'The night clubs all closed. Black wreaths on the Statue of Civic Virtue. Please work hard and be remarkably happy.'

'Dear Jacob,' she wired back, 'miss you so. You are the nicest man that ever lived and I mean it, dear. Please don't forget me. Love from Jenny.'

Winter came. The picture Jenny had made in the East was released, together with preliminary interviews and articles in the fan magazines. Jacob sat in his apartment, playing the Kreutzer Sonata over and over on his new phonograph, and read her meager and stilted but affectionate letters and the articles which said she was a discovery of Billy Farrelly's. In February he became engaged to an old friend, now a widow.

They went to Florida and were suddenly snarling at each other in hotel corridors and over bridge games, so they decided not to go through with it after all. In the spring he took a stateroom on the Paris, but three days before sailing he disposed of it and went to California.

IV

Jenny met him at the station, kissed him and clung to his arm in the car all the way to the Ambassador Hotel. 'Well, the man came,' she cried. 'I never thought I'd get him to come. I never did.'

Her accent betrayed an effort at control. The emphatic 'Geeze!' with all the wonder, horror, disgust or admiration she could put in it was gone, but there was no mild substitute, no 'swell' or 'grand.' If her mood required expletives outside her repertoire, she kept silent.

But at seventeen, months are years and Jacob perceived a change in her; in no sense was she a child any longer. There were fixed things in her mind—not distractions, for she was instinctively too polite for that, but simply things there. No longer was the studio a lark and a wonder and a divine

(171)

accident; no longer 'for a nickel I wouldn't turn up tomorrow.' It was part of her life. Circumstances were stiffening into a career which went on independently of her casual hours.

'If this picture is as good as the other—I mean if I make a personal hit again, Hecksher'll break the contract. Everybody that's seen the rushes says it's the first one I've had sex appeal in.'

'What are the rushes?'

'When they run off what they took the day before. They say it's the first time I've had sex appeal.'

'I don't notice it,' he teased her.

'You wouldn't. But I have.'

'I know you have,' he said, and, moved by an ill-considered impulse, he took her hand.

She glanced quickly at him. He smiled—half a second too late. Then she smiled and her glowing warmth veiled his mistake.

'Jake,' she cried, 'I could bawl, I'm so glad you're here! I got you a room at the Ambassador. They were full, but they kicked out somebody because I said I had to have a room. I'll send my car back for you in half an hour. It's good you came on Sunday, because I got all day free.'

They had luncheon in the furnished apartment she had leased for the winter. It was 1920 Moorish, taken over complete from a favorite of yesterday. Someone had told her it was horrible, for she joked about it; but when he pursued the matter he found that she didn't know why.

'I wish they had more nice men out here,' she said once during luncheon. 'Of course there's a lot of nice ones, but I mean——Oh, you know, like in New York—men that know even more than a girl does, like you.'

After luncheon he learned that they were going to tea. 'Not today,' he objected. 'I want to see you alone.'

'All right,' she agreed doubtfully. 'I suppose I could telephone. I thought——It's a lady that writes for a lot of newspapers and I've never been asked there before. Still, if you don't want to——'

Her face had fallen a little and Jacob assured her that he couldn't be more willing. Gradually he found that they were going not to one party but to three.

'In my position, it's sort of the thing to do,' she explained. 'Otherwise you don't see anybody except the people on your own lot, and that's narrow.' He smiled. 'Well, anyhow,' she finished—'anyhow, you smart Aleck, that's what everybody does on Sunday afternoon.'

At the first tea, Jacob noticed that there was an enormous preponderance of women over men, and of supernumeraries —lady journalists, cameramen's daughters, cutters' wives— over people of importance. A young Latin named Raffino appeared for a brief moment, spoke to Jenny and departed; several stars passed through, asking about children's health with a domesticity that was somewhat overpowering. Another group of celebrities posed immobile, statue-like, in a corner. There was a somewhat inebriated and very much excited author apparently trying to make engagements with one girl after another. As the afternoon waned, more people were suddenly a little tight; the communal voice was higher in pitch and greater in volume as Jacob and Jenny went out the door.

At the second tea, young Raffino—he was an actor, one of innumerable hopeful Valentinos—appeared again for a minute, talked to Jenny a little longer, a little more attentively this time, and went out. Jacob gathered that this party was not considered to have quite the swagger of the other. There was a bigger crowd around the cocktail table. There was more sitting down.

Jenny, he saw, drank only lemonade. He was surprised and pleased at her distinction and good manners. She talked to one person, never to everyone within hearing; then she listened, without finding it necessary to shift her eyes about. Deliberate or not on her part, he noticed that at both teas she was sooner or later talking to the guest of most consequence. Her seriousness, her air of saying 'This is my opportunity of learning something,' beckoned their egotism imperatively near.

When they left to drive to the last party, a buffet supper, it was dark and the electric legends of hopeful real-estate brokers were gleaming to some vague purpose on Beverly Hills. Outside Grauman's Theater a crowd was already gathered in the thin, warm rain.

'Look! Look!' she cried. It was the picture she had finished a month before.

They slid out of the thin Rialto of Hollywood Boulevard and into the deep gloom of a side street; he put his arm about her and kissed her.

'Dear Jake.' She smiled up at him.

'Jenny, you're so lovely; I didn't know you were so lovely.'

She looked straight ahead, her face mild and quiet. A wave of annoyance passed over him and he pulled her toward him urgently, just as the car stopped at a lighted door.

They went into a bungalow crowded with people and smoke. The impetus of the formality which had begun the afternoon was long exhausted; everything had become at once vague and strident.

'This is Hollywood,' explained an alert talkative lady who had been in his vicinity all day. 'No airs on Sunday afternoon.' She indicated the hostess. 'Just a plain, simple, sweet girl.' She raised her voice: 'Isn't that so, darling—just a plain, simple, sweet girl?'

The hostess said, 'Yeah. Who is?' And Jacob's informant lowered her voice again: 'But that little girl of yours is the wisest one of the lot.'

The totality of the cocktails Jacob had swallowed was affecting him pleasantly, but try as he might, the plot of the party—the key on which he could find ease and tranquillity—eluded him. There was something tense in the air—something competitive and insecure. Conversations with the men had a way of becoming empty and overjovial or else melting off into a sort of suspicion. The women were nicer. At eleven o'clock, in the pantry, he suddenly realized that he hadn't seen Jenny for an hour. Returning to the living room, he saw her come in, evidently from outside, for she tossed a raincoat from her shoulders. She was with Raffino. When she came up, Jacob saw that she was out of breath and her eyes were very bright. Raffino smiled at Jacob pleasantly and negligently; a few moments later, as he turned to go, he bent and whispered in Jenny's ear and she looked at him without smiling as she said good night.

'I got to be on the lot at eight o'clock,' she told Jacob presently. 'I'll look like an old umbrella unless I go home. Do you mind, dear?'

'Heavens, no!'

Their car drove over one of the interminable distances of the thin, stretched city.

'Jenny,' he said, 'you've never looked like you were to-night. Put your head on my shoulder.'

'I'd like to. I'm tired.'

'I can't tell you how radiant you've got to be.'

'I'm just the same.'

'No, you're not.' His voice suddenly became a whisper, trembling with emotion. 'Jenny, I'm in love with you.'

'Jacob, don't be silly.'

'I'm in love with you. Isn't it strange, Jenny? It happened just like that.'

'You're not in love with me.'

'You mean the fact doesn't interest you.' He was conscious of a faint twinge of fear.

She sat up out of the circle of his arm. 'Of course it interests me; you know I care more about you than anything in the world.'

'More than about Mr Raffino?'

'Oh—my—gosh!' she protested scornfully. 'Raffino's nothing but a baby.'

'I love you, Jenny.'

'No, you don't.'

He tightened his arm. Was it his imagination or was there a small instinctive resistance in her body? But she came close to him and he kissed her.

'You know that's crazy about Raffino.'

'I suppose I'm jealous.' Feeling insistent and unattractive, he released her. But the twinge of fear had become an ache. Though he knew that she was tired and that she felt strange at this new mood in him, he was unable to let the matter alone. 'I didn't realize how much a part of my life you were. I didn't know what it was I missed—but I know now. I wanted you near.'

'Well, here I am.'

He took her words as an invitation, but this time she relaxed wearily in his arms. He held her thus for the rest of the way, her eyes closed, her short hair falling straight back, like a girl drowned.

'The car'll take you to the hotel,' she said when they reached the apartment. 'Remember, you're having lunch with me at the studio tomorrow.'

Suddenly they were in a discussion that was almost an argument, as to whether it was too late for him to come in. Neither could yet appreciate the change that his declaration had made in the other. Abruptly they had become like different people, as Jacob tried desperately to turn back the clock to that night in New York six months before, and Jenny watched this mood, which was more than jealousy and less than love, snow under, one by one, the qualities of consideration and understanding which she knew in him and with which she felt at home.

'But I don't love you like that,' she cried. 'How can you come to me all at once and ask me to love you like that?'

'You love Raffino like that!'

'I swear I don't! I never even kissed him—not really!'

'H'm!' He was a gruff white bird now. He could scarcely

(176)

credit his own unpleasantness, but something illogical as love itself urged him on. 'An actor!'

'Oh, Jake,' she cried, 'please lemme go. I never felt so terrible and mixed up in my life.'

'I'll go,' he said suddenly. 'I don't know what's the matter, except that I'm so mad about you that I don't know what I'm saying. I love you and you don't love me. Once you did, or thought you did, but that's evidently over.'

'But I do love you.' She thought for a moment; the red-and-green glow of a filling station on the corner lit up the struggle in her face. 'If you love me that much, I'll marry you tomorrow.'

'Marry me!' he exclaimed. She was so absorbed in what she had just said that she did not notice.

'I'll marry you tomorrow,' she repeated. 'I like you better than anybody in the world and I guess I'll get to love you the way you want me to.' She uttered a single half-broken sob. 'But—I didn't know this was going to happen. Please let me alone tonight.'

Jacob didn't sleep. There was music from the Ambassador grill till late and a fringe of working girls hung about the carriage entrance waiting for their favorites to come out. Then a long-protracted quarrel between a man and a woman began in the hall outside, moved into the next room and continued as a low two-toned mumble through the intervening door. He went to the window sometime toward three o'clock and stared out into the clear splendor of the California night. Her beauty rested outside on the grass, on the damp, gleaming roofs of the bungalows, all around him, borne up like music on the night. It was in the room, on the white pillow, it rustled ghostlike in the curtains. His desire recreated her until she lost all vestiges of the old Jenny, even of the girl who had met him at the train that morning. Silently, as the night hours went by, he molded her over into an image of love—an image that would endure as long as love itself, or even longer—not to perish till he could say, 'I never really loved her.' Slowly he created it with this and that illusion from his youth, this and that sad old yearning, until she stood before him identical with her old self only by name.

Later, when he drifted off into a few hours' sleep, the image he had made stood near him, lingering in the room, joined in mystic marriage to his heart.

V

'I won't marry you unless you love me,' he said, driving back from the studio. She waited, her hands folded tranquilly in her lap. 'Do you think I'd want you if you were unhappy and unresponsive, Jenny—knowing all the time you didn't love me?'

'I do love you. But not that way.'

'What's "that way"?'

She hesitated, her eyes were far off. 'You don't—thrill me, Jake. I don't know—there have been some men that sort of thrilled me when they touched me, dancing or anything. I know it's crazy, but——'

'Does Raffino thrill you?'

'Sort of, but not so much.'

'And I don't at all?'

'I just feel comfortable and happy with you.'

He should have urged her that that was best, but he couldn't say it, whether it was an old truth or an old lie.

'Anyhow, I told you I'll marry you; perhaps you might thrill me later.'

He laughed, stopped suddenly. 'If I didn't thrill you, as you call it, why did you seem to care so much last summer?'

'I don't know. I guess I was young. You never know how you once felt, do you?'

She had become elusive to him, with that elusiveness that gives a hidden significance to the least significant remarks. And with the clumsy tools of jealousy and desire, he was trying to create the spell that is ethereal and delicate as the dust on a moth's wing.

'Listen, Jake,' she said suddenly. 'That lawyer my sister had—that Scharnhorst—called up the studio this afternoon.'

'Your sister's all right,' he said absently, and he added: 'So a lot of men thrill you.'

'Well, if I've felt it with a lot of men, it couldn't have anything to do with real love, could it?' she said hopefully.

'But your theory is that love couldn't come without it.'

'I haven't got any theories or anything. I just told you how I felt. You know more than me.'

'I don't know anything at all.'

There was a man waiting in the lower hall of the apartment house. Jenny went up and spoke to him; then, turning back to Jake, said in a low voice: 'It's Scharnhorst. Would you mind waiting downstairs while he talks to me? He says it won't take half an hour.'

He waited, smoking innumerable cigarettes. Ten minutes passed. Then the telephone operator beckoned him.

'Quick!' she said. 'Miss Prince wants you on the telephone.'

Jenny's voice was tense and frightened. 'Don't let Scharnhorst get out,' she said. 'He's on the stairs, maybe in the elevator. Make him come back here.'

Jacob put down the receiver just as the elevator clicked. He stood in front of the elevator door, barring the man inside. 'Mr Scharnhorst?'

'Yeah.' the face was keen and suspicious.

'Will you come up to Miss Prince's apartment again? There's something she forgot to say.'

'I can see her later.' He attempted to push past Jacob. Seizing him by the shoulders, Jacob shoved him back into the cage, slammed the door and pressed the button for the eighth floor.

'I'll have you arrested for this!' Scharnhorst remarked. 'Put into jail for assault!'

Jacob held him firmly by the arms. Upstairs, Jenny, with panic in her eyes, was holding open her door. After a slight struggle, the lawyer went inside.

'What is it?' demanded Jacob.

'Tell him, you,' she said. 'Oh, Jake, he wants twenty thousand dollars!'

'What for?'

'To get my sister a new trial.'

'But she hasn't a chance!' exclaimed Jacob. He turned to Scharnhorst. 'You ought to know she hasn't a chance.'

'There are some technicalities,' said the lawyer uneasily—'things that nobody but an attorney would understand. She's very unhappy there, and her sister so rich and successful. Mrs Choynski thought she ought to get another chance.'

'You've been up there working on her, heh?'

'She sent for me.'

'But the blackmail idea was your own. I suppose if Miss Prince doesn't feel like supplying twenty thousand to retain your firm, it'll come out that she's the sister of the notorious murderess.'

Jenny nodded. 'That's what he said.'

'Just a minute!' Jacob walked to the phone. 'Western Union, please. Western Union? Please take a telegram.' He gave the name and address of a man high in the political world of New York. 'Here's the message:

The convict Choynski threatening her sister, who is a picture actress, with exposure of relationship stop Can you arrange it with warden that she be cut off from visitors until I can get East and explain the situation stop Also wire me if two witnesses to an attempted blackmailing scene are enough to disbar a lawyer in New York if charges proceed from such a quarter as Read, Van Tyne, Biggs & Company, or my uncle the surrogate stop Answer Ambassador Hotel, Los Angeles.

Jacob C. K. Booth

He waited until the clerk had repeated the message. 'Now, Mr Scharnhorst,' he said, 'the pursuit of art should not be interrupted by such alarms and excursions. Miss Prince, as you see, is considerably upset. It will show in her work tomorrow and a million people will be just a little disappointed. So we won't ask her for any decisions. In fact you and I will leave Los Angeles on the same train tonight.'

VI

The summer passed. Jacob went about his useless life, sustained by the knowledge that Jenny was coming East in the fall. By fall there would have been many Raffinos, he supposed, and she would find that the thrill of their hands and eyes—and lips—was much the same. They were the equivalent, in a different world, of the affairs at a college house party, the undergraduates of a casual summer. And if it was still true that her feeling for him was less than romantic, then he would take her anyway, letting romance come after marriage as—so he had always heard—it had come to many wives before.

Her letters fascinated and baffled him. Through the ineptitude of expression he caught gleams of emotion—an ever-present gratitude, a longing to talk to him, and a quick, almost frightened reaction toward him, from—he could only imagine—some other man. In August she went on location; there were only post cards from some lost desert in Arizona, then for a while nothing at all. He was glad of the break. He had thought over all the things that might have repelled her—of his portentousness, his jealousy, his manifest misery. This time it would be different. He would keep control of the situation. She would at least admire him again, see in him the incomparably dignified and well adjusted life.

Two nights before her arrival Jacob went to see her latest picture in a huge nightbound vault on Broadway. It was a college story. She walked into it with her hair knotted on the crown of her head—a familiar symbol for dowdiness—inspired the hero to a feat of athletic success and faded out of it, always subsidiary to him, in the shadow of the cheering stands. But there was something new in her performance; for the first time the arresting quality he had noticed in her voice a year before had begun to get over on the screen. Every move she made, every gesture, was poignant and important. Others in the audience saw it too. He fancied he could tell this by some change in the quality of their breathing, by a reflection of her clear, precise expression in their casual and indifferent faces. Reviewers, too, were aware of it, though most of them were incapable of any precise definition of a personality.

But his first real consciousness of her public existence came from the attitude of her fellow passengers disembarking from the train. Busy as they were with friends or baggage, they found time to stare at her, to call their friends' attention, to repeat her name.

She was radiant. A communicative joy flowed from her and around her, as though her perfumer had managed to imprison ecstasy in a bottle. Once again there was a mystical transfusion, and blood began to course again through the hard veins of New York—there was the pleasure of Jacob's chauffeur when she remembered him, the respectful frisking of the bell boys at the Plaza, the nervous collapse of the head waiter at the restaurant where they dined. As for Jacob, he had control of himself now. He was gentle, considerate and polite, as it was natural for him to be—but as, in this case, he had found it necessary to plan. His manner promised and outlined an ability to take care of her, a will to be leaned on.

After dinner, their corner of the restaurant cleared gradually of the theater crowd and the sense of being alone settled over them. Their faces became grave, their voices very quiet.

(182)

'It's been five months since I saw you.' He looked down at his hands thoughtfully. 'Nothing has changed with me, Jenny. I love you with all my heart. I love your face and your faults and your mind and everything about you. The one thing I want in this world is to make you happy.'

'I know,' she whispered. 'Gosh, I know!'

'Whether there's still only affection in your feeling toward me, I don't know. If you'll marry me, I think you'll find that the other things will come, will be there before you know it—and what you called a thrill will seem a joke to you, because life isn't for boys and girls, Jenny, but for men and women.'

'Jacob,' she whispered, 'you don't have to tell me. I know.'

He raised his eyes for the first time. 'What do you mean—you know?'

'I get what you mean. Oh, this is terrible! Jacob, listen! I want to tell you. Listen, dear, don't say anything. Don't look at me. Listen, Jacob, I fell in love with a man.'

'What?' he asked blankly.

'I fell in love with somebody. That's what I mean about understanding about a silly thrill.'

'You mean you're in love with me?'

'No.'

The appalling monosyllable floated between them, danced and vibrated over the table: 'No—no—no—no—no!'

'Oh, this is awful!' she cried. 'I fell in love with a man I met on location this summer. I didn't mean to—I tried not to, but first thing I knew there I was in love and all the wishing in the world couldn't help it. I wrote you and asked you to come, but I didn't send the letter, and there I was, crazy about this man and not daring to speak to him, and bawling myself to sleep every night.'

'An actor?' he heard himself saying in a dead voice. 'Raffino?'

'Oh, no, no, no! Wait a minute, let me tell you. It went on

for three weeks and I honestly wanted to kill myself, Jake. Life wasn't worth while unless I could have him. And one night we got in a car by accident alone and he just caught me and made me tell him I loved him. He knew—he couldn't help knowing.'

'It just—swept over you,' said Jacob steadily. 'I see.'

'Oh, I knew you'd understand, Jake! You understand everything. You're the best person in the world, Jake, and don't I know it?'

'You're going to marry him?'

Slowly she nodded her head. 'I said I'd have to come East first and see you.' As her fear lessened, the extent of his grief became more apparent to her and her eyes filled with tears. 'It only comes once, Jake, like that. That's what kept in my mind all those weeks I didn't hardly speak to him—if you lose it once, it'll never come like that again and then what do you want to live for? He was directing the picture—he was the same about me.'

'I see.'

As once before, her eyes held his like hands. 'Oh, Ja-a-ake!' In that sudden croon of compassion, all-comprehending and deep as a song, the first force of the shock passed off. Jacob's teeth came together again and he struggled to conceal his misery. Mustering his features into an expression of irony, he called for the check. It seemed an hour later they were in a taxi going toward the Plaza Hotel.

She clung to him. 'Oh, Jake, say it's all right! Say you understand! Darling Jake, my best friend, my only friend, say you understand!'

'Of course I do, Jenny.' His hand patted her back automatically.

'Oh-h-h, Jake, you feel just awful, don't you?'

'I'll survive.'

'Oh-h-h, Jake!'

They reached the hotel. Before they got out Jenny glanced at her face in her vanity mirror and turned up the

(184)

collar of her fur cape. In the lobby, Jacob ran into several people and said, 'Oh, I'm so sorry,' in a strained, unconvincing voice. The elevator waited. Jenny, her face distraught and tearful, stepped in and held out her hand toward him with the fist clenched helplessly.

'Jake,' she said once more.

'Good night, Jenny.'

She turned her face to the wire wall of the cage. The gate clanged.

'Hold on!' he almost said. 'Do you realize what you're doing, starting that car like that?'

He turned and went out the door blindly. 'I've lost her,' he whispered to himself, awed and frightened. 'I've lost her!'

He walked over Fifty-ninth Street to Columbus Circle and then down Broadway. There were no cigarettes in his pocket —he had left them at the restaurant—so he went into a tobacco store. There was some confusion about the change and someone in the store laughed.

When he came out he stood for a moment puzzled. Then the heavy tide of realization swept over him and beyond him, leaving him stunned and exhausted. It swept back upon him and over him again. As one rereads a tragic story with the defiant hope that it will end differently, so he went back to the morning, to the beginning, to the previous year. But the tide came thundering back with the certainty that she was cut off from him forever in a high room at the Plaza Hotel.

He walked down Broadway. In great block letters over the porte-cochère of the Capitol Theater five words glittered out into the night: 'Carl Barbour and Jenny Prince.'

The name startled him, as if a passer-by had spoken it. He stopped and stared. Other eyes rose to that sign, people hurried by him and turned in.

Jenny Prince.

Now that she no longer belonged to him, the name assumed a significance entirely its own.

(185)

It hung there, cool and impervious, in the night, a challenge, a defiance.

Jenny Prince.

'Come and rest upon my loveliness,' it said. 'Fulfill your secret dreams in wedding me for an hour.'

Jenny Prince.

It was untrue—she was back at the Plaza Hotel, in love with somebody. But the name, with its bright insistence, rode high upon the night.

'I love my dear public. They are all so sweet to me.'

The wave appeared far off, sent up whitecaps, rolled toward him with the might of pain, washed over him. 'Never any more. Never any more.' The wave beat upon him, drove him down, pounding with hammers of agony on his ears. Proud and impervious, the name on high challenged the night.

Jenny Prince.

She was there! All of her, the best of her—the effort, the power, the triumph, the beauty.

Jacob moved forward with a group and bought a ticket at the window.

Confused, he stared around the great lobby. Then he saw an entrance and walking in, found himself a place in the fast-throbbing darkness.

SCOTT

The Swimmers

(The Saturday Evening Post,
19 October 1929)

In the Place Benoît, a suspended mass of gasoline exhaust
cooked slowly by the June sun. It was a terrible thing, for,
unlike pure heat, it held no promise of rural escape, but
suggested only roads choked with the same foul asthma. In
the offices of The Promissory Trust Company, Paris Branch,
facing the square, an American man of thirty-five inhaled it,
and it became the odor of the thing he must presently do. A
black horror suddenly descended upon him, and he went up
to the washroom, where he stood, trembling a little, just
inside the door.

Through the washroom window his eyes fell upon a sign—
1000 Chemises. The shirts in question filled the shop
window, piled, cravated and stuffed, or else draped with
shoddy grace on the show-case floor. 1000 Chemises—
Count them! To the left he read Papeterie, Pâtisserie,
Solde, Réclame, and Constance Talmadge in Déjeuner
de Soleil; and his eye, escaping to the right, met yet
more somber announcements: Vêtements Ecclésiastiques,
Déclaration de Décès, and Pompes Funèbres. Life and
Death.

Henry Marston's trembling became a shaking; it would be
pleasant if this were the end and nothing more need be done,
he thought, and with a certain hope he sat down on a stool.
But it is seldom really the end, and after a while, as he became too exhausted to care, the shaking stopped and he was
better. Going downstairs, looking as alert and self-possessed

as any other officer of the bank, he spoke to two clients he knew, and set his face grimly toward noon.

'Well, Henry Clay Marston!' A handsome old man shook hands with him and took the chair beside his desk.

'Henry, I want to see you in regard to what we talked about the other night. How about lunch? In that green little place with all the trees.'

'Not lunch, Judge Waterbury; I've got an engagement.'

'I'll talk now, then; because I'm leaving this afternoon. What do these plutocrats give you for looking important around here?'

Henry Marston knew what was coming.

'Ten thousand and certain expense money,' he answered.

'How would you like to come back to Richmond at about double that? You've been over here eight years and you don't know the opportunities you're missing. Why both my boys——'

Henry listened appreciatively, but this morning he couldn't concentrate on the matter. He spoke vaguely about being able to live more comfortably in Paris and restrained himself from stating his frank opinion upon existence at home.

Judge Waterbury beckoned to a tall, pale man who stood at the mail desk.

'This is Mr Wiese,' he said. 'Mr Wiese's from downstate; he's a halfway partner of mine.'

'Glad to meet you, suh.' Mr Wiese's voice was rather too deliberately Southern. 'Understand the judge is makin' you a proposition.'

'Yes,' Henry answered briefly. He recognized and detested the type—the prosperous sweater, presumably evolved from a cross between carpet-bagger and poor white. When Wiese moved away, the judge said almost apologetically:

'He's one of the richest men in the South, Henry.' Then, after a pause: 'Come home, boy.'

'I'll think it over, judge.' For a moment the gray and ruddy head seemed so kind; then it faded back into something one-dimensional, machine-finished, blandly and bleakly un-European. Henry Marston respected that open kindness —in the bank he touched it with daily appreciation, as a curator in a museum might touch a precious object removed in time and space; but there was no help in it for him; the questions which Henry Marston's life propounded could be answered only in France. His seven generations of Virginia ancestors were definitely behind him every day at noon when he turned home.

Home was a fine high-ceiling apartment hewn from the palace of a Renaissance cardinal in the Rue Monsieur—the sort of thing Henry could not have afforded in America. Choupette, with something more than the rigid tradition-alism of a French bourgeois taste, had made it beautiful, and moved through gracefully with their children. She was a frail Latin blonde with fine large features and vividly sad French eyes that had first fascinated Henry in a Grenoble *pension* in 1918. The two boys took their looks from Henry, voted the handsomest man at the University of Virginia a few years before the war.

Climbing the two broad flights of stairs, Henry stood panting a moment in the outside hall. It was quiet and cool here, and yet it was vaguely like the terrible thing that was going to happen. He heard a clock inside his apartment strike one, and inserted his key in the door.

The maid who had been in Choupette's family for thirty years stood before him, her mouth open in the utterance of a truncated sigh.

'*Bonjour*, Louise.'

'Monsieur!' He threw his hat on a chair. 'But, monsieur— but I thought monsieur said on the phone he was going to Tours for the children!'

'I changed my mind, Louise.'

He had taken a step forward, his last doubt melting away at the constricted terror in the woman's face.

'Is madame home?'

Simultaneously he perceived a man's hat and stick on the hall table and for the first time in his life he heard silence—a loud, singing silence, oppressive as heavy guns or thunder. Then, as the endless moment was broken by the maid's terrified little cry, he pushed through the portières into the next room.

An hour later Doctor Derocco, *de la Faculté de Médecine*, rang the apartment bell. Choupette Marston, her face a little drawn and rigid, answered the door. For a moment they went through French forms; then:

'My husband has been feeling unwell for some weeks,' she said concisely. 'Nevertheless, he did not complain in a way to make me uneasy. He has suddenly collapsed; he cannot articulate or move his limbs. All this, I must say, might have been precipitated by a certain indiscretion of mine—in all events, there was a violent scene, a discussion, and sometimes when he is agitated, my husband cannot comprehend well in French.'

'I will see him,' said the doctor; thinking: 'Some things are comprehended instantly in all languages.'

During the next four weeks several people listened to strange speeches about one thousand chemises, and heard how all the population of Paris was becoming etherized by cheap gasoline—there was a consulting psychiatrist, not inclined to believe in any underlying mental trouble; there was a nurse from the American Hospital, and there was Choupette, frightened, defiant and, after her fashion, deeply sorry. A month later, when Henry awoke to his familiar room, lit with a dimmed lamp, he found her sitting beside his bed and reached out for her hand.

'I still love you,' he said—'that's the odd thing.'

'Sleep, male cabbage.'

'At all costs,' he continued with a certain feeble irony, 'you can count on me to adopt the Continental attitude.'

'Please! You tear at my heart.'

When he was sitting up in bed they were ostensibly close together again—closer than they had been for months.

'Now you're going to have another holiday,' said Henry to the two boys, back from the country. 'Papa has got to go to the seashore and get really well.'

'Will we swim?'

'And get drowned, my darlings?' Choupette cried. 'But fancy, at your age. Not at all!'

So, at St Jean de Luz they sat on the shore instead, and watched the English and Americans and a few hardy French pioneers of *le sport* voyage between raft and diving tower, motorboat and sand. There were passing ships, and bright islands to look at, and mountains reaching into cold zones, and red and yellow villas, called Fleur des Bois, Mon Nid, or Sans-Souci; and farther back, tired French villages of baked cement and gray stone.

Choupette sat at Henry's side, holding a parasol to shelter her peach-bloom skin from the sun.

'Look!' she would say, at the sight of tanned American girls. 'Is that lovely? Skin that will be leather at thirty—a sort of brown veil to hide all blemishes, so that everyone will look alike. And women of a hundred kilos in such bathing suits! Weren't clothes intended to hide Nature's mistakes?'

Henry Clay Marston was a Virginian of the kind who are prouder of being Virginians than of being Americans. That mighty word printed across a continent was less to him than the memory of his grandfather, who freed his slaves in '58, fought from Manassas to Appomattox, knew Huxley and Spencer as light reading, and believed in caste only when it expressed the best of race.

To Choupette all this was vague. Her more specific criticisms of his compatriots were directed against the women.

'How would you place them?' she exclaimed. 'Great ladies, bourgeoises, adventuresses—they are all the same.

Look! Where would I be if I tried to act like your friend, Madame de Richepin? My father was a professor in a provincial university, and I have certain things I wouldn't do because they wouldn't please my class, my family. Madame de Richepin has other things she wouldn't do because of her class, her family.' Suddenly she pointed to an American girl going into the water: 'But that young lady may be a stenographer and yet be compelled to warp herself, dressing and acting as if she had all the money in the world.'

'Perhaps she will have, some day.'

'That's the story they are told; it happens to one, not to the ninety-nine. That's why all their faces over thirty are discontented and unhappy.'

Though Henry was in general agreement, he could not help being amused at Choupette's choice of target this afternoon. The girl—she was perhaps eighteen—was obviously acting like nothing but herself—she was what his father would have called a thoroughbred. A deep, thoughtful face that was pretty only because of the irrepressible determination of the perfect features to be recognized, a face that could have done without them and not yielded up its poise and distinction.

In her grace, at once exquisite and hardy, she was that perfect type of American girl that makes one wonder if the male is not being sacrificed to it, much as, in the last century, the lower strata in England were sacrificed to produce the governing class.

The two young men, coming out of the water as she went in, had large shoulders and empty faces. She had a smile for them that was no more than they deserved—that must do until she chose one to be the father of her children and gave herself up to destiny. Until then—Henry Marston was glad about her as her arms, like flying fish, clipped the water in a crawl, as her body spread in a swan dive or doubled in a jackknife from the springboard and her head appeared from the depth, jauntily flipping the damp hair away.

The two young men passed near.

'They push water,' Choupette said, 'then they go elsewhere and push other water. They pass months in France and they couldn't tell you the name of the President. They are parasites such as Europe has not known in a hundred years.'

But Henry had stood up abruptly, and now all the people on the beach were suddenly standing up. Something had happened out there in the fifty yards between the deserted raft and the shore. The bright head showed upon the surface; it did not flip water now, but called: '*Au secours!* Help!' in a feeble and frightened voice.

'Henry!' Choupette cried. 'Stop! Henry!'

The beach was almost deserted at noon, but Henry and several others were sprinting toward the sea; the two young Americans heard, turned and sprinted after them. There was a frantic little time with half a dozen bobbing heads in the water. Choupette, still clinging to her parasol, but managing to wring her hands at the same time, ran up and down the beach crying: 'Henry! Henry!'

Now there were more helping hands, and then two swelling groups around prostrate figures on the shore. The young fellow who pulled in the girl brought her around in a minute or so, but they had more trouble getting the water out of Henry, who had never learned to swim.

II

'This is the man who didn't know whether he could swim, because he'd never tried.'

Henry got up from his sun chair, grinning. It was next morning, and the saved girl had just appeared on the beach with her brother. She smiled back at Henry, brightly casual, appreciative rather than grateful.

'At the very least, I owe it to you to teach you how,' she said.

(193)

'I'd like it. I decided that in the water yesterday, just before I went down the tenth time.'

'You can trust me. I'll never again eat chocolate ice cream before going in.'

As she went on into the water, Choupette asked: 'How long do you think we'll stay here? After all, this life wearies one.'

'We'll stay till I can swim. And the boys too.'

'Very well. I saw a nice bathing suit in two shades of blue for fifty francs that I will buy you this afternoon.'

Feeling a little paunchy and unhealthily white, Henry, holding his sons by the hand, took his body into the water. The breakers leaped at him, staggering him, while the boys yelled with ecstasy; the returning water curled threateningly around his feet as it hurried back to sea. Farther out, he stood waist deep with other intimidated souls, watching the people dive from the raft tower, hoping the girl would come to fulfill her promise, and somewhat embarrassed when she did.

'I'll start with your eldest. You watch and then try it by yourself.'

He floundered in the water. It went into his nose and started a raw stinging; it blinded him; it lingered afterward in his ears, rattling back and forth like pebbles for hours. The sun discovered him, too, peeling long strips of parchment from his shoulders, blistering his back so that he lay in a feverish agony for several nights. After a week he swam, painfully, pantingly, and not very far. The girl taught him a sort of crawl, for he saw that the breast stroke was an obsolete device that lingered on with the inept and the old. Choupette caught him regarding his tanned face in the mirror with a sort of fascination, and the youngest boy contracted some sort of mild skin infection in the sand that retired him from competition. But one day Henry battled his way desperately to the float and drew himself up on it with his last breath.

'That being settled,' he told the girl, when he could speak, 'I can leave St Jean tomorrow.'

'I'm sorry.'

'What will you do now?'

'My brother and I are going to Antibes; there's swimming there all through October. Then Florida.'

'And swim?' he asked with some amusement.

'Why, yes. We'll swim.'

'Why do you swim?'

'To get clean,' she answered surprisingly.

'Clean from what?'

She frowned. 'I don't know why I said that. But it feels clean in the sea.'

'Americans are too particular about that,' he commented.

'How could anyone be?'

'I mean we've got too fastidious even to clean up our messes.'

'I don't know.'

'But tell me why you——' He stopped himself in surprise. He had been about to ask her to explain a lot of other things— to say what was clean and unclean, what was worth knowing and what was only words—to open up a new gate to life. Looking for a last time into her eyes, full of cool secrets, he realized how much he was going to miss these mornings, without knowing whether it was the girl who interested him or what she represented of his ever-new, ever-changing country.

'All right,' he told Choupette that night. 'We'll leave tomorrow.'

'For Paris?'

'For America.'

'You mean I'm to go too? And the children?'

'Yes.'

'But that's absurd,' she protested. 'Last time it cost more than we spend in six months here. And then there were only three of us. Now that we've managed to get ahead at last——'

'That's just it. I'm tired of getting ahead on your skimping

(195)

and saving and going without dresses. I've got to make more money. American men are incomplete without money.'

'You mean we'll stay?'

'It's very possible.'

They looked at each other, and against her will, Choupette understood. For eight years, by a process of ceaseless adaptation, he had lived her life, substituting for the moral confusion of his own country, the tradition, the wisdom, the sophistication of France. After that matter in Paris, it had seemed the bigger part to understand and to forgive, to cling to the home as something apart from the vagaries of love. Only now, glowing with a good health that he had not experienced for years, did he discover his true reaction. It had released him. For all his sense of loss, he possessed again the masculine self he had handed over to the keeping of a wise little Provençal girl eight years ago.

She struggled on for a moment.

'You've got a good position and we really have plenty of money. You know we can live cheaper here.'

'The boys are growing up now, and I'm not sure I want to educate them in France.'

'But that's all decided,' she wailed. 'You admit yourself that education in America is superficial and full of silly fads. Do you want them to be like those two dummies on the beach?'

'Perhaps I was thinking more of myself, Choupette. Men just out of college who brought their letters of credit into the bank eight years ago, travel about with ten-thousand-dollar cars now. I didn't use to care. I used to tell myself that I had a better place to escape to, just because, we knew that lobster armoricaine was really lobster américaine.* Perhaps I haven't that feeling any more.'

---

* The *Post* printed this as 'lobster American was really lobster American'—which has no point. Lobster with 'sauce à l'américaine' was invented in 1867 by chef Noel Peters, but some French restaurateurs balked at the name and called it 'sauce à l'armoricaine' from the old name for Brittany, l'Armorique.

She stiffened. 'If that's it——'

'It's up to you. We'll make a new start.'

Choupette thought for a moment. 'Of course my sister can take over the apartment.'

'Of course.' He waxed enthusiastic. 'And there are sure to be things that'll tickle you—we'll have a nice car, for instance, and one of those electric ice boxes, and all sorts of funny machines to take the place of servants. It won't be bad. You'll learn to play golf and talk about children all day. Then there are the movies.'

Choupette groaned.

'It's going to be pretty awful at first,' he admitted, 'but there are still a few good nigger cooks, and we'll probably have two bathrooms.'

'I am unable to use more than one at a time.'

'You'll learn.'

A month afterward, when the beautiful white island floated toward them in the Narrows, Henry's throat grew constricted with the rest and he wanted to cry out to Choupette and all foreigners, 'Now, you see!'

III

Almost three years later, Henry Marston walked out of his office in the Calumet Tobacco Company and along the hall to Judge Waterbury's suite. His face was older, with a suspicion of grimness, and a slight irrepressible heaviness of body was not concealed by his white linen suit.

'Busy, judge?'

'Come in, Henry.'

'I'm going to the shore tomorrow to swim off this weight. I wanted to talk to you before I go.'

'Children going too?'

'Oh, sure.'

'Choupette'll go abroad, I suppose.'

'Not this year. I think she's coming with me, if she doesn't stay here in Richmond.'

The judge thought: 'There isn't a doubt but what he knows everything.' He waited.

'I wanted to tell you, judge, that I'm resigning the end of September.'

The judge's chair creaked backward as he brought his feet to the floor.

'You're quitting, Henry?'

'Not exactly. Walter Ross wants to come home; let me take his place in France.'

'Boy, do you know what we pay Walter Ross?'

'Seven thousand.'

'And you're getting twenty-five.'

'You've probably heard I've made something in the market,' said Henry deprecatingly.

'I've heard everything between a hundred thousand and half a million.'

'Somewhere in between.'

'Then why a seven-thousand-dollar job? Is Choupette homesick?'

'No, I think Choupette likes it over here. She's adapted herself amazingly.'

'He knows,' the judge thought. 'He wants to get away.'

After Henry had gone, he looked up at the portrait of his grandfather on the wall. In those days the matter would have been simpler. Dueling pistols in the old Wharton meadow at dawn. It would be to Henry's advantage if things were like that today.

Henry's chauffeur dropped him in front of a Georgian house in a new suburban section. Leaving his hat in the hall, he went directly out on the side veranda.

From the swaying canvas swing Choupette looked up with a polite smile. Save for a certain alertness of feature and a certain indefinable knack of putting things on, she might have passed for an American. Southernisms overlay her

French accent with a quaint charm; there were still college boys who rushed her like a debutante at the Christmas dances

Henry nodded at Mr Charles Wiese, who occupied a wicker chair, with a gin fizz at his elbow.

'I want to talk to you,' he said, sitting down.

Wiese's glance and Choupette's crossed quickly before coming to rest on him.

'You're free, Wiese,' Henry said. 'Why don't you and Choupette get married?'

Choupette sat up, her eyes flashing.

'Now wait.' Henry turned back to Wiese. 'I've been letting this thing drift for about a year now, while I got my financial affairs in shape. But this last brilliant idea of yours makes me feel a little uncomfortable, a little sordid, and I don't want to feel that way.'

'Just what do you mean?' Wiese inquired.

'On my last trip to New York you had me shadowed. I presume it was with the intention of getting divorce evidence against me. It wasn't a success.'

'I don't know where you got such an idea in your head, Marston; you——'

'Don't lie!'

'Suh——' Wiese began, but Henry interrupted impatiently:

'Now don't "Suh" me, and don't try to whip yourself up into a temper. You're not talking to a scared picker full of hookworm. I don't want a scene; my emotions aren't sufficiently involved. I want to arrange a divorce.'

'Why do you bring it up like this?' Choupette cried, breaking into French. 'Couldn't we talk of it alone, if you think you have so much against me?'

'Wait a minute; this might as well be settled now,' Wiese said. 'Choupette does want a divorce. Her life with you is unsatisfactory, and the only reason she has kept on is because she's an idealist. You don't seem to appreciate that fact, but it's true; she couldn't bring herself to break up her home.'

(199)

'Very touching.' Henry looked at Choupette with bitter amusement. 'But let's come down to facts. I'd like to close up this matter before I go back to France.'

Again Wiese and Choupette exchanged a look.

'It ought to be simple,' Wiese said. 'Choupette doesn't want a cent of your money.'

'I know. What she wants is the children. The answer is, You can't have the children.'

'How perfectly outrageous!' Choupette cried. 'Do you imagine for a minute I'm going to give up my children?'

'What's your idea, Marston?' demanded Wiese. 'To take them back to France and make them expatriates like yourself?'

'Hardly that. They're entered for St. Regis School and then for Yale. And I haven't any idea of not letting them see their mother whenever she so desires—judging from the past two years, it won't be often. But I intend to have their entire legal custody.'

'Why?' they demanded together.

'Because of the home.'

'What the devil do you mean?'

'I'd rather apprentice them to a trade than have them brought up in the sort of home yours and Choupette's is going to be.'

There was a moment's silence. Suddenly Choupette picked up her glass, dashed the contents at Henry and collapsed on the settee, passionately sobbing.

Henry dabbed his face with his handkerchief and stood up.

'I was afraid of that,' he said, 'but I think I've made my position clear.'

He went up to his room and lay down on the bed. In a thousand wakeful hours during the past year he had fought over in his mind the problem of keeping his boys without taking those legal measures against Choupette that he could not bring himself to take. He knew that she wanted the children only because without them she would be suspect, even *déclassée,* to her family in France; but with that quality of detachment peculiar to old stock, Henry recognized this as a perfectly legitimate motive. Furthermore, no public scandal must touch the mother of his sons—it was this that had rendered his challenge so ineffectual this afternoon.

When difficulties became insurmountable, inevitable, Henry sought surcease in exercise. For three years, swimming had been a sort of refuge, and he turned to it as one man to music or another to drink. There was a point when he would resolutely stop thinking and go to the Virginia coast for a week to wash his mind in the water. Far out past the breakers he could survey the green-and-brown line of the Old Dominion with the pleasant impersonality of a porpoise. The burden of his wretched marriage fell away with the buoyant tumble of his body among the swells, and he would begin to move in a child's dream of space. Sometimes remembered playmates of his youth swam with him; sometimes, with his two sons beside him, he seemed to be setting off along the bright pathway to the moon. Americans, he liked to say, should be born with fins, and perhaps they were—perhaps money was a form of fin. In England property begot a strong place sense, but Americans, restless and with shallow roots, needed fins and wings. There was even a recurrent idea in America about an education that would leave out history and the past, that should be a sort of equipment for aerial adventure, weighed down by none of the stowaways of inheritance or tradition.

Thinking of this in the water the next afternoon brought Henry's mind to the children; he turned and at a slow trudgen started back toward shore. Out of condition, he rested, panting, at the raft, and glancing up, he saw familiar eyes. In a moment he was talking with the girl he had tried to rescue four years ago.

He was overjoyed. He had not realized how vividly he remembered her. She was a Virginian—he might have guessed it abroad—the laziness, the apparent casualness that masked an unfailing courtesy and attention; a good form devoid of forms was based on kindness and consideration. Hearing her name for the first time, he recognized it—an Eastern Shore name, 'good' as his own.

Lying in the sun, they talked like old friends, not about races and manners and the things that Henry brooded over Choupette, but rather as if they naturally agreed about those things; they talked about what they liked themselves and about what was fun. She showed him a sitting-down, standing-up dive from the high springboard, and he emulated her inexpertly—that was fun. They talked about eating soft-shelled crabs, and she told him how, because of the curious acoustics of the water, one could lie here and be diverted by conversations on the hotel porch. They tried it and heard two ladies over their tea say:

'Now, at the Lido——'

'Now, at Asbury Park——'

'Oh, my dear, he just scratched and scratched all night; he just scratched and scratched——'

'My dear, at Deauville——'

'——scratched and scratched all night.'

After a while the sea got to be that very blue color of four o'clock, and the girl told him how, at nineteen, she had been divorced from a Spaniard who locked her in the hotel suite when he went out at night.

'It was one of those things,' she said lightly. 'But speaking more cheerfully, how's your beautiful wife? And the boys— did they learn to float? Why can't you all dine with me tonight?'

'I'm afraid I won't be able to,' he said, after a moment's hesitation. He must do nothing, however trivial, to furnish Choupette weapons, and with a feeling of disgust, it occurred to him that he was possibly being watched this afternoon. Nevertheless, he was glad of his caution when she unexpectedly arrived at the hotel for dinner that night.

After the boys had gone to bed, they faced each other over coffee on the hotel veranda.

'Will you kindly explain why I'm not entitled to a half share in my own children?' Choupette began. 'It is not like you to be vindictive, Henry.'

It was hard for Henry to explain. He told her again that she could have the children when she wanted them, but that he must exercise entire control over them because of certain old-fashioned convictions—watching her face grow harder, minute by minute, he saw there was no use, and broke off. She made a scornful sound.

'I wanted to give you a chance to be reasonable before Charles arrives.'

Henry sat up. 'Is he coming here this evening?'

'Happily. And I think perhaps your selfishness is going to have a jolt, Henry. You're not dealing with a woman now.'

When Wiese walked out on the porch an hour later, Henry saw that his pale lips were like chalk; there was a deep flush on his forehead and hard confidence in his eyes. He was cleared for action and he wasted no time. 'We've got something to say to each other, suh, and since I've got a motor-boat here, perhaps that'd be the quietest place to say it.'

Henry nodded coolly; five minutes later the three of them were headed out into Hampton Roads on the wide fairway of the moonlight. It was a tranquil evening, and half a mile from shore Wiese cut down the engine to a mild throbbing, so that they seemed to drift without will or direction through the bright water. His voice broke the stillness abruptly:

'Marston, I'm going to talk to you straight from the shoulder. I love Choupette and I'm not apologizing for it. These things have happened before in this world. I guess you understand that. The only difficulty is this matter of the custody of Choupette's children. You seem determined to try and take them away from the mother that bore them and raised them'—Wiese's words became more clearly articulated, as if they came from a wider mouth—'but you left one thing out of your calculations, and that's me. Do

(203)

you happen to realize that at this moment I'm one of the richest men in Virginia?'

'I've heard as much.'

'Well, money is power, Marston. I repeat, suh, money is power.'

'I've heard that too. In fact, you're a bore, Wiese.' Even by the moon Henry could see the crimson deepen on his brow.

'You'll hear it again, suh. Yesterday you took us by surprise and I was unprepared for your brutality to Choupette. But this morning I received a letter from Paris that puts the matter in a new light. It is a statement by a specialist in mental diseases, declaring you to be of unsound mind, and unfit to have the custody of children. The specialist is the one who attended you in your nervous breakdown four years ago.'

Henry laughed incredulously, and looked at Choupette, half expecting her to laugh, too, but she had turned her face away, breathing quickly through parted lips. Suddenly he realised that Wiese was telling the truth—that by some extraordinary bribe he had obtained such a document and fully intended to use it.

For a moment Henry reeled as if from a material blow. He listened to his own voice saying, 'That's the most ridiculous thing I ever heard,' and to Wiese's answer: 'They don't always tell people when they have mental troubles.'

Suddenly Henry wanted to laugh, and the terrible instant when he had wondered if there could be some shred of truth in the allegation passed. He turned to Choupette, but again she avoided his eyes.

'How could you, Choupette?'

'I want my children,' she began, but Wiese broke in quickly:

'If you'd been halfway fair, Marston, we wouldn't have resorted to this step.'

'Are you trying to pretend you arranged this scurvy trick since yesterday afternoon?'

'I believe in being prepared, but if you had been reasonable; in fact, if you will be reasonable, this opinion needn't be used.' His voice became suddenly almost paternal, almost kind: 'Be wise, Marston. On your side there's an obstinate prejudice; on mine there are forty million dollars. Don't fool yourself. Let me repeat, Marston, that money is power. You were abroad so long that perhaps you're inclined to forget that fact. Money made this country, built its great and glorious cities, created its industries, covered it with an iron network of railroads. It's money that harnesses the forces of Nature, creates the machine and makes it go when money says go, and stop when money says stop.'

As though interpreting this as a command, the engine gave forth a sudden hoarse sound and came to rest.

'What is it?' demanded Choupette.

'It's nothing.' Wiese pressed the self-starter with his foot. 'I repeat, Marston, that money——The battery is dry. One minute while I spin the wheel.'

He spun it for the best part of fifteen minutes while the boat meandered about in a placid little circle.

'Choupette, open that drawer behind you and see if there isn't a rocket.'

A touch of panic had crept into her voice when she answered that there was no rocket. Wiese eyed the shore tentatively.

'There's no use in yelling; we must be half a mile out. We'll just have to wait here until someone comes along.'

'We won't wait here.' Henry remarked.

'Why not?'

'We're moving toward the bay. Can't you tell? We're moving out with the tide.'

'That's impossible!' said Choupette sharply.

'Look at those two lights on shore—one passing the other now. Do you see?'

'Do something!' she wailed, and then, in a burst of French: '*Ah, c'est épouvantable! N'est-ce pas qu'il y a quelque chose qu'on peut faire?*'

(205)

The tide was running fast now, and the boat was drifting down the Roads with it toward the sea. The vague blots of two ships passed them, but at a distance, and there was no answer to their hail. Against the western sky a lighthouse blinked, but it was impossible to guess how near to it they would pass.

'It looks as if all our difficulties would be solved for us,' Henry said.

'What difficulties?' Choupette demanded. 'Do you mean there's nothing to be done? Can you sit there and just float away like this?'

'It may be easier on the children, after all.' He winced as Choupette began to sob bitterly, but he said nothing. A ghostly idea was taking shape in his mind.

'Look here, Marston. Can you swim?' demanded Wiese, frowning.

'Yes, but Choupette can't.'

'I can't either—I didn't mean that. If you could swim in and get to a telephone, the coast-guard people would send for us.'

Henry surveyed the dark, receding shore.

'It's too far,' he said.

'You can try!' said Choupette.

Henry shook his head.

'Too risky. Besides, there's an outside chance that we'll be picked up.'

The lighthouse passed them, far to the left and out of earshot. Another one, the last, loomed up half a mile away.

'We might drift to France like that man Gerbault,' Henry remarked. 'But then, of course, we'd be expatriates— and Wiese wouldn't like that, would you, Wiese?'

Wiese, fussing frantically with the engine, looked up.

'See what you can do with this,' he said.

'I don't know anything about mechanics,' Henry answered. 'Besides, this solution of our difficulties grows on me. Just suppose you were dirty dog enough to use that statement

(206)

and got the children because of it—in that case I wouldn't have much impetus to go on living. We're all failures—I as head of my household, Choupette as a wife and a mother, and you, Wiese, as a human being. It's just as well that we go out of life together.'

'This is no time for a speech, Marston.'

'Oh, yes, it's a fine time. How about a little more house-organ oratory about money being power?'

Choupette sat rigid in the bow; Wiese stood over the engine, biting nervously at his lips.

'We're not going to pass that lighthouse very close.' An idea suddenly occurred to him. 'Couldn't you swim to that, Marston?'

'Of course he could!' Choupette cried.

Henry looked at it tentatively.

'I might. But I won't.'

'You've got to!'

Again he flinched at Choupette's weeping; simultaneously he saw the time had come.

'Everything depends on one small point,' he said rapidly. 'Wiese, have you got a fountain pen?'

'Yes. What for?'

'If you'll write and sign about two hundred words at my dictation, I'll swim to the lighthouse and get help. Otherwise, so help me God, we'll drift out to sea! And you better decide in about one minute.'

'Oh, anything!' Choupette broke out frantically. 'Do what he says, Charles; he means it. He always means what he says. Oh, please don't wait!'

'I'll do what you want'—Wiese's voice was shaking— 'only, for God's sake, go on. What is it you want—an agreement about the children? I'll give you my personal word of honor——'

'There's no time for humor,' said Henry savagely. 'Take this piece of paper and write.'

The two pages that Wiese wrote at Henry's dictation

relinquished all lien on the children thence and forever for himself and Choupette. When they had affixed trembling signatures Wiese cried:

'Now go, for God's sake, before it's too late!'

'Just one thing more: The certificate from the doctor.'

'I haven't it here.'

'You lie.'

Wiese took it from his pocket.

'Write across the bottom that you paid so much for it, and sign your name to that.'

A minute later, stripped to his underwear, and with the papers in an oiled-silk tobacco pouch suspended from his neck, Henry dived from the side of the boat and struck out toward the light.

The waters leaped up at him for an instant, but after the first shock it was all warm and friendly, and the small murmur of the waves was an encouragement. It was the longest swim he had ever tried, and he was straight from the city, but the happiness in his heart buoyed him up. Safe now, and free. Each stroke was stronger for knowing that his two sons, sleeping back in the hotel, were safe from what he dreaded. Divorced from her own country, Choupette had picked the things out of American life that pandered best to her own self-indulgence. That, backed by a court decree, she should be permitted to hand on this preposterous moral farrago to his sons was unendurable. He would have lost them forever.

Turning on his back, he saw that already the motorboat was far away, the blinding light was nearer. He was very tired. If one let go—and, in the relaxation from strain, he felt an alarming impulse to let go—one died very quickly and painlessly, and all these problems of hate and bitterness disappeared. But he felt the fate of his sons in the oiled-silk pouch about his neck, and with a convulsive effort he turned over again and concentrated all his energies on his goal.

Twenty minutes later he stood shivering and dripping in

the signal room while it was broadcast out to the coast patrol that a launch was drifting in the bay.

'There's not much danger without a storm,' the keeper said. 'By now they've probably struck a cross current from the river and drifted into Peyton Harbor.'

'Yes,' said Henry, who had come to this coast for three summers. 'I knew that too.'

IV

In October, Henry left his sons in school and embarked on the Majestic for Europe. He had come home as to a generous mother and had been profusely given more than he asked—money, release from an intolerable situation, and the fresh strength to fight for his own. Watching the fading city, the fading shore, from the deck of the Majestic, he had a sense of overwhelming gratitude and of gladness that America was there, that under the ugly débris of industry the rich land still pushed up, incorrigibly lavish and fertile, and that in the heart of the leaderless people the old generosities and devotions fought on, breaking out sometimes in fanaticism and excess, but indomitable and undefeated. There was a lost generation in the saddle at the moment, but it seemed to him that the men coming on, the men of the war, were better; and all his old feeling that America was a bizarre accident, a sort of historical sport, had gone forever. The best of America was the best of the world.

Going down to the purser's office, he waited until a fellow passenger was through at the window. When she turned, they both started, and he saw it was the girl.

'Oh, hello!' she cried. 'I'm glad you're going! I was just asking when the pool opened. The great thing about this ship is that you can always get a swim.'

'Why do you like to swim?' he demanded.

'You always ask me that.' She laughed.

'Perhaps you'd tell me if we had dinner together tonight.'

But when, in a moment, he left her he knew that she could never tell him—she or another. France was a land, England was a people, but America, having about it still that quality of the idea, was harder to utter—it was the graves at Shiloh and the tired, drawn, nervous faces of its great men, and the country boys dying in the Argonne for a phrase that was empty before their bodies withered. It was a willingness of the heart.

ZELDA

The Original Follies Girl

(College Humor,

July 1929*)

The thing that made you first notice Gay was that manner she had, as though she was masquerading as herself. All her clothes and jewelry were so good that she wore them 'on the surface,' as superficially as a Christmas tree supports its ornaments. She could do that because she, too, was awfully good quality and had nothing to conceal except her past. That is to say, she had unquestionably the best figure in New York, otherwise she'd never have made all that money for just standing on the stage lending an air of importance to two yards of green tulle. And her hair was that blond color that's no color at all but a reflector of light, so that she seldom bothered to have it waved or 'done.'

The first time I saw her she was eating raspberries and cream in the Japanese Garden at the Ritz. There was a cool sound on the air from the tiny fountain and the clink of jeweled bracelets, and the vaporous hush of mid-summer had settled over the voices. I thought how appropriate she was—so airy, as if she had a long time ago dismissed herself as something decorative and amusing, and not to be confused with the vital elements of American life.

Her eyes were far apart and small. All of her was small, though she wasn't in the least restricted or economized upon, rather, polished away. She was quite tall, and all of her fitted together with delightful precision, like the seeds

* Published as by 'F. Scott and Zelda Fitzgerald', but written by Zelda.

of a pomegranate. I suppose that *objet d'art* quality was what drew about her a long string of men-about-town.

But she had another quality which you couldn't help feeling would betray her sooner or later. It was the quality that made her like intellectual men, though I'm sure that she never read a book through and preferred beer to all other drinks; a quality that made her love 'dives' and learn French and waver back and forth between Theosophy and Catholicism.

She wasn't at all the tabloid sort of person. From the first, the men who liked her were very distinguished. She had learned discretion at the start, almost as if it were a thing she wanted for herself, to use so as to be freer therewith—the aristocratic viewpoint.

And then, though undeniably an adventuress of a quiet order, she was financially safe, which relieved her from the taint of hysteria that goes so often with her kind of life. Of course she hadn't always had enough to live on, but in the early years, before producers found out that she made the rest of the chorus look like bologna sausages, there had been a husband with a gift of fantasy that cost him five thousand dollars a year for the rest of her life. That left Gay free to pay her respects to the primrose path, undoubting.

Those first years she came quite near destroying her value. She went to all the parties recorded in the Sunday supplement, and the press photographs of her were so startling that the mysterious notoriety about her was almost turned into vulgarity. But she learned to like absinthe cocktails and to want a serious stage career, which turned her towards successful people and saved her from the usual marriage-to-pugilist end.

She was very kaleidoscopic. There were times when she'd just sit and drink and drink, ending the evening with a heavy British accent, and there were other times when she'd drink nothing but would eat great trays of asparagus hollandaise and swear she was going to enter a convent. Once, when she seemed particularly serious about taking the veil, I asked her why and she said: 'Because I've never done *that*.'

This was in the stage of her career when she lived in a silver apartment with mulberry carpets and lots of billowing old-blue taffeta, so you see how bored she must have been with her Louis XVI tea service and her grand piano, the huge silver vase that must have calla lilies in it and the white bear skin rug.

Gay was swamped in a flood of interior decorators' pastel restraints. She knew she didn't like the apartment, but the vanity of taking her friends there made her stick for quite a while. It had so obviously cost a lot.

In the vestibule the only French telephone in New York modestly hid itself. You worked the elevator yourself, which in Gay's circle was very *recherché* and showed a fine disdain for American commercialism. She must have passed eternities just waiting in all this carefully faded finery, though she kept an engagement book and always had to look all through the Wednesdays and Sundays when you asked her to tea. There was a purple address book on the marble mantel shelf, chock full of phone numbers from Naples to Nantucket; *couturières* and ex-patriates, millionaires and hair dressers, the restaurants in Rome and the summer homes of producers. It was her attempt at system and gave her a sense of the solidity of organized life. Once you were inscribed in that book you were Gay's friend and theoretically available for bridge or ocean crossings, or any unforeseen contingency such as making the extra man for the Fourth of July in Timbuctoo.

But in spite of all the names and numbers, she lived mostly alone, and to soften the harsh loneliness she soon began to live in a great many places at once. She spent a year on the London stage, with a suite in Paris and innumerable trips to New York, carrying about with her an air of urgency and mystery that made her very elusive.

Gay *en route* meant the arrival of countless band-boxes, mountains of tissue paper, telephone calls in a rapid foreign tongue, people dropping in who didn't know she was going and whom she hadn't seen for years, and always newspaper reporters because they liked Gay and made up important sounding little stories about her. The pictures that went above these anecdotes nowadays were heads, well groomed, unpretentious heads, and the 'Miss' was always printed in front of her name.

In Paris she lived in a blue velvet trunk. Lost in the intricate fragility of France's imitation of its lost grandeur, there was a cold looking bath hiding in the corner of a banquet sized room, that all Gay's bottles and atomizers and bright dressing gowns couldn't make informal. Next to that there was a gray and gilt sitting room which she always kept full of South Americans. The marble top tables were covered with champagne cocktails and big paper like magenta roses with stems like pipes.

In her bedroom there was a picture of her sister's child, a little girl with Gay's wide eyes, lost in the square of a huge red leather frame.

She found the hotel apartment much less oppressive than the silver walls in New York, because it did not belong to her and she could wipe cold cream on the towels and rub her shoes with the bath mat.

At this time she was making an awful struggle to hang onto something that had never crystallized for her—it was the past. She wanted to get her hands on something tangible, to be able to say, 'That is real, that is part of my experience, that goes into this or that category, this that happened to me is part of my memories.' She could not correlate the events that had made up her life, so now when she was beginning to feel time passing she felt as though she had just been born; born without a family, without a friendly house about her, without any scheme to settle into or to rebel against. The isolation of each day made her incapable of feeling surprise and caused her to be wonderfully tolerant, which is another way of saying that she was sick with spiritual boredom.

The blue velvet trunk became so plastered with hotel labels that it had to be revarnished. Then Gay filled it again with three thousand dollars' worth of sunburn georgette crêpe cobwebs and a statue that she went to Florence for, and set out for Biarritz. She was jaunty and courageous, and whenever the corners of life got stuffed up with laundry lists and stale cigarettes, she would be off for a new place with an ever changing, starchy maid whom she pretended had been with her for years.

She felt that people should be used to their surroundings, and should like old things. The intense obligation she felt of being appreciative was a thing she had learned by finding out, afterwards, how many of the things she hadn't instinctively liked were of recognized merit.

Gay came back from Biarritz that year looking very pale. She was one of the few people who could have managed so many long hours on a beach and emerge positively bleached. It was part of a sadistic interpretation of Anglo Saxon self-discipline that she should always be Hawaïan brown in winter and as white as the fox on the collars of her transparent coats, in summer.

If she had lived longer, she would have owned innumerable lace parasols, long beige gloves, floppy hats and a perroquet. Gay liked style, fluttering, feminine style, better than anything she knew, and she never even once suspected that she had it because she dealt so completely in fundamentals—how many children you'd had or how many millions you'd made, how many rôles you'd acted or the number of lions you'd tamed.

All these wanderings about took time, and Gay was being forgotten in New York like all people are who are not constantly being casually run into. There were other girls from fresher choruses, with wide clear eyes and free boyish laughs, and you heard less and less about Gay. If you asked for news of her, a blank look or a look of hesitancy would cross the face opposite you as if its owner didn't know whether he should have news of Gay or not, since her present status was undetermined. People said she was older than she was, when they talked about her—men, mostly, who were anxious that she should belong to a finished past.

She couldn't possibly be the ages they said, because I saw her not long ago under the trees in the Champs-Elysées. She looked like a daffodil. She was taking a yellow linen sports thing for an airing and she reeked of a lemony perfume and bacardi cocktails. She wouldn't come to tea with me because her favorite barber had been ill for a long time and Gay was taking him the money for a month in the country.

Before I had half finished looking at all the little tailored bows that made the yellow thing just right for Gay, she was pressed up the broad avenue by the mist from the fountains and the glitter of bright flowers in the shadow, the curling blue haze and the smell of excitement that make a Paris summer dusk. I thought she seemed pale and fragile, but Gay was always on some sort of an ascetic diet to keep her beautiful figure. These long régimes would bore her so that afterwards she'd go on a terrific spree and have to spend two weeks at a rest cure. She wore herself out with the struggle between her desire for physical perfection and her desire to use it.

The next news of Gay was a small bit on the bottom of the front page. It was an obituary notice from Paris. The papers were sketchy and said pneumonia. Later, I saw an old friend of hers who had been with her just before she died, and she told me that Gay had wanted the baby. Well, the child lived. And Gay still lives, too—in all the restless souls who follow the season in its fashionable pilgrimage, who look for the lost spell of brown backs and summer beaches in musty cathedrals, who seek the necessity for solidity and accomplishment but never quite believe in it, in all of those who make the Ritz what it is, and ocean travel an informal affair of dinner clothes and diamond bracelets.

She was very courageous—braver than the things that happened to her, always—and since courage has a way of pushing itself out, I suppose that's why she wanted a child. But it must have been awful, dying alone under the gilt curlicues of a Paris hotel, no matter how expensive the gilt, nor how used to them she was.

Gay was too good a companion and too pretty to go dying like that for a romanticism that she was always half afraid would slip away from her.

ZELDA

Southern Girl

(College Humor,
October 1929*)

The solid South stretches away for miles from Jeffersonville, long clay roads climbing slow hills covered with straggling pines, broad, blank cotton fields, isolated cabins in patches of sand, and far off in the distance the blue promise of hills. The town is lost beside a wide brown swirling river which cuts swiftly under its high red banks on either side. Deep trees overhang the brown foam at the edges, and shadows lie long and sleepily under the Spanish moss where darting hard shelled insects fall down from the branches. Brown mud oozes between the cobblestones of the ponderous width of Jackson Street where it curls down to the riverside, lined with decaying wharves from the time when there was much shipping on the river.

Every springtime the brown water, with foam and twirling twigs and bits of feather, seeps slowly up the street until finally it reaches the gutters in front of the biggest hotel in Jeffersonville; then the inhabitants know that all the red clay bottoms for miles around are under water.

Wistaria meets over the warm asphalt in summer, and the young people swim in the luke warm creeks. The drug stores are bright at night with the organdie balloons of girls' dresses under the big electric fans. Automobiles stand along the curbs in front of open frame houses at dusk, and sounds of supper being prepared drift through the soft splotches of

* Published as by 'F. Scott and Zelda Fitzgerald', but written by Zelda.

(218)

darkness to the young world that moves every evening out of doors. Telephones ring, and the lacy blackness under the trees disgorges young girls in white and pink, leaping over the squares of warm light toward the tinkling sound with an expectancy that people have only in places where any event is a pleasant one.

Nothing seems ever to happen in Jeffersonville; the days pass, lazily gossiping in the warm sun. A lynching, an election, a wedding, catastrophes and business booms all take on the same value, rounded, complete, dusted by the lush softness of the air in a climate too hot for any but sporadic effort, too beneficent for any but the most desultory competition.

In my youth, number Twenty State Street had a pincushion of grass pushing up on either side of the straight brick path, and two cracked concrete steps leading to the blue and white octagonal paving blocks that formed the side-walk. The roots of big water elms cracked the blocks, and we children skating home from school fell over the crevices. The house was an apologetic one for sheltering big families that had grown faster than the family income in that way obligations have of increasing their proportions more rapidly than the hopes and abilities that begot them.

Number Twenty was where Harriet and a fragile mother and Harriet's younger sister lived in one room and a latticed back porch. The rest of the house, all the three cornered bed-rooms and back hallways and waste space under the stairs, was rented. It was, in fact, a boarding-house of a very friendly Sunday dinner sort, and as we grew up and Harriet's mother softly became an invalid, it grew to be Harriet's responsibility. If the boarders weren't friendly when they came, they soon fell into the note of shy bravado about the long table, and they never seemed able to dispense with it even after they realized how uncomfortable they were, what with Harriet's squeezing them in between her beaux and her half day job teaching school. The young men waiting to be married and old couples living on one railroad bond, and all the cheerful lot who came in the evening to sit about the stove in the parlor, seemed to find an ease and relaxation in Harriet's jovial irony and in the big horse laugh she gave any pretentiousness.

Her manner with the old was free and impeccable. To the rest, she gave the right to all the self deceptions they found necessary for their peace of mind, so long as they granted her that sudden, blatant laugh that began with a sort of ticklish chuckling and ended with a series of in-drawn screeches bordering on hysteria. The roots of it lay deep in fatigue and strain, and if it didn't spare anyone's nerves, well, ever since Harriet walked for the last time with the rest of us between the blind eyed Venus and plaster Minerva that were just inside the high school door, she had never spared her own.

People early wondered why she didn't go in for something more satisfactory and spectacular than teaching school and supervising a boarding-house. It seemed to us such a waste of her energy and ability. The reason was probably that she was incapable of giving up anything; of relinquishing the smallest part of a conception or a phase of her life until she felt that it had been completed. She left school with all sorts of convictions about sticking to things until the ultimate desired effect was produced, and it kept her hoeing a hard row, sticking by the hopeless patch-work of the various responsibilities that were hers instead of trying to turn them into one bigger unit of a job.

Every place has its hours: there's Rome in the glassy sun of a winter noon and Paris under the blue gauze of spring twilight, and there's the red sun flowing through the chasms of a New York dawn. So in Jeffersonville there existed then, and I suppose now, a time and quality that appertains to nowhere else. It began about half past six on an early summer night, with the flicker and splutter of the corner street lights going on, and it lasted until the great incandescent globes were black inside with moths and beetles and the children were called in to bed from the dusty streets.

The leaves of the elms stenciled black friezes over the side-walks, and men in shirt sleeves threw arcs of warm rubber smelling water onto the moon-vines and Bermuda grass until the air was fresher with a baked, grassy scent, and the ladies behind the thick flowering vines had a moment's respite from their fanning. The town waited for the nine o'clock breeze in a floating stillness so complete that you could hear the grinding wheels of a trolley-car climbing a hill six blocks away. Inside, girls in preparation for the evening dance struggled between the difficulties of the spasmodic sweep of an electric fan and the dripping heat.

That was how it happened that one night during the war, when Harriet was still only nineteen and at the beginning of her effort, the door-bell rang and she answered it in a pair of blue bloomers and a huge bath towel. The door-bell before nine could only mean a telegram or something that could be reached around for. She swung the door back in front of her as a screen, and there stood Dan Stone, all the high spots of him lighted up and shining with the light from the hall. He was a big, square soldier, fine legs like a Greek athlete, and a handsome Ohio face with a chin and a big arena of teeth.

He had behind him a girl who, even in the dark, Harriet knew was not Southern. Her black hair was too sleek to have known the muddy water of summer creeks, and her dark clothes were cut with a precision and directness which could not have been interrupted by frequent half hour respites from the heat. Harriet was swept with an exultant embarrassment that she always felt in a situation promising adventure. She laughed and he laughed, and the gray eyes back of his shoulder started a little to hear so much instantaneous comradeship bouncing down the worn veranda.

He explained about himself to Harriet, about how he was

engaged to the cloudless eyes in the faultless *tailleur*, and how the hotel lobbies filled with fan draped flags and khaki hats and Red Cross posters were not the place to leave his fiancée. His mother had intended coming South, but she was ill. The regiment was leaving any time now, so couldn't Harriet's mother find a place for Louise among the hot biscuits and iced tea and fresh vegetables.

So Louise and Harriet, living in the same house, became friends for three weeks—which is a long time in war time— and Harriet initiated Louise into our dawdling late yellow afternoons of Jeffersonville; into the automobile rides past dusty mock-orange hedges, the beveled fruit rotting beneath; into the sweet tartness of Coca-Cola cooling in wooden tubs beside a country store; into the savory vapors of Mexican hot dog stands, and into all the mysteries of a town that, to escape the heat, sleeps nine months a year under its banks of four petal roses.

We knew all about each other in Jeffersonville: how each other swam and danced and what time our parents wanted us to be home at night, and what each one of us liked to eat and drink and talk about, so that we all were one against the taller, broader, older youth in uniform which had begun from boredom to invade the ice-cream parlors and the country-club dances, and to change into something serious the casualness of an intimate social world founded on the fact that people like filling the same hours with the same things. We swam at five o'clock because the glare of the sun on the water was too hot to permit swimming before that, but with the advent of a colder-climate-organization that five o'clock swim and the six o'clock soda became self-conscious rituals that moved along more robustly than the long legged, affable young men of Jeffersonville could follow with ease.

There weren't enough girls to go around. Girls too tall or too prim for the taste of Jeffersonville were dragged from their spinsterly pursuits to dance with the soldiers and make them feel less lonely through the summer nights. You can imagine how the popular ones fared! Harriet's sagging veranda was almost completely in uniform. It looked like a recruiting station.

During the weeks that Louise spent in the vine-clad smouldering depths of the South, Dan was always there at Harriet's, lounging over the front banisters with the loose longness of a rubber man, or standing under the stairs, his face in a beam, while he waited for the girls to materialize out of the dust of powder and squeaks and slamming of doors that always began when they heard him in the hall below. He came every day in the fire-fly hush before supper, and he stayed until the last trolley rolled its cargo of summer light down the dim streets and out to camp.

At first, he and Louise fought shy of the lazy groups of us banging the screen door and laughing and shouting plans back and forth. They would have dinner in town under big fans like airplane propellers, waiting for the steaming corn on the cob to cool and the ice-cream to melt, unable to eat in the lush, fertile heat. Gradually, they became part of the restless inertia of Harriet's porch. Dan liked it, and little by little Louise of the indigo hair and aquamarine eyes was left lost and baffled in the horsey smell of men in khaki and the heavy fragrance of white flowers in the semi-tropics. From soft shaded corners, the great rolling, enveloping laugh of Dan swept out, coming closer all the time, the way thunder seems to come nearer as you hear it passing over; and then out of the same lacy, geometric dusk, the audacious friendliness of Harriet's kidding horse laugh.

They were always together, and for the last few days before Louise left, a sort of desperation hung about the trio. It seemed as if Dan was driven by some inner necessity for honesty to wound and hurt Louise in Harriet's presence. Not that he was cross or ungracious or even impolite, but he simply unchained a robustness that he knew would terrify her, a quality that she thought of as masculine and frightening and that he though of as particular to himself.

They couldn't seem to agree even about why they were not happy together any more.

At last one hot five o'clock, he hurried Louise over the pulpy boards of the station platform and into a long sleek train with a special name like a race horse. While he waited for the train to pull out, they sat opposite each other on the green, prickly, cindery seats, and broke their engagement. There must have been some protecting quality about the Northern solidity of the steel and screens and humming fans that gave Louise the confidence and courage to face the fact that Dan was breaking their engagement. And he found something in the cart of dripping ice beside the steaming train, in the lounging, muddy river beside the tracks, in the low brick station with its long shed over the freight cars and drowsy porters, to keep him from minding that he was changing her life at a word into something quite different from how she had thought of it for two years. When the in-drawn siren call of ''Board' swept along from the back of the long train, Dan swung down the steps with no remorse.

He was only ten minutes behind his usual time of arriving at Harriet's, which meant to him simply that he had lost his seat in the creaking swing and that she was ten minutes deeper in the freshness of rose southern organdie when they swung off together into the light and dark of the ambling street. They were in love.

Months afterwards when the war got itself over in one way or another, and after Dan had been to the port of embarkation and tasted New York on the eve of a departure that never came off, and after Harriet had had a dozen other beaux and a hundred other heartaches, he wrote for her to come to Ohio to visit his mother.

They had been engaged so long now, had written so many letters to each other from so far away, that their relationship had become a background for their lives rather than a reality, but Harriet decided to make the trip, searching vaguely to recreate those moments of mutual discovery that she and

Dan had shared. From Jeffersonville, deserted in August, rows of newspapers yellowing in the heat before closed doorways, neglected lawns parching under the burning sun, shut window-panes ricocheting the sun's rays onto the already burning pavements, Harriet set out for the North to recapture the balm and beauty of war nights under an Alabama moon. In Ohio she sought the hoarse croaking of frogs in the cypress swamps, the glint of moonlight on black scummy water, the smell of pine rolling up from lone cabin chimneys and, above all, the sveltness of youth in leather and uniform —young, strange foreign soldiers, conquerors of her most enthusiastic years.

Dan, she wrote home, met her in the huge glass and tile station. The nearest thing like it that Harriet had ever seen was an operating room, and immediately a sense of alarm arose out of the back of her neck and undermined the easy delight with which she had been looking forward to seeing him. The blue white rays from the station skylight pelted mercilessly on rouge more convincing in the soft, fuzzy light of the South, and all his politeness could scarcely keep out of his eyes the dubious quality that men feel when they find themselves with women from a different financial plane than themselves. In the quiet beige heaviness, avenues lined with small clipped trees and gleaming white façades slid past until at last he helped her out in front of a gleaming glass and grilled door. Inside his mother waited.

Dan's mother was as concise and formal and as black and white as a printed page, and Harriet, who was used to the old being tired and worn, fell into a panic. She lost her attention amongst the myriad silver picture frames and the bright backs of books that lined the walls, and her eyes kept hiding in corners behind the baskets of flowers or under the bearskin rug. It was an inauspicious beginning. She wanted to run, and in all the days she spent in the big red brick house, she never quite conquered the feeling that she, on confronting its mistress, might jump suddenly out of the window.

The summer nights passed in cabarets or circling about between rows of geraniums down the broad gravel drives of country-clubs. People were away and there weren't many parties, so they even sought Louise, for old time's sake, to complete a foursome.

They drove sometimes over the trim tar roads to an amusement park. Harriet liked that best of all because there, floating over the smell of the hot butter from the popcorn, the acrid smoke from the shooting gallery and the tart brassness of the merry-go-round, their two laughs sounded together on the night air like an echo from the war. But those moments were rare.

Louise and Dan rediscovered a common taste for the wicker chairs and long frosted glasses of club verandahs. Gradually they lapsed together into a silent, fashionable sentimentality amidst the clatter of golf clubs and automobile horns and the dim chink of poker chips drifting from the bar.

To Harriet it all seemed like an illustration, an advertisement that reads under the bottom, 'In Palm Beach they all smoke Melliflors.' This one would read, 'In Ohio we have more and better of the best young people.' She was surprised at the robustness of her own laugh and distressed by the freeness of her Southern manner. She felt foreign to herself in finding herself so foreign to the others. She, never having been rich and 'marriageable,' had never learned the protective formalities and reserves of expensive society. She was a lonely appendage to these white flannel afternoons.

With a sense of relief, she entered into the last week of her visit. Louise was constantly about the house now, her quiet voice muffled on the thick carpeted stairs or languidly discussing with Dan's mother leagues and organizations and societies for the prevention of things. She belonged in that quiet house. The candlelight singing in the globular sides of silver bowls, the gleam of a gold plate under the strawberries, the feel of water heavier than the glass that contained it, called out no overpowering confusion, no overwhelmed inadequacy in her calm twilight eyes.

Harriet sensed all that, and so it was that she was less hurt and surprised than Dan had supposed she would be when he told her that he wanted to marry Louise. All she wanted at that moment were the bare floors of Jeffersonville, the succulence of a Sunday baked ham, the familiar clatter of green-rimmed dishes on the boarding-house table.

When she got home, she told us all about the clubs and motor cars and how people dressed in the North, and she said simply that she and Dan had decided not to marry. She didn't feel that she could leave her mother.

I left Jeffersonville about then, but I can imagine how the winter came and the groups about the parlor at Harriet's grew bigger and perhaps younger. At holiday time there were dozens of college boys, joking and shooting dice and teasing the girls, so that if Harriet wanted to be alone she had to leave the house. At the Saturday night dances she often passed from one pair of arms to another without dancing a step. Everybody was fond of her, of her tireless good humor and impersonal intimacies.

Old people said they didn't see how she found the courage to work all day and dance all night and look after the boarding house in odd moments, and always to be laughing and happy. She saved the money she earned, a little at a time, and twice every year she went to some big city. One summer she visited me in New York. She learned a vague species of French and bought all the fashionable magazines. She was determined to find for herself a bigger sophistication than Jeffersonville had to offer.

Five more summers and winters steamed off the slow river and passed like a gentle mist over the salvia beds and cherokee hedges and ribbon-grass of the town, and now the children she had drawn paper dolls for crowded the country-club dances, and most of her contemporaries had kids of their own.

From time to time I went home and found the girls she grew up with vaguely pitying her about their bridge tables and over their bassinets, speculating about why she had not married this man or that, and wondering why she preferred long chalky hours in a primary school and the gentility of aged boarders' complaints to the gilded radiators and flowered chintz of a suburban bungalow.

People went away and came back; friends of hers who had married or boys she had known in the army said she hadn't changed a bit. The people she saw now formed an expensive white bungalow ring about the city, and they all owned silver cocktail glasses and dined by candlelight and liked the taste of preserved caviar. They gave teas and dinners and parties late at night for strangers in Jeffersonville who had arrived with cards to the club or letters of introduction, or who had come to give a concert or a lecture.

Charles was one of the ones who came with a letter. He was an architect. Jeffersonville is as famous for its old stairways and fan lights over its doorways as it is for its hospitality. Harriet met him in an odd sort of way. He just came bounding in one night, the light from the hall lighting up his square shoulders and an arena of big white teeth. He was tall and he laughed outrageously at her because she was all wrapped up in a bath towel with a few fluttery things underneath. She hadn't known, naturally, that he would bounce in so un-expectedly, demanding a room. They laughed together, and evidently she felt the fear of losing interest in life scurry away down the worn verandah, worsted by the heartiness of two ringing battle laughs.

They were seen about together so constantly that nobody was much surprised when they ran away and got married. You see, he lived in Ohio, and he didn't want to wait while a lot of elaborate preparations were made. That happened about two years ago, and the news is that they are perfectly happy —as she always showed herself and so deserved to be. They live behind an expensive grilled door with his mother, a black taffeta widow who is very rich and formidable, and Harriet seems to spend a great deal of time working for leagues and societies of all sorts.

Their life is full of candlelight and gleaming bright things. And, of course, she has the baby who, from his pictures, is big and square even for his age. She called him Dan 'because,' she wrote me, 'it's the only name that really suits him.'

ZELDA

The Girl the Prince Liked

(College Humor,
February 1930*)

Helena always said that all she had from her father was the
big clock that stood in the hall, engraved with a touching
testimonial from his employees, but she forgot the eight
million dollars and the driving, restless ambition that had led
him to accumulate his money so relentlessly. She had also
from him a pair of mystic, deep-set eyes and an unbroken,
round hair line and a deep, straight crease above her lips
when she laughed. These showed very plainly in her wedding
photographs, when she was still completely under his living
influence.

When I first knew her she was already twenty-seven, and
the corners and ridges of a successful personality had been
modulated and polished by a Parisian finishing school,
seven years in *Town Topics*, two children and an enormous
collection of second prizes from golf tournaments. Heaven
knows what the force of her must have been in its aboriginal
state! She once showed me lots of grayish brown photographs of a huge frame house whose ground plan must have
looked like a roller coaster, so much was it of the billowing
nineties. Here she had spent a dynamic, motherless childhood. It was easy to imagine her skipping rope on the circling verandas, while the summer rain trickled down the tin
gutters onto the deep hydrangea beds. She must have been
a small, slight little girl full of sudden flashing indications

* Published as by 'F. Scott and Zelda Fitzgerald', but written by
Zelda.

(230)

of a firm and constant energy, because she was still like that years after when I got to know her.

At first it was disconcerting because her vitality did not come and go like most people's, but simply changed from one sort to another. From a vibrant excitement that she could convey when she wanted to be disturbing, it would quiet down into a smouldering yellow light back of her light eyelashes, back of her yellow-brown eyes crouching there independent of Helena, watching you, always taking note of everything.

That was one of the ways she established social dominance over people: she would sit and watch until she frightened them, and then suddenly be friendly and free and just as charming as she had been formidable.

The summer that I knew her best, she was already in the direct line of succession to the social throne of the big wind-swept Middle Western city where she had lived since her husband had taken her there after their wedding. It was not such an easy place to subjugate; the people there were terribly rich and awfully proud of their fine possessions. Everybody who counted had everything; their houses were full of sea green bowls of fragile things that grew in their own conservatories, and their walls were lit with those expensive globules of light that only millionaires' architects seem able to invent. There were marble bathrooms and painted ones whose pictures were in *Town and Country*, and there were dozens of houses with rooms as long and still and thick as a very fashionable hotel lobby. The cream brick façades and the concrete drives, punctuated with heavy powerful roadsters, forged a chain about the rendezvous of the people of importance, whom Helena wore like a string of glass beads. The others loved that nonchalance of hers.

The winter I was there, they liked going to dinner at her house. It was always a sort of boyish affair where Helena sat half holding her breath in the hope that perhaps the menu would be different from what she had ordered, suppressing in herself a feeling of guilt that she had not given her afternoon to improving it, impatient with the Nordic progress of the Swedish maids about the table, pleased and jocular after the first mishap which released her of feeling that somehow, in spite of her carelessness, the meal might achieve perfection, as a race that's run releases the rambler's tension.

Helena's personality was so strong that the most insensitive of her guests could never relax if she was nervous; they must all await the figurative plate-breaking. That excitement in her did not come from shyness. I've seen her walk into a Christmas cotillion and butlers and footmen fall about her at the door like a flurry of early snow, and I've asked myself what it was that gave her so much instantaneous authority, because even on the most formal occasions of the winter she never looked any way except like a very young person with very clean ears.

She went through her winter time *beaux* with the same air of impassibility and detachment. On the list of her admirers there were sober, efficient young men who organized balls, and middle aged men with fine figures and a devoted reticence, and tall, trim men from New Orleans, and two or three admirable pianists, and an almost magnificent tenor. She had around her, too, lots of young boys still in college—very attractive, straight young athletes, mostly, who were afraid of the difficulties that lay in sentimental relations with girls their own age. In winter she kidded these young ones mercilessly and asked them one at a time to the parties she gave and sometimes went to their sleigh rides, all bundled up in tawny, fluffy wool, with her feet in doeskin moccasins. In summer she kissed them—on flag walks beside fresh water lakes; in the webbed moonlight spun into fragile patterns by pine needles, beside a cool wide river; on long asphalt roads beaten by the sun till the tar and rubber melted and the automobile wheels whirred like telephone wires as they rode along.

Helena was far too personal to like dancing, and often from the screened balcony of the Yacht Club during the Saturday night celebration, I've watched her strolling along the jetty, with a pair of flannel trousers; with a few truncated gestures, changing a likely candidate for the diplomatic corps into a hopeless *gigolo* who would speak his lines for life like a person talking a jazz ballad. Inconstant, consequent Helena! The others fared just as badly.

It was hard to find and keep chauffeurs in our state at that time (I think they were all in Congress), so Helena used to borrow the great, rolling, padded cells of the portentous men of affairs, who kept the vases inside these limousines full of orchids for her. Her own garage had a place for three cars and there was one that was always broken, but she liked using other people's things, not for what she got out of them but for the sense of power it gave her to have somebody doing things for her. She was like a beautiful general on a tour of inspection when she picked the finest car she could for paying her Sunday calls—sipping the egg-nog in one place, nibbling the cinnamon toast in another, her gray fur coat trailing behind her like a Greek toga, everything gray but her black suede slippers and herself. She was rose-gold.

All through the winter she went about talking of how dull life was and how she wanted to go away. People listened to her with the same rapt hope of illumination with which unaccustomed sinners listen to the *Lord's Prayer*.

When summer came, all the people who liked summer time moved out to the huge, clear lake not far from town, and lived there in long, flat cottages surrounded with dank shrubbery and pine trees, and so covered by screened verandas that they made you think of small pieces of cheese under large meat-safes. All the people came who liked to play golf or sail on the lake, or who had children to shelter from the heat. All the young people came whose parents had given them for wedding presents white bungalows hid

(233)

in the green—and all the old people who liked the flapping sound of the water at the end of their hollyhock walks. All the bachelors who liked living over the cheerful clatter of plates and clinking locker doors in the Yacht Club basement came, and a great many handsome, sun-dried women of forty or fifty with big families and smart crisp linen costumes that stuck to the seats of their roadsters when they went to meet their husbands escaping from town in the five o'clock heat.

With all those people, you see how it was that there were always so many parties during the summer time. Helena never tried much to be a good hostess; she was content always to be the perfect guest and liked saving her energies for being attractive. An important part of her line was kidding things about her and that was easier when she wasn't at home; in her own house a great chorus of 'Oh, no's' arose when she put on that very surprised look and made some horrid remark about the dinner. Sympathetic protestations slowed her up; she liked better to be somewhere else and, saying things in that explosive way of hers, to start giggles and whispers scurrying about the long lace tablecloths.

I remember one summer when Helena had a green dress with patches sewed all over it, in which she used to play golf. When she stood on the first tee to drive off over the embankment, she gave the effect of clean laundry in a March wind, there was so little of her and so much of crispness silhouetted against the Queen's Checker Board of the golf course. Her hard gold hair did not escape into the sunshine but lay close to her head like a protective helmet. That and her tanned skin and a 'stripped for action' quality she had made me think of a pine wood, when I saw her blowing in and out of bunkers, up and down the long grass aisles.

It was the same summer of the big regatta on the lake. Canadians in blue blazers and Americans from all around the Great Lakes and from all over the West came with their fast, graceful boats and sun-beaten faces, and Helena captivated

(234)

them all. She seemed awfully happy, running about in her big station wagon, supervising the seating of people for dinners, choosing between orchestras for dances and pretending she would have nothing to do with the arrangements.

I think that was the last summer that she got any real pleasure out of doing what she liked with us all, because towards autumn when the deep woods began to smell of Indian camp-fires from the past, and goldenrod lined the dusty roads, she was less and less with us. She started riding again and became awfully serious about golf. Her parties weren't the same either; at some of them there were even people quite obviously tight. Helena usually kidded those propensities out of her guests, forcing them to behave to their best advantage, but now she didn't seem to care.

By the time the tiny purple asters baked in the yellow autumn sun, she was so definitely bored that night after night she didn't go out at all, leaving the dregs of the summer moon to a disbanding crowd—a crowd becoming every day less harmonious, a crowd without a leader, breaking up into small groups, drifting with their individual inclinations now that Helena had lost her former interest in being our center.

When everybody moved back to town, Helena bought a new house, a huge stone place with a fountain in the conservatory and a series of gloomy velvet rooms, all with official titles: the Music Room, the Library, the Study—and there was a stairway that should have been in an Embassy. She said she meant to do it over, but I think it got to seem a sort of protection from the intimacies of a town where in every familiar face you saw, you could trace the family likeness. What she did over was her list of friends. The charades that rose against the heavy paneling of the dining-room took on a suggestion of obscenity in the expensive candle-shadows, and Helena's parties gave off that aroma of danger that only people already in the age of security can afford.

Handsome men who spent their mornings telephoning

fortunes to New York and San Francisco, spent their evenings in defiant supplication of chance, nature and God to place in the pearls of their friends' wives just one disastrous gleam. They were all too used to each other to furnish much mutual excitement, so it was easy for Helena, with her affrontal gallantry of a boy of thirteen and her uncomplaining husband, to become indispensable to that roster of owners of railroads and banks and nation wide trademarks that made up the older set in search of pleasure.

After Christmas, when the snow wears gray and glassy and the cold is so severe that even the biggest houses get full of week old steam heat, she and her family and her dogs and her maid and chauffeur, and the children's maid and nurse, and the valet that she thought her husband should have, all set out for Florida. All that retinue must have given the press photographers the same impression that it gave us, of a young prince and playmates traveling, because every Sunday, for the two months she was away, there were brown pictures of them in all the papers big enough to boast a rotogravure section.

Of course all of us were jealous, and we said how silly and affected it was of Helena suddenly to become so doggy. The real affectation had been when she ran about the lake pretending she was not as rich and powerful as infinite charm and inexhaustible funds could make her.

So Florida was a series of successes. There were two Knickerbocker names, and a cruise on a world famous yacht that became public property, and I don't know what private triumphs. It was natural that she should find us dull when she came back to the dripping, crunching slush of our late spring, and that she should turn her eyes toward theaters more worthy of her talents.

Chicago took her just about two weeks, I should say. I was living in the East then and I saw her only occasionally for lunch on the flying shopping trips she made. She would sit chuckling and smoking over a green sea of salad, the rise of the social barometer plainly visible in the immaculateness of her hair line, in the quiet insistence of her very correct accessories. She was trimmer and prettier than ever, and formidable! She could devastate a person with an apparently harmless little story about his personal eccentricities, and annihilate another with a broad, good natured joke about his physique.

Judging from the way she looked when I last saw her, with her smooth gold hair drawn tight from the middle over her ears and her yellow eyes full of the promise of sun in the winter and cool summer shadows, she should have had a good ten years of organization ahead of her. But then she met the most famous young man in England.

We heard several versions of the story about how he singled her out of a party in Chicago and sat talking with her through a heavy, silhouetting moon, on a balcony, both of them dangling their legs over the Renaissance balustrade and making wise-cracks. He stayed only a few days and after he left, the rumors whirred about like humming birds' wings. People exaggerated and pretended they were sorry for a husband in so obviously helpless a plight. Even the few people who had not been interested in Helena became consumed with curiosity to gauge the charm that had thrilled the young-man-who-had-everything.

Their overtures weren't very long in boring Helena to a terrific impatience. One morning, with very little warning, she packed the white lace film in which she'd first laid eyes on that famous boyish face, and with that and all her household goods, stepped briskly over the bent back of Chicago into a big white house that sat in the center of a mystic maze of pebble walks in the most fashionable corner of Long Island.

Motoring home on summer evenings through the blue dusk that turns New York to a city under the sea, she would roll over the scalloped bridge hanging like draped lace between the stenographers and the families of American capitalists. From it she could see a sign flashing forth its mechanical pride in the product of her father's ingenuity. I remember her telling me once that that sign made her feel safe and secure. She had always thought of herself as an Easterner. It must have been pleasant and familiar to her to step out of the big car and guess who was waiting on the dusky porch, by the timbers of their voices. There would be the crunch of shaved ice in the sweating silver glasses and the smell of mint, and they would all stay for a summer supper under the spell of Helena. She must have had a vague sensation of comfortable recognition such as you would feel on finding yourself in a place where you'd been in a dream, but it was not a life she'd ever really led—that drifting and whirling through the piles of raw material and great plans drawn in the sky that make New York so glamorous.

However, it was the environment in which she was born, and the atmosphere of the place in which we pass our earliest youth seeps into us through the slats of our cradles. But I don't believe she was happy even here, back in the place she came from. There is something infinitely disturbing in the phosphorescent rosiness that surrounds the successful and the great, a mystic magnetism that promises the same freedom from doubt and trouble that is part of themselves to all who surround them. Hundreds of people must have felt it at one time or another about Helena in her triumphant progress across half a continent and back, and now, contact with a personal power more compelling than her own left her wanting to seek its mystery in the rhythm of railroad wheels and the creaking beams of ships at sea.

One night in Paris she found him again. A sudden summer rain fell, drenching the *gala fleuri* at the Chateau de Madrid, passing through the colored lights like a blurring hand over a wet picture, forcing the trick shadows to disgorge their secrets. From behind the gauze of fountains and from out of the dark, under elms, streamed the incognitos, the maharajas, the figurants of current scandals and many millionaires who knew what to buy with their money. Then, just as the nicest presents on a Christmas tree are hidden far under the branches, Helena saw his boyish face, covered with raindrops, charging into the light where she stood. That meeting marked the beginning of a time when they were seen about Paris together a lot.

When the time came that this most famous person had to leave, he probably said to Helena, 'Well, if you ever are in my part of the world, look me up, won't you?' And she promised she would, and she *did*, because not very long after the good times they'd had in Paris had come to an end, she found herself quite by accident in the great gray city where the magic person lived and had his palace. He was awfully pleased and excited at the prospect of seeing her again, and insisted that she come to tea. Helena was charming: she told him that she was desperately afraid of so many butlers and lackeys and footmen and guards, and he could only persuade her to come when he promised to send them all away.

Picture to yourself Helena, trim, golden, dynamic, getting out of a yellow taxi in front of a palace so big and full of spires that to stand in front of it gives you the feeling that you are one of those dots of people in the engravings of Biblical market squares. And picture the most romantic young man of our era, sitting whistling on the top of the second flight of long steps, without a butler or a soldier or a lackey in sight.

And that is the last news I had of Helena, though she is often on the passenger list of the fashionable trans-Atlantic liners and is usually registered at the Ritz in Paris and New York in between seasons, or in some small, unpretentious hotel on the Left Bank, that costs more. You will know her immediately, if you should run into her, by the raillery in her confident voice and by the awkward, stuffy way you feel before her.

If you are famous or rich or very, very handsome, she will annex you and give you a good time and hurt your feelings.

If you just meet her because chance has thrown you into her path without exciting her curiosity about you, she will simply hurt your feelings, and you will never be part of that fine group of Helena's intimates all over the world, whose insides fit their outsides as they should.

When she's finished with dashing about, disturbing the susceptible, making susceptible the disturbing, perhaps you will find her one day enveloped in Venetian shawls, hugging the most elaborate heating system that money can buy and ending her tales with, 'Of course it's true; it happened to me.' But she will have to be a very old grandmother, indeed, because she doesn't like talking about herself and has so little of the romantic about her that, so the story goes, she took the bracelet (which she will always keep as proof that romance has not passed out of the world) into a jeweler's to have it valued.

I wonder if the reflections of the palace lying in the depths of the stones added to the weight in the jeweler's scale, or if that added importance is only for Helena, to help her remember her best fairy story when life leaves her time for telling it.

ZELDA

The Girl with Talent

(College Humor,
April 1930*)

The febrile winter sun felt its way along the basement stairways, digging out the corners of the cold stone steps into
live cubistic patterns. Tentatively it flicked the red and green
electric bulbs that framed a Chinese restaurant into glassy
momentary life. It slipped on the gilt of a second story
costumer's sign and fell with a splash under the canopy of a
Forty-third Street theater. Then it wound itself in and out
around the noise and smells of trucks and taxis, a hurdy-
gurdy, a porcelain lunch-room, a gigantic tooth over a
dentist's window—slithering its way through the warm oily
fumes of a coiffeur's, glinting the glass rectangle of a cheap
photographer's show-case. With cold calculation it avoided
the alley up which I turned and left it sunless, trafficless,
bounded with a network of fire escapes and filled with a
stolid gray silence like a street in Dickens' England.

It was a theatrical alley, lined with green baize doors;
in its gutters bits of program from yesterday's matinée
floated morosely. Where the words, *Stage Entrance*, were
hollowed out in green glass I went in.

The theater was dark and on the stage in the half gloom a
girl with short black hair raced about, tapping out the
rhythm of a mountain cataract to the tune of the hit of the
winter. As she moved, her hair flowed back from her pert,
serious face like the hair of a person coming up from a dive.

* Published as by 'F. Scott and Zelda Fitzgerald', but written by
Zelda.

(241)

She stopped suddenly and a deep chuckle rose from somewhere and enveloped her. All her gestures were involuntary like that, as if superimposed on a colossal dignity and restraint and as much a surprise to her as to the rest of the world. That quality was known to theatrical managers as hot stuff, to a large and discerning public as physical magnetism and to a widish circle of enemies from lower theatrical planes as lack of talent. 'Why,' they loved saying, 'she can't *do* anything. She doesn't know how to sing or dance, and she's built like a beef-eating beer bottle——' Which libelous slander had hindered her progress to the stars' dressing-room not at all.

Lou found her way through the maze of steel cables and slack ropes and bits of painted garden to the place where I waited against the bare concrete wall. I followed her courageous little lilt along the long stone corridor full of electric switches and signs about smoking, past a water cooler and a pile of lily cups and an old man in a tilted chair, past two men with their hands in their pockets and a fire-extinguishing apparatus to a gray door with a star stenciled high up in the center and *Miss Laurie* in a box underneath. Two soft blue ballet skirts formed amorphous clouds against the door and a light swung in a cage, like a golden bird, above a long mirror framed with cards and papers. Among them I saw a poem written on the back of an old program, a lacy Victorian valentine, two long telegrams for austerity, a few calling cards, a beautiful picture of a baby playing in long curly grass and by its side a newspaper picture of a handsome young husband, rich and famous enough to have claimed a good quarter of the front page.

All these things were hers. There was, as well, a grinning Bahama maid emanating an aura of irregularity, and the soft seduction of a gray squirrel coat hovering over the radiator in the corner. A big decisive automobile waited beyond the alley. I couldn't restrain an involuntary, 'Such a lucky girl—you've got everything,' as I ran my mind slowly over the delectable list of Lou's possessions.

She had a band of gauze about her hair and she was digging away at a big tin of cold cream. She answered me from the mirror. 'Yes,' she said, 'except a cocktail. Let's go and have a drink.'

Out of the quiet resonance of the passage and down a short flight of stairs, we followed the loopings of the tinsel January sun and left it at the entrance to a dark dining-room that smelt of orange juice and gin. Lou's dancing partner was there, hard at work on creating a smoke screen about himself. They laughed and pushed each other about with friendly little pats, talking shop in a professional lingo that I only half understood. She was fond of him, I knew, and we were all having a good time, but even so she gave the impression of constraint and of awaiting the passage of time as one waits for the five fifteen. Her partner was reading her a half kidding lecture about drinking too much gin, and finally it made her angry and we left. Outside she stood on the curb like a fine, high bred hunter picking up a cosmic scent on the early winter night, the bright silver buckles on her slippers twinkling and twinkling with a restlessness to be off. 'Oh, hell,' she said obscenely, 'I wish there were——'

High up over Central Park the beautiful baby was eating carrot soup with nice crispy things in it that caused the tiny mouth to weave a rhythmic circle to and fro, almost obliterating its startling likeness to Lou. A cardboard Nanny stood over the small wicker chair, waving a spoon about with the delicate emphasis of an orchestra leader and speculating mildly on the whereabouts of madam. In the Tudor splendor and oaken shadows of the tall living-room, a handsome young husband sat straining his cheek bones white against the gloom and feeling strongly the poignancy of his tilted, famous chin. Three expensive dresses lay pressing their Alice-blue pleats and twinkling buttons against discreet box tops.

Still no Lou—that is, no Lou in the high and fine apartment. No Lou running a noisy shower, changing the sterile

(243)

tiles of the bath to a broadcasting apparatus for slushes and gurgles and burst of a piercing, unmusical whistle. No Lou wandering in and out of the massive shadows, overawed and defiant, shoulders pressed back and rounded out by the weight of the sky itself into a noble dignity of line that accepted no mastery from paneling or marble hearths. No Lou to feel sorry for such a little baby eating such a lot of soup.

At that moment she sat incredibly immobile in a beige corner of her snug limousine and turned wide eyes like holes in a frozen lake on the cross-stitching of the elevated, on the red and yellow lights that went round and round and the green lights that made squares and the lights that outlined stars and words and shapes of things. I supposed she was brooding, or maybe enjoying that delicious feeling of motion that makes children hum in motor cars, so I didn't disturb her. We went all the way home in silence, crawling the pharmaceutical smells and the smell of hot bread, of gasoline and city dust, the overpowering smell of friction and all the used-up smells that escape into the New York streets with the letting down of business hour discipline.

We were late, and her husband was terribly annoyed when we finally got there. I suppose meeting her at the door all ready to be cross and finding himself frustrated by the presence of a stranger gave him a sensation like finding oneself at a ball in pyjamas, or waking up in a dinner coat on a bright sunny morning.

'You'll be late for the theater,' he said automatically.

'I know. I'll hurry. Did my dresses come? I thought we'd all have dinner together.'

'Dinner! My God, it's eight o'clock! Luckily gin's very nourishing, I believe.'

'Absolutely no calibers at all—I mean calorics. Oh, don't nag. I never nag, nag, nag at you.'

The buckled shoes beat out a lively rhythm. There were tears in the big, translucent eyes; back and forth flew the quiet angry words like a game of kitty o'cat. The sternness of a North American Indian settled over the famous profile.

'I wouldn't care,' he said, 'if it wasn't always these cheap theatrical folks. I don't see how Lou stands them—sitting on their laps, slobbering over them.'

Somehow feeling included in the sweeping condemnation, I felt emboldened to protest.

'There was once,' I began, 'a house of such wonderful shining glass that it was almost a diamond——'

He froze to precision before my eyes and bade us good night with the austere benevolence of an early colonial minister saying goodbye to his flock as he softly closed the door. Lou's 'Well, I suppose that's that' made me think morosely that she might be able to sing mammy songs with moving conviction.

The winter went on and packets of pansy seeds and tulip bulbs cluttered the bird stores along Sixth Avenue. Swift sudden winds lifted the sunshine high in the air and crumpled together the violet and yellow petals in the flower-sellers' baskets. Lou's show had shut, that amateurish, fresh flavor that she had on the stage proving not strong enough to carry a star part through a winter of the caprices of a New York public. I thought when I read that the show was leaving that she would probably sink back into a more peaceful domesticity, away from the detested theatrical world. But nothing of the kind. Later in the spring, when the time came that any two people meeting on the street greeted each other with 'What boat are you going on?', I bumped into Lou on a corner of Fifth Avenue.

'Oh, hello!' she gurgled. 'When are you sailing?'

A gray cape floated out behind her, like a fairy story illustration, and the cool sun dusted the bits of metal about her costume. I knew by her exuberance that she was on her way from the steamship booking office.

'I'll see you there before long,' I promised.

'Sure you will, because I'll be dancing at *Les Arcades*, and you'll be needing to go there to keep up with the *monde*——'

The lights changed and she, like a visiting officer in the front line trenches, dashed appraisingly across the line of cars.

'Are you *all* going?' I called after her.

'Oh, no,' she grinned, and then, not smiling any more, she added, 'Oh, no!'

Now a Paris night club during the season is a very serious affair. The seriousness begins with the waiters. If you are not known, they have an awful time finding you just the right table for your station in life, and if you are known they have an awful time giving your table to somebody else. The strain shows in their earnest white faces. There are clients who must be hidden without their knowledge behind palms and screens and may be even behind the cold buffet, and there are other clients who must be exploited and forced to like being put in the position of a sort of social sponsor to the party in spite of their inclination towards inaccessible corners.

Then there is the question of the orchestra: suave and supple it must be and conduct itself with grave decorum in moments of calculated abandon. It must transfer through the convolutions of its golden hours the certain hopes of the past into the uncertain expectancies of the future. It must make people want to eat and dance and drink and do what other people want them to, particularly what proprietors of night clubs want them to. Naturally, all this responsibility makes fashionable orchestras pale and solicitous and scoops great bays deep into the hair of their foreheads.

Lastly there is the *décor* adding to the solemnity, being sometimes so restrained as to be almost inside out. Every night quite late, in any one of these sophisticated rendezvous, a powerful white spotlight falls blindly toward the dance floor, bodily picking out big men with cigars who turn themselves sideways and try not to smile, and thin hanging women who cover their eyes with long white hands, and fat women who fluff up their features, and sleek girls' eyes giving back the glare from the dark like the eyes of an animal. The light

(246)

lumps them all at the far, impersonal end of a telescope. Swooping about amid gilded chair legs and many strata of smoke, the fluffy ends of summer gowns and the sharp crease of black broadcloth, it finally fixes itself a transparent geometric cone, rising like a prestidigitator's hat from the shining floor.

At *Les Arcades* it performed its magic for Lou. Straight into the suspended gravity of adults amusing themselves, she walked each midnight with the air of a child saying, 'Now you can watch me play.' No heavenward smiling, no sidewise grimaces, no attempt to let the audience in on her secret. She moved about under the light with preoccupied exaltation, twirling and finding it pleasant; twirling again, then beating swiftly on the floor like a hammer tapping the turns into place. A pleasurable effort shone in the infinitesimal strain on her face, and her outstretched arms seemed to be resting on something soft and supporting, so clearly did you sense their weight and their pulling on the shoulder sockets.

'I like to dance,' she seemed to say. 'There's nothing so much fun as this is.'

Of course, she was an enormous success. People beat on the table with little hammers and, enchanted with the noise, beat louder. Lou asked for more money and got it, and asked for rake-offs in formidable *couturières'* and got them. She bought dark blue dresses with Peter Pan collars, and bright red dresses with skirts like carnations, and big hats that flopped over one eye and small ones that half covered the other. She bought *masseurs* to rub her in the morning, and too many 'side-cars' before lunch, and underwear in which to find herself dead. There her expenses stopped. Her beaux bought champagne and taxis and curried chicken at *Voisin's* and half the perfume in *Babani's*. There wasn't really much they could buy for her because she was such a boyish little person, with black hair turning up like a bell back of her jaws, so that only a fishing-rod or a pocket knife

(247)

would have been really appropriate. She liked best the men who bought her eating and drinking and excitement.

One day she got soaking wet in a leaden Paris rain and stopped into my place to dry her stockings. I tried making one of those appropriate drinks like mulled claret, and while we were waiting for the foul thing to cool, I said to her, 'Lou, does your husband know you're raising Cain over here?'

'Cain?' she echoed incredulously. 'Why, I am so good as to make a Mother Superior seem like a glandular phenomenon.'

It was a week after that that she disappeared.

It seemed as if all Paris had been on a big bust all during the week, and the survivors of dozens of small groups were meeting every night under the pale late lights, driven by common fear of the stillness of a bedroom between midnight and dawn to hunt the morning over the cobblestones and pointed alleys of Montmartre. Now Lou was always a survivor, and one night, when it had got so late that we all sat huddled over the drum in a Negro joint, like people engaged in a tribal rite, we annexed another.

He was tall and dark, as neat as the washed flower-beds around *Les Ambassadeurs*, as romantically presented as a soft waltz at *Armenonville*, and he shone like a prize apple even at six in the morning. I half expected to see him take a strip of dingy flannel from his immaculate dinner coat, spit in his palm and begin polishing his head, rolling it round on the inside of his arms like a kitten washing itself, then swiftly sawing the cloth back and forth over his forehead. Instead, he sat down next to Lou so softly that I had a momentary illusion that he had come down on wires from heaven. He spoke low to her, bending himself almost to his knees with each word as if forcing the words out like notes from an accordion. There was a pained and questioning group of shadows just above his eyes and about the corners of his nose, and Lou talked to him with her face straight ahead and only moving her eyes in his direction. 'Love at first sight, undoubtedly,' I thought philosophically.

We had all drunk enough champagne to keep us in bed for a day, and had begun saying quarrelsome things to each other, pretending that we were being friendly and frank, so when somebody suggested that we leave, everybody was ready to go. Standing in the corridor with the door swinging open and shut on a street full of yellowish blue, and the glitter of a red sunrise coursing along the flowing gutters, we shook off the gloom that had settled over the party and said robust good nights and felt rather fine and cozy and suddenly sleepy as we rolled off down the hill in rickety old red taxis.

The morning held a cool, fragile mist that did not permeate it but lay along its promise of heat like drops of water on a sprinkled rose. The July sun peeled the tops of trees to orange-gold, and warmed and shrunk the slim shadows tracing the buildings. All over, beyond and above the cracking red in the East, the sky was the dense and colorless blue of a dawn inalienably identified in my mind with the dawn of battles. I was so absorbed with all these things, and with the sweet smell of the woods and ferns given off by a cart piled high with raspberries on its way to the market, that I didn't notice that Lou and the man with the high patina were not with us any more.

She had been staying with some very discreet mutual friends of ours, and if the telephone hadn't got mixed up in the affair probably nobody would have known about it. The manager of the night club started it, naturally, by phoning all the people he'd ever seen Lou with to know what he should do about his grand gala. All the silk dolls and little hammers and balloons and, oh, my God, the champagne! Lou's name out in front a mile high and Lou's chiffon dresses floating out at the opening of the dressing-room like colored papers on an electric fan—and Lou vanished off the face of the earth.

We couldn't find her either, though there was no place

that we could look except up and down the labyrinthine corridors of our friend's apartment, in and out of speckled French bedrooms, searching through a maze of splitting yellow satin and deep sepulchral beds. She simply wasn't there—until after five days of looking, just as we were about to notify the police, she suddenly *was* there again, stretched across the bed in such a state of fatigue that to look at the small body sleeping you would have thought it moulded from lead so heavy did it seem. She slept for hours and hours and hours, and I never saw her again until after her divorce.

It's hard to tell what brave people think. Courage is almost like a sixth directing sense, and I think sometimes that their judgments and decisions wait on its dictates. I hadn't been back to America the winter that Lou was getting her divorce, but stories of a desperate sort of dissipation slid down back of the leather cushions in the bar chairs of pompous ocean liners and reached Paris like a new edition of the *Arabian Nights*. It must have been hard, selling all that mess of pottage for a birthright, and Lou probably went through some pretty nightmarish times. Of course she was dancing all the time in a big hit and she didn't have to be eternally fabricating complex philosophical reasons for why she cared about the things she liked.

When she came back to France she seemed taciturn, but Lou was always that way, as if she was afraid of what ecstatic sounds might escape that primitive throat of hers. To my mind, people never change until they actually look different, so I didn't find her greatly modified. She missed the baby terribly. I suppose we always feel a deep regret for the things we leave behind incompleted, but it is a regret inextricably mixed with human disappointment at human imperfections and fastens itself to one thing in the past as readily as to another. She had never seen much of the child.

I saw her when she was passing through Paris, filling up her trunks like an engine drawing water. One day I found her helpless in the hands of two dressmakers. They were sticking mouthfuls of pins into her, and all about her feet were the white lights and deep apricot folds of gold satin. She stood there as rigid as a lighthouse, and I wondered vaguely where those fine muscles came from. Suddenly I remembered stories of a past trailing away over the water under ripe Hawaiian moons, doubling over itself like a game of hare and hounds about half the army posts of the Western world. She must have been brought up on baking horseback trails and bamboo verandas and swims miles long in fruitful Southern waters—a good school of unrest for adventurous, restless spirits.

'Well, Lou, or Brunhilde, or whatever your name is, what do you intend to do now?'

'I am going to work so hard that my spirit will be completely broken, and I am going to be a very fine dancer,' she answered, trying to look as if she saw visions. 'I have a magnificent contract in a magnificent casino on the *Cote d'Azur*, and I am now on my way to work and make money magnificently.'

Thinking that those were excellent defense plans that would never be carried out because of lack of attack, I made no comment. Neither could I think of anything appropriate to say later when somebody told me critically that just in the middle of a big success, when Lou was making an unprecedented hit, she ran off to China with a tall blond Englishman. Now, I believe, they have a beautiful baby almost big enough to eat carrot soup from a spoon.

ZELDA

A Millionaire's Girl

(*The Saturday Evening Post*,
7 May 1930*)

Twilights were wonderful just after the war. They hung above New York like indigo wash, forming themselves from asphalt dust and sooty shadows under the cornices and limp gusts of air exhaled from closing windows, to hang above the streets with all the mystery of white fog rising off a swamp. The far-away lights from buildings high in the sky burned hazily through the blue, like golden objects lost in deep grass, and the noise of hurrying streets took on that hushed quality of many footfalls in a huge stone square. Through the gloom people went to tea. On all the corners around the Plaza Hotel, girls in short squirrel coats and long flowing skirts and hats like babies' velvet bathtubs waited for the changing traffic to be suctioned up by the revolving doors of the fashionable grill. Under the scalloped portico of the Ritz, girls in short ermine coats and fluffy, swirling dresses and hats the size of manholes passed from the nickel glitter of traffic to the crystal glitter of the lobby.

In front of the Lorraine and the St Regis, and swarming about the mad-hatter doorman under the warm orange lights of the Biltmore façade, were hundreds of girls with marcel waves, with colored shoes and orchids, girls with pretty faces, dangling powder boxes and bracelets and lank young men from their wrists—all on their way to tea. At that time, tea was a public levee. There were tea personalities—

* Published as by 'F. Scott Fitgerald', but written by Zelda.

young leaders who, though having no claim to any particular social or artistic distinction, swung after them long strings of contemporary silhouettes like a game of crack-the-whip. Under the somber, ironic parrots of the Biltmore the halo of golden bobs absorbed the light from heavy chandeliers, dark heads lost themselves in corner shadows, leaving only the rim of young faces against the winter windows—all of them scurrying along the trail of one or two dynamic youngsters.

Caroline was one of those. She was then about sixteen, and dressed herself always in black dresses—dozens of them—falling away from her slim, perfect body like strips of clay from a sculptor's thumb. She had invented a new way to dance, shaking her head from side to side in dreamy, tentative emphasis and picking her feet up quickly off the floor. It would have made you notice her, even if she hadn't had that lovely Bacchanalian face to turn and nod and turn away into the smoky walls. I watched her for ages before I asked who she was. There was a sense of adventure in the way her high heels sat so precisely in the center of the backs of her long silk legs, and a sense of drama in her conical eyebrows, and she was much too young to have learned such complete self-possession in any legitimate way.

Her story, to date, was short and hysterical—a runaway marriage—annulled immediately—a year in small parts on the New York stage, and the scandalous journalism that followed that affair of Brooklyn Bridge. It must have demanded a good bit of vitality to bring all that to the attention of so many people in such a short time, especially since she started out empty-handed, equipped with only the love and despair in her father's vague eyes. He was one of those people who distinguish themselves in an obscure profession, and Caroline was far from considering Who's Who an adequate substitute for the Social Register. She was ambitious, she was extravagant, and she was just about the prettiest thing you ever saw. I never could decide whether she was

(253)

calculating or not. I suppose any young person in a red-flower hat who suddenly, in the midst of an undergraduate hullabaloo, meets the heir to fantastic millions, and who thereupon smiles poetically into his brown eyes, could be called calculating, but Caroline had made the same gestures so many times before without material considerations.

They looked fine together; they were both dusted with soft golden brown like bees' wings, and they were tall, and the color under their skins was apricot, and there was harmony in the way he leaned forward and she leaned back against the red-leather bench. You could see that he was rich and that he liked her, and you could see that she was poor and that she knew he did. That, at their first meeting, was all there was to be seen; though psychics might have found an aura of tragedy whirling above their two young heads even then. They seemed too perfect.

The winter got old and frayed the edges of the palms in the quiet clinking of the Plaza lobby. The steam heat twisted their tips into little brown mustache ends, and people waiting for other people ripped short slits about their lower leaves. Caroline had worn out two big branches since the day she discovered that Barry was not even regular about being late. It was a nuisance, that; it meant that she had to sit there rigid, being stared at by men without knees, in spats, and bell boys without necks, in billiard-table covers, and clerks without shoulders, in cages, while Barry did something somewhere to one of his automobiles. He had three, so underslung that riding in them was like climbing a mountain in a cable car. They used to go together for mad rides up and down Long Island, or splitting the green of Connecticut hills in the spring; Caroline so lost in the snake-skin cushions that she seemed deflated; Barry steering the monstrous thing as if he were sketching in charcoal, and both of them singing chorus after chorus of monotonous Negro blues.

One late winter Sunday when the glare of the afternoon

snow forced the shadows into great banks in the corners of the living room, Caroline and Barry drove out to see us. They came in breathing off a refrigerated crispness of lettuce just off the ice chest; the moisture on the tips of their long-haired furs refracting the hall lights to a purplish halo.

'Hello,' she said. 'Is this Fitzgerald's roadhouse?'

Her voice was as full of varied emotions as sinking into a soft cold bed after a strenuous day. Over its voluptuous nuances brooded the purring monotone of well-bred New York.

'It is,' I affirmed, 'and there's cold turkey and asparagus for supper; so come in and get warm while you wait.'

Barry sat under the one light in the far end of the long living room, turning over a great pile of phonograph records, and Caroline sat rigid in the pink shadows, both of them so conscious of each other that they gave the impression of two hidden enemies waiting to attack. We listened to the big logs popping in the quiet like wet firecrackers, and to the clinking of the furnace being fixed for the night, and to the sound of a bath running on the second floor. Supper was being laid in the dining room opposite, and an intimate unwarranted friendliness stole into our low monosyllabic conversation. I felt like reciting "'Twas the night before Christmas' and going to sleep on the rug, when suddenly Barry, from way over there under the light, asked Caroline to marry him. The slow dignity of her acceptance made us realize the seriousness of the affair; there was nothing to do but try to garnish our Sunday scraps into an engagement supper.

They were both absorbed and quiet during the meal, and, not knowing quite what to say, I began thinking of all sorts of things—of Caroline the winter before, in creamy white georgette and a fog of gray squirrel, coming down the steps of a narrow Fifth Avenue mansion, freezing her tears on the clear winter air. It was a debut party, and she had tried crashing too formidable a gate. New York butlers are not hired for their response to beauty and this one had turned her away decisively. I thought of Barry calling for his mother at an Embassy tea in Rome—of Barry, nineteen, elegant, impeccable, preferred of all the mothers of girls whose families chose for them their paths of light. He was spoiled and wild, but since he had probably met Caroline on some sort of jag, that was no reason why there should be any miscomprehension between them on that score. I wondered how he would explain his intimacy with so lovely and scandalous a person to his austere family, and if they would accept Caroline with no matter what explanation he could invent.

That winter to me is a memory of endless telephone calls and of slipping and sliding over the snow between the low white fences of Long Island, which means that we were running around a lot. We met Caroline and Barry in town occasionally, in the aquarium lights of an expensive night club or under the glare of a theater portico. People said they were always together and never went out without each other. She was one of the few women I've known who was both fluffy enough and concise enough to look pretty in ermine, and when you saw them stepping together into his huge automobile it made you think of musical-comedy principalities or glamorous suppers from Renaissance paintings.

Of course, all the scandal sheets had a dig at them. There were venomous little paragraphs in most of the Broadway oracles, particularly after people found out how strongly his family disapproved. I believe they tried buying her off, and it was something to do with that that precipitated that awful row in Ciro's. As is mostly the case when something dreary happens to you, all their friends seemed to be there that night. It was an absurd place, done with the most pretentious simplicity, so that you saw quite clearly what was happening around you, and, to make matters worse, Caroline and Barry were directly facing the whole room over by the orchestra. First she threw her glass on the floor, then, unwinding her beautiful figure from an enormous napkin, a slim chair back and a dozen scattering cigarettes, she fixed on Barry a look of such malevolent hatred that the saxophone player blasted a wild siren cry into his silver horn and the maître d'hôtel came hopping up to represent the management. She was utterly furious and kept demanding her car, as if it could be driven straight on to the waxed floor. Barry told them to take her away, as if she'd been something inedible served from the kitchen.

Everybody was delighted with so public and melo-dramatic a *crise* in a romance that had inspired so much envy. Before they left, even the waiters in the place had gleaned the story of Caroline's foolish acceptance of a nice big check and an automobile from Barry's father. She claimed, to Barry, that she had not understood it was to have been the reward for letting him go, and he claimed in no uncertain terms that she was fundamentally, hopelessly and irreclaimably dishonest. It seems too bad they couldn't have done their claiming at home, because then they might have patched up the mess. But too many people had wit-nessed the scene for either of them to give in an inch.

Several days later Barry shut the bumpings and thumpings of the embryo delirium tremens that usually follows a complete disillusionment into a golden-oak suite of one of the biggest transatlantic liners, en route for Paris. Two weeks later, as I was bumping along the walnut panelings of a trans-continental express on my way to California, I slipped along the rounded corner and bang into Caroline. I don't know how I had expected to find her, but I was terribly surprised with her air of elegant martyrdom. She was royalty in exile. From the slope of her shoulders to the eloquent inactivity of her hands her whole person cried out, 'This is the way I am, and I'm going to stick by it.' Now I knew that Caroline had not a bit of that fading-violets, closing-episode note of the minor lyric poet that makes people run from things in her erstwhile personality, and I wondered what determination had sent her scurrying from a world that she knew, but that didn't know her, across a continent to a world that knew her from her escapades, but that she didn't know. It seemed to me an unreasonable exchange. If it was not escape that motivated her, then it must be vengeance, I told myself, and it was all I could do to keep from asking her on the spot.

Thinking of that long ride to California, it does not appear remarkable that people should lose their sense of proportion on the way. The pattern of the tracks at the beginning lies like featherstitching along the borders of a land suggesting the tin scenic effects that are sold with mechanical trains; a green-and-brown hill, a precipitate tunnel, a brick station too small for the train, an odd gate, a lamp-post and a little lead dog. The first night there is a feeling of accomplishment that you are installed in your apple-green compartment, moving in a phosphorescent line through the red and purple streaks of a Western dark. The dining car glistens with bright new food; the train is still a part of its advertising pamphlets and has not yet settled down to its own dynamic ends. You can still smoke without tasting brass cartridges in the back of your mouth. I didn't see Caroline at first, to victimize her by my curiosity. We were both fascinated by the limitations of life on the train, probably; but later, when even Mr Harvey's ingenuity could invent no name for hash-brown potatoes exotic enough to tempt our cindery palates, we sat in mutual lamentation amongst the catchup bottles and vinegar cruets of the diner.

The countryside was changing. The faraway hills did not meet the horizon, and the trees and houses on the green mountain-sides seemed on probation. Caroline was suddenly fed up with the quiet reserve that her getting-away-from-it-all manner had imposed upon her and was bursting to talk. She told me she had a part in a movie and was going West to work. In the course of a long conversation I gathered that she was completely determined to distinguish herself and force Barry to realize the enormity of his error in leaving her so precipitately. She talked and talked, fascinating herself with the idea of success, until by the end of the trip I think she never wanted to see me again, so full had she filled me with her hopes and plans. I could see her changing personalities behind the first onrush of people in the Los Angeles station, marking herself with the silent wary confidence so necessary in a world of competitive struggle.

We found ourselves at the same hotel. About the central mass there lay shimmering in the rarefied sun low lines of bungalows like the tentacles of a sea monster crystallizing itself in the humid heat. Grass like wet paint covered the gushing squares of earth between the cement paths in the court, and from one doorway to another white rose vines stretched and aspired along a trellising of flaky zinc pipes. Caroline's rooms were opposite mine, and I could tell by the number of waiters who were always scurrying in and out that she was auspiciously launched in her new *milieu*. I had to pass her door on my way in, and there was always a paper envelope hanging on her knob, bulging with telephone messages. More and more often there were yellow roses under the yellow curtains at her window. I knew which director preferred yellow roses and referred to them, amusingly, as 'radishes.'

Sometimes I burrowed my way through the candy stores and barber shops and glass cases filled with the curlicues of Oriental art to the great supper room of the hotel. There, in the brightly lit darkness of an artificial Hawaii, was always Caroline, sitting, listening, elegant and fragile, *connaisseuse* of perfumes and parades. People knew her by name; her career was getting under way. She drank little and spent the mornings having herself pummeled and pounded into a nervously receptive state that was, for film purposes, the equivalent of dramatic ability. She learned to accentuate a slight defect in her lovely face with heavy make-up, so that her wide cheek-bones gave her a Tatar look under the thick, creamy powder. She learned to be distrait and aloof and passed those two qualities off as sophistication and disillusionment. Hollywood was captivated. I'd been out there about two months when I heard that Caroline was not able to work and was holding up a costly production with uncontrolled flares of nerves. I concluded she was about to get fired, so I ran to stick my finger in the pie. I persuaded her to drive to the sea with me.

I don't know what there is about California that makes it seem so inland. I suppose it's that sparse attempt to inclose so much space with two orange trees and an oil well. Anyway, I felt that it would do her good to escape that feeling of being in a vacuum that the wide-spaced city gives me, and she had never seen the Pacific, so we hired an open car and became part of an unbroken line of automobiles weaving along under the vast sky, like an invasion of beetles, toward Long Beach. She was hardly interested in the flatness of a country that was bright like a dirty mirror from its lack of color in the sun, and I could see that the chauffeur's fast driving made her nervous. Having wrecked my own nerves years ago, I like advising other people about their own.

'You're going too hard,' I told her, 'and if you keep on living at such tension that you can't sit in an automobile without grabbing the sides you won't last long at your work.' The sun curved along her high cheekbones and dug a white triangle under her lifted chin. A big bunch of pink sweet peas tattered themselves against the brim of her white felt hat in the wind and blew against her shining face as she turned and cheerfully agreed with me that she would probably collapse before long.

'But it isn't the work,' she said enigmatically.

'Oh, gosh,' I thought, 'she's going to start proving she's right again.'

We had luncheon in a dingy dining room facing a brick wall, with pictures of the ocean painted about the ceiling.

There was nowhere else in Long Beach on the sea to have luncheon, since nonalcoholic races are too suspicious of reality to face even the ocean. We both tried temporizing with a soggy shrimp cocktail. Caroline leaned over the table and asked me suddenly for news of New York in such an apologetic, eager way that I sensed what she really wanted to talk about. It was Barry. People had, naturally, avoided the subject with her, I suppose, and I was feeling complacent enough to say what she wanted.

'Aren't you over that yet?' I asked.

She smiled with detached desperation.

'Oh, yes, of course, but I hate to lose touch with him,' she answered. 'Ever since I met him everything I do or that happens to me has seemed because of him. Now I am going to make a hit so that I can choose him again, because I'm going to have him somehow. I wanted to say that to somebody, so I'd have to do it. I'm sorry to spoil your ride, but it's made me able to go back to work again. You see, I haven't any friends,' she finished simply.

When she left me at the door of her bungalow that night so much sadness sank into the shadows about her eyes and so much unsurety sounded in her footfalls along the cement steps that a surge of hatred swept over me against trim seaside hotels, and even old Balboa, and the East and the West and love affairs. As she climbed the stairs the heels of her slippers echoed as if the shoes were empty. I spectrally crossed over the fog to my own door.

Next day it began to rain in California, much against the better judgment of the most influential citizens—not just ordinary rain the way it rains in other places, but great brown bulks of water flowing down the gutters like hot molasses candy. At the bottom of hills where two streets met, the water came up to the running boards of automobiles. It seethed through umbrellas in a fine spray and covered the sidewalks with slippery mud deltas. If the sun came out for a minute the air steamed with hot vapor and the sodden cushions of grass smoked under its discouraged rays. Naturally, going about was unpleasant, so I spent most of my time in my room, washing down quantities of spring onions and alligator pears with California Bordeaux. When I traveled the flood again Caroline's picture was finished and March was powdering the air with spring dust. I had heard talk about the film; apparently she came off with flying colors. The director had been so pleased with her work that, with the final assembling of the picture, her part had grown to star proportions, and there was nothing between her and a successful career. I was pleased that she was glad to see me again and that she gave me seats to the opening. It was surprising that such a prospect hadn't erased that distant distress in her eyes but had only superimposed an air of excitement on the placidity of her lovely white features.

A Hollywood opening night is a fairy-tale affair. A street is flooded with blue-white diamond light that glints over the trees and lies like mica over their foliage and along their trunks. There are festoons of ordinary lights like strings of golden oranges swung from pole to pole in the ether whiteness, and all is broken into a million cones and triangles by the headlights of hundreds of automobiles. The shadows fall short about their objects—thick gluey puddles under the cars and people. A red carpet bridges the pavement between automobiles and the theater door, and grinding cameras envelop the arriving celebrities. A gigantic megaphone cries out famous names to the crowd waiting on the edge of the light, and they, in turn, respond with loud applause or rustling silence—a sort of trial by fire. Fine, uncharitable ladies in silver shoes and ermine may be greeted with protesting murmurs from under the trees, and gay young girls in coral velvet that people know have helped their kind may start the clatter of many hands swelling from far around the corner, in the approval of a public that considers itself humanitarian.

There is no expectancy in the air; it is the dumb hero worship of fans gathered in the gloom like medieval serfs awaiting a conquering baron that dominates the atmosphere —that and the shining assurance that insecure people must assume in places of authority. I had never been to an opening before, so I stood for an hour watching from across the way. It was like an elegant feminine circus breaking ground. I wanted terribly to see Caroline come in. It was her night, and I knew she would have something amusing to contribute— some little unpretentious trick of pinning her flowers in an unexpected corner, of forcing her hair to interrogative angles, of wearing some funny thing like a dagger, or a tiny bell at the side of her slippers—but the line of cars moved faster and faster before the door and the cheaper cars were making their appearance, so I knew I'd be late if I didn't go inside.

The picture was fine. Caroline's beautiful Biblical eyes dimmed and shone over teacups and decanters and through the spray of shower baths and dominated the mists of a good art director. I felt a secret jealousy of such assured success. I came outside in the *entr'acte* to see if I could find her in the crowded lobby. She was nowhere around, and feeling rather gloomy at being alone among so many people using so many adjectives, I went along bareheaded through the moist spring air to the corner drug store. It was like all drug stores—gift cases of perfume and powder, writing paper and books, round tables of incense burners and picture frames and all the things you couldn't imagine buying in a drug store—and I don't know why that sudden sense of disaster came over me. I felt as if I were in an exiled and floating world, isolated from all necessities of life except the one of buying things. To bring myself back to reality I went to the cigar counter and chose the late edition of an evening paper. On the front page was a big picture of Barry and his fiancée, telegraphed from Paris. Heirs of Two Great Fortunes to Have Quiet Ceremony. I was glad Caroline had made such a killing in the film and I wondered if she'd mind much when she saw those blaring headlines.

The picture was thoroughly amusing. There was always that horizon quality in her eyes, and nobody ever had a more symmetrical body to help her to stardom, or one that she could work so well. It was like a splendid mechanical installation in its trim, impersonal fitness. Toward the end she surprised me with an intensely moving scene—some sort of stuff about two young lovers being separated by a misunderstanding. The audience was moved and would have been even more affected, I think, except for the violent clanging of an ambulance bell, jarring throughout the quiet of a pathetic episode. It was a pity; it took half the value away from the scene.

Next morning I hurried out for all the papers, from a malicious curiosity to see whether Caroline or Barry would have the choicest space. She won, hands down. The dramatic columns were full of laudatory accounts of the film, obviously written the night before; and the front pages were full of last-minute headlines and two-column stories of her attempted suicide on the night of her successful debut. The sob sisters made a very dramatic episode out of her clanging past the theater in an ambulance on the opening night.

Two weeks later, when she was well enough to receive visitors, I called at the hospital to see her. I almost had to engage a room for myself when I ran into Barry. For he was there, very solicitous and proprietary, and you'd never have guessed from his manner that he was responsible for her half death or half responsible for her death, so I didn't stay long. I left, pondering all the way back to town over the wonders that long-distance telephones and a dramatic sense can accomplish when brought in close proximity. One of those friends that Caroline disclaimed must have called up Paris for her.

She married him, of course, and since she left the films on that occasion, they have both had much to reproach each other for. That was three years ago, and so far they have kept their quarrels out of the divorce courts, but I somehow think you can't go on forever protecting quarrels, and that romances born in violence and suspicion will end themselves on the same note; though, of course, I am a cynical person and, perhaps, no competent judge of idyllic young love affairs.

ZELDA

Poor Working Girl

(*College Humor*,
January 1931*)

Eloise Everette Elkins stood on a dilapidated pair of wooden steps that belonged to a faded frame house with rain colored trimmings. Eloise and the house were standing in the middle of a community that had of recent years grown very prosperous and so outgrown the capabilities of its older inhabitants. This was why all the good jobs in town were held by imported young men, who in turn imported their sweethearts from large neighboring cities and felt no necessity to know Eloise socially. And that was why all the boys whom she could have married were inadequate for marrying purposes and spent their lives limping along on a salary that she thought she could have earned herself. Industries, when they get started, grow faster than men or towns and do not allow the time for lying fallow which people seem to need when they have always lived in close proximity to cultivated fields.

Eloise was twenty and carefully protected but unprovided for. Her two aunts and her grandmother nagged her quite a bit about her laziness, but there wasn't really much that she could do. Mamma and Father had seen to it that she had an education in a college for girls down state, and nature had done well by the storehouse for all this knowledge. It must have been quite a strain for so Anglo-Saxon and flawless a skin to contain the verse and choruses of all the popular songs

* Published as by 'F. Scott and Zelda Fitzgerald', but written by Zelda.

for five years back, together with a real talent for the ukulele, a technical knowledge of football, ten poetic declamations and a lyric taste in dress. Eloise knew shorthand, too, but she fumbled about in it and was pleased with herself when it worked, like a famous person making a speech in a foreign language. She knew how to get breakfast if the stove was electric and not overpoweringly large and if things could be cooked one at a time.

Her eyes were so clear that you could see right through to the mechanics of them, and she was altogether remarkably pretty and new looking even for an American girl of her age. She had twelve-year-old legs, like Mary Pickford's, that were intriguing when they grew out of those square rubber bottom shoes which give strangers the idea that we are a sturdy race, but these same little girl legs had too much curve on the outside when she put on the tall heeled silver slippers which go with tulle and taffeta.

Anyway, she poked them out in front of her this morning and sat down on the third step because it had less splinters along the worn edge and wouldn't send runs climbing along the back seams of her stockings, which shows that she had it in her to be more painstaking than she was. She opened *Every Evening* from yesterday. She had decided to go to work and she was looking for the want ads. She read with mingled suspicion, fear and personal interest about all the people who wanted chocolate dippers and part time maids and people to make fortunes selling unnamed things that sounded secret and complicated. Eloise knew she could *never* sell *anything*, and her light eyes moved lazily on down the column. Then she found a neat little square with all the dignity of a calling card, which announced tersely and dramatically that Mr and Mrs Goatbeck were looking for Eloise.

It seemed that they had a very refined child in a refined but isolated home with nobody refined to play with, so that Eloise could earn seventy-five dollars a month for just being

natural and keeping a little girl from running over automobiles. She thought of all the refinement to be bought with
seventy-five dollars: the twenty-five dollar dresses and the
ten dollar perfume. Then she multiplied by four and five
and thought of New York and Broadway. That brought her
around after awhile to thinking of the night after the com-
mencement play when the college president himself had told
her what a real dramatic gift she had.

All that ambitious thinking made it much easier for Eloise
to contribute the outstanding excitement of months to the
family dinner table. Over the sweet potatoes and meat pie
and muffins wavered the announcement that she was going
to leave home. Even when she was 'in college' she had
always slept at home and so it was not hard to understand
why Mamma pictured Eloise in a strange land with a strange
disease, somewhat like pneumonia only much more painful,
and with nobody to look after her. There was indignation in
Mamma's mental picture. It somehow included the law and
all the hygienic societies and the pound. Father didn't see
why girls didn't stay at home, but he had his own worries and
he made it a rule never to complain until afterwards.

The aunts thought that serious employment would be
fine for Eloise. She had always helped them with their
children and she could save her money and it wasn't as if
there weren't telephones, so finally all was agreed upon.
When everybody had got all he could of his own righteous-
ness out of the situation, she set out with her semi-fiancé
in his second-hand car to interview the Goatbecks.

Eloise had been half engaged for four years now to numer-
ous editions of the same young man. He always had a second-hand car, a fur coat, that irregular cast of feature known
as an open countenance, and a gold football on his watch
chain. Having him waiting outside in his long gray car while
she went in to her interview reinforced her in a feeling of
reduced circumstances. So many young Americans have
that feeling as their sole equipment for meeting reality:

(268)

the sense of being in circumstances reduced from the dreams and pamperings of parents still guided by the wisdom of an epoch when the mere fact of children to run the farm was an asset; reduced circumstances with its half whine and its fierce swallowed pride which robs the children of the old Americans of the clarity so necessary to success, and which inevitably nourishes the sulkiness that follows the first failure.

But it is a feeling that goes very well with taking care of refined offspring. Eloise told the lady humbly how she had to work and how she loved children, and the lady told Eloise that she was much too pretty to bury herself in a nursery. Eloise liked that idea and felt pleased and bravely sorry for herself. She made up her mind to be perfect and to live up to her reduced circumstances in all things.

When she started out for home again with the young man, she felt positively married to him. He had seen her ask for a job. They had gone through an overwhelming adventure together. As she put her arm under his on the steering wheel everything seemed changed to her, as if she'd already worked at her job, at all jobs, and now wanted to settle down with the fur coat and the football and cook breakfast on a ukulele for the rest of her life.

If you asked Eloise what happened for the next six months, she would say she worked and worked and got so nervous that life didn't seem worth living. If you asked Mrs Goatbeck she would say that Eloise didn't keep her shoes in a row and that providence alone protected her refined child from a series of accidents.

But Eloise stuck to her job and did her best when she hadn't been up too late the night before, and it really looked as though all her reading of dramatic school prospectuses might help her formulate a future after all. She was gravely saving money to study in New York.

But then spring came right in the middle of things, as it always does, and the manufacturers flooded the showcases with shoes for tramping golf courses, and the smell of chocolate began to seep through the more open doors of drugstores, and music from the phonographs in the ten cent stores became audible above the noise of the trolleys, and Eloise succumbed.

The first thing she bought was a tan coat much too thin to wear until it would be too hot to wear it. To make up for that, she wrote for more dramatic school prospectuses and wore the coat anyway, so she got the grippe. After that she had an awful attack of loneliness on account of having been in bed, and spent a lot of her money on some blue things with feathers and something green with pink hanging off. And there was a little rounded hat that was too old for her and another one that she wore on one side so it looked like the rings around Saturn on her head. Self-expression, that was, and it runs expensive. But she told the lady that she was going to save every cent of her money for the next three months and go to New York in the summer.

The self-expression served one purpose: it renewed her confidence in college presidents as dramatic critics and, just for good measure, attached some new young men to Eloise —one with a face as open as a cracked safe, and one who recited *The Ladies* to Eloise.

Finally, she felt so sure that she was going to save enough money to keep her safely in New York while she studied that she went home to consult her family about it. Father's idea of the stage was founded on the stereopticon slides of 1890, and Mamma's was positively Biblical. You would have thought Morris Gest wanted to produce *The Miracle* in the front parlor! Eloise drew courage from all the gold footballs and signed photographs in her bureau drawer and went back to work in such a dynamic frame of mind that the refined child learned two multiplication tables in a day. Nothing remained but to save her salary.

Long days went by. In the mornings there were lessons, a correspondence course for children which gave Eloise a sort of missionary pleasure. The half hour of mythology she especially liked. To hear the labyrinthine Greek names twisting the tongue of the child always left her with a feeling that life was perhaps a bizarre affair after all.

Eloise had grown quite fond of her charge, so fond of her that she could forget her entirely on the long afternoon walks in the country and project herself into a dream that consisted of all the hazy, unsolved things of the past and an unresolved future state—not rosy nor misty nor anything definite, but just a flooding of a gentle light, as a blind person must feel when he finds himself in a pale spring sun.

At night there was the bath hour and several choruses of *What's the Use?* and then, often, when the family wasn't going out, there were the movies or dancing at the local hotel with her current beau. Eloise loved ice-cream. It was extraordinary how her skin stayed like that with her eating it on top of pie and under cake and around bananas, and disguised as stews and soups and puddings. But it was certainly not a taste for simplicity that made her enjoy so many simple things.

Now spring came in earnest and America began to look like the inside of a small boy's pocket to Mr and Mrs Goatbeck. The migratory instinct settled over the house until the suburban stillness teemed like flies in a bottle. Eloise went out more and more at night, so by the time the air began to melt and settle and touch the earth as capriciously as falling toy balloons, her ambition fell away to the same tempo. In spite of her determination to finish her job well, now that the Goatbecks had decided to go abroad, her lapses began to catch up with each other so that soon she was floundering about in a void of things-not-done, with the child following after like an inquisitive puppy sniffing at the unusual.

The row came when there were only four days more to go. There were recriminations on the stairway and nonchalance in the day nursery and tears in the hallways, and finally cryptic telephone calls in a deeply injured tone of voice. It seems the cupboards weren't in order and the child had no clean socks and there was eight dollars' worth of telephoning to numbers unknown to the Goatbecks—a formidable list of misdemeanors. Eloise tried awfully hard to care (she admitted to Mrs Goatbeck that she hadn't been doing her duty lately), but it was too near the end for that, so she left one afternoon in a battleship gray second-hand car, with all her photographs and dance cards and some letters that Mr Goatbeck had given her to theatrical managers in New York—enough letters to get her into forty choruses and a house of correction.

But to Eloise, all motivating power was of divine origin and people waited for its coming like a prisoner for a trial, with the expectation of release or a sense of black misgiving. Both these sensations were merged in her when she found herself at home again. She couldn't decide whether or not she was as wonderful as she thought she was, and New York seemed awfully far from the yellow frame house full of the sweetness of big Sunday meals and the noise of the cleaning in the mornings and black shadows from an open fire.

New York seemed so far away that it was a full three months before Eloise stretched out her rubber soled shoes and let herself gently down into a patch of sunshine on the third step. Then she opened *Every Evening* and once again began on the want ads.

When the Goatbeck family came back months later, she was working in the capacity of pretty girl in the local power plant. All the second-hand automobiles that waited out front at five thirty added quite a lot to the traffic congestion around that quarter.

The refined child saw her one day in a theater lobby; she didn't remember her fair flaxen skin and eyes like transparent pearls, though she remembered several governesses she had before Miss Elkins. The blood in Eloise's veins had worn itself out pumping against the apathy of weary generations of farmers and little lawyers and doctors and a mayor, and she couldn't really imagine achieving anything. She came from our worn-out stock. But perhaps there are lovely faces whose real place is in the power company; perhaps Eloise wasn't destined for Broadway after all.

SCOTT

The Hotel Child

(The Saturday Evening Post,
31 January 1931)

It is a place where one's instinct is to give a reason for being there—'Oh, you see, I'm here because——' Failing that, you are faintly suspect, because this corner of Europe does not draw people; rather, it accepts them without too many inconvenient questions—live and let live. Routes cross here—people bound for private *cliniques* or tuberculosis resorts in the mountains, people who are no longer *persona grata* in Italy or France. And if that were all——

Yet on a gala night at the Hotel des Trois Mondes a new arrival would scarcely detect the current beneath the surface. Watching the dancing there would be a gallery of English-women of a certain age, with neckbands, dyed hair and faces powdered pinkish gray; a gallery of American women of a certain age, with snowy-white transformations, black dresses and lips of cherry red. And most of them with their eyes swinging right or left from time to time to rest upon the ubiquitous Fifi. The entire hotel had been made aware that Fifi had reached the age of eighteen that night.

Fifi Schwartz. An exquisitely, radiantly beautiful Jewess whose fine, high forehead sloped gently up to where her hair, bordering it like an armorial shield, burst into lovelocks and waves and curlicues of soft dark red. Her eyes were bright, big, clear, wet and shining; the color of her cheeks and lips was real, breaking close to the surface from the strong young pump of her heart. Her body was so assertively adequate that one cynic had been heard to remark that she always looked as if she had nothing on underneath her dresses; but he was probably wrong, for Fifi had been as thoroughly equipped for beauty by man as by God. Such dresses—cerise for Chanel, mauve for Molyneux, pink for Patou; dozens of them, tight at the hips, swaying, furling, folding just an eighth of an inch off the dancing floor. Tonight she was a woman of thirty in dazzling black, with long white gloves dripping from her forearms. 'Such ghastly taste,' the whispers said. 'The stage, the shop window, the manikins' parade. What can her mother be thinking? But, then, look at her mother.'

Her mother sat apart with a friend and thought about Fifi and Fifi's brother, and about her other daughters, now married, whom she considered to have been even prettier than Fifi. Mrs Schwartz was a plain woman; she had been a Jewess a long time, and it was a matter of effortless indifference to her what was said by the groups around the room. Another large class who did not care were the young men— dozens of them. They followed Fifi about all day in and out of motorboats, night clubs, inland lakes, automobiles, tea rooms and funiculars, and they said, 'Hey, look, Fifi!' and showed off for her, or said, 'Kiss me, Fifi,' or even, 'Kiss me again, Fifi,' and abused her and tried to be engaged to her.

Most of them, however, were too young, since this little city, through some illogical reasoning, is supposed to have an admirable atmosphere as an educational center.

Fifi was not critical, nor was she aware of being criticized herself. Tonight the gallery in the great, crystal, horseshoe room made observations upon her birthday party, being somewhat querulous about Fifi's entrance. The table had been set in the last of a string of dining rooms, each accessible from the central hall. But Fifi, her black dress shouting and halloing for notice, came in by way of the first dining room, followed by a whole platoon of young men of all possible nationalities and crosses, and at a sort of little run that swayed her lovely hips and tossed her lovely head, led them bumpily through the whole vista, while old men choked on fish bones, old women's facial muscles sagged, and the protest rose to a roar in the procession's wake.

They need not have resented her so much. It was a bad party, because Fifi thought she had to entertain everybody and be a dozen people, so she talked to the entire table and broke up every conversation that started, no matter how far away from her. So no one had a good time, and the people in the hotel needn't have minded so much that she was young and terribly happy.

Afterward, in the salon, many of the supernumerary males floated off with a temporary air to other tables. Among these was young Count Stanislas Borowki, with his handsome, shining brown eyes of a stuffed deer, and his black hair already dashed with distinguished streaks like the keyboard of a piano. He went to the table of some people of position named Taylor and sat down with just a faint sigh, which made them smile.

'Was it ghastly?' he was asked.

The blond Miss Howard who was traveling with the Taylors was almost as pretty as Fifi and stitched up with more consideration. She had taken pains not to make Miss Schwartz's acquaintance, although she shared several of the same young men. The Taylors were career people in the diplomatic service and were now on their way to London, after the League Conference at Geneva. They were presenting Miss Howard at court this season. They were very Europeanized Americans; in fact, they had reached a position where they could hardly be said to belong to any nation at all; certainly not to any great power, but perhaps to a sort of Balkanlike state composed of people like themselves. They considered that Fifi was as much of a gratuitous outrage as a new stripe in the flag.

The tall Englishwoman with the long cigarette holder and the half-paralyzed Pekingese presently got up, announcing to the Taylors that she had an engagement in the bar, and strolled away, carrying her paralyzed Pekingese and causing, as she passed, a chilled lull in the seething baby talk that raged around Fifi's table.

About midnight, Mr Weicker, the assistant manager, looked into the bar, where Fifi's phonograph roared new German tangoes into the smoke and clatter. He had a small face that looked into things quickly, and lately he had taken a cursory glance into the bar every night. But he had not come to admire Fifi; he was engaged in an inquiry as to why matters were not going well at the Hotel des Trois Mondes this summer.

There was, of course, the continually sagging American Stock Exchange. With so many hotels begging to be filled, the clients had become finicky, exigent, quick to complain, and Mr Weicker had had many fine decisions to make recently. One large family had departed because of a night-going phonograph belonging to Lady Capps-Karr. Also there was presumably a thief operating in the hotel; there had been complaints about pocketbooks, cigarette cases, watches and rings. Guests sometimes spoke to Mr Weicker as if they would have liked to search his pockets. There were empty suites that need not have been empty this summer.

His glance fell dourly, in passing, upon Count Borowki, who was playing pool with Fifi. Count Borowki had not paid his bill for three weeks. He had told Mr Weicker that he was expecting his mother, who would arrange every-thing. Then there was Fifi, who attracted an undesirable crowd—young students living on pensions who often charged drinks, but never paid for them. Lady Capps-Karr, on the contrary, was a *grande cliente*; one could count three bottles of whisky a day for herself and entourage, and her father in London was good for every drop of it. Mr Weicker decided to issue an ultimatum about Borowki's bill this very night, and withdrew. His visit had lasted about ten seconds.

Count Borowki put away his cue and came close to Fifi, whispering something. She seized his hand and pulled him to a dark corner near the phonograph.

'My American dream girl,' he said. 'We must have you painted in Budapest the way you are tonight. You will hang with the portraits of my ancestors in my castle in Transylvania.'

One would suppose that a normal American girl, who had been to an average number of moving pictures, would have detected a vague ring of familiarity in Count Borowki's persistent wooing. But the Hotel des Trois Mondes was full of people who were actually rich and noble, people who did fine embroidery or took cocaine in closed apartments and meanwhile laid claim to European thrones and half a dozen mediatized German principalities, and Fifi did not choose to doubt the one who paid court to her beauty. Tonight she was surprised at nothing: not even his precipitate proposal that they get married this very week.

'Mamma doesn't want that I should get married for a year. I only said I'd be engaged to you.'

'But my mother wants me to marry. She is hard-boiling, as you Americans say; she brings pressure to bear that I marry Princess This and Countess That.'

Meanwhile Lady Capps-Karr was having a reunion across the room. A tall, stooped Englishman, dusty with travel, had just opened the door of the bar, and Lady Capps-Karr, with a caw of 'Bopes!' had flung herself upon him: 'Bopes, I say!'

'Capps, darling. Hi, there, Rafe——' this to her companion. 'Fancy running into you, Capps.'

'Bopes! Bopes!'

Their exclamations and laughter filled the room, and the bartender whispered to an inquisitive American that the new arrival was the Marquis Kinkallow.

Bopes stretched himself out in several chairs and a sofa and called for the barman. He announced that he had driven from Paris without a stop and was leaving next morning to meet the only woman he had ever loved, in Milan. He did not look in a condition to meet anyone.

'Oh, Bopes, I've been so blind,' said Lady Capps-Karr pathetically. 'Day after day after day. I flew here from Cannes, meaning to stay one day, and I ran into Rafe here and some other Americans I knew, and it's been two weeks, and now all my tickets to Malta are void. Stay here and save me! Oh, Bopes! Bopes! Bopes!'

The Marquis Kinkallow glanced with tired eyes about the bar.

'Ah, who is that?' he demanded. 'The lovely Jewess? And who is that item with her?'

'She's an American,' said the daughter of a hundred earls. 'The man is a scoundrel of some sort, but apparently he's a cat of the stripe; he's a great pal of Schenzi, in Vienna. I sat up till five the other night playing two-handed *chemin de fer* with him here in the bar and he owes me a mille Swiss.'

'Have to have a word with that wench,' said Bopes twenty minutes later. 'You arrange it for me, Rafe, that's a good chap.'

Ralph Berry had met Miss Schwartz, and, as the opportunity for the introduction now presented itself, he rose obligingly. The opportunity was that a *chasseur* had just requested Count Borowki's presence in the office; he managed to beat two or three young men to her side.

'The Marquis Kinkallow is so anxious to meet you. Can't you come and join us?'

Fifi looked across the room, her fine brow wrinkling a little. Something warned her that her evening was full enough already. Lady Capps-Karr had never spoken to her; Fifi believed she was jealous of her clothes.

'Can't you bring him over here?'

A minute later Bopes sat down beside Fifi with a shadow of fine tolerance settling on his face. This was nothing he could help; in fact, he constantly struggled against it, but it was something that happened to his expression when he met

(279)

Americans. 'The whole thing is too much for me,' it seemed to say. 'Compare my confidence with your uncertainty, my sophistication with your naïveté, and yet the whole world has slid into your power.' Of later years he found that his tone, unless carefully guarded, held a smoldering resentment.

Fifi eyed him brightly and told him about her glamorous future.

'Next I'm going to Paris,' she said, announcing the fall of Rome, 'to, maybe, study at the Sorbonne. Then, maybe, I'll get married; you can't tell. I'm only eighteen. I had eighteen candles on my birthday cake tonight. I wish you could have been here. . . . I've had marvelous offers to go on the stage, but of course a girl on the stage gets talked about so.'

'What are you doing tonight?' asked Bopes.

'Oh, lots more boys are coming in later. Stay around and join the party.'

'I thought you and I might do something. I'm going to Milan tomorrow.'

Across the room, Lady Capps-Karr was tense with displeasure at the desertion.

'After all,' she protested, 'a chep's a chep, and a chum's a chum, but there are certain things that one simply doesn't do. I never saw Bopes in such frightful condition.'

She stared at the dialogue across the room.

'Come along to Milan with me,' the marquis was saying. 'Come to Tibet or Hindustan. We'll see them crown the King of Ethiopia. Anyhow, let's go for a drive right now.'

'I got too many guests here. Besides, I don't go out to ride with people the first time I meet them. I'm supposed to be engaged. To a Hungarian count. He'd be furious and would probably challenge you to a duel.'

Mrs Schwartz, with an apologetic expression, came across the room to Fifi.

'John's gone,' she announced. 'He's up there again.'

Fifi gave a yelp of annoyance. 'He gave me his word of honor he would not go.'

'Anyhow, he went. I looked in his room and his hat's gone. It was that champagne at dinner.' She turned to the marquis. 'John is not a vicious boy, but vurry, vurry weak.'

'I suppose I'll have to go after him,' said Fifi resignedly.

'I hate to spoil your good time tonight, but I don't know what else. Maybe this gentleman would go with you. You see, Fifi is the only one that can handle him. His father is dead and it really takes a man to handle a boy.'

'Quite,' said Bopes.

'Can you take me?' Fifi asked. 'It's just up in town to a café.'

He agreed with alacrity. Out in the September night, with her fragrance seeping through an ermine cape, she explained further:

'Some Russian woman's got hold of him; she claims to be a countess, but she's only got one silver-fox fur, that she wears with everything. My brother's just nineteen, so whenever he's had a couple glasses champagne he says he's going to marry her, and mother worries.'

Bopes' arm dropped impatiently around her shoulder as they started up the hill to the town.

Fifteen minutes later the car stopped at a point several blocks beyond the café and Fifi stepped out. The marquis' face was now decorated by a long, irregular finger-nail scratch that ran diagonally across his cheek, traversed his nose in a few sketchy lines and finished in a sort of grand terminal of tracks upon his lower jaw.

'I don't like to have anybody get so foolish,' Fifi explained. 'You needn't wait. We can get a taxi.'

'Wait!' cried the marquis furiously. 'For a common little person like you? They tell me you're the laughingstock of the hotel, and I quite understand why.'

Fifi hurried along the street and into the café, pausing in the door until she saw her brother. He was a reproduction of Fifi without her high warmth; at the moment he was sitting at a table with a frail exile from the Caucasus and two Serbian consumptives. Fifi waited for her temper to rise to an executive pitch; then she crossed the dance floor, conspicuous as a thundercloud in her bright black dress.

'Mamma sent me after you, John. Get your coat.'

'Oh, what's biting her?' he demanded, with a vague eye.

'Mamma says you should come along.'

He got up unwillingly. The two Serbians rose also; the countess never moved; her eyes, sunk deep in Mongol cheek bones, never left Fifi's face; her head crouched in the silver-fox fur which Fifi knew represented her brother's last month's allowance. As John Schwartz stood there swaying unsteadily the orchestra launched into *Ich bin von Kopf bis Fuss*. Diving into the confusion of the table, Fifi emerged with her brother's arm, marched him to the coat room and then out toward the taxi stand.

It was late, the evening was over, her birthday was over, and driving back to the hotel, with John slumped against her shoulder, Fifi felt a sudden depression. By virtue of her fine health she had never been a worrier, and certainly the Schwartz family had lived so long against similar backgrounds that Fifi felt no insufficiency in the Hotel des Trois Mondes as cloud and community—and yet the evening was suddenly all wrong. Didn't evenings sometimes end on a high note and not fade out vaguely in bars? After ten o'clock every night she felt she was the only real being in a colony of ghosts, that she was surrounded by utterly intangible figures who retreated whenever she stretched out her hand.

The doorman assisted her brother to the elevator. Stepping in, Fifi saw, too late, that there were two other people inside. Before she could pull John out again, they had both brushed past her as if in fear of contamination. Fifi heard 'Mercy!' from Mrs Taylor and 'How revolting!' from Miss Howard. The elevator mounted. Fifi held her breath until it stopped at her floor.

It was, perhaps, the impact of this last encounter that caused her to stand very still just inside the door of the dark apartment. Then she had the sense that someone else was there in the blackness ahead of her, and after her brother had stumbled forward and thrown himself on a sofa, she still waited.

'Mamma,' she called, but there was no answer; only a sound fainter than a rustle, like a shoe scraped along the floor.

A few minutes later, when her mother came upstairs, they called the *valet de chambre* and went through the rooms together, but there was no one. Then they stood side by side in the open door to their balcony and looked out on the lake with the bright cluster of Evian on the French shore and the white caps of snow on the mountains.

'I think we've been here long enough,' said Mrs Schwartz suddenly. 'I think I'll take John back to the States this fall.'

Fifi was aghast. 'But I thought John and I were going to the Sorbonne in Paris?'

'How can I trust him in Paris? And how could I leave you behind alone there?'

'But we're used to living in Europe now. Why did I learn to talk French? Why, mamma, we don't even know any people back home any more.'

'We can always meet people. We always have.'

'But you know it's different; everybody is so bigoted there. A girl hasn't the chance to meet the same sort of men, even if there were any. Everybody just watches everything you do.'

'So they do here,' said her mother. 'That Mr Weicker just stopped me in the hall; he saw you come in with John, and he talked to me about how you must keep out of the bar, you were so young. I told him you only took lemonade, but he said it didn't matter; scenes like tonight made people leave the hotel.'

'Oh, how perfectly mean!'

'So I think we better go back home.'

The empty word rang desolately in Fifi's ears. She put her arms around her mother's waist, realizing that it was she and

(283)

not her mother, with her mother's clear grip on the past, who was completely lost in the universe. On the sofa her brother snored, having already entered the world of the weak, of the leaners together, and found its fetid and mercurial warmth sufficient. But Fifi kept looking at the alien sky, knowing that she could pierce it and find her own way through envy and corruption. For the first time she seriously considered marrying Borowki immediately.

'Do you want to go downstairs and say good night to the boys?' suggested her mother. 'There's lots of them still there asking where you are.'

But the Furies were after Fifi now—after her childish complacency and her innocence, even after her beauty—out to break it all down and drag it in any convenient mud. When she shook her head and walked sullenly into her bedroom, they had already taken something from her forever.

II

The following morning Mrs Schwartz went to Mr Weicker's office to report the loss of two hundred dollars in American money. She had left the sum on her chiffonier upon retiring; when she awoke, it was gone. The door of the apartment had been bolted, but in the morning the bolt was found drawn, and yet neither of her children was awake. Fortunately, she had taken her jewels to bed with her in a chamois sack.

Mr Weicker decided that the situation must be handled with care. There were not a few guests in the hotel who were in straitened circumstances and inclined to desperate remedies, but he must move slowly. In America one has money or hasn't; in Europe the heir to a fortune may be unable to stand himself a haircut until the collapse of a fifth cousin, yet be a sure risk and not to be lightly offended. Opening the office copy of the Almanack de Gotha, Mr Weicker found Stanislas Karl Joseph Borowki hooked firmly

(284)

on to the end of a line older than the crown of St Stephen. This morning, in riding clothes that were smart as a hussar's uniform, he had gone riding with the utterly correct Miss Howard. On the other hand, there was no doubt as to who had been robbed, and Mr Weicker's indignation began to concentrate on Fifi and her family, who might have saved him this trouble by taking themselves off some time ago. It was even conceivable that the dissipated son, John, had nipped the money.

In all events, the Schwartzes were going home. For three years they had lived in hotels—in Paris, Florence, St Raphael, Como, Vichy, La Baule, Lucerne, Baden-Baden and Biarritz. Everywhere there had been schools—always new schools—and both children spoke in perfect French and scrawny fragments of Italian. Fifi had grown from a large-featured child of fourteen to a beauty; John had grown into something rather dismal and lost. Both of them played bridge, and somewhere Fifi had picked up tap dancing. Mrs Schwartz felt that it was all somehow unsatisfactory, but she did not know why. So, two days after Fifi's party, she announced that they would pack their trunks, go to Paris for some new fall clothes and then go home.

That same afternoon Fifi came to the bar to get her phonograph, left there the night of her party. She sat up on a high stool and talked to the barman while she drank a ginger ale.

'Mother wants to take me back to America, but I'm not going.'

'What will you do?'

'Oh, I've got a little money of my own, and then I may get married.' She sipped her ginger ale moodily.

'I hear you had some money stolen,' he remarked. 'How did it happen?'

'Well, Count Borowki thinks the man got into the apartment early and hid in between the two doors between us and the next apartment. Then, when we were asleep, he took the money and walked out.'

'Ha!'

Fifi sighed. 'Well, you probably won't see me in the bar any more.'

'We'll miss you, Miss Schwartz.'

Mr Weicker put his head in the door, withdrew it and then came in slowly.

'Hello,' said Fifi coldly.

'A-ha, young lady.' He waggled his finger at her with affected facetiousness. 'Didn't you know I spoke to your mother about your coming in to the bar? It's merely for your own good.'

'I'm just having a ginger ale,' she said indignantly.

'But no one can tell what you're having. It might be whisky or what not. It is the other guests who complain.'

She stared at him indignantly—the picture was so different from her own—of Fifi as the lively center of the hotel, of Fifi in clothes that ravished the eye, standing splendid and unattainable amid groups of adoring men. Suddenly Mr Weicker's obsequious, but hostile, face infuriated her.

'We're getting out of this hotel!' she flared up. 'I never saw such a narrow-minded bunch of people in my life; always criticizing everybody and making up terrible things about them, no matter what they do themselves. I think it would be a good thing if the hotel caught fire and burned down with all the nasty cats in it.'

Banging down her glass, she seized the phonograph case and stalked out of the bar.

In the lobby a porter sprang to help her, but she shook her head and hurried on through the salon, where she came upon Count Borowki.

'Oh, I'm so furious!' she cried. 'I never saw so many old cats! I just told Mr Weicker what I thought of them!'

'Did someone dare to speak rudely to you?'

'Oh, it doesn't matter. We're going away.'

'Going away!' He started. 'When?'

'Right away. I don't want to, but mamma says we've got to.'

'I must talk to you seriously about this,' he said. 'I just called your room. I have brought you a little engagement present.'

Her spirits returned as she took the handsome gold-and-ivory cigarette case engraved with her initials.

'How lovely!'

'Now, listen; what you tell me makes it more important that I talk to you immediately. I have just received another letter from my mother. They have chosen a girl for me in Budapest—a lovely girl, rich and beautiful and of my own rank who would be very happy at the match, but I am in love with you. I would never have thought it possible, but I have lost my heart to an American.'

'Well, why not?' said Fifi, indignantly. 'They call girls beautiful here if they have one good feature. And then, if they've got nice eyes or hair, they're usually bow-legged or haven't got nice teeth.'

'There is no flaw or fault in you.'

'Oh, yes,' said Fifi modestly. 'I got a sort of big nose. Would you know I was Jewish?'

With a touch of impatience, Borowki came back to his argument: 'So they are bringing pressure to bear for me to marry. Questions of inheritance depend on it.'

'Besides, my forehead is too high,' observed Fifi abstractedly. 'It's so high it's got sort of wrinkles in it. I knew an awfully funny boy who used to call me "the highbrow."'

'So the sensible thing,' pursued Borowki, 'is for us to marry immediately. I tell you frankly there are other American girls not far from here who wouldn't hesitate.'

'Mamma would be about crazy,' Fifi said.

'I've thought about that too,' he answered her eagerly. 'Don't tell her. If we drove over the border tonight we could be married tomorrow morning. Then we come back and you show your mother the little gilt coronets painted on

(287)

your luggage. My own personal opinion is that she'll be delighted. There you are, off her hands, with social position second to none in Europe. In my opinion, your mother has probably thought of it already, and may be saying to herself: "Why don't those two young people just take matters into their own hands and save me all the fuss and expense of a wedding?" I think she would like us for being so hard-boiled.'

He broke off impatiently as Lady Capps-Karr, emerging from the dining room with her Pekingese, surprised them by stopping at their table. Count Borowki was obliged to introduce them. As he had not known of the Marquis Kinkallow's defection the other evening, nor that His Lordship had taken a wound to Milan the following morning, he had no suspicion of what was coming.

'I've noticed Miss Schwartz,' said the Englishwoman in a clear, concise voice. 'And of course I've noticed Miss Schwartz's clothes.'

'Won't you sit down?' said Fifi.

'No, thank you.' She turned to Borowki. 'Miss Schwartz's clothes make us all appear somewhat drab. I always refuse to dress elaborately in hotels. It seems such rotten taste. Don't you think so?'

'I think people always ought to look nice,' said Fifi, flushing.

'Naturally. I merely said that I consider it rotten taste to dress elaborately, save in the houses of one's friends.'

She said 'Good-by-e-e' to Borowki and moved on, emitting a mouthed cloud of smoke and a faint fragrance of whisky.

The insult had been as stinging as the crack of a whip, and as Fifi's pride of her wardrobe was swept away from her, she heard all the comments that she had not heard, in one great resurgent whisper. Then they said that she wore her clothes here because she had nowhere else to wear them. That was why the Howard girl considered her vulgar and did not care to know her.

For an instant her anger flamed up against her mother for not telling her, but she saw that her mother did not know either.

'I think she's so dowdy,' she forced herself to say aloud, but inside she was quivering. 'What is she, anyhow? I mean, how high is her title? Very high?'

'She's the widow of a baronet.'

'Is that high?' Fifi's face was rigid. 'Higher than a countess?'

'No. A countess is much higher—infinitely higher.' He moved his chair closer and began to talk intently.

Half an hour later Fifi got up with indecision on her face.

'At seven you'll let me know definitely,' Borowki said, 'and I'll be ready with a car at ten.'

Fifi nodded. He escorted her across the room and saw her vanish into a dark hall mirror in the direction of the lift.

As he turned away, Lady Capps-Karr, sitting alone over her coffee, spoke to him:

'I want a word with you. Did you, by some slip of the tongue, suggest to Weicker that in case of difficulties I would guarantee your bills?'

Borowki flushed. 'I may have said something like that, but——'

'Well, I told him the truth—that I never laid eyes on you until a fortnight ago.'

'I, naturally, turned to a person of equal rank——'

'Equal rank! What cheek! The only titles left are English titles. I must ask you not to make use of my name again.'

He bowed. 'Such inconveniences will soon be for me a thing of the past.'

'Are you getting off with that vulgar little American?'

'I beg your pardon,' he said stiffly.

'Don't be angry. I'll stand you a whisky-and-soda. I'm getting in shape for Bopes Kinkallow, who's just telephoned he's tottering back here.'

Meanwhile, upstairs, Mrs Schwartz was saying to Fifi:

(289)

'Now that I know we're going away I'm getting excited about it. It will be so nice seeing the Hirsts and Mrs Bell and Amy and Marjorie and Gladys again, and the new baby. You'll be happy, too; you've forgotten how they're like. You and Gladys used to be great friends. And Marjorie——'

'Oh, mamma, don't talk about it,' cried Fifi miserably. 'I can't go back.'

'We needn't stay. If John was in a college like his father wanted, we could, maybe, go to California.'

But for Fifi all the romance of life was rolled up into the last three impressionable years in Europe. She remembered the tall guardsmen in Rome and the old Spaniard who had first made her conscious of her beauty at the Villa d'Este at Como, and the French naval aviator at St Raphael who had dropped her a note from his plane into their garden, and the feeling that she had sometimes, when she danced with Borowki, that he was dressed in gleaming boots and a white-furred dolman.

She had seen many American moving pictures and she knew that the girls there always married the faithful boy from the old home town, and after that there was nothing.

'I won't go,' she said aloud.

Her mother turned with a pile of clothes in her arms. 'What talk is that from you, Fifi? You think I could leave you here alone?' As Fifi didn't answer, she continued, with an air of finality: 'That talk doesn't sound nice from you. Now you stop fretting and saying such things, and get me this list of things uptown.'

But Fifi had decided. It was Borowki, then, and the chance of living fully and adventurously. He could go into the diplomatic service, and then one day when they encountered Lady Capps-Karr and Miss Howard at a legation ball, she could make audible the observation that for the moment seemed so necessary to her: 'I hate people who always look as if they were going to or from a funeral.'

'So run along,' her mother continued. 'And look in at that café and see if John is up there, and take him to tea.'

Fifi accepted the shopping list mechanically. Then she went into her room and wrote a little note to Borowki which she would leave with the concierge on the way out.

Coming out, she saw her mother struggling with a trunk, and felt terribly sorry for her. But there were Amy and Gladys in America, and Fifi hardened herself.

She walked out and down the stairs, remembering halfway that in her distraction she had omitted an official glance in the mirror; but there was a large mirror on the wall just outside the grand salon, and she stopped in front of that instead.

She was beautiful—she learned that once more, but now it made her sad. She wondered whether the dress she wore this afternoon was in bad taste, whether it would minister to the superiority of Miss Howard or Lady Capps-Karr. It seemed to her a lovely dress, soft and gentle in cut, but in color a hard, bright, metallic powder blue.

Then a sudden sound broke the stillness of the gloomy hall and Fifi stood suddenly breathless and motionless.

III

At eleven o'clock Mr Weicker was tired, but the bar was in one of its periodical riots and he was waiting for it to quiet down. There was nothing to do in the stale office or the empty lobby; and the salon, where all day he held long conversations with lonely English and American women, was deserted; so he went out the front door and began to make the circuit of the hotel. Whether due to his circumambient course or to his frequent glances up at the twinkling bedroom lights and into the humble, grilled windows of the kitchen floor, the promenade gave him a sense of being in .control of the hotel, of being adequately responsible, as though it were a ship and he was surveying it from a quarterdeck.

He went past a flood of noise and song from the bar, past a

window where two bus boys sat on a bunk and played cards over a bottle of Spanish wine. There was a phonograph somewhere above, and a woman's form blocked out a window; then there was the quiet wing, and turning the corner, he arrived back at his point of departure. And in front of the hotel, under the dim porte-cochère light, he saw Count Borowki.

Something made him stop and watch—something incongruous—Borowki, who couldn't pay his bill, had a car and a chauffeur. He was giving the chauffeur some sort of detailed instructions, and then Mr Weicker perceived that there was a bag in the front seat, and came forward into the light.

'You are leaving us, Count Borowki?'

Borowki started at the voice. 'For the night only,' he answered. 'I'm going to meet my mother.'

'I see.'

Borowki looked at him reproachfully. 'My trunk and hat box are in my room, you'll discover. Did you think I was running away from my bill?'

'Certainly not. I hope you will have a pleasant journey and find your mother well.'

But inside he took the precaution of dispatching a *valet de chambre* to see if the baggage was indeed there, and even to give it a thoughtful heft, lest its kernel were departed.

He dozed for perhaps an hour. When he woke up, the night concierge was pulling at his arm and there was a strong smell of smoke in the lobby. It was some moments before he could get it through his head that one wing of the hotel was on fire.

Setting the concierge at the alarms, he rushed down the hall to the bar, and through the smoke that poured from the door he caught sight of the burning billiard table and the flames licking along the floor and flaring up in alcoholic ecstasy every time a bottle on the shelves cracked with the heat. As he hastily retreated he met a line of half-dressed *chasseurs* and bus boys already struggling up from the lower depths with buckets of water. The concierge shouted that the fire department was on its way. He put two men at the telephones to awaken the guests, and as he ran back to form a bucket line at the danger point, he thought for the first time of Fifi.

Blind rage consumed him—with a precocious Indianlike cruelty she had carried out her threat. Ah, he would deal with that later; there was still law in the country. Meanwhile a clangor outdoors announced that the engines had arrived, and he made his way back through the lobby, filled now with men in pajamas carrying brief cases, and women in bedclothes carrying jewel boxes and small dogs; the number swelling every minute and the talk rising from a cadence heavy with sleep to the full staccato buzz of an afternoon soirée.

A *chasseur* called Mr Weicker to the phone, but the manager shook him off impatiently.

'It's the commissionaire of police,' the boy persisted. 'He says you must speak to him.'

With an exclamation, Mr Weicker hurried into the office. ''Allo!'

'I'm calling from the station. Is this the manager?'

'Yes, but there's a fire here.'

'Have you among your guests a man calling himself Count Borowki?'

'Why, yes——'

'We're bringing him there for identification. He was picked up on the road on some information we received.'

'But——'

'We picked up a girl with him. We're bring them both down there immediately.'

'I tell you——'

The receiver clicked briskly in his ear and Mr Weicker hurried back to the lobby, where the smoke was diminishing. The reassuring pumps had been at work for five minutes and the bar was a wet charred ruin. Mr Weicker began passing here and there among the guests, tranquilizing and

(293)

persuading; the phone operators began calling the rooms again, advising such guests as had not appeared that it was safe to go back to bed; and then, at the continued demands for an explanation, he thought again of Fifi, and this time of his own accord he hurried to the phone.

Mrs Schwartz's anxious voice answered; Fifi wasn't there. That was what he wanted to know. He rang off brusquely. There was the story, and he could not have wished for anything more sordidly complete—an incendiary blaze and an attempted elopement with a man wanted by the police. It was time for paying, and all the money of America couldn't make any difference. If the season was ruined, at least Fifi would have no more seasons at all. She would go to a girls' institution where the prescribed uniform was rather plainer than any clothing she had ever worn.

As the last of the guests departed into the elevators, leaving only a few curious rummagers among the soaked débris, another procession came in by the front door. There was a man in civilian clothes and a little wall of policemen with two people behind. The commissionaire spoke and the screen of policemen parted.

'I want you to identify these two people. Has this man been staying here under the name of Borowki?'

Mr Weicker looked. 'He has.'

'He's been wanted for a year in Italy, France and Spain. And this girl?'

She was half hidden behind Borowki, her head hanging, her face in shadow. Mr Weicker craned toward her eagerly. He was looking at Miss Howard.

A wave of horror swept over Mr Weicker. Again he craned his head forward, as if by the intensity of his astonishment he could convert her into Fifi, or look through her and find Fifi. But this would have been difficult, for Fifi was far away. She was in front of the café, assisting the stumbling and reluctant John Schwartz into a taxi. 'I should say you can't go back. Mother says you should come right home.'

Count Borowki took his incarceration with a certain grace, as though, having lived so long by his own wits, there was a certain relief in having his days planned by an external agency. But he resented the lack of intercourse with the outer world, and was overjoyed when, on the fourth day of his imprisonment, he was led forth to find Lady Capps-Karr.

'After all,' she said, 'a chep's a chep and a chum's a chum, whatever happens. Luckily, our consul here is a friend of my father's, or they wouldn't have let me see you. I even tried to get you out on bail, because I told them you went to Oxford for a year and spoke English perfectly, but the brutes wouldn't listen.'

'I'm afraid there's no use,' said Count Borowki gloomily. 'When they've finished trying me I'll have had a free journey all over Europe.'

'But that's not the only outrageous thing,' she continued. 'Those idiots have thrown Bopes and me out of the Trois Mondes, and the authorities are trying to get us to leave the city.'

'What for?'

'They're trying to put the full blame of that tiresome fire on us.'

'Did you start it?'

'We did set some brandy on fire because we wanted to cook some potato chips in alcohol, and the bartender had gone to bed and left us there. But you'd think, from the way the swine talk, that we'd come there with the sole idea of burning everyone in their beds. The whole thing's an outrage and Bopes is furious. He says he'll never come here again. I went to the consulate and they agreed that the whole affair was perfectly disgraceful, and they've wired the Foreign Office.'

Borowki considered for a moment. 'If I could be born over again,' he said slowly, 'I think without any doubt I should choose to be born an Englishman.'

(295)

'I could choose to be anything but an American! By the way, the Taylors are not presenting Miss Howard at court because of the disgraceful way the newspapers played up the matter.'

'What puzzles me is what made Fifi suspicious,' said Borowki.

'Then it was Miss Schwartz who blabbed?'

'Yes. I thought I had convinced her to come with me, and I knew that if she didn't, I had only to snap my fingers to the other girl. . . . That very afternoon Fifi visited the jeweler's and discovered I'd paid for the cigarette case with a hundred-dollar American note I'd lifted from her mother's chiffonier. She went straight to the police.'

'Without coming to you first! After all, a chep's a chep——'

'But what I want to know is what made her suspicious enough to investigate, what turned her against me.'

Fifi, at that moment sitting on a high stool in a hotel bar in Paris and sipping a lemonade, was answering that very question to an interested bartender.

'I was standing in the hall looking in the mirror,' she said, 'and I heard him talking to the English lady—the one who set the hotel on fire. And I heard him say, "After all, my one nightmare is that she'll turn out to look like her mother."' Fifi's voice blazed with indignation. 'Well, you've seen my mother, haven't you?'

'Yes, and a very fine woman she is.'

'After that I knew there was something the matter with him, and I wondered how much he'd paid for the cigarette case. So I went up to see. They showed me the bill he paid with.'

'And you will go to America now?' the barman asked.

Fifi finished her glass; the straw made a gurgling sound in the sugar at the bottom.

'We've got to go back and testify, and we'll stay a few months anyhow.' She stood up. 'Bye-bye; I've got a fitting.'

They had not got her—not yet. The Furies had withdrawn

a little and stood in the background with a certain gnashing of teeth. But there was plenty of time.

Yet, as Fifi tottered out through the lobby, her face gentle with new hopes, as she went out looking for completion under the impression that she was going to the *couturier*, there was a certain doubt among the eldest and most experienced of the Furies if they would get her, after all.

SCOTT

A New Leaf

(The Saturday Evening Post,

4 July 1931)

It was the first day warm enough to eat outdoors in the Bois
de Boulogne, while chestnut blossoms slanted down across
the tables and dropped impudently into the butter and the
wine. Julia Ross ate a few with her bread and listened to the
big goldfish rippling in the pool and the sparrows whirring
about an abandoned table. You could see everybody again—
the waiters with their professional faces, the watchful
Frenchwomen all heels and eyes, Phil Hoffman opposite her
with his heart balanced on his fork, and the extraordinarily
handsome man just coming out on the terrace.

——the purple noon's transparent might.
The breath of the moist air is light
Around each unexpanded bud——

Julia trembled discreetly; she controlled herself; she
didn't spring up and call, 'Yi-yi-yi-yi! Isn't this grand?' and
push the maître d'hôtel into the lily pond. She sat there, a
well-behaved woman of twenty-one, and discreetly trembled.

Phil was rising, napkin in hand. 'Hi there, Dick!'

'Hi, Phil!'

It was the handsome man; Phil took a few steps forward
and they talked apart from the table.

'——seen Carter and Kitty in Spain——'

'——poured on to the Bremen——'

(298)

'——so I was going to——'

The man went on, following the head waiter, and Phil sat down.

'Who is that?' she demanded.

'A friend of mine—Dick Ragland.'

'He's without doubt the handsomest man I ever saw in my life.'

'Yes, he's handsome,' he agreed without enthusiasm.

'Handsome! He's an archangel, he's a mountain lion, he's something to eat. Just why didn't you introduce him?'

'Because he's got the worst reputation of any American in Paris.'

'Nonsense; he must be maligned. It's all a dirty frame-up —a lot of jealous husbands whose wives got one look at him. Why, that man's never done anything in his life except lead cavalry charges and save children from drowning.'

'The fact remains he's not received anywhere—not for one reason but for a thousand.'

'What reasons?'

'Everything. Drink, women, jails, scandals, killed somebody with an automobile, lazy, worthless——'

'I don't believe a word of it,' said Julia firmly. 'I bet he's tremendously attractive. And you spoke to him as if you thought so too.'

'Yes,' he said reluctantly, 'like so many alcholics, he has a certain charm. If he'd only make his messes off by himself somewhere—except right in people's laps. Just when somebody's taken him up and is making a big fuss over him, he pours the soup down his hostess' back, kisses the serving maid and passes out in the dog kennel. But he's done it too often. He's run through about everybody, until there's no one left.'

'There's me,' said Julia.

There was Julia, who was a little too good for anybody and sometimes regretted that she had been quite so well endowed. Anything added to beauty has to be paid for—that is

(299)

to say, the qualities that pass as substitutes can be liabilities when added to beauty itself. Julia's brilliant hazel glance was enough, without the questioning light of intelligence that flickered in it; her irrepressible sense of the ridiculous detracted from the gentle relief of her mouth, and the loveliness of her figure might have been more obvious if she had slouched and postured rather than sat and stood very straight, after the discipline of a strict father.

Equally perfect young men had several times appeared bearing gifts, but generally with the air of being already complete, of having no space for development. On the other hand, she found that men of larger scale had sharp corners and edges in youth, and she was a little too young herself to like that. There was, for instance, this scornful young egotist, Phil Hoffman, opposite her, who was obviously going to be a brilliant lawyer and who had practically followed her to Paris. She liked him as well as anyone she knew, but he had at present all the overbearance of the son of a chief of police.

'Tonight I'm going to London, and Wednesday I sail,' he said. 'And you'll be in Europe all summer, with somebody new chewing on your ear every few weeks.'

'When you've been called for a lot of remarks like that you'll begin to edge into the picture,' Julia remarked. 'Just to square yourself, I want you to introduce that man Ragland.'

'My last few hours!' he complained.

'But I've given you three whole days on the chance you'd work out a better approach. Be a little civilized and ask him to have some coffee.'

As Mr Dick Ragland joined them, Julia drew a little breath of pleasure. He was a fine figure of a man, in coloring both tan and blond, with a peculiar luminosity to his face. His voice was quietly intense; it seemed always to tremble a little with a sort of gay despair; the way he looked at Julia made her feel attractive. For half an hour, as their sentences floated

(300)

pleasantly among the scent of violets and snowdrops, forget-me-nots and pansies, her interest in him grew. She was even glad when Phil said:

'I've just thought about my English visa. I'll have to leave you two incipient love birds together against my better judgment. Will you meet me at the Gare St Lazare at five and see me off?'

He looked at Julia hoping she'd say, 'I'll go along with you now.' She knew very well she had no business being alone with this man, but he made her laugh, and she hadn't laughed much lately, so she said: 'I'll stay a few minutes; it's so nice and springy here.'

When Phil was gone, Dick Ragland suggested a *fine* champagne.

'I hear you have a terrible reputation?' she said impulsively.

'Awful. I'm not even invited out any more. Do you want me to slip on my false mustache?'

'It's so odd,' she pursued. 'Don't you cut yourself off from all nourishment? Do you know that Phil felt he had to warn me about you before he introduced you? And I might very well have told him not to.'

'Why didn't you?'

'I thought you seemed so attractive and it was such a pity.'

His face grew bland; Julia saw that the remark had been made so often that it no longer reached him.

'It's none of my business,' she said quickly. She did not realize that his being a sort of outcast added to his attraction for her—not the dissipation itself, for never having seen it, it was merely an abstraction—but its result in making him so alone. Something atavistic in her went out to the stranger to the tribe, a being from a world with different habits from hers, who promised the unexpected—promised adventure.

'I'll tell you something else,' he said suddenly. 'I'm going permanently on the wagon on June fifth, my twenty-eighth

birthday. I don't have fun drinking any more. Evidently I'm
not one of the few people who can use liquor.'

'You sure you can go on the wagon?'

'I always do what I say I'll do. Also I'm going back to
New York and go to work.'

'I'm really surprised how glad I am.' This was rash, but
she let it stand.

'Have another *fine*?' Dick suggested. 'Then you'll be
gladder still.'

'Will you go on this way right up to your birthday?'

'Probably. On my birthday I'll be on the Olympic in
mid-ocean.'

'I'll be on that boat too!' she exclaimed.

'You can watch the quick change; I'll do it for the ship's
concert.'

The tables were being cleared off. Julia knew she should
go now, but she couldn't bear to leave him sitting with that
unhappy look under his smile. She felt, maternally, that she
ought to say something to help him keep his resolution.

'Tell me why you drink so much. Probably some obscure
reason you don't know yourself.'

'Oh, I know pretty well how it began.'

He told her as another hour waned. He had gone to the war
at seventeen and, when he came back, life as a Princeton
freshman with a little black cap was somewhat tame. So he
went up to Boston Tech and then abroad to the Beaux Arts;
it was there that something happened to him.

'About the time I came into some money I found that with
a few drinks I got expansive and somehow had the ability to
please people, and the idea turned my head. Then I began
to take a whole lot of drinks to keep going and have everybody think I was wonderful. Well, I got plastered a lot and
quarreled with most of my friends, and then I met a wild
bunch and for a while I was expansive with them. But I was
inclined to get superior and suddenly think "What am I
doing with this bunch?" They didn't like that much. And

(302)

when a taxi that I was in killed a man, I was sued. It was just a graft, but it got in the papers, and after I was released the impression remained that I'd killed him. So all I've got to show for the last five years is a reputation that makes mothers rush their daughters away if I'm at the same hotel.'

An impatient waiter was hovering near and she looked at her watch.

'Gosh, we're to see Phil off at five. We've been here all the afternoon.'

As they hurried to the Gare St Lazare, he asked: 'Will you let me see you again; or do you think you'd better not?'

She returned his long look. There was no sign of dissipation in his face, in his warm cheeks, in his erect carriage.

'I'm always fine at lunch,' he added, like an invalid.

'I'm not worried,' she laughed. 'Take me to lunch day after tomorrow.'

They hurried up the steps of the Gare St Lazare, only to see the last carriage of the Golden Arrow disappearing toward the Channel. Julia was remorseful, because Phil had come so far.

As a sort of atonement, she went to the apartment where she lived with her aunt and tried to write a letter to him, but Dick Ragland intruded himself into her thoughts. By morning the effect of his good looks had faded a little; she was inclined to write him a note that she couldn't see him. Still, he had made her a simple appeal and she had brought it all on herself. She waited for him at half-past twelve on the appointed day.

Julia had said nothing to her aunt, who had company for luncheon and might mention his name—strange to go out with a man whose name you couldn't mention. He was late and she waited in the hall, listening to the echolalia of chatter from the luncheon party in the dining room. At one she answered the bell.

There in the outer hall stood a man whom she thought she had never seen before. His face was dead white and erratically shaven, his soft hat was crushed bunlike on his head, his shirt collar was dirty, and all except the band of his tie was out of sight. But at the moment when she recognized the figure as Dick Ragland she perceived a change which dwarfed the others into nothing; it was in his expression. His whole face was one prolonged sneer—the lids held with difficulty from covering the fixed eyes, the drooping mouth drawn up over the upper teeth, the chin wabbling like a made-over chin in which the paraffin had run—it was a face that both expressed and inspired disgust.

'H'lo,' he muttered.

For a minute she drew back from him; then, at a sudden silence from the dining room that gave on the hall, inspired by the silence in the hall itself, she half pushed him over the threshold, stepped out herself and closed the door behind them.

'Oh-h-h!' she said in a single, shocked breath.

'Haven't been home since yest'day. Got involve' on a party at——'

With repugnance, she turned him around by his arm and stumbled with him down the apartment stairs, passing the concierge's wife, who peered out at them curiously from her glass room. Then they came out into the bright sunshine of the Rue Guynemer.

Against the spring freshness of the Luxembourg Gardens opposite, he was even more grotesque. He frightened her; she looked desperately up and down the street for a taxi, but one turning the corner of the Rue de Vaugirard disregarded her signal.

'Where'll we go lunch?' he asked.

'You're in no shape to go to lunch. Don't you realize? You've got to go home and sleep.'

'I'm all right. I get a drink I'll be fine.'

A passing cab slowed up at her gesture.

'You go home and go to sleep. You're not fit to go anywhere.'

(304)

As he focused his eyes on her, realizing her suddenly as something fresh, something new and lovely, something alien to the smoky and turbulent world where he had spent his recent hours, a faint current of reason flowed through him. She saw his mouth twist with vague awe, saw him make a vague attempt to stand up straight. The taxi yawned.

'Maybe you're right. Very sorry.'

'What's your address?'

He gave it and then tumbled into a corner, his face still struggling toward reality. Julia closed the door.

When the cab had driven off, she hurried across the street and into the Luxembourg Gardens as if someone were after her.

II

Quite by accident, she answered when he telephoned at seven that night. His voice was strained and shaking:

'I suppose there's not much use apologizing for this morning. I didn't know what I was doing, but that's no excuse. But if you could let me see you for a while somewhere tomorrow—just for a minute—I'd like the chance of telling you in person how terribly sorry——'

'I'm busy tomorrow.'

'Well, Friday then, or any day.'

'I'm sorry, I'm very busy this week.'

'You mean you don't ever want to see me again?'

'Mr Ragland, I hardly see the use of going any further with this. Really, that thing this morning was a little too much. I'm very sorry. I hope you feel better. Good-by.'

She put him entirely out of her mind. She had not even associated his reputation with such a spectacle—a heavy drinker was someone who sat up late and drank champagne and maybe in the small hours rode home singing. This spectacle at high noon was something else again. Julia was through.

Meanwhile there were other men with whom she lunched at Ciro's and danced in the Bois. There was a reproachful letter from Phil Hoffman in America. She liked Phil better for having been so right about this. A fortnight passed and she would have forgotten Dick Ragland, had she not heard his name mentioned with scorn in several conversations. Evidently he had done such things before.

Then, a week before she was due to sail, she ran into him in the booking department of the White Star Line. He was as handsome—she could hardly believe her eyes. He leaned with an elbow on the desk, his fine figure erect, his yellow gloves as stainless as his clear, shining eyes. His strong, gay personality had affected the clerk who served him with fascinated deference; the stenographers behind looked up for a minute and exchanged a glance. Then he saw Julia; she nodded, and with a quick, wincing change of expression he raised his hat.

They were together by the desk a long time and the silence was oppressive.

'Isn't this a nuisance?' she said.

'Yes,' he said jerkily, and then: 'You going by the Olympic?'

'Oh, yes.'

'I thought you might have changed.'

'Of course not,' she said coldly.

'I thought of changing; in fact, I was here to ask about it.'

'That's absurd.'

'You don't hate the sight of me? So it'll make you seasick when we pass each other on the deck?'

She smiled. He seized his advantage:

'I've improved somewhat since we last met.'

'Don't talk about that.'

'Well then, you have improved. You've got the loveliest costume on I ever saw.'

This was presumptuous, but she felt herself shimmering a little at the compliment.

(306)

'You wouldn't consider a cup of coffee with me at the café next door, just to recover from this ordeal?'

How weak of her to talk to him like this, to let him make advances. It was like being under the fascination of a snake.

'I'm afraid I can't.' Something terriby timid and vulnerable came into his face, twisting a little sinew in her heart.

'Well, all right,' she shocked herself by saying.

Sitting at the sidewalk table in the sunlight, there was nothing to remind her of that awful day two weeks ago. Jekyll and Hyde. He was courteous, he was charming, he was amusing. He made her feel, oh, so attractive! He presumed on nothing.

'Have you stopped drinking?' she asked.

'Not till the fifth.'

'Oh!'

'Not until I said I'd stop. Then I'll stop.'

When Julia rose to go, she shook her head at his suggestion of a further meeting.

'I'll see you on the boat. After your twenty-eighth birthday.'

'All right; one more thing: It fits in with the high price of crime that I did something inexcusable to the one girl I've ever been in love with in my life.'

She saw him the first day on board, and then her heart sank into her shoes as she realized at last how much she wanted him. No matter what his past was, no matter what he had done. Which was not to say that she would ever let him know, but only that he moved her chemically more than anyone she had ever met, that all other men seemed pale beside him.

He was popular on the boat; she heard that he was giving a party on the night of his twenty-eighth birthday. Julia was not invited; when they met they spoke pleasantly, nothing more.

It was the day after the fifth that she found him stretched in his deck chair looking wan and white. There were wrinkles on his fine brow and around his eyes, and his hand, as he reached out for a cup of bouillon, was trembling. He was still there in the late afternoon, visibly suffering, visibly miserable. After three times around, Julia was irresistibly impelled to speak to him:

'Has the new era begun?'

He made a feeble effort to rise, but she motioned him not to and sat on the next chair.

'You look tired.'

'I'm just a little nervous. This is the first day in five years that I haven't had a drink.'

'It'll be better soon.'

'I know,' he said grimly.

'Don't weaken.'

'I won't.'

'Can't I help you in any way? Would you like a bromide?'

'I can't stand bromides,' he said almost crossly. 'No, thanks, I mean.'

Julia stood up: 'I know you feel better alone. Things will be brighter tomorrow.'

'Don't go, if you can stand me.'

Julia sat down again.

'Sing me a song—can you sing?'

'What kind of a song?'

'Something sad—some sort of blues.'

She sang him Libby Holman's 'This is how the story ends,' in a low, soft voice.

'That's good. Now sing another. Or sing that again.'

'All right. If you like, I'll sing to you all afternoon.'

III

The second day in New York he called her on the phone. 'I've missed you so,' he said. 'Have you missed me?'

'I'm afraid I have,' she said reluctantly.

'Much?'

'I've missed you a lot. Are you better?'

'I'm all right now. I'm still just a little nervous, but I'm starting work tomorrow. When can I see you?'

'When you want.'

'This evening then. And look—say that again.'

'What?'

'That you're afraid you have missed me.'

'I'm afraid that I have,' Julia said obediently.

'Missed me,' he added.

'I'm afraid I have missed you.'

'All right. It sounds like a song when you say it.'

'Good-by, Dick.'

'Good-by, Julia dear.'

She stayed in New York two months instead of the fortnight she had intended, because he would not let her go. Work took the place of drink in the daytime, but afterward he must see Julia.

Sometimes she was jealous of his work when he telephoned that he was too tired to go out after the theater. Lacking drink, night life was less than nothing to him— something quite spoiled and well lost. For Julia, who never drank, it was a stimulus in itself—the music and the parade of dresses and the handsome couple they made dancing together. At first they saw Phil Hoffman once in a while; Julia considered that he took the matter rather badly; then they didn't see him any more.

A few unpleasant incidents occurred. An old schoolmate, Esther Cary, came to her to ask if she knew of Dick Ragland's reputation. Instead of growing angry, Julia invited her to meet Dick and was delighted with the ease with which Esther's convictions were changed. There were other, small, annoying episodes, but Dick's misdemeanors had, fortunately, been confined to Paris and assumed here a far-away unreality. They loved each other deeply now—the memory of that morning slowly being effaced from Julia's imagination— but she wanted to be sure.

'After six months, if everything goes along like this, we'll announce our engagement. After another six months we'll be married.'

'Such a long time,' he mourned.

'But there were five years before that,' Julia answered. 'I trust you with my heart and with my mind, but something else says wait. Remember, I'm also deciding for my children.'

Those five years—oh, so lost and gone.

In August, Julia went to California for two months to see her family. She wanted to know how Dick would get along alone. They wrote every day; his letters were by turns cheerful, depressed, weary and hopeful. His work was going better. As things came back to him, his uncle had begun really to believe in him, but all the time he missed his Julia so. It was when an occasional note of despair began to appear that she cut her visit short by a week and came East to New York.

'Oh, thank God you're here!' he cried as they linked arms and walked out of the Grand Central station. 'It's been so hard. Half a dozen times lately I've wanted to go on a bust and I had to think of you, and you were so far away.'

'Darling—darling, you're so tired and pale. You're working too hard.'

'No, only that life is so bleak alone. When I go to bed my mind churns on and on. Can't we get married sooner?'

'I don't know; we'll see. You've got your Julia near you now, and nothing matters.'

After a week, Dick's depression lifted. When he was sad, Julia made him her baby, holding his handsome head against her breast, but she liked it best when he was confident and could cheer her up, making her laugh and feel taken care of and secure. She had rented an apartment with another girl and she took courses in biology and domestic science in Columbia. When deep fall came, they went to football games and the new shows together, and walked through the first snow in Central Park, and several times a week spent long evenings together in front of her fire. But time was going by and they were both impatient. Just before Christmas, an unfamiliar visitor—Phil Hoffman—presented himself at her door. It was the first time in many months. New York, with its quality of many independent ladders set side by side, is unkind to even the meetings of close friends; so, in the case of strained relations, meetings are easy to avoid.

And they were strange to each other. Since his expressed skepticism of Dick, he was automatically her enemy; on another count, she saw that he had improved, some of the hard angles were worn off; he was now an assistant district attorney, moving around with increasing confidence through his profession.

'So you're going to marry Dick?' he said. 'When?'

'Soon now. When mother comes East.'

He shook his head emphatically. 'Julia, don't marry Dick. This isn't jealousy—I know when I am licked—but it seems awful for a lovely girl like you to take a blind dive into a lake full of rocks. What makes you think that people change their courses? Sometimes they dry up or even flow into a parallel channel, but I've never known anybody to change.'

'Dick's changed.'

'Maybe so. But isn't that an enormous "maybe"? If he was unattractive and you liked him, I'd say go ahead with it. Maybe I'm all wrong, but it's so darn obvious that what fascinates you is that handsome pan of his and those attractive manners.'

'You don't know him,' Julia answered loyally. 'He's different with me. You don't know how gentle he is, and responsive. Aren't you being rather small and mean?'

'Hm.' Phil thought for a moment. 'I want to see you again in a few days. Or perhaps I'll speak to Dick.'

'You let Dick alone,' she cried. 'He has enough to worry him without your nagging him. If you were his friend you'd try to help him instead of coming to me behind his back.'

'I'm your friend first.'

'Dick and I are one person now.'

But three days later Dick came to see her at an hour when he would usually have been at the office.

'I'm here under compulsion,' he said lightly, 'under threat of exposure by Phil Hoffman.'

Her heart dropping like a plummet. 'Has he given up?' she thought. 'Is he drinking again?'

'It's about a girl. You introduced me to her last summer and told me to be very nice to her—Esther Cary.'

Now her heart was beating slowly.

'After you went to California I was lonesome and I ran into her. She'd liked me that day, and for a while we saw quite a bit of each other. Then you came back and I broke it off. It was a little difficult; I hadn't realized that she was so interested.'

'I see.' Her voice was starved and aghast.

'Try and understand. Those terribly lonely evenings. I think if it hadn't been for Esther, I'd have fallen off the wagon. I never loved her—I never loved anybody but you—but I had to see somebody who liked me.'

He put his arm around her, but she felt cold all over and he drew away.

'Then any woman would have done,' Julia said slowly. 'It didn't matter who.'

'No!' he cried.

'I stayed away so long to let you stand on your own feet and get back your self-respect by yourself.'

'I only love you, Julia.'

'But any woman can help you. So you don't really need me, do you?'

His face wore that vulnerable look that Julia had seen several times before; she sat on the arm of his chair and ran her hand over his cheek.

'Then what do you bring me?' she demanded. 'I thought that there'd be the accumulated strength of having beaten your weakness. What do you bring me now?'

'Everything I have.'

She shook her head. 'Nothing. Just your good looks—and the head waiter at dinner last night had that.'

They talked for two days and decided nothing. Sometimes she would pull him close and reach up to his lips that she loved so well, but her arms seemed to close around straw.

'I'll go away and give you a chance to think it over,' he said despairingly. 'I can't see any way of living without you, but I suppose you can't marry a man you don't trust or believe in. My uncle wanted me to go to London on some business——'

The night he left, it was sad on the dim pier. All that kept her from breaking was that it was not an image of strength that was leaving her; she would be just as strong without him. Yet as the murky lights fell on the fine structure of his brow and chin, as she saw the faces turn toward him, the eyes that followed him, an awful emptiness seized her and she wanted to say: 'Never mind, dear; we'll try it together.'

But try what? It was human to risk the toss between failure and success, but to risk the desperate gamble between adequacy and disaster——

'Oh, Dick, be good and be strong and come back to me. Change, change, Dick—change!'

'Good-by, Julia—good-by.'

She last saw him on the deck, his profile cut sharp as a cameo against a match as he lit a cigarette.

IV

It was Phil Hoffman who was to be with her at the beginning and the end. It was he who broke the news as gently as it could be broken. He reached her apartment at half-past eight and carefully threw away the morning paper outside. Dick Ragland had disappeared at sea.

After her first wild burst of grief, he became purposely a little cruel.

'He knew himself. His will had given out; he didn't want

life any more. And, Julia, just to show you how little you can possibly blame yourself, I'll tell you this: He'd hardly gone to his office for four months—since you went to California. He wasn't fired because of his uncle; the business he went to London on was of no importance at all. After his first enthusiasm was gone he'd given up.'

She looked at him sharply. 'He didn't drink, did he? He wasn't drinking?'

For a fraction of a second Phil hesitated. 'No, he didn't drink; he kept his promise—he held on to that.'

'That was it,' she said. 'He kept his promise and he killed himself doing it.'

Phil waited uncomfortably.

'He did what he said he would and broke his heart doing it,' she went on chokingly. 'Oh, isn't life cruel sometimes—so cruel, never to let anybody off. He was so brave—he died doing what he said he'd do.'

Phil was glad he had thrown away the newspaper that hinted of Dick's gay evening in the bar—one of many gay evenings that Phil had known of in the past few months. He was relieved that was over, because Dick's weakness had threatened the happiness of the girl he loved; but he was terribly sorry for him—even understanding how it was necessary for him to turn his maladjustment to life toward one mischief or another—but he was wise enough to leave Julia with the dream that she had saved out of wreckage.

There was a bad moment a year later, just before their marriage, when she said:

'You'll understand the feeling I have and always will have about Dick, won't you, Phil? It wasn't just his good looks. I believed in him—and I was right in a way. He broke rather than bent; he was a ruined man, but not a bad man. In my heart I knew when I first looked at him.'

Phil winced, but he said nothing. Perhaps there was more behind it than they knew. Better let it all alone in the depths of her heart and the depths of the sea.

ZELDA

Miss Ella

(Scribner's Magazine,
December 1931)

Bitter things dried behind the eyes of Miss Ella like garlic on
a string before an open fire. The acrid fumes of sweet
memories had gradually reddened their rims until at times
they shone like the used places in copper saucepans. Withal
she was not a kitchen sort of person, nor even a person whom
life had found much use in preserving. She was elegant,
looking exactly like one of the ladies in a two-tone print on
the top of a fancy glove box. Her red hair stuck out of a
choir cap on Sundays in a tentative attempt to color the
etching of her personality.

When I was young I loved Miss Ella. Her fine high instep
curved into her white canvas shoes in summer with the
voluptuous smoothness of a winter snow-bank. She had a
lace parasol and was so full of birdlike animation that she
teetered on her feet when she spoke to you—sometimes
she had meals with us and I remember her twittering about
on our hearth after supper, dodging the popping bits of blue
flame from our bituminous coal, believing ardently that
'one' could keep fit by standing up twenty minutes after
eating.

All the people in the world who were not her blood
relations were impersonally 'one' to Miss Ella. She was
severe with the world and had she ordered the universe she
would have kept it at runners' tension toeing the chalk
starting-mark forever. I don't know which would have upset
her equanimity more: the materialization of a race or the

realization that there wasn't going to be any. In any case, 'one' must keep fit for all problematical developments.

Even her moments of relaxation were arduous, so much so as to provoke her few outbursts of very feminine temper and considerable nervous agitation. She was essentially Victorian. Passing along the sidewalk in the heat of the afternoon and seeing Miss Ella far away in her hammock in the shade of the big elms by the house, her white skirt dusting a white flutter off the snowball bushes as she rocked herself back and forth, you would never have guessed how uncomfortable she was or how intensely she disliked hammocks. It always took at least three tries before she was tolerably ensconced: the first invariably loosened the big silver buckle that held her white-duck skirt in place; the second was wasted because it might result in immodest exposure of her fragile legs, by furling too tightly around her the white canvas lengths. After that she simply climbed into the hammock and did her arranging afterward, which is about as easy as dressing in a Pullman berth. The hammock fanned its red and yellow fringe in a triumphant crescent motion that discomfited Miss Ella. By holding tightly to the strings at one end and desperately straining her foot against the worn patch of clay in the grass underneath, she managed to preserve a more or less static position. With her free hand she opened letters and held her book and brushed away things that fell from the trees and scratched the itchings that always commence when stillness is imperative.

These were Miss Ella's hours of daytime rest. She never allowed herself to be disturbed until the sun had got well to the west and down behind the big house, its last light pulsing through the square hall-ways in the back windows and out the front, vivisected by the cold iron tracery of the upstairs balcony, to fall in shimmering splinters on the banana-shrubs below. At five a decisive old lady rolled up the drive in a delicate carriage, high and springy, with a beige parasol top. Her hair was snow-white and her face was white and pink with ante-bellum cosmetics. Even from far away they emanated the pleasant smell of oris root and iris. She held the reins absent-mindedly in one hand, the big diamonds in their old-fashioned settings poking up through her beige silk gloves. Her other arm made a formal, impersonal nest for a powdered spitz. When she called to Miss Ella the words slid along the sun rays with the sound of a softly drawn curtain on brass rings. 'Ella! It's time to cool off, my child. The dust is settled by now. And oh, Ella, be a good girl and find Aunt Ella's fan, will you?'

So Miss Ella and Aunt Ella and the white dog went for their afternoon drive leaving the sweet cool of the old garden to the aromatic shrubs, the fireflies and the spiders who made their webs in the box-wood, to the locusts tuning the air for night vibrations and to three romantic children who waited every day for the carriage to roll out of sight before scaling the highest bit of wall that surrounded the grounds.

We loved that garden. Under two mulberry trees where the earth was slippery beneath our bare feet there stood a wooden play-house, relic of Miss Ella's youth. To me it never seemed an actual play-house but to represent the houses associated with childhood in homely stories; it was in my imagination the little red schoolhouse, the farmhouse, the kindly orphan asylum, literary locales that never materialized in my own life. I never went inside but once, because of a horror of the fat summer worms that fell squashing from the mulberry trees. It was dry and dusty, scattered traces of a frieze of apple-blossoms still sticking to the walls where Miss Ella had pasted them long ago.

No one but us ever went near the play-house, not even the grand-nieces of Aunt Ella when they came occasionally to visit. Almost buried in a tangle of jonquils and hyacinths dried brown from the summer heat, its roof strewn with the bruised purple bells of a hibiscus overhanging its tiny gables, the house stood like a forgotten sarcophagus, guarding with

(317)

the reticent dignity that lies in all abandoned things a paint-less, rusty shotgun. Here was a rough oasis apart from the rest of the orderly garden. From out of the delicate concision there foamed and billowed feathery shell-colored bushes that effervesced in the spring like a strawberry soda; there were round beds of elephants-ears with leaves that held the water after a rain and changed it to silver balls of mercury running over the flat surface. There were pink storm-lilies on their rubbery stems, and snowdrops, and shrubs with bottle-green leaves that ripped like stitching when you tore them. Japonicas dropped brown flowers into the damp about the steps of the square, sombre house, and wistaria vines leaned in heavy plaits against the square columns. In the early morning Miss Ella came with a flat Mexican basket and picked the freshest flowers for the church. She said she tended the garden, but it was really Time and a Negro contemporary of his, who did that. In front of the kitchen door, the old black man had a star-shaped bed of giant yellow cannas covered with brown spots and in a crescent were purple pansies. He scolded appallingly when he caught us on the grounds: he was most proprietary about the place and guarded the play-house like some cherished shrine.

That was the atmosphere that enveloped the life of Miss Ella. Nobody knew why she found it sufficient; why she did not follow the path of the doctor's coupé that divided its time between the downtown club and the curb in front of her shadowy lawn. The reason was Miss Ella's story, which like all women's stories was a love story and like most love stories took place in the past. Love is for most people as elusive as the jam in 'Alice in Wonderland'—jam yesterday, jam to-morrow, but no jam to-day. Anyhow, that was how it was with Miss Ella, living titularly on the jam of some time ago, skimming over life's emotions like a bird flying low over the water detaching bright sprays into the air with its wings.

In her youth she was as slim and smooth as a figure in blown glass. Compact in long organdies that buoyed themselves out on the bars of a waltz, she stood firm in the angular aloof arm of her fiancé.

He pyramided above her, two deep lines from the corners of his eyes, his mouth closed tight over many unuttered words, a deep triangle about the bridge of his nose. In the autumn he stood for hours up to his knees in the greasy backwash from the river, the long barrel of his gun trained skyward on wide files of green-backed ducks flying south over the marshes. He brought his loot to Miss Ella in bunches and she had them cooked in her white-pine kitchen, steeped in port and bitters and orange peel, till the brown delicious odor warmed the whole house. They sat together over an enormous table, eating shyly in the dim rings of light that splattered the silver and crept softly over the heavy frames of the dark still-lifes that lined the wall. They were formally in love. There was a passive dignity in the currents that passed between them that quieted the air like a summer Sunday morning. The enveloping consideration of him, the luminous fragility of her, they made a harmonious pair.

In those days the town was small, and elegant ladies agitated their rockers with pleasure back of box-wood gardens as Miss Ella and her beau whipped past in his springy carriage, the light pouring over the polished spokes of the wheels like the flowing glint of water over a mill.

He called her 'dear'; she never called him anything but Mr Hendrix. In the soft chasm of the old hall after a late party, he reverently held her hands, hands filled with a dance card, a butterfly pin, a doll in feathers, trinkets of the dance, souvenirs of dreamy rhythms that wavered in her head with the fluctuations of watered silk propelled by the warmth of quiet happiness. They poured the plans for their life together into the moulds of the thick tree shadows and turned them out on the midnight air marked with the delicate tracings of the leaves—modest stable plans of two in love. He told her how things were to be, and she acquiesced, pleased with his quiet voice piling up in mid-air like smoke in an airless room.

They were both religious to a fashionable restrained extent, and it was the church which drew Andy Bronson across the strings of their devotion, to saw them and haggle them and finally leave the broken ends twisting upward, frayed and ruined, dangling loose in tragedy with the resonance of twisted catgut. Miss Ella and Mr Hendrix planned to be married in the square white church in the spring. Entering from the back where the iron banisters led to the balcony, they planned to walk in solemnity through the misty gusts of face powder, the green smell of lilies, the holiness of candles, to barter with God at the altar; toil and amiability for emotional sanctity. He said that there would be beauty and peace forever after and she said 'Yes.'

Sorting their dreams absent-mindedly, like putting clean linen in a cupboard, they stood side by side dreaming of that at Christmas time. A church festival was going on and there were eggnog and lemonade and silver cake-baskets filled with sliced fruit cake and bonbonnières of nuts and candy in the Sunday-school room. The church was hot, and young men drifted out and in again, bringing with them the odor of overcoats and cigarettes smoked in the cold, and fumes of Bourbon. There in the smoky feminine confusion stood Andy Bronson, the excitement of Christmas hanging bright wreaths about his cheek bones, a mysterious quiet certitude proclaiming nefarious motives.

Miss Ella was conscious of him in a still world beyond reality, even as she talked with animation of all the years that would churn behind the honeymoon boat that plied between Savannah and New York. From that tremulous duality she shivered into the confusion that followed the bang of the giant firecracker that Andy had lit beneath the steps that led to the balcony. A spark caught in her flimsy Dolly Varden and Ella's dress was in flames. Through the slow split groups laughing, disapproving, explaining, not knowing what had

(320)

happened, Andy was the first to reach her burning skirts, clapping the blaze between his palms until only a black, charred fringe was left.

The day after Christmas, hid in an enormous box of roses so deep in red and remorse that their petals shone like the purple wings of an insect, he sent her yards and yards of silk from Persia, and then he sent her ivory beads, a fan with Dresden ladies swinging between mother-of-pearl sticks, a Phi Beta Kappa key, an exquisite miniature of himself when his face was smaller than his great soft eyes—treasures. Finally he brought her a star-sapphire (which she tied about her neck in a chamois bag lest Mr Hendrix should know) and she loved him with desperate suppression. One night he kissed her far into the pink behind her ears and she folded herself in his arms, a flag without a breeze about its staff.

For weeks she could not tell Mr Hendrix, saving and perfecting dramatically the scene she hopefully dreaded. When she did tell him, his eyes swung back in his head with the distant pendulousness of a sea-captain's. Looking over her small head through far horizons with the infinite sadness of a general surrendering his sword, finding no words or thoughts with which to fill her expectant pathos, he turned and slowly rolled the delicate air of early spring down the gravel path before him and out into the open road. Afterward he came to call one Sunday and sat stiffly in a bulbous mahogany chair, gulping a frosted mint julep. The depression about him made holes in the air, and Miss Ella was glad when he left her free to laugh again.

The southern spring passed, the violets and the yellow white pear trees and the jonquils and cape jasmine gave up their tenderness to the deep green lullaby of early May. Ella and Andy were being married that afternoon in her long living-room framed by the velvet portières and empire mirrors encasing the aroma of lives long past. The house had been cleaned and polished, and shadows and memories each put in their proper place. The bride cake nested on southern smilax in the dining-room and decanters of port studded the long sideboard mirrors with garnets. Between the parlor and the dining-room calla lilies and babies'-breath climbed about a white tulle trellis and came to a flowery end on either side of the improvised altar.

Upstairs, Miss Ella was deep in the cedar and lavender of a new trunk; fine linen night-gowns and drawn-work chemises were lifted preciously into the corners and little silk puffs of sachet perched tentatively over the newness. A Negress enamoured of the confusion stood in the window drinking in the disorder from behind dotted Swiss curtains, looking this way and that, stirring the trees with the excitement of her big black eyes and quieting the room with the peace they stole from the garden.

Miss Ella heard the curtains rip as the strong black hands tore them from the fragile pole. 'O Lawd—O Lawd—O Lawd.' She lay in a heap of fright. By the time Ella reached the heavy mass, the woman could only gesticulate toward the window and hide her face. Ella rushed to the window in terror.

The bushes swished softly in the warmth. On the left there was nothing remarkable; a carriage crawling away far down the road, and plants growing in quiet now that their flowers were shed. Reassurance of the coming summer pushed her leaping heart back into place. Ella looked across the drive. There on the play-house steps lay Mr Hendrix, his brains falling over the earth in a bloody mess. His hands were clinched firmly about his old shotgun, and he as dead as a door nail.

Years passed but Miss Ella had no more hope for love. She fixed her hair more lightly about her head and every year her white skirts and peek-a-boo waists were more stiffly starched. She drove with Auntie Ella in the afternoons, took an interest in the tiny church, and all the time the rims about her eyes grew redder and redder, like those of a person leaning over a hot fire, but she was not a kitchen sort of person, withal.

ZELDA

The Continental Angle

(*The New Yorker*,

4 June 1932)

Gastronomic delight and sartorial pleasure radiated from the two people. They sat at a table on a polished dais under a canopy of horse-chestnuts eating of the fresh noon sunlight which turned the long, yellow bars of their asparagus to a chromatic xylophone. The hot, acrid sauce and the spring air disputed and wept together, Tweedledum and Tweedledee, over the June down that floated here and there before their vision like frayed places in a tapestry.

'Do you remember,' she said, 'the Ducoed chairs of Southern tearooms and the left-over look of the Sunday gingerbread that goes with a dollar dinner, the mustardy linen and the waiters' spotted dinner coats of a Broadway chophouse, the smell of a mayonnaise you get with a meal in the shopping district, the pools of blue milk like artificial opals on a drugstore counter, the safe, plebeian intimacy of chocolate on the air, and the greasy smell of whipped cream in a sandwich emporium? There's the sterility of upper Broadway with the pancakes at Childs drowned in the pale hospital light, and Swiss restaurants with walls like a merry-go-round backdrop, and Italian restaurants latticed like the lacing of a small and pompous Balkan officer, and green peppers curling like garter snakes in marshy hors-d'oeuvre compartments, and piles of spaghetti like the sweepings from a dance hall under the red lights and paper flowers.'

'Yes,' he said, but with nostalgia, 'and there are strips of bacon curling over the country sausage in the luminous

(323)

filterings from the princely windows of the Plaza, and honey-dew melon with just a whiff of lemon from narrow red benches that balustrade Park Avenue restaurants, and there's the impersonal masculinity of lunch at the Chatham, the diplomacy of dinner at the St Regis; there are strawberries in winter on buffets that rise like fountains in places named Versailles and Trianon and Fontainebleu, and caviar in blocks of ice.'

'If you eat late on Sunday at the Lafayette,' she continued blandly, 'the tables are covered with coffee cups and the deep windows let in the wheezing asphalt and you look over boxes of faded artificial flowers onto the tables where people have eaten conversation and dumped their ashes in their saucers while they talked, and at the Brevoort men with much to think about have eaten steak, thick, chewing like a person's footfalls in a heavily padded corridor. In all the basements where old English signs hang over the stairs, years ago they buried puddings, whereas if you have the energy to climb a flight of stairs, there are motherly nests of salad and perhaps something Hawaiian.'

'Ah, and at Delmonicos there were meals with the flavor of a transatlantic liner,' he said; 'at Hicks there are illustration salads, gleaming, tumbling over the plate like a rajah's jewels, cream cheese and alligator pear and cherries floating about like balls on a Christmas tree. And *filet de sole* paves the Fifties, and shrimp cobbles Broadway, and grapefruits roll about the roof and turn roof gardens to celestial bowling alleys. There is cold salmon with the elegance of a lady's boudoir in the infinity of big hotel dining-rooms, and Mephistophelean crab cocktails that give you the sweat of a long horseback ride and pastry that spurts like summer showers in restaurants famed for their chef.'

'And there are waffles spongy under syrups as aromatic as the heat that rises in a hedged lane after a July rain, and

(324)

chicken in the red brick of Madison Avenue,' she pursued. 'And I have eaten in old places under stained-glass windows where the palm fronds reflected in my cream-of-tomato soup reminded me of embalming parlors, and I've gulped sweet potatoes in the Pennsylvania Station, ice-tea and pineapple salad under the spinning fans blowing travellers to a standstill, tomato skins in a club sandwich and the smell of pickles in the Forties.'

'Yes,' he said, 'and raspberries trickling down the fountain at the Ritz, bubbling up and falling like the ball in a shooting-gallery spray, and eggs in a baked potato for ladies and——'

'*Pardon, est-ce que Madame a bien déjeuné?*'

'*C'était exquis, merci bien.*'

'*Et Monsieur, il se plaît chez vous?*'

'What the hell did he say, my dear? I learned my French in America and it doesn't seem to be completely adequate.'

'Ah, sir, I understand perfectly. I be so bold as to ask if Monsieur like our restaurant, perhaps?' answered the waiter.

ZELDA

A Couple of Nuts

(*Scribner's Magazine*,

August 1932)

The summer of 1924 shrivelled the trees in the Champs-
Elysées to a misty blue till they swayed before your eyes as if
they were about to go down under the gasoline fumes. Before
July was out, dead leaves floated over the square of St
Sulpice like paper ashes from a bonfire. The nights lifted
themselves exhausted from the pavements; restless mid-
nights settled over the city like the fall of a cooling soufflé in
the bowl of early morning. Sleep was impossible and I
wasted lots of time in Montmartre. The grass in the Bois was
as baked from the heat as pressed flowers under a bell, and
bed was only possible comparatively, so I lethalized myself in
boîtes-de-nuit night after night that I might find my apartment bearable afterward. That was how I got to know Larry
and Lola.

They already had a certain clientele. I mean there were
groups who drifted into their 'club' specially to hear them
play and offered them drinks and asked for their favorite
tunes. The two kids sat in a state of watchful collapse
holding on to the dying spring excitement as if they were
having a tug of war with itinerant Americans who would
have dragged it south. They were nothing but kids, either of
them. She was a protruding Irish beauty, full and carnivorous,
with black hair slicking up her conical brows, and hunter's
eyes that trapped and slew her mouth. She moved the masses
of her body with the slow admiration of a baby discovering
its toes, deliberately, like a person at chess, so that it gave no

(326)

impression of movement, just constant arrangement and rearrangement. You would have thought she had learned to breathe on the piano bench.

They played me the old war tunes and I jounced my youth upon my knee as if it had been a lusty grandchild instead of a string of intangible memories. We got to be sentimental friends. Sometimes very late when the place was deserted and shirt fronts sailed the thick smoke like racing yachts in a fog, they asked me for definitions of love and success and beauty. Larry would say tentatively, 'Now, Lola, I think *she's* beautiful.' Lola, piling herself very high, dismissed us tolerantly. 'Of course we don't know much about life. We've always had each other.' As if that were a sop to fate!

In those days of going to pieces and general disintegration it was charming to see them together. Their friends were divided into two camps as to whose stamina it was that kept them going and comparatively equilibrated in that crazy world of ours playing at prisoner's base across the Atlantic Ocean. Some people thought they weren't married, they were so young and decorative. They had walked across Panama on their honeymoon. A sort of practical imagination they shared pulled them in and nearly out of all their adventures, through the muddlings of high society's private checking accounts and through the sordid backwash that people rich enough to take their amusements seriously scatter behind them like wrappings from candy eaten along the way. If she had told for instance how she got the ruby bracelet she wore as a memento of a party they once played for on Long Island, a famous millionaire would have buried his face in the Sound, and I happen to know that it was a Duchess who paid for his sunstroke. But they themselves were at that time innocent children as faithful to each other as two aristocratic Borzoi on the same leash. Larry was wonderful looking. He humped his shoulders over his banjo like a football player huddling a ball. When he sang he opened his mouth sideways and howled and broke the notes and fitted them back together with the

(327)

easy precision of cogs slipping into place, shaking the tones loose on the air as if he were freeing his fingers from some ticklish substance. If he had been born twenty years before, or in a country town, he might have worn a blond pompadour and clerked in the village drug store. Instead, he shared our generation's intellectual yearnings and was a little ashamed of his metier. 'Oh!—oh—oh' he sang, luring the boldness of great ladies from mulatto staccato to Spanish persuasion and 'tum—diddle—um—dum' he urged them back again till they didn't know what they felt. He was a banjo-player, and they were the people who rose with the moon and swamped his soul in uncategorical dismay. He had the nicest face opening out beneath his eyes like wide and friendly prairies in a copper glow. His smile tucked up his skin back of one ear like satin skirts held high from a rainy pavement.

Well, they managed to stick together through everything when they couldn't pay for their sheet music and had to refuse the champagne that was offered them because of their empty stomachs. Afterward when unhappiness used up the unexplored regions in their laughter and hardened their gestures into remembered mimicry they got to love telling people about the hard time they had had getting started. It must have brought them closer for a moment, retracing the days when they knew they couldn't have borrowed five dollars.

When they first floated up on the heat wave they made music in a dump that prides itself on discovering new people. Their patrons later turned out to be the heroes and heroines of half our modern novels and their fortunes rose on the insatiability of the Paris lion-hunters. So long as there is money to buy leisure there is the necessity to forget we have it, and Lola and Larry might still be successfully blasting Time from the stones of the rue Pigalle if they hadn't gradually become obsessed by their 'rights.'

That was what engaged them in an eternal round of petty quarrels. It was either the drummer who wanted to get them fired or the bartender whom they suspected of making dirty cracks about them, or the manager who was an impossible person. The domestic element in Lola's life was replaced by these pitiful bickerings, and I suppose that for him they satisfied some instinct of taking things in hand, the same as paying the weekly bills does for most of us. They seemed to forget the ultimate dispensability of jazz singers. One night they lost their job—drinking, I think. When I came in, Lola's cheeks were floating over the room like two red clouds, her eyes playing about the edges of the manager like an Indian sword-thrower, picking out his bulky form against the desolate room. The boîte somehow seemed inside out in the confusion, bolstered together like the wrong side of stage scenery. You could see the joints in everything, even the people. Larry was all for a placative attitude. He stuffed his hands in his pockets as if he gathered back his words in fistfuls to carry away with him. I heard him say to Lola: 'There's nothing to say. You can't argue with a kike like him. Get your coat, that's all.' I walked along with them under the dripping shadows of a Paris night, mauve and rose-quartz under the street lamps, pattery, clattery before the yellow cafés, droning, groaning, sucking its breath up the dark side streets, and I lent them twenty dollars to pay their board bill when I left them at their dingy pension.

'That old crab,' Lola exploded, 'he just wanted to get rid of us, said we sat around with all of you too much and didn't play enough to suit him. Sometimes I sang so much that my voice sounded like convicts breaking rocks by morning— and out we go at the end.' She turned to Larry like a well-behaved child who had upset his glass at the table. 'Well, what'll we do now—what will Larry and Lola do now?'

Jeff Daugherty was the answer to that—a genial expatriate who counted his spotted ties in hundreds and expatiated his existence with discoveries of the last word in entertainment. All of us who had ever been short-changed out of a five-franc note or tried to cash a check at lunch time or had any dealings with a French post office brought our violence to Jeff, confident that he could tell us where to find echoes from America to soothe our nostalgic lamentations. Larry and Lola took him by storm.

You would have thought they were buying a seat on the stock exchange if you'd heard them discussing how much they were going to ask him, to play at his dinner. They fixed on the absurdity of twenty-five dollars. It was the first time Jeff had been presented with a bill as small as that since college; it moved him to a patronly feeling. 'I've got rather a nice little place on the Riviera, where I'll be in a week,' he said, tracing their future on one of his calling cards. 'Come down and play for me there.' Jeff drew a magic circle round his phone number. 'That,' he said, 'is the combination of my private safe.' They told me that they ran all the way home that night, their feet just tickling the pavement like the feet of marionettes, strung with happiness at the possibility of getting out of Paris.

It was late in the summer when I got away to Cannes. All the gay and glamorous people had floated off on the fumes of alcohol to Biarritz and Switzerland, Vichy and Aix-les-Bains to steam and sweat and look with satiated moralism over other gambling tables than those that wilted in Mediterranean vapors. I hadn't been long at my hotel when Jeff phoned me for dinner. He had never been a great friend of mine but the season was disintegrating, already split into quarrelling groups and cliques intent on their private affairs, and I was glad to fit in somewhere. 'I've got hold of two lambs,' he said, 'and I'm giving a slaughter. If your sanguinary tastes are nicely developed you might drop in.' Since I have for years considered all of Jeff's friends more or less of a menagerie, I never thought twice to ask for details. After a day on the parched beach I squirmed my dinner clothes over my puffy, sunburned back and with my shoulders feeling like a package of live fish and my arms running up and down themselves like vibrating rubber and I damned

(330)

Jeff as an animal-fancying exile, who meant no good to us who intended to escape from life. By the time I arrived, a group about the piano were whipping the party round and round like one of those gyroscope affairs to keep an airplane from falling. There was a lush hardness in the voice that sustained it, a voice removed from personal appeal, a prince and princess quality, gracious and cavalier. Most of those ingratiating voices that hang on the air like juicy ripening fruit hold a promise of initiation—this one didn't. It was a secret you could never share, as detached from its owner as from you. I knew it was Lola. Nobody else could sing like that. So Jeff was going in for troubadours! The confident notes whipped the summer night to a negroid frenzy and she sang about 'loving you—you—you.' She put on a show about being glad to see me and made the party roar with an account of how she'd cheated their landlady out of my twenty dollars and blown into Cannes on the profit. I thought she was over-exuberant and after a while I decided that they were both respectably but quite definitely drunk. When Jeff drinks it's because he has been drinking for so long that liquor is as much a part of his daily ritual as his morning massage, and when I drink it is to fill up the gaps in human relations, but Lola and Larry were drinking to create the illusion that they had some reason for it. I suppose it didn't make any eventual difference, since somebody else paid for their drinks, but they hadn't yet staked out a claim for themselves on the face of this difficult earth, and it depressed me to see barriers go crashing before they were constructed. Jeff hung over the piano, svelte and proprietary. Even when he joined the scattered tables you could feel Lola's attention following him, participating in his security. Larry seemed flattered, or thought he should be, by Jeff's attention to his wife. Anyhow, he talked to me in alcoholic modesty for a long time, and when the party shattered itself on the back of the August night, I drove him home. We left Lola in the midst of innumerable 'My dears' and promiscuous 'Darlings' tidying up the immaculate Jeff as if he'd

(331)

been a cabinet of bibelots, and he extremely passive even for a cabinet. Next morning Larry was very determined in his attempt to be worldly about the fact that Lola got home after breakfast, had skated in on his fried eggs, so to speak.

Well, the rest of that summer Larry's rôle was not to care. He was awfully good at it and grew as stolid as a substitute half-back; toward the end he didn't even seem to expect to be called into the play. Financially, they had done very well by themselves, playing at private parties and finally organizing a short-lived club which rocked itself to a lonely, delirious death to the tune of her garrulous blues. It was pounded out of existence by the roar of the autumn sea. Jeff left with his fatuous coterie. We three shivered alone in the prickly sunshine of the beach. The ocean turned muddy and our bathing clothes didn't dry from one brisk swim to another; we grew irritable with the unspent tang of the sea. They made certain pretensions at a sophisticated coldness between them, but I could see how necessary they were to each other even in their disagreements. Larry behaved as if he'd been brought up on the Murad advertisements, and Lola was proud of his pseudo worldliness in spite of her inflation at Jeff's attention. Being always a little bit chilly was ruining my disposition and I decided to move on. They didn't know where they were going that winter so when I left I offered to drive them to Monte Carlo. The first day of school hung in the air, crisp and anticipatory, and resuscitated our dog-eared hopes as we drove along. We stopped for beer and cheese along the way and looked sentimentally on the fall concision of the Mediterranean. Those white and blistered palaces that line the Nice sea front had opened their shutters once more and the gray rocks about the coast were no longer vaporous bathings of sunshine but scenery preening itself in an invitation to be appreciated as obvious as the coquetries of a marriageable daughter. The country was selling itself. We absorbed its bright confidence, a sort of transfusion of light after the summer gulling.

When I rode off into the carnation-padded hills of Italy and left them there in the subdued hubbub of Monte Carlo, I had somehow a feeling that they were all right, safe with the rich and privileged. My emotion may have been evoked by the outlandish number of policemen there were about. Have you ever noticed what a lot of watching the rich seem to need?

II

In Rome I had a letter. 'Jeff got us a wonderful job at a café de Paris, but we haven't been able to save any money. We hate to bother you like this but Lola's in trouble and if you could spare us forty dollars, you know how grateful we'd be. We can't afford a child at present, though we both feel terrible about it.' Of course I sent it and they continued to write me from time to time. In the course of our correspondence, it developed that the last of some Pharaohic dynasty had lent them one of those apartments consisting entirely of boudoirs, whose blinding fronts corset the pompous hills of Monaco with musical comedy stairs. They were apparently living in royal disarray, drinking and playing, and howling like Banshee from the yachts in the harbor. They referred to the Egyptian as their 'nigger friend,' and taught him the Charleston and in spite of their hang-overs remained dependent on each other. Their stuff was spectacularly American and they made a killing at it, being simple kids. It wasn't until another spring that I saw them again in Paris. Frankly, Larry looked as if he'd just slept out the year in a cloak-room. The stagnant smoke of nightclubs had worn an embalmed, unearthly swirl over his head and he was as glazed as the surface of a delicatessen mince-pie. They were prosperous and very much in vogue. Both of them had acquired a calculating quality and I missed the old 'nothing to lose' bravery that used to be in their music when they tipped over their chair-backs and sang. I asked them out with me but they were always busy. Life had become a sort of Virginia reel of

(333)

dissolute counts and American millionaires and disillusioned English—and Jeff. Larry was funny about Jeff. He treated him now as if he'd been a rare find from some obscure curio shop that he'd managed to buy for Lola with cautious saving. Of course, Jeff wasn't serious about Lola, but he followed her everywhere, batting her cigarette ashes with his signet ring and picking up the little bits of her that seemed to detach themselves whenever she moved.

'What do you think of this fellow Daugherty?' Larry asked me one night, assuming a confidential air as if Jeff had come up for a club election. 'Well, I don't know,' I answered. Jeff was an older, if more casual, friend of mine than Larry and I wasn't going into the days when he had had an artificial shower arrangement outside his windows to keep girls from leaving his apartment, and was only saved by his youth and suavity from the accusation of lechery. 'He's a charming person, really. He used to write musical comedies years ago.'

'Oh! did he? Were they any good?' Larry's face fell in blank incredulity. He couldn't bear it that Jeff should have had ambitions, and perhaps talents, the same human attributes as his own.

'Well, yes, I believe they were good—something very special and sophisticated for that time.'

'Why did he give it up? You know, I think *Europe* is a bad influence. I mean, life's so easy over here. I've been trying to get Lola to go home.' You could tell by the way he balanced the words and tentatively meted them out that the idea had just come into his head. I supposed he wanted to get Lola away from their environment and Jeff. I cannot tolerate buoyant comedy characters when they lapse into that attitude of baffled seriousness just 'to show you the stuff they're really made of,' so I paid my check and walked off, feeling rather pleased with myself that I hadn't betrayed Jeff: I so often do make nasty cracks about my friends. I didn't see Larry again until June.

That spring the lilacs dumped their skirts over the walls in the Boulevard St Germain and wanderlust sprinkled the air. I wanted to stop at every 'Rendezvous des Cochers' and 'Paradis des Chauffeurs' I passed as I strolled along. It was like walking with a child beside you, the morning was so tender. I had got as far as the Café des Deux Magots, enjoying the people airing themselves on the sidewalk, when Larry caught up to me. I expected some coldness when I remembered the abrupt end of our last meeting, but he was beaming away in the daylight like a beacon left burning from the night before. 'We're going,' he said triumphantly, as if we'd never parted. 'Sailing at noon tomorrow. At first Lola didn't want to for a damn, but I finally got her to see that if we're ever going to make a name for ourselves we've got to go home now while we're known and settle down.'

'I think you're very sensible,' I said cautiously, in surprise. It seemed rather silly to me that they should tear off just now when people were beginning to recognize them over here but of course I guessed his motives. There had been some malicious talk about Jeff and Lola. He slipped his hand under my arm and we slid down one of those brown streets padded with humanity that mark dark vistas to the Seine. The shadows cooled the inside of my nose like a breath of melting snow; the sun was fragile as a blown glass casing around the world. Larry stopped and lit a cigarette. Something in his movements suggested a boy scout about to perform a good deed. I waited. 'Say,' he said, 'if you see Jeff any time soon you might tell him I'm sorry I was rude the other night. I'm afraid I was awful. I thought he was pawing Lola but as soon as I sobered up I saw how absurd I was. You will tell him, won't you, and that Lola sends her love? And say, I'm gonna send him a check for what I owe as soon as we get to America.' He seemed relieved after that as if he had somehow discharged all obligations and could now withdraw from the scene with a clear conscience. I left him by the river where it flows like a typewriter ribbon printing the alphabet of Paris on the city itself, wishing them good luck and bon voyage.

As it happened I hadn't seen and didn't see Jeff for six more months.

I woke up one Sunday morning having lost my superiority on Saturday night and I thought it would make me feel more respectable to look at the cold equilibrium of the Luxembourg statues. So I did every surface thing a person can to myself and delivered my interior chimney-sweepishness onto the sidewalks. Symphonic taxi horns blew the muffled suppression of Sunday calmly through the narrow streets as I trod the quiet tones through the soles of my shoes. I ran into Jeff by accident outside the Museum and we decided to lunch together. I suppose people with like habits discover the same escapes from them. We went to Foyot's where we devoted two hours to eating ourselves into a lethargy. We soon exhausted our categoric conversation, and searching the past for tit-bits, I remembered Larry's message. Jeff smiled with dubious scepticism and when he saw that I disapproved of that particular conquest he began to expand in self-justification. Jeff is a bore when he expands; he usually goes into details about how much it cost in telegrams to extricate himself and leaves you guessing as to the situation but I was interested in the kids and it was a long time since I'd had any news of them. 'Lola and Larry,' he commenced, 'are a couple of museum pieces, early Neathandral* I make them. I don't see why they can't take life like adults. I was very fond of her, you know, and he seemed a nice sort of chap, so when they left Europe, I sent out mail-order blanks to some friends who used to put on my fiascos in the days when failure was still a novelty to me, trying to get them a decent job. Maybe you know "les Arcades?" Well, it's so chic that people sit about in a gun-man hush and sense the satisfaction that they're paying ten dollars more for their champagne than all the other people similarly seated in similar circumstances. They were supposed to sing and pass

* Thus in the *Scribner's Magazine* text.

(336)

themselves off as society toughs. They got away with it beautifully for a while. I mean, they fitted all the current adjectives, "hectic and delirious and killing" and all that, and people went there in droves to keep from having to think up new epithets for their conversation. Everything went along like fire-works in an oven until my ex-wife appeared on the scene, or until the scene swallowed her up, I can't make out which. Mabel, you know, rejoices in her quaint Victorian ways and I suppose it hurt her pride that there should be a man in America she hadn't slept with besides myself. So she began making passes at that handsome exterior of Larry's, which, I believe, were eventually fatal. She'd turn up every night with Lord Ashes of Alley or the Hon Hick-ups, and graciously surrender them to Lola. The four of them spent evening after evening gloomily soaking cigarette butts in the dregs of their high-balls, happily quarrelling. Mabel is a glamorous person, and she eventually located Larry's Achilles heel in Brett's Peerage. At any rate, Lola became pugilistic when she found she was losing Larry. When the situation got to the stale mustard point, the clientele, bored with the unpleasant aura, wandered off. I mean, everybody knew the four of them wanted to bash each other's faces in, and no reasonable person is going to squander a hundred dollars a night for the privilege of being sorry for two clowns. So they got fired. Well, one must live, and bread and whiskey are expensive since the war. Lola got a Broadway jackal to bring suit for alienation, and it looks as if the whole thing were going to cost some hundred thousand dollars. Mabel hasn't got a penny outside her alimony and the price is extravagant even for an eccentricity. Of course, I can't afford to have the mud-slinging in the papers. Really, these days I never know when my breakfast rolls will be loaded with dynamite. I suppose, however, it is my just deserts for fooling around with such a couple of nuts.'

Jeff is a genial individual who learned his philosophy from check books and I confess that I envied him the equanimity with which he accepted his schooling. He drove placidly off in a taxi and I stood there in the skeleton sun terribly conscious of the frailty of human relations. I was wondering about the kids. They had possessed something precious that most of us never have: a jaunty confidence in life and in each other like the plaiting together of a lovely cravat from an assortment of shoe-string. What did Lola want? It seemed to me her broken heart came a bit high—a hundred thousand, Jeff had said, but I somehow couldn't believe she was the kind that cared much about money. Nevertheless, the blue surface of her eyes was jagged with a predetermination not to care, a vengeful quality like sharp rocks where the water is too shallow to dive. Larry was a nice fellow. I wondered if he had given in to Mabel to be vindictive. The whole thing oppressed me. I disliked thinking that where there had been something pleasant and clean and crisp as an autumn morning now there was nothing. To see them again would be like revisiting the scenes of my youth and finding my mother's house no longer there, so I put them out of my mind, as I would have dismissed a false conception when I found that it was wrong.

Three weeks later I picked up the paper and saw that ghastly tragedy staring out from the front page. The fact that it was Mabel's yacht made it headline news. They had all put off in a hurricane, Mabel and Larry and some of those imported brummagen of hers and the high sea swallowed them up like gulls pouncing on the refuse from an ocean liner. It was horrible. A boy who almost drowned once told me that while he was trying to keep himself afloat, birds settled on his head and pecked at his eyes. The papers said the sea that drowned them was the worst in forty years, so I hope they sank at once and weren't left there a long time struggling. Larry's body was never found, nor any of the others—only Lola. She lay for weeks in a recuperating hospital. Lola wrote me a pathetic letter when she got well again. 'Can you spare me some money? I think I've got a job in a new show that's

opening in the spring, but you know we never saved anything and I've got to get along until then. You've always been
so kind to us and now that I haven't got Larry any more all of
our friends seem to have disappeared. I could ask Jeff but
sometimes I feel that if we'd never known him none of this
would ever have happened. He and his wife were such a
couple of nuts. What were we doing on a yacht? Before we
met Mabel we could always quarrel well enough at home and
forget about it afterward.'

Lola and Larry! No, they never saved anything. Well, I
sent her the money and I suppose she'll be all right for
another five years. She'll be pretty that long anyway. It takes
time a good thirty years to batter down a woman's looks and
crumple the charm she acquires from moving in a world she
finds rich in that fantastic quality. Poor kids! Their Paris
address turned up just the other day when I was looking for
my trunk keys, along with some dirty post-cards and a torn
fifty-franc note and an expired passport. I remembered the
night Larry gave it to me: I had promised to send them some
songs from home—songs about love and success and beauty.

SCOTT
What a Handsome Pair!

(The Saturday Evening Post,
27 August 1932)

At four o'clock on a November afternoon in 1902, Teddy Van
Beck got out of a hansom cab in front of a brownstone
house on Murray Hill. He was a tall, round-shouldered
young man with a beaked nose and soft brown eyes in a
sensitive face. In his veins quarreled the blood of colonial
governors and celebrated robber barons; in him the synthesis
had produced, for that time and place, something different
and something new.

His cousin, Helen Van Beck, waited in the drawing-room.
Her eyes were red from weeping, but she was young enough
for it not to detract from her glossy beauty—a beauty that
had reached the point where it seemed to contain in itself the
secret of its own growth, as if it would go on increasing forever. She was nineteen and, contrary to the evidence, she was
extremely happy.

Teddy put his arm around her and kissed her cheek, and
found it changing into her ear as she turned her face away.
He held her for a moment, his own enthusiasm chilling; then
he said:

'You don't seem very glad to see me.'

Helen had a premonition that this was going to be one of
the memorable scenes of her life, and with unconscious
cruelty she set about extracting from it its full dramatic value.
She sat in a corner of the couch, facing an easy-chair.

'Sit there,' she commanded, in what was then admired as a
'regal manner,' and then, as Teddy straddled the piano

stool: 'No, don't sit there. I can't talk to you if you're going to revolve around.'

'Sit on my lap,' he suggested.

'No.'

Playing a one-handed flourish on the piano, he said, 'I can listen better here.'

Helen gave up hopes of beginning on the sad and quiet note.

'This is a serious matter, Teddy. Don't think I've decided it without a lot of consideration. I've got to ask you—to ask you to release me from our understanding.'

'What?' Teddy's face paled with shock and dismay.

'I'll have to tell you from the beginning. I've realized for a long time that we have nothing in common. You're interested in your music, and I can't even play chopsticks.' Her voice was weary as if with suffering; her small teeth tugged at her lower lip.

'What of it?' he demanded, relieved. 'I'm musician enough for both. You wouldn't have to understand banking to marry a banker, would you?'

'This is different,' Helen answered. 'What would we do together? One important thing is that you don't like riding; you told me you were afraid of horses.'

'Of course I'm afraid of horses,' he said, and added reminiscently: 'They try to bite me.'

'It makes it so——'

'I've never met a horse—socially, that is—who didn't try to bite me. They used to do it when I put the bridle on; then, when I gave up putting the bridle on, they began reaching their heads around trying to get at my calves.'

The eyes of her father, who had given her a Shetland at three, glistened, cold and hard, from her own.

'You don't even like the people I like, let alone the horses,' she said.

'I can stand them. I've stood them all my life.'

'Well, it would be a silly way to start a marriage. I don't see any grounds for mutual—mutual——'

(341)

'Riding?'

'Oh, not that.' Helen hesitated, and then said in an unconvinced tone, 'Probably I'm not clever enough for you.'

'Don't talk such stuff!' He demanded some truth: 'Who's the man?'

It took her a moment to collect herself. She had always resented Teddy's tendency to treat women with less ceremony than was the custom of the day. Often he was an unfamiliar, almost frightening young man.

'There is someone,' she admitted. 'It's someone I've always known slightly, but about a month ago, when I went to Southampton, I was—thrown with him.'

'Thrown from a horse?'

'Please, Teddy,' she protested gravely. 'I'd been getting more unhappy about you and me, and whenever I was with him everything seemed all right.' A note of exaltation that she would not conceal came into Helen's voice. She rose and crossed the room, her straight, slim legs outlined by the shadows of her dress. 'We rode and swam and played tennis together—did the things we both liked to do.'

He stared into the vacant space she had created for him. 'Is that all that drew you to this fellow?'

'No, it was more than that. He was thrilling to me like nobody ever has been.' She laughed. 'I think what really started me thinking about it was one day we came in from riding and everybody said aloud what a nice pair we made.'

'Did you kiss him?'

She hesitated. 'Yes, once.'

He got up from the piano stool. 'I feel as if I had a cannon ball in my stomach,' he exclaimed.

The butler announced Mr Stuart Oldhorne.

'Is he the man?' Teddy demanded tensely.

She was suddenly upset and confused. 'He should have come later. Would you rather go without meeting him?'

But Stuart Oldhorne, made confident by his new sense of proprietorship, had followed the butler.

(342)

The two men regarded each other with a curious impotence of expression; there can be no communication between men in that position, for their relation is indirect and consists in how much each of them has possessed or will possess of the woman in question, so that their emotions pass through her divided self as through a bad telephone connection.

Stuart Oldhorne sat beside Helen, his polite eyes never leaving Teddy. He had the same glowing physical power as she. He had been a star athlete at Yale and a Rough Rider in Cuba, and was the best young horseman on Long Island. Women loved him not only for his points but for a real sweetness of temper.

'You've lived so much in Europe that I don't often see you,' he said to Teddy. Teddy didn't answer and Stuart Oldhorne turned to Helen: 'I'm early; I didn't realize——'

'You came at the right time,' said Teddy rather harshly. 'I stayed to play you my congratulations.'

To Helen's alarm, he turned and ran his fingers over the keyboard. Then he began.

What he was playing, neither Helen nor Stuart knew, but Teddy always remembered. He put his mind in order with a short résumé of the history of music, beginning with some chords from The Messiah and ending with Debussy's La Plus Que Lent, which had an evocative quality for him, because he had first heard it the day his brother died. Then, pausing for an instant, he began to play more thoughtfully, and the lovers on the sofa could feel that they were alone—that he had left them and had no more traffic with them—and Helen's discomfort lessened. But the flight, the elusiveness of the music, piqued her, gave her a feeling of annoyance. If Teddy had played the current sentimental song from Erminie, and had played it with feeling, she would have understood and been moved, but he was plunging her suddenly into a world of mature emotions, whither her nature neither could nor wished to follow.

She shook herself slightly and said to Stuart: 'Did you buy the horse?'

'Yes, and at a bargain. . . . Do you know I love you?'

'I'm glad,' she whispered.

The piano stopped suddenly. Teddy closed it and swung slowly around: 'Did you like my congratulations?'

'Very much,' they said together.

'It was pretty good,' he admitted. 'That last was only based on a little counterpoint. You see, the idea of it was that you make such a handsome pair.'

He laughed unnaturally; Helen followed him out into the hall.

'Good-by, Teddy,' she said. 'We're going to be good friends, aren't we?'

'Aren't we?' he repeated. He winked without smiling, and with a clicking, despairing sound of his mouth, went out quickly.

For a moment Helen tried vainly to apply a measure to the situation, wondering how she had come off with him, realizing reluctantly that she had never for an instant held the situation in her hands. She had a dim realization that Teddy was larger in scale; then the very largeness frightened her and, with relief and a warm tide of emotion, she hurried into the drawing-room and the shelter of her lover's arms.

Their engagement ran through a halcyon summer. Stuart visited Helen's family at Tuxedo, and Helen visited his family in Wheatley Hills. Before breakfast, their horses' hoofs sedately scattered the dew in sentimental glades, or curtained them with dust as they raced on dirt roads. They bought a tandem bicycle and pedaled all over Long Island—which Mrs Cassius Ruthven, a contemporary Cato, considered 'rather fast' for a couple not yet married. They were seldom at rest, but when they were, they reminded people of His Move on a Gibson pillow.

Helen's taste for sport was advanced for her generation. She rode nearly as well as Stuart and gave him a decent game in tennis. He taught her some polo, and they were golf crazy when it was still considered a comic game. They liked to feel fit and cool together. They thought of themselves as a team, and it was often remarked how well mated they were. A chorus of pleasant envy followed in the wake of their effortless glamour.

They talked.

'It seems a pity you've got to go to the office,' she would say. 'I wish you did something we could do together, like taming lions.'

'I've always thought that in a pinch I could make a living breeding and racing horses,' said Stuart.

'I know you could, you darling.'

In August he brought a Thomas automobile and toured all the way to Chicago with three other men. It was an event of national interest and their pictures were in all the papers. Helen wanted to go, but it wouldn't have been proper, so they compromised by driving down Fifth Avenue on a sunny September morning, one with the fine day and the fashionable crowd, but distinguished by their unity, which made them each as strong as two.

'What do you suppose?' Helen demanded. 'Teddy sent me the oddest present—a cup rack.'

Stuart laughed. 'Obviously, he means that all we'll ever do is win cups.'

'I thought it was rather a slam,' Helen ruminated. 'I saw that he was invited to everything, but he didn't answer a single invitation. Would you mind very much stopping by his apartment now? I haven't seen him for months and I don't like to leave anything unpleasant in the past.'

He wouldn't go in with her. 'I'll sit and answer questions about the auto from passers-by.'

The door was opened by a woman in a cleaning cap, and Helen heard the sound of Teddy's piano from the room beyond. The woman seemed reluctant to admit her.

'He said don't interrupt him, but I suppose if you're his cousin——'

Teddy welcomed her, obviously startled and somewhat upset, but in a minute he was himself again.

'I won't marry you,' he assured her. 'You've had your chance.'

'All right,' she laughed.

'How are you?' He threw a pillow at her. 'You're beautiful! Are you happy with this—this centaur? Does he beat you with his riding crop?' He peered at her closely. 'You look a little duller than when I knew you. I used to whip you up to a nervous excitement that bore a resemblance to intelligence.'

'I'm happy, Teddy. I hope you are.'

'Sure, I'm happy; I'm working. I've got MacDowell on the run and I'm going to have a shebang at Carnegie Hall next September.' His eyes became malicious. 'What did you think of my girl?'

'Your girl?'

'The girl who opened the door for you.'

'Oh, I thought it was a maid.' She flushed and was silent.

He laughed. 'Hey, Betty!' he called. 'You were mistaken for the maid!'

'And that's the fault of my cleaning on Sunday,' answered a voice from the next room.

Teddy lowered his voice. 'Do you like her?' he demanded.

'Teddy!' She teetered on the arm of the sofa, wondering whether she should leave at once.

'What would you think if I married her?' he asked confidentially.

'Teddy!' She was outraged; it had needed but a glance to place the woman as common. 'You're joking. She's older than you. . . . You wouldn't be such a fool as to throw away your future that way.'

He didn't answer.

'Is she musical?' Helen demanded. 'Does she help you with your work?'

(346)

'She doesn't know a note. Neither did you, but I've got enough music in me for twenty wives.'

Visualizing herself as one of them, Helen rose stiffly.

'All I can ask you is to think how your mother would have felt—and those who care for you . . . . Good-by, Teddy.'

He walked out the door with her and down the stairs.

'As a matter of fact, we've been married for two months,' he said casually. 'She was a waitress in a place where I used to eat.'

Helen felt that she should be angry and aloof, but tears of hurt vanity were springing to her eyes.

'And do you love her?'

'I like her; she's a good person and good for me. Love is something else. I loved you, Helen, and that's all dead in me for the present. Maybe it's coming out in my music. Some day I'll probably love other women—or maybe there'll never be anything but you. Good-by, Helen.'

The declaration touched her. 'I hope you'll be happy, Teddy. Bring your wife to the wedding.'

He bowed noncommittally. When she had gone, he returned thoughtfully to his apartment.

'That was the cousin that I was in love with,' he said.

'And was it?' Betty's face, Irish and placid, brightened with interest. 'She's a pretty thing.'

'She wouldn't have been as good for me as a nice peasant like you.'

'Always thinking of yourself, Teddy Van Beck.'

He laughed. 'Sure I am, but you love me, anyhow?'

'That's a big wur-red.'

'All right. I'll remember that when you come begging around for a kiss. If my grandfather knew I married a bog trotter, he'd turn over in his grave. Now get out and let me finish my work.'

He sat at the piano, a pencil behind his ear. Already his face was resolved, composed, but his eyes grew more intense minute by minute, until there was a glaze in them, behind which they seemed to have joined his ears in counting and hearing. Presently there was no more indication in his face that anything had occurred to disturb the tranquillity of his Sunday morning.

II

Mrs Cassius Ruthven and a friend, veils flung back across their hats, sat in their auto on the edge of the field.

'A young woman playing polo in breeches.' Mrs Ruthven sighed. 'Amy Van Beck's daughter. I thought when Helen organized the Amazons she'd stop at divided skirts. But her husband apparently has no objections, for there he stands, egging her on. Of course, they always have liked the same things.'

'A pair of thoroughbreds, those two,' said the other woman complacently, meaning that she admitted them to be her equals. 'You'd never look at them and think that anything had gone wrong.'

She was referring to Stuart's mistake in the panic of 1907. His father had bequeathed him a precarious situation and Stuart had made an error of judgment. His honor was not questioned and his crowd stood by him loyally, but his usefulness in Wall Street was over and his small fortune was gone.

He stood in a group of men with whom he would presently play, noting things to tell Helen after the game—she wasn't turning with the play soon enough and several times she was unnecessarily ridden off at important moments. Her ponies were sluggish—the penalty for playing with borrowed mounts—but she was, nevertheless, the best player on the field, and in the last minute she made a save that brought applause.

'Good girl! Good girl!'

Stuart had been delegated with the unpleasant duty of chasing the women from the field. They had started an hour late and now a team from New Jersey was waiting to

(348)

play; he sensed trouble as he cut across to join Helen and walked beside her toward the stables. She was splendid, with her flushed cheeks, her shining, triumphant eyes, her short, excited breath. He temporized for a minute.

'That was good—that last,' he said.

'Thanks. It almost broke my arm. Wasn't I pretty good all through?'

'You were the best out there.'

'I know it.'

He waited while she dismounted and handed the pony to a groom.

'Helen, I believe I've got a job.'

'What is it?'

'Don't jump on the idea till you think it over. Gus Myers wants me to manage his racing stables. Eight thousand a year.'

Helen considered. 'It's a nice salary; and I bet you could make yourself up a nice string from his ponies.'

'The principal thing is that I need the money; I'd have as much as you and things would be easier.'

'You'd have as much as me,' Helen repeated. She almost regretted that he would need no more help from her. 'But with Gus Myers, isn't there a string attached? Wouldn't he expect a boost up?'

'He probably would,' answered Stuart bluntly, 'and if I can help him socially, I will. As a matter of fact, he wants me at a stag dinner tonight.'

'All right, then,' Helen said absently. Still hesitating to tell her her game was over, Stuart followed her glance toward the field, where a runabout had driven up and parked by the ropes.

'There's your old friend, Teddy,' he remarked dryly— 'or rather, your new friend, Teddy. He's taking a sudden interest in polo. Perhaps he thinks the horses aren't biting this summer.'

'You're not in a very good humor,' protested Helen. 'You know, if you say the word, I'll never see him again. All I want in the world is for you and I to be together.'

(349)

'I know,' he admitted regretfully. 'Selling horses and giving up clubs put a crimp in that. I know the women all fall for Teddy, now he's getting famous, but if he tries to fool around with you I'll break his piano over his head. . . . Oh, another thing,' he began, seeing the men already riding on the field. 'About your last chukker——'

As best he could, he put the situation up to her. He was not prepared for the fury that swept over her.

'But it's an outrage! I got up the game and it's been posted on the bulletin board for three days.'

'You started an hour late.'

'And do you know why?' she demanded. 'Because your friend Joe Morgan insisted that Celie ride sidesaddle. He tore her habit off her three times, and she only got here by climbing out the kitchen window.'

'I can't do anything about it.'

'Why can't you? Weren't you once a governor of this club? How can women ever expect to be any good if they have to quit every time the men want the field? All the men want is for the women to come up to them in the evening and tell them what a beautiful game they played!'

Still raging and blaming Stuart, she crossed the field to Teddy's car. He got out and greeted her with concentrated intensity:

'I've reached the point where I can neither sleep nor eat from thinking of you. What point is that?'

There was something thrilling about him that she had never been conscious of in the old days; perhaps the stories of his philanderings had made him more romantic to her.

'Well, don't think of me as I am now,' she said. 'My face is getting rougher every day and my muscles lean out of an evening dress like a female impersonator. People are beginning to refer to me as handsome instead of pretty. Besides, I'm in a vile humor. It seems to me women are always just edged out of everything.'

Stuart's game was brutal that afternoon. In the first five

minutes, he realized that Teddy's runabout was no longer there, and his long slugs began to tally from all angles. Afterward, he bumped home across country at a gallop; his mood was not assuaged by a note handed him by the children's nurse:

> *Dear:* Since your friends made it impossible for us to play, I wasn't going to sit there just dripping; so I had Teddy bring me home. And since you'll be out to dinner, I'm going into New York with him to the theater. I'll either be out on the theater train or spend the night at mother's.
> HELEN.

Stuart went upstairs and changed into his dinner coat. He had no defense against the unfamiliar claws of jealousy that began a slow dissection of his insides. Often Helen had gone to plays or dances with other men, but this was different. He felt toward Teddy the faint contempt of the physical man for the artist, but the last six months had bruised his pride. He perceived the possibility that Helen might be seriously interested in someone else.

He was in a bad humor at Gus Myers' dinner—annoyed with his host for talking so freely about their business arrangement. When at last they rose from the table, he decided that it was no go and called Myers aside.

'Look here. I'm afraid this isn't a good idea, after all.'

'Why not?' His host looked at him in alarm. 'Are you going back on me? My dear fellow——'

'I think we'd better call it off.'

'And why, may I ask? Certainly I have the right to ask why.'

Stuart considered. 'All right, I'll tell you. When you made that little speech, you mentioned me as if you had somehow bought me, as if I was a sort of employe in your office. Now, in the sporting world that doesn't go; things are more— more democratic. I grew up with all these men here tonight, and they didn't like it any better than I did.'

(351)

'I see,' Mr Myers reflected carefully—'I see.' Suddenly he clapped Stuart on the back. 'That is exactly the sort of thing I like to be told; it helps me. From now on I won't mention you as if you were in my—as if we had a business arrangement. Is that all right?'

After all, the salary was eight thousand dollars.

'Very well, then,' Stuart agreed. 'But you'll have to excuse me tonight. I'm catching a train to the city.'

'I'll put an automobile at your disposal.'

A ten o'clock he rang the bell of Teddy's apartment on Forty-eighth Street.

'I'm looking for Mr Van Beck,' he said to the woman who answered the door. 'I know he's gone to the theater, but I wonder if you can tell me——' Suddenly he guessed who the woman was. 'I'm Stuart Oldhorne,' he explained. 'I married Mr Van Beck's cousin.'

'Oh, come in,' said Betty pleasantly. 'I know all about who you are.'

She was just this side of forty, stoutish and plain of face, but full of a keen, brisk vitality. In the living room they sat down.

'You want to see Teddy?'

'He's with my wife and I want to join them after the theater. I wonder if you know where they went?'

'Oh, so Teddy's with your wife.' There was a faint, pleasant brogue in her voice. 'Well, now, he didn't say exactly where he'd be tonight.'

'Then you don't know?'

'I don't—not for the life of me,' she admitted cheerfully. 'I'm sorry.'

He stood up, and Betty saw the thinly hidden anguish in his face. Suddenly she was really sorry.

'I did hear him say something about the theater,' she said ruminatively. 'Now sit down and let me think what it was. He goes out so much and a play once a week is enough for me, so that one night mixes up with the others in my head. Didn't your wife say where to meet them?'

'No. I only decided to come in after they'd started. She said she'd catch the theater train back to Long Island or go to her mother's.'

'That's it,' Betty said triumphantly, striking her hands together like cymbals. 'That's what he said when he called up—that he was putting a lady on the theater train for Long Island, and would be home himself right afterward. We've had a child sick and it's driven things from my mind.'

'I'm very sorry I bothered you under those conditions.'

'It's no bother. Sit down. It's only just after ten.'

Feeling easier, Stuart relaxed a little and accepted a cigar.

'No, if I tried to keep up with Teddy, I'd have white hair by now,' Betty said. 'Of course, I go to his concerts, but often I fall asleep—not that he ever knows it. So long as he doesn't take too much to drink and knows where his home is, I don't bother about where he wanders.' As Stuart's face grew serious again, she changed her tone: 'All and all, he's a good husband to me and we have a happy life together, without interfering with each other. How would he do working next to the nursery and groaning at every sound? And how would I do going to Mrs Ruthven's with him, and all of them talking about high society and high art?'

A phrase of Helen's came back to Stuart: 'Always together —I like for us to do everything together.'

'You have children, haven't you, Mr Oldhorne?'

'Yes. My boy's almost big enough to sit a horse.'

'Ah, yes; you're both great for horses.'

'My wife says that as soon as their legs are long enough to reach stirrups, she'll be interested in them again.' This didn't sound right to Stuart and he modified it: 'I mean she always has been interested in them, but she never let them monopolize her or come between us. We've always believed that marriage ought to be founded on companionship, on having the same interests. I mean, you're musical and you help your husband.'

(353)

Betty laughed. 'I wish Teddy could hear that. I can't read a note or carry a tune.'

'No?' He was confused. 'I'd somehow got the impression that you were musical.'

'You can't see why else he'd have married me?'

'Not at all. On the contrary.'

After a few minutes, he said good night, somehow liking her. When he had gone, Betty's expression changed slowly to one of exasperation; she went to the telephone and called her husband's studio:

'There you are, Teddy. Now listen to me carefully. I know your cousin is with you and I want to talk with her. . . . Now, don't lie. You put her on the phone. Her husband has been here, and if you don't let me talk to her, it might be a serious matter.'

She could hear an unintelligible colloquy, and then Helen's voice:

'Hello.'

'Good evening, Mrs Oldhorne. Your husband came here, looking for you and Teddy. I told him I didn't know which play you were at, so you'd better be thinking which one. And I told him Teddy was leaving you at the station in time for the theater train.'

'Oh, thank you very much. We——'

'Now, you meet your husband or there's trouble for you, or I'm no judge of men. And—wait a minute. Tell Teddy, if he's going to be up late, that Josie's sleeping light, and he's not to touch the piano when he gets home.'

Betty heard Teddy come in at eleven, and she came into the drawing-room smelling of camomile vapor. He greeted her absently; there was a look of suffering in his face and his eyes were bright and far away.

'You call yourself a great musician, Teddy Van Beck,' she said, 'but it seems to me you're much more interested in women.'

'Let me alone, Betty.'

(354)

'I do let you alone, but when the husbands start coming here, it's another matter.'

'This was different, Betty. This goes way back into the past.'

'It sounds like the present to me.'

'Don't make any mistake about Helen,' he said. 'She's a good woman.'

'Not through any fault of yours, I know.'

He sank his head wearily in his hands. 'I've tried to forget her. I've avoided her for six years. And then, when I met her a month ago, it all rushed over me. Try and understand, Bet. You're my best friend; you're the only person that ever loved me.'

'When you're good I love you,' she said.

'Don't worry. It's over. She loves her husband; she just came to New York with me because she's got some spite against him. She follows me a certain distance just like she always has, and then——Anyhow, I'm not going to see her any more. Now go to bed, Bet. I want to play for a while.'

He was on his feet when she stopped him.

'You're not to touch the piano tonight.'

'Oh, I forgot about Josie,' he said remorsefully. 'Well, I'll drink a bottle of beer and then I'll come to bed.'

He came close and put his arm around her.

'Dear Bet, nothing could ever interfere with us.'

'You're a bad boy, Teddy,' she said. 'I wouldn't ever be so bad to you.'

'How do you know, Bet? How do you know what you'd do?'

He smoothed down her plain brown hair, knowing for the thousandth time that she had none of the world's dark magic for him, and that he couldn't live without her for six consecutive hours. 'Dear Bet,' he whispered. 'Dear Bet.'

III

The Oldhornes were visiting. In the last four years, since Stuart had terminated his bondage to Gus Myers, they had become visiting people. The children visited Grandmother Van Beck during the winter and attended school in New York. Stuart and Helen visited friends in Asheville, Aiken and Palm Beach, and in the summer usually occupied a small cottage on someone's Long Island estate. 'My dear, it's just standing there empty. I wouldn't dream of accepting any rent. You'll be doing us a favor by occupying it.'

Usually, they were; they gave out a great deal of themselves in that eternal willingness and enthusiasm which makes a successful guest—it became their profession. Moving through a world that was growing rich with the war in Europe, Stuart had somewhere lost his way. Twice playing brilliant golf in the national amateur, he accepted a job as professional at a club which his father had helped to found. He was restless and unhappy.

This week-end they were visiting a pupil of his. As a consequence of a mixed foursome, the Oldhornes went upstairs to dress for dinner surcharged with the unpleasant accumulation of many unsatisfactory months. In the afternoon, Stuart had played with their hostess and Helen with another man—a situation which Stuart always dreaded, because it forced him into competition with Helen. He had actually tried to miss that putt on the eighteenth—to just miss it. But the ball dropped in the cup. Helen went through the superficial motions of a good loser, but she devoted herself pointedly to her partner for the rest of the afternoon.

Their expressions still counterfeited amusement as they entered their room.

When the door closed, Helen's pleasant expression faded and she walked toward the dressing table as though her own reflection was the only decent company with which to forgather. Stuart watched her, frowning.

'I know why you're in a rotten humor,' he said; 'though I don't believe you know yourself.'

'I'm not in a rotten humor,' Helen responded in a clipped voice.

'You are; and I know the real reason—the one you don't know. It's because I holed that putt this afternoon.'

She turned slowly, incredulously, from the mirror.

'Oh, so I have a new fault! I've suddenly become, of all things, a poor sport!'

'It's not like you to be a poor sport,' he admitted, 'but otherwise why all this interest in other men, and why do you look at me as if I'm—well, slightly gamy?'

'I'm not aware of it.'

'I am.' He was aware, too, that there was always some man in their life now—some man of power and money who paid court to Helen and gave her the sense of solidity which he failed to provide. He had no cause to be jealous of any particular man, but the pressure of many was irritating. It annoyed him that on so slight a grievance, Helen should remind him by her actions that he no longer filled her entire life.

'If Anne can get any satisfaction out of winning, she's welcome to it,' said Helen suddenly.

'Isn't that rather petty? She isn't in your class; she won't qualify for the third flight in Boston.'

Feeling herself in the wrong, she changed her tone.

'Oh, that isn't it,' she broke out. 'I just keep wishing you and I could play together like we used to. And now you have to play with dubs, and get their wretched shots out of traps. Especially'—she hesitated—'especially when you're so unnecessarily gallant.'

The faint contempt in her voice, the mock jealousy that covered a growing indifference was apparent to him. There had been a time when, if he danced with another woman, Helen's stricken eyes followed him around the room.

'My gallantry is simply a matter of business,' he answered. 'Lessons have brought in three hundred a month all summer. How could I go to see you play at Boston next week, except that I'm going to coach other women?'

'And you're going to see me win,' announced Helen. 'Do you know that?'

'Naturally, I want nothing more,' Stuart said automatically. But the unnecessary defiance in her voice repelled him, and he suddenly wondered if he really cared whether she won or not.

At the same moment, Helen's mood changed and for a moment she saw the true situation—that she could play in amateur tournaments and Stuart could not, that the new cups in the rack were all hers now, that he had given up the fiercely competitive sportsmanship that had been the breath of life to him in order to provide necessary money.

'Oh, I'm so sorry for you, Stuart!' There were tears in her eyes. 'It seems such a shame that you can't do the things you love, and I can. Perhaps I oughtn't to play this summer.'

'Nonsense,' he said. 'You can't sit home and twirl your thumbs.'

She caught at this: 'You wouldn't want me to. I can't help being good at sports; you taught me nearly all I know. But I wish I could help you.'

'Just try to remember I'm your best friend. Sometimes you act as if we were rivals.'

She hesitated, annoyed by the truth of his words and unwilling to concede an inch; but a wave of memories rushed over her, and she thought how brave he was in his eked-out, pieced-together life; she came and threw her arms around him.

'Darling, darling, things are going to be better. You'll see.'

Helen won the finals in the tournament at Boston the following week. Following around with the crowd, Stuart was very proud of her. He hoped that instead of feeding her egotism, the actual achievement would make things easier between them. He hated the conflict that had grown out of their wanting the same excellences, the same prizes from life.

Afterward he pursued her progress toward the clubhouse, amused and a little jealous of the pack that fawned around her. He reached the club among the last, and a steward accosted him. 'Professionals are served in the lower grill, please,' the man said.

'That's all right. My name's Oldhorne.'

He started to walk by, but the man barred his way.

'Sorry, sir. I realize that Mrs Oldhorne's playing in the match, but my orders are to direct the professionals to the lower grill, and I understand you are a professional.'

'Why, look here——' Stuart began, wildly angry, and stopped. A group of people were listening. 'All right; never mind,' he said gruffly, and turned away.

The memory of the experience rankled; it was the determining factor that drove him, some weeks later, to a momentous decision. For a long time he had been playing with the idea of joining the Canadian Air Force, for service in France. He knew that his absence would have little practical bearing on the lives of Helen and the children; happening on some friends who were also full of the restlessness of 1915, the matter was suddenly decided. But he had not counted on the effect upon Helen; her reaction was not so much one of grief or alarm, but as if she had been somehow outwitted.

'But you might have told me!' she wailed. 'You leave me dangling; you simply take yourself away without any warning.'

Once again Helen saw him as the bright and intolerably blinding hero, and her soul winced before him as it had when they first met. He was a warrior; for him, peace was only the interval between wars, and peace was destroying him. Here was the game of games beckoning him——Without throwing over the whole logic of their lives, there was nothing she could say.

'This is my sort of thing,' he said confidently, younger with his excitement. 'A few more years of this life and I'd go to pieces, take to drink. I've somehow lost your respect, and I've got to have that, even if I'm far away.'

She was proud of him again; she talked to everyone of his impending departure. Then, one September afternoon, she

came home from the city, full of the old feeling of comradeship and bursting with news, to find him buried in an utter
depression.

'Stuart,' she cried, 'I've got the——' She broke off. 'What's
the matter, darling? Is something the matter?'

He looked at her dully. 'They turned me down,' he said.
'What?'

'My left eye.' He laughed bitterly. 'Where that dub
cracked me with the brassie. I'm nearly blind in it.'

'Isn't there anything you can do?'

'Nothing.'

'Stuart!' She stared at him aghast. 'Stuart, and I was
going to tell you! I was saving it for a surprise. Elsa Prentice
has organized a Red Cross unit to serve with the French, and
I joined it because I thought it would be wonderful if we
both went. We've been measured for uniforms and bought
our outfits, and we're sailing the end of next week.'

IV

Helen was a blurred figure among other blurred figures on a
boat deck, dark against the threat of submarines. When the
ship had slid out into the obscure future, Stuart walked
eastward along Fifty-seventh Street. His grief at the sever-
ance of many ties was a weight he carried in his body, and he
walked slowly, as if adjusting himself to it. To balance this
there was a curious sensation of lightness in his mind. For
the first time in twelve years he was alone, and the feeling
came over him that he was alone for good; knowing Helen
and knowing war, he could guess at the experiences she
would go through, and he could not form any picture of a
renewed life together afterward. He was discarded; she had
proved the stronger at last. It seemed very strange and sad
that his marriage should have such an ending.

He came to Carnegie Hall, dark after a concert, and his eye
caught the name of Theodore Van Beck, large on the posted

bills. As he stared at it, a green door opened in the side of the building and a group of people in evening dress came out. Stuart and Teddy were face to face before they recognized each other.

'Hello, there!' Teddy cried cordially. 'Did Helen sail?'

'Just now.'

'I met her on the street yesterday and she told me. I wanted you both to come to my concert. Well, she's quite a heroine, going off like that. . . . Have you met my wife?'

Stuart and Betty smiled at each other.

'We've met.'

'And I didn't know it,' protested Teddy. 'Women need watching when they get toward their dotage. . . . Look here, Stuart; we're having a few people up to the apartment. No heavy music or anything. Just supper and a few debutantes to tell me I was divine. It will do you good to come. I imagine you're missing Helen like the devil.'

'I don't think I——'

'Come along. They'll tell you you're divine too.'

Realizing that the invitation was inspired by kindliness, Stuart accepted. It was the sort of gathering he had seldom attended, and he was surprised to meet so many people he knew. Teddy played the lion in a manner at once assertive and skeptical. Stuart listened as he enlarged to Mrs Cassius Ruthven on one of his favorite themes:

'People tried to make marriages coöperative and they've ended by becoming competitive. Impossible situation. Smart men will get to fight shy of ornamental women. A man ought to marry somebody who'll be grateful, like Betty here.'

'Now don't talk so much, Theodore Van Beck,' Betty interrupted. 'Since you're such a fine musician, you'd do well to express yourself with music instead of rash words.'

'I don't agree with your husband,' said Mrs Ruthven. 'English girls hunt with their men and play politics with them on absolutely equal terms, and it tends to draw them together.'

(361)

'It does not,' insisted Teddy. 'That's why English society is the most disorganized in the world. Betty and I are happy because we haven't any qualities in common at all.'

His exuberance grated on Stuart, and the success that flowed from him swung his mind back to the failure of his own life. He could not know that his life was not destined to be a failure. He could not read the fine story that three years later would be carved proud above his soldier's grave, or know that his restless body, which never spared itself in sport or danger, was destined to give him one last proud gallop at the end.

'They turned me down,' he was saying to Mrs Ruthven. 'I'll have to stick to Squadron A, unless we get drawn in.'

'So Helen's gone.' Mrs Ruthven looked at him, reminiscing. 'I'll never forget your wedding. You were both so handsome, so ideally suited to each other. Everybody spoke of it.'

Stuart remembered; for the moment it seemed that he had little else that it was fun to remember.

'Yes,' he agreed, nodding his head thoughtfully, 'I suppose we were a handsome pair.'

SCOTT

Last Kiss

(*Collier's*, 16 April 1949*)

The sound of revelry fell sweet upon James Leonard's ear. He alighted, a little awed by his new limousine, and walked down the red carpet through the crowd. Faces strained forward, weird in the split glare of the drum lights—but after a moment they lost interest in him. Once Jim had been annoyed by his anonymity in Hollywood. Now he was pleased with it.

Elsie Donohue, a tall, lovely, gangling girl, had a seat reserved for him at her table. 'If I had no chance before,' she said, 'what chance have I got now that you're so important?' She was half teasing—but only half.

'You're a stubborn man,' she said. 'When we first met, you put me in the undesirable class. Why?' She tossed her shoulders despairingly as Jim's eyes lingered on a little Chinese beauty at the next table. 'You're looking at Ching Loo Poo-poo, Ching Loo Poo-poo! And for five long years I've come out to this ghastly town——'

'They couldn't keep you away,' Jim objected. 'It's on your swing around—the Stork Club, Palm Beach and Dave Chasen's.'

Tonight something in him wanted to be quiet. Jim was thirty-five and suddenly on the winning side of all this. He was one of those who said how pictures should go, what they should say. It was a fine pure feeling to be on top.

One was very sure that everything was for the best, that the lights shone upon fair ladies and brave men, that pianos

---

* Written in 1940.

dripped the right notes and that the young lips singing them spoke for happy hearts.

They absolutely must be happy, these beautiful faces. And then in a twilight rumba, a face passed Jim's table that was not quite happy. It had gone before Jim formulated this opinion, yet it remained fixed on his memory for some seconds. It was the head of a girl almost as tall as he was, with opaque brown eyes and cheeks as porcelain as those of the little Chinese.

'At least you're back with the white race,' said Elsie, following his eyes.

Jim wanted to answer sharply: *You've had your day— three husbands. How about me? Thirty-five and still trying to match every woman with a childhood love who died, still finding fatally in every girl the similarities and not the differences.*

The next time the lights were dim he wandered through the tables to the entrance hall. Here and there friends hailed him—more than the usual number of course, because his rise had been in the Reporter that morning, but Jim had made other steps up and he was used to that. It was a charity ball, and by the stairs was the man who imitated wallpaper about to go in and do a number, and Bob Bordley with a sandwich board on his back: At Ten Tonight In the Hollywood Bowl SONJA HENIE Will Skate on HOT SOUP.

By the bar Jim saw the producer whom he was displacing tomorrow having an unsuspecting drink with the agent who had contrived his ruin. Next to the agent was the girl whose face had seemed sad as she danced by in the rumba.

'Oh, Jim,' said the agent, 'Pamela Knighton—your future star.'

She turned to him with professional eagerness. What the agent's voice had said to her was: 'Look alive! This *is* somebody.'

'Pamela's joined my stable,' said the agent. 'I want her to change her name to Boots.'

(364)

'I thought you said Toots,' the girl laughed.

'Toots or Boots. It's the *oo-oo* sound. Cutie shoots Toots. Judge Hoots. No conviction possible. Pamela is English. Her real name is Sybil Higgins.'

It seemed to Jim that the deposed producer was looking at him with an infinite something in his eyes—not hatred, not jealousy, but a profound and curious astonishment that asked: Why? Why? For Heaven's sake, why? More disturbed by this than by enmity, Jim surprised himself by asking the English girl to dance. As they faced each other on the floor his exultation of the early evening came back.

'Hollywood's a good place,' he said, as if to forestall any criticism from her. 'You'll like it. Most English girls do— they don't expect too much. I've had luck working with English girls.'

'Are you a director?'

'I've been everything—from press agent on. I've just signed a producer's contract that begins tomorrow.'

'I like it here,' she said after a minute. 'You can't help expecting things. But if they don't come I could always teach school again.'

Jim leaned back and looked at her—his impression was of pink-and-silver frost. She was so far from a schoolmarm, even a schoolmarm in a Western, that he laughed. But again he saw that there was something sad and a little lost within the triangle formed by lips and eyes.

'Whom are you with tonight?' he asked.

'Joe Becker,' she answered, naming the agent. 'Myself and three other girls.'

'Look—I have to go out for half an hour. To see a man— this is not phony. Believe me. Will you come along for company and night air?'

She nodded.

On the way they passed Elsie Donohue, who looked

(365)

inscrutably at the girl and shook her head slightly at Jim. Out in the clear California night he liked his big car for the first time, liked it better than driving himself. The streets through which they rolled were quiet at this hour. Miss Knighton waited for him to speak.

'What did you teach in school?' he asked.

'Sums. Two and two are four and all that.'

'It's a long jump from that to Hollywood.'

'It's a long story.'

'It can't be very long—you're about eighteen.'

'Twenty.' Anxiously she asked, 'Do you think that's too old?'

'Lord, no! It's a beautiful age. I know—I'm twenty-one myself and the arteries haven't hardened much.'

She looked at him gravely, estimating his age and keeping it to herself.

'I want to hear the long story,' he said.

She sighed. 'Well, a lot of old men fell in love with me. Old, old men—I was an old man's darling.'

'You mean old gaffers of twenty-two?'

'They were between sixty and seventy. This is all true. So I became a gold digger and dug enough money out of them to go to New York. I walked into 21 the first day and Joe Becker saw me.'

'Then you've never been in pictures?' he asked.

'Oh, yes—I had a test this morning,' she told him.

Jim smiled. 'And you don't feel bad taking money from all those old men?' he inquired.

'Not really,' she said, matter-of-fact. 'They enjoyed giving it to me. Anyhow it wasn't really money. When they wanted to give me presents I'd send them to a certain jeweler, and afterward I'd take the presents back to the jeweler and get four-fifths of the cash.'

'Why, you little chiseler!'

'Yes,' she admitted. 'Somebody told me how. I'm out for all I can get.'

'Didn't they mind—the old men, I mean—when you didn't wear their presents?'

'Oh, I'd wear them—once. Old men don't see very well, or remember. But that's why I haven't any jewelry of my own.' She broke off. 'This I'm wearing is rented.'

Jim looked at her again and then laughed aloud. 'I wouldn't worry about it. California's full of old men.'

They had twisted into a residential district. As they turned a corner Jim picked up the speaking tube. 'Stop here.' He turned to Pamela, 'I have some dirty work to do.'

He looked at his watch, got out and went up the street to a building with the names of several doctors on a sign. He went past the building walking slowly, and presently a man came out of the building and followed him. In the darkness between two lamps Jim went close, handed him an envelope and spoke concisely. The man walked off in the opposite direction and Jim returned to the car.

'I'm having all the old men bumped off,' he explained. 'There're some things worse than death.'

'Oh, I'm not free now,' she assured him. 'I'm engaged.'

'Oh.' After a minute he asked, 'To an Englishman?'

'Well—naturally. Did you think——' She stopped herself but too late.

'Are we that uninteresting?' he asked.

'Oh, no.' Her casual tone made it worse. And when she smiled, at the moment when a street light shone in and dressed her beauty up to a white radiance, it was more annoying still.

'Now you tell *me* something,' she asked. 'Tell me the mystery.'

'Just money,' he answered almost absently. 'That little Greek doctor keeps telling a certain lady that her appendix is bad—we need her in a picture. So we bought him off. It's the last time I'll ever do anyone else's dirty work.'

She frowned. 'Does she really need her appendix out?'

He shrugged. 'Probably not. At least that rat wouldn't know. He's her brother-in-law and he wants the money.'

(367)

After a long time Pamela spoke judicially. 'An Englishman wouldn't do that.'

'Some would,' he said shortly, '—and some Americans wouldn't.'

'An English gentleman wouldn't,' she insisted.

'Aren't you getting off on the wrong foot,' he suggested, 'if you're going to work here?'

'Oh, I like Americans all right—the civilized ones.'

From her look Jim took this to include him, but far from being appeased he had a sense of outrage. 'You're taking chances,' he said. 'In fact, I don't see how you dared come out with me. I might have had feathers under my hat.'

'You didn't bring a hat,' she said placidly. 'Besides, Joe Becker said to. There might be something in it for me.'

After all he was a producer and you didn't reach eminence by losing your temper—except on purpose. 'I'm sure there's something in it for you,' he said, listening to a stealthily treacherous purr creep into his voice.

'Are you?' she demanded. 'Do you think I'll stand out at all—or am I just one of the thousands?'

'You stand out already,' he continued on the same note. 'Everyone at the dance was looking at you.' He wondered if this was even faintly true. Was it only he who had fancied some uniqueness? 'You're a new type,' he went on. 'A face like yours might give American pictures a—a more civilized tone.'

This was his arrow—but to his vast surprise it glanced off.

'Oh, do you think so?' she cried. 'Are you going to give me a chance?'

'Why, certainly.' It was hard to believe that the irony in his voice was missing its mark. 'But after tonight there'll be so much competition that——'

'Oh, I'd rather work for you,' she declared. 'I'll tell Joe Becker——'

'Don't tell him anything,' he interrupted.

'Oh, I won't. I'll do just as you say,' she promised.

Her eyes were wide and expectant. Disturbed, he felt that words were being put in his mouth or slipping from him unintended. That so much innocence and so much predatory toughness could go side by side behind this gentle English voice.

'You'd be wasted in bits,' he began. 'The thing is to get a fat part——' He broke off and started again, 'You've got such a strong personality that——'

'Oh, don't!' He saw tears blinking in the corners of her eyes. 'Let me just keep this to sleep on tonight. You call me in the morning—or when you need me.'

The car came to rest at the carpet strip in front of the dance. Seeing Pamela, the crowd bulged forward grotesquely, autograph books at the ready. Failing to recognize her, it sighed back behind the ropes.

In the ballroom he danced her to Becker's table.

'I won't say a word,' she answered. From her evening case she took a card with the name of her hotel penciled on it. 'If any other offers come I'll refuse them.'

'Oh, no,' he said quickly.

'Oh, yes.' She smiled brightly at him and for an instant the feeling Jim had had on seeing her came back. It was an impression of a rich warm sympathy, of youth and suffering side by side. He braced himself for a final quick slash to burst the scarcely created bubble.

'After a year or so——' he began. But the music and her voice overrode him.

'I'll wait for you to call. You're the—you're the most civilized American I've ever met.'

She turned her back as if embarrassed by the magnificence of her compliment. Jim started back to his table—then seeing Elsie Donohue talking to a woman across his empty chair, he turned obliquely away. The room, the evening had gone raucous—the blend of music and voices seemed inharmonious and accidental and his eyes covering the room saw only

(369)

jealousies and hatreds—egos tapping like drumbeats up to a fanfare. He was not above the battle as he had thought.

He started for the coatroom thinking of the note he would dispatch by waiter to his hostess: 'You were dancing.' Then he found himself almost upon Pamela Knighton's table, and turning again he took another route toward the door.

A picture executive can do without intelligence but he cannot do without tact. Tact now absorbed Jim Leonard to the exclusion of everything else. Power should have pushed diplomacy into the background, leaving him free, but instead it intensified all his human relations—with the executives, with the directors, writers, actors and technical men assigned to his unit, with department heads, censors and 'men from the East' besides. So the stalling off of one lone English girl, with no weapon except the telephone and a little note that reached him from the entrance desk, should have been no problem at all.

Just passing by the studio and thought of you and of our ride. There have been some offers but I keep stalling Joe Becker. If I move I will let you know.

A city full of youth and hope spoke in it—in its two transparent lies, the brave falsity of its tone. It didn't matter to her—all the money and glory beyond the impregnable walls. She had just been passing by—just passing by.

That was after two weeks. In another week Joe Becker dropped in to see him. 'About that little English girl, Pamela Knighton—remember? How'd she strike you?'

'Very nice.'

'For some reason she didn't want me to talk to you.' Joe looked out the window. 'So I suppose you didn't get along so well that night.'

'Sure we did.'

'The girl's engaged, you see, to some guy in England.'

'She told me that,' said Jim, annoyed. 'I didn't make any passes at her if that's what you're getting at.'

'Don't worry—I understand those things. I just wanted to tell you something about her.'

'Nobody else interested?'

'She's only been here a month. Everybody's got to start. I just want to tell you that when she came into 21 that day the barflies dropped like—like flies. Let me tell you—in one minute she was the talk of café society.'

'It must have been great,' Jim said dryly.

'It was. And Lamarr was there that day too. Listen—Pam was all alone, and she had on English clothes, I guess, nothing you'd look at twice—rabbit fur. But she shone through it like a diamond.'

'Yeah?'

'Strong women,' Joe went on, 'wept into their Vichyssoise. Elsa Maxwell—'

'Joe, this is a busy morning.'

'Will you look at her test?'

'Tests are for make-up men,' said Jim, impatiently. 'I never believe a good test. And I always suspect a bad one.'

'Got your own ideas, eh?'

'About that,' Jim admitted. 'There've been a lot of bad guesses in projection rooms.'

'Behind desks, too,' said Joe rising.

A second note came after another week: '*When I phoned yesterday one secretary said you were away and one said you were in conference. If this is a run-around tell me. I'm not getting any younger. Twenty-one is staring me in the face—and you must have bumped off all the old men.*'

Her face had grown dim now. He remembered the delicate cheeks, the haunted eyes, as from a picture seen a long time ago. It was easy to dictate a letter that told of changed plans, of new casting, of difficulties which made it impossible——

(371)

He didn't feel good about it but at least it was finished business. Having a sandwich in his neighborhood drugstore that night, he looked back at his month's work as good. He had reeked of tact. His unit functioned smoothly. The shades who controlled his destiny would soon see.

There were only a few people in the drugstore. Pamela Knighton was the girl at the magazine rack. She looked up at him, startled, over a copy of The Illustrated London News.

Knowing of the letter that lay for signature on his desk Jim wished he could pretend not to see her. He turned slightly aside, held his breath, listened. But though she had seen him, nothing happened, and hating his Hollywood cowardice he turned again presently and lifted his hat.

'You're up late,' he said.

Pamela searched his face momentarily. 'I live around the corner,' she said. 'I've just moved—I wrote you today.'

'I live near here, too.'

She replaced the magazine in the rack. Jim's tact fled. He felt suddenly old and harassed and asked the wrong question.

'How do things go?' he asked.

'Oh, very well,' she said. 'I'm in a play—a real play at the New Faces theater in Pasadena. For the experience.'

'Oh, that's very wise.'

'We open in two weeks. I was hoping you could come.'

They walked out the door together and stood in the glow of the red neon sign. Across the autumn street newsboys were shouting the result of the night football.

'Which way?' she asked.

The other way from you, he thought, but when she indicated her direction he walked with her. It was months since he had seen Sunset Boulevard, and the mention of Pasadena made him think of when he had first come to California ten years ago, something green and cool.

Pamela stopped before some tiny bungalows around a central court. 'Good night,' she said. 'Don't let it worry you if you can't help me. Joe has explained how things are, with the war and all. I know you wanted to.'

He nodded solemnly—despising himself.

'Are you married?' she asked.

'No.'

'Then kiss me good night.'

As he hesitated she said, 'I like to be kissed good night. I sleep better.'

He put his arms around her shyly and bent down to her lips, just touching them—and thinking hard of the letter on his desk which he couldn't send now—and liking holding her.

'You see it's nothing,' she said. 'Just friendly. Just good night.'

On his way to the corner Jim said aloud, 'Well, I'll be damned,' and kept repeating the sinister prophecy to himself for some time after he was in bed.

On the third night of Pamela's play Jim went to Pasadena and bought a seat in the last row. A likely crowd was jostling into the theater and he felt glad that she would play to a full house, but at the door he found that it was a revival of Room Service—Pamela's play was in the Experiment Hall up the stairs.

Meekly he climbed to a tiny auditorium and was the first arrival except for fluttering ushers and voices chattering amid the hammers backstage. He considered a discreet retirement but was reassured by the arrival of a group of five, among them Joe Becker's chief assistant. The lights went out; a gong was beaten; to an audience of six the play began.

It was about some Mexicans who were being deprived of relief. Concepcione (Pamela Knighton) was having a child by an oil magnate. In the old Horatio Alger tradition, Pedro was reading Marx so someday he could be a bureaucrat and have offices at Palm Springs.

Pedro: '*We stay here. Better Boss Ford than Renegade Trotsky.*'

Concepcione: (Miss Knighton): 'But who will live to inherit?'

Pedro: 'Perhaps the great-grandchildren, or the grandchildren of the great-grandchildren. Quién sabe?'

Through the gloomy charade Jim watched Pamela; in front of him the party of five leaned together and whispered after her scenes. Was she good? Jim had no notion—he should have taken someone along, or brought in his chauffeur. What with pictures drawing upon half the world for talent there was scarcely such a phenomenon as a 'natural.' There were only possibilities—and luck. He was luck. He was maybe this girl's luck—if he felt that her pull at his insides was universal.

Stars were no longer created by one man's casual desire as in the silent days, but stock girls were, tests were, chances were. When the curtain finally dropped, domestically as a Venetian blind, he went backstage by the simple process of walking through a door on the side. She was waiting for him.

'I was hoping you wouldn't come tonight,' she said. 'We've flopped. But the first night it was full and I looked for you.'

'You were fine,' he said stiffly.

'Oh, no. You should have seen me then.'

'I saw enough,' he said suddenly. 'I can give you a little part. Will you come to the studio tomorrow?'

He watched her expression. Once more it surprised him. Out of her eyes, out of the curve of her mouth gleamed a sudden and overwhelming pity.

'Oh,' she said. 'Oh, I'm terribly sorry. Joe brought some people over and next day I signed up with Bernie Wise.'

'You *did?*'

'I knew you wanted me and at first I didn't realize you were just a sort of supervisor. I thought you had more power —you know?' She could not have chosen sharper words out

(374)

of deliberate mischief. 'Oh, I like you better *personally*,' she assured him. 'You're much more civilized than Bernie Wise.'

All right then he was civilized. He could at least pull out gracefully. 'Can I drive you back to Hollywood?'

They rode through an October night soft as April. When they crossed a bridge, its walls topped with wire screens, he gestured toward it and she nodded.

'I know what it is,' she said. 'But how stupid! English people don't commit suicide when they don't get what they want.'

'I know. They come to America.'

She laughed and looked at him appraisingly. Oh, she could do something with him all right. She let her hand rest upon his.

'Kiss tonight?' he suggested after a while.

Pamela glanced at the chauffeur insulated in his compartment. 'Kiss tonight,' she said. . . .

He flew East next day, looking for a young actress just like Pamela Knighton. He looked so hard that any eyes with an aspect of lovely melancholy, any bright English voice, predisposed him; he wandered as far afield as a stock company in Erie and a student play at Wellesley—it came to seem a desperate matter that he should find someone exactly like this girl. Then when a telegram called him impatiently back to Hollywood, he found Pamela dumped in his lap.

'You got a second chance, Jim,' said Joe Becker. 'Don't miss it again.'

'What was the matter over there?'

'They had no part for her. They're in a mess—change of management. So we tore up the contract.'

Mike Harris, the studio head, investigated the matter. Why was Bernie Wise, a shrewd picture man, willing to let her go?

'Bernie says she can't act,' he reported to Jim. 'And what's more she makes trouble. I keep thinking of Simone and those two Austrian girls.'

'I've seen her act,' insisted Jim. 'And I've got a place for her. I don't even want to build her up yet. I want to spot her in this little part and let you see.'

A week later Jim pushed open the padded door of Stage III and walked in. Extras in dress clothes turned toward him in the semidarkness; eyes widened.

'Where's Bob Griffin?'

'In that bungalow with Miss Knighton.'

They were sitting side by side on a couch in the glare of the make-up light, and from the resistance in Pamela's face Jim knew the trouble was serious.

'It's *nothing*,' Bob insisted heartily. 'We get along like a couple of kittens, don't we, Pam? Sometimes I roll over her but she doesn't mind.'

'You smell of onions,' said Pamela.

Griffin tried again. 'There's an English way and an American way. We're looking for the happy mean—that's all.'

'There's a nice way and a silly way,' Pamela said shortly. 'I don't want to begin by looking like a fool.'

'Leave us alone, will you, Bob?' Jim said.

'Sure. All the time in the world.'

Jim had not seen her in this busy week of tests and fittings and rehearsals, and he thought now how little he knew about her and she of them.

'Bob seems to be in your hair,' he said.

'He wants me to say things no sane person would say.'

'All right—maybe so,' he agreed. 'Pamela, since you've been working here have you ever blown up in your lines?'

'Why—everybody does sometimes.'

'Listen, Pamela—Bob Griffin gets almost ten times as much money as you do—for a particular reason. Not because he's the most brilliant director in Hollywood—he isn't—but because he never blows up in his lines.'

(376)

'He's not an actor,' she said, puzzled.

'I mean his lines in real life. I picked him for this picture because once in a while I blow up. But not Bob. He signed a contract for an unholy amount of money—which he doesn't deserve, which nobody deserves. But smoothness is the fourth dimension of this business and Bob has forgotten the word "I." People of three times his talent—producers and troupers and directors—go down the sink because they can't forget it.'

'I know I'm being lectured to,' she said uncertainly. 'But I don't seem to understand. An actress has her own personality——'

He nodded. 'And we pay her five times what she could get for it anywhere else—*if* she'll only keep it off the floor where it trips the rest of us up. You're tripping us all up, Pamela.'

I thought you were my friend, her eyes said.

He talked to her a few minutes more. Everything he said he believed with all his heart, but because he had twice kissed those lips, he saw that it was support and protection they wanted from him. All he had done was to make her a little shocked that he was not on her side. Feeling rather baffled, and sorry for her loneliness he went to the door of the bungalow and called: 'Hey, Bob!'

Jim went about other business. He got back to his office to find Mike Harris waiting.

'Again that girl's making trouble.'

'I've been over there.'

'I mean in the last five minutes!' cried Harris. 'Since you left she's made trouble! Bob Griffin had to stop shooting for the day. He's on his way over.'

Bob came in. 'There's one type you can't seem to get at—can't find what makes them that way. I'm afraid it's either Pamela or me.'

There was a moment's silence. Mike Harris, upset by the whole situation, suspected that Jim was having an affair with the girl.

(377)

'Give me till tomorrow morning,' said Jim. 'I think I can find what's back of this.'

Griffin hesitated but there was a personal appeal in Jim's eyes—an appeal to associations of a decade. 'All right, Jim,' he agreed.

When they had gone Jim called Pamela's number. What he had almost expected happened, but his heart sank none the less when a man's voice answered the phone. . . .

Excepting a trained nurse, an actress is the easiest prey for the unscrupulous male. Jim had learned that in the background of their troubles or their failures there was often some plausible confidence man, some soured musician, who asserted his masculinity by way of interference, midnight nagging, bad advice. The technique of the man was to belittle the woman's job and to question endlessly the motives and intelligence of those for whom she worked.

Jim was thinking of all this when he reached the bungalow hotel in Beverly Hills where Pamela had moved. It was after six. In the court a cold fountain splashed senselessly against the December fog and he heard Major Bowes's voice loud from three radios.

When the door of the apartment opened Jim stared. The man was old—a bent and withered Englishman with ruddy winter color dying in his face. He wore an old dressing gown and slippers and he asked Jim to sit down with an air of being at home. Pamela would be in shortly.

'Are you a relative?' Jim asked wonderingly.

'No, Pamela and I met here in Hollywood. We were strangers in a strange land. Are you employed in pictures, Mr—Mr——'

'Leonard,' said Jim. 'Yes. At present I'm Pamela's boss.'

A change came into the man's eyes—the watery blink became conspicuous, there was a stiffening of the old lids. The lips curled down and backward and Jim was gazing into an expression of utter malignancy. Then the features became old and bland again.

(378)

'I hope Pamela is being handled properly?'

'You've been in pictures?' Jim asked.

'Till my health broke down. But I am still on the rolls at Central Casting and I know everything about this business and the souls of those who own it——' He broke off.

The door opened and Pamela came in. 'Well, hello,' she said in surprise. 'You've met? The Honorable Chauncey Ward—Mr Leonard.'

Her glowing beauty, borne in from outside like something snatched from wind and weather, make Jim breathless for a moment.

'I thought you told me my sins this afternoon,' she said with a touch of defiance.

'I wanted to talk to you away from the studio.'

'Don't accept a salary cut,' the old man said. 'That's an old trick.'

'It's not that, Mr Ward,' said Pamela. 'Mr Leonard has been my friend up to now. But today the director tried to make a fool of me, and Mr Leonard backed him up.'

'They all hang together,' said Mr Ward.

'I wonder——' began Jim. 'Could I possibly talk to you alone?'

'I trust Mr Ward,' said Pamela frowning. 'He's been over here twenty-five years and he's practically my business manager.'

Jim wondered from what deep loneliness this relationship had sprung. 'I hear there was more trouble on the set,' he said.

'Trouble!' She was wide-eyed. 'Griffin's assistant swore at me and I heard it. So I walked out. And if Griffin sent apologies by you I don't want them—our relation is going to be strictly business from now on.'

'He didn't send apologies,' said Jim uncomfortably. 'He sent an ultimatum.'

'An ultimatum!' she exclaimed. 'I've got a contract, and you're his boss, aren't you?'

'To an extent,' said Jim, '—but, of course, making pictures is a joint matter——'

'Then let me try another director.'

'Fight for your rights,' said Mr Ward. 'That's the only thing that impresses them.'

'You're doing your best to wreck this girl,' said Jim quietly.

'You can't frighten me,' snapped Ward. 'I've seen your type before.'

Jim looked again at Pamela. There was exactly nothing he could do. Had they been in love, had it ever seemed the time to encourage the spark between them, he might have reached her now. But it was too late. In the Hollywood darkness outside he seemed to feel the swift wheels of the industry turning. He knew that when the studio opened tomorrow, Mike Harris would have new plans that did not include Pamela at all.

For a moment longer he hesitated. He was a well-liked man, still young, and with a wide approval. He could buck them about this girl, send her to a dramatic teacher. He could not bear to see her make such a mistake. On the other hand he was afraid that somewhere people had yielded to her too much, spoiled her for this sort of career.

'Hollywood isn't a very civilized place,' said Pamela.

'It's a jungle,' agreed Mr Ward. 'Full of prowling beasts of prey.'

Jim rose. 'Well, this one will prowl out,' he said. 'Pam, I'm very sorry. Feeling like you do, I think you'd be wise to go back to England and get married.'

For a moment a flicker of doubt was in her eyes. But her confidence, her young egotism, was greater than her judgment—she did not realize that this very minute was opportunity and she was losing it forever.

For she had lost it when Jim turned and went out. It was weeks before she knew how it happened. She received her salary for some months—Jim saw to that—but she did not set foot on that lot again. Nor on any other. She was placed quietly on that black list that is not written down but that functions at backgammon games after dinner, or on the way to the races. Men of influence stared at her with interest at restaurants here and there but all their inquiries about her reached the same dead end.

She never gave up during the following months—even long after Becker had lost interest and she was in want, and no longer seen in the places where people go to be looked at. It was not from grief or discouragement but only through commonplace circumstances that in June she died. . . .

When Jim heard about it, it seemed incredible and terrible. He learned accidentally that she was in the hospital with pneumonia—he telephoned and found that she was dead. 'Sybil Higgins, actress, English. Age twenty-one.'

She had given old Ward as the person to be informed and Jim managed to get him enough money to cover the funeral expenses, on the pretext that some old salary was still owing. Afraid that Ward might guess the source of the money he did not go to the funeral but a week later he drove out to the grave.

It was a long bright June day and he stayed there an hour. All over the city there were young people just breathing and being happy and it seemed senseless that the little English girl was not one of them. He kept on trying and trying to twist things about so that they would come out right for her but it was too late. He said good-by aloud and promised that he would come again.

Back at the studio he reserved a projection room and asked for her tests and for the bits of film that had been shot on her picture. He sat in a big leather chair in the darkness and pressed the button for it to begin.

In the test Pamela was dressed as he had seen her that first night at the dance. She looked very happy and he was glad she had had at least that much happiness. The reel of takes from the picture began and ran jerkily with the sound of Bob Griffin's voice off scene and with prop boys showing the number of blocks for the scenes. Then Jim started as the next to the last one came up, and he saw her turn from the camera and whisper: 'I'd rather die than do it that way.'

Jim got up and went back to his office where he opened the three notes he had from her and read them again.

'—*just passing by the studio and thought of you and of our ride.*'

Just passing by. During the spring she had called him twice on the phone, he knew, and he had wanted to see her. But he could do nothing for her and could not bear to tell her so.

'I am not very brave,' Jim said to himself. Even now there was fear in his heart that this would haunt him like that memory of his youth, and he did not want to be unhappy.

Several days later he worked late in the dubbing room, and afterward he dropped into his neighborhood drugstore for a sandwich. It was a warm night and there were many young people at the soda counter. He was paying his check when he became aware that a figure was standing by the magazine rack looking at him over the edge of a magazine. He stopped —he did not want to turn for a closer look only to find the resemblance at an end. Nor did he want to go away.

He heard the sound of a page turning and then out of the corner of his eye he saw the magazine cover, The Illustrated London News.

He felt no fear—he was thinking too quickly, too desperately. If this were real and he could snatch her back, start from there, from that night.

'Your change, Mr Leonard.'

'Thank you.'

Still without looking he started for the door and then he heard the magazine close, drop to a pile and he heard someone breathe close to his side. Newsboys were calling an extra across the street and after a moment he turned the wrong way, her way, and he heard her following—so plain that he slowed his pace with the sense that she had trouble keeping up with him.

In front of the apartment court he took her in his arms and drew her radiant beauty close.

'Kiss me good night,' she said. 'I like to be kissed good night. I sleep better.'

Then sleep, he thought, as he turned away—sleep. I couldn't fix it. I tried to fix it. When you brought your beauty here I didn't want to throw it away, but I did somehow. There is nothing left for you now but sleep.

SCOTT

Dearly Beloved

(*Fitzgerald/Hemingway Annual 1969**)

O my Beauty Boy—reading Plato so divine! O, dark, oh fair, colored golf champion of Chicago. Over the rails he goes at night, steward of the club car, and afterwards in the dim smoke by the one light and the smell of stale spittoons, writing west to the Rosecrucian Brotherhood. Seeking ever.

O Beauty Boy here is your girl, not one to soar like you, but a clean swift serpent who will travel as fast on land and look toward you in the sky.

Lilymary loved him, oft invited him and they were married in St Jarvis' church in North Englewood. For years they bettered themselves, running along the tread-mill of their race, becoming only a little older and no better than before. He was loaned the Communist Manifesto by the wife of the advertising manager of a Chicago daily but for preference give him Plato—the Phaedo and the Apologia, or else the literature of the Rosecrucian Brotherhood of Sacramento, California, which burned in his ears as the rails clicked past Alton, Springfield and Burlington in the dark.

Bronze lovers, never never canst thou have thy bronze child—or so it seemed for years. Then the clock struck, the gong rang and Dr Edwin Burch of South Michigan Avenue agreed to handle the whole thing for two hundred dollars. They looked so nice—so delicately nice, neither of them ever hurting the other and gracefully expert in the avoidance. Beauty Boy took fine care of her in her pregnancy—paid his sister to watch with her while he did double work on the road

* Probably written in 1940.

and served for caterers in the city; and one day the bronze baby was born.

O Beauty Boy, Lilymary said, here is your beauty boy. She lay in a four bed ward in the hospital with the wives of a prize fighter, an undertaker and a doctor. Beauty Boy's face was so twisted with radiance; his teeth shining so in his smile and his eyes so kind that it seemed that nothing and nothing could ever.

Beauty Boy sat beside her bed when she slept and read Thoreau's Walden for the third time. Then the nurse told him he must leave. He went on the road that night and in Alton going to mail a letter for a passenger he slipped under the moving train and his leg was off above the knee.

Beauty Boy lay in the hospital and a year passed. Lilymary went back to work again cooking. Things were tough, there was even trouble about his workman's compensation, but he found lines in his books that helped them along for awhile when all the human beings seemed away.

The little baby flourished but he was not beautiful like his parents; not as they had expected in those golden dreams. They had only spare-time love to give the child so the sister more and more and more took care of him. For they wanted to get back where they were, they wanted Beauty Boy's leg to grow again so it would all be like it was before. So that he could find delight in his books again and Lilymary could find delight in hoping for a little baby.

Some years passed. They were so far back on the tread-mill that they would never catch up. Beauty Boy was a night-watchman now but he had six operations on his stump and each new artificial limb gave him constant pain. Lilymary worked fairly steadily as a cook. Now they had become just ordinary people. Even the sister had long since forgotten that Beauty Boy was formerly colored golf champion of Chicago. Once in cleaning the closet she threw out all his books—the Apologia and the Phaedo of Plato, and the Thoreau and the Emerson and all the leaflets and correspondence with the Rosecrucian

(385)

Brotherhood. He didn't find out for a long time that they were gone. And then he just stared at the place where they had been and said 'Say, man . . . say man.'

For things change and get so different that we can hardly recognize them and it seems that only our names remain the same. It seemed wrong for them still to call each other Beauty Boy and Lilymary long after the delight was over.

Some years later they both died in an influenza epidemic and went to heaven. They thought it was going to be all right then—indeed things began to happen in exactly the way that they had been told as children. Beauty Boy's leg grew again and he became golf champion of all heaven, both white and black, and drove the ball powerfully from cloud to cloud through the blue fairway. Lilymary's breasts became young and firm, she was respected among the other angels, and her pride in Beauty Boy became as it had been before.

In the evening they sat and tried to remember what it was they missed. It was not his books, for here everyone knew all those things by heart, and it was not the little boy for he had never really been one of them. They couldn't remember so after a puzzled time they would give up trying, and talk about how nice the other one was, or how fine a score Beauty Boy would make tomorrow.

So things go.